THE WRATH OF RIVERS

THE SEVEN ISLES
BOOK THREE

A.R. KNIGHT

CHAPTER I
THE RIVER CITY

Wax, Vis Renewal, potential world savior, was broke. His satchel hung empty from his shoulders, blowing in the occasional Rana wind, and his Guardians were little better. They sat, clad in the scratchy linen layers bought by trading their remaining Foti loot, around a gilded fountain. Six small jets spouting into the chill morning surrounded a larger geyser, labeled for its home isle. Sweeping alabaster buildings played with sharp angles, banners declaring family names and businesses flew in radiant splendor. The square around them seemed not the slightest bit concerned with their hero's plight, the traders, workers, and families maximizing the dwindling days left until winter set on in full.

And that was the problem.

"Not a single one," Torny said, the bandit pulling up her knees and wrapping them with her arms as she sat. "Asked all the drivers again this morning, and the few that even said they could cart our sorry butts up north demanded more than we've got."

'Even when you promised more later?' Bliss signed,

though the slapdash fingers suggested she knew the answer.

"Guess the Rana only believe in payment upfront." Torny shrugged, sighed. "You have anything stashed away for lunch, Wax, or shall I . . . ?"

That fade played to a suggestion Torny had been making the last two days, once it became clear Wax's not-so-merry band wouldn't be getting a celebratory jaunt up to the Whirlpool, the eternal vortex where Rana's skars, those mysterious stones, were held. The bandit hadn't forgotten her former life when she'd joined up with Wax's group, when he'd accepted her ask to become a Guardian, and now every need seemingly could be solved with a few light fingers, a few lifted purses.

"You know what the Rana do to thieves," Quik, Wax's older brother and the surly, muscle-bound member of their group, growled. "They'll string you up or cast you into the sea without a question. As they should."

"Only if they catch me. Bet they wouldn't."

"I'll take that bet."

"Nobody's stealing a damn thing," Wax said, cutting the argument. "We need to get north, and we can't walk it." That'd been the first sure thing they'd learned since the Foti galleon dropped them in Riroca four days back. Rana, the isle, ran on its omnipresent waterways, and while bridges existed, a hike to the Whirlpool would be both dangerous and long. "Which means we have to earn our passage the hard way."

'Which is what we've been doing,' Bliss signed. 'It's never enough.'

True. The few jobs Rana offered to non-locals left them with little more than enough to buy shelter and food. Wax and Quik had burned days moving cargo on and off ships, and even after a successful shift, the Riroca dockmaster offered little more than pittance and no promise of work the next day. Begging for another round seemed an almost unbearable option, but what else did they have?

"No street fights for you this time?" Quik asked his younger sister, and Bliss shook her head.

'None that I can find. Not that they let me into the places I'd think would have them.'

"This damn isle." Quik smacked a flat hand on the cool gray stone. "We could trade our weapons?"

The Foti blade, Bliss's staff, Quik's gauntlets, and Torny's daggers? Might be enough to get passage, but fiends were everywhere these days. Going on a journey with hands and feet seemed to be asking for a swift death.

Riroca knew it too. Rana's curling avenues, thin and alternating with canals and their boats, had guards posted everywhere. Trios marched or rode in gondolas, two sabers and a crossbowman in each group. Their efforts hadn't been all successful either: the port had lost three piers and two warehouses to fiend attacks, and during their walks, Wax had seen more damage along the city's outskirts.

Little laughter hung on the air. A dry, inevitable fear clung to the place, despite the colors.

"Can't do that," Wax said.

"Which means it's what, business as usual?" Torny asked. "Because if we're burning another day, best get on it. I want something tastier than soup tonight."

"Steal it, then," Quik added.

"If I do, I'll eat it real slow in front of you. Savor every bite."

Wax stood up. Went to scratch his shoulder and found the linens there. Getting used to wearing full clothing all the time took, well, time. He sighed. So much adventure.

"Quik and I will hit the docks again. Torny, you and Bliss see if you can't grab a shift at an inn. Maybe the Angler's Rest again?"

"If that cook makes another pass at me, Wax, I'll gut him," Torny said.

Wax grimaced, saw a simmering anger in Bliss's eyes as she signed a similar accusation.

"Then a different one," Wax replied. "We'll figure something out. Meet back here at sunset."

"You got it, boss." Torny snapped up, Bliss right along with her, and the pair broke right, heading deeper into the city.

"Those two," Quik muttered, watching them walk away. "Torny's getting into her head."

"With what?" Wax asked, starting off the walk down to the dock.

"Ideas."

Wax laughed, "How's that dangerous?"

"Don't know, but Torny's not one of us, Wax. She's not from Vis."

"Got that, thanks. When there's something I need to worry about, Quik, tell me, okay?"

THE DOCKS HUSTLED much like the city above. Riroca sprawled on a downward slope where rushing water met the ocean in a swirling delta, one overbuilt now with huge piers filled flush with ships from every isle save one: Whent.

Wax probably wouldn't have noticed that except everything going wrong on these docks prompted a curse aimed at the bulky isle to the northeast. A rockbiter's sneeze caused this crate to fall over, another one's trip and fall pushed a boat a bit too far from its berth. If a Foti-forged seal failed, it was because some Whent had screwed it up first.

Wax and Quik learned to ignore the banter, even add to it when they had a chance, if only because it made the rest of the handlers look at them with a little less ire.

The brothers scored some luck when they hit the port, the dockmaster waving them over and pointing towards a massive Foti galleon stocked with fresh arms and armor, metals to be dyed Rana's sea-green. Crate after crate needed moving, and the two Vis had earned the right to shift the biggest, worst packages from the galleon's deepest holds.

"Lucky us," Quik said.

"That's right," the dockmaster replied. "Get on it."

Wax didn't protest, held secret his own relief at the job. Simple labor had an added benefit now, one contingent on moving the same ways for hours. Lift, walk, climb ramps and set down near the carts that'd take the gear to Riroca artisans. Easy enough to do without much thought.

Which left Wax time to listen to the whispers in his head.

Two skars lay hidden on a necklace beneath his weathered gray tunic, a Vis emerald and a Foti ruby, though neither matched a true gem's sedate beauty. Instead, they pulsed with life, warm to the touch, and they talked like they had stories to tell.

At first Wax found their whispers interchangeable, a flurry in his head like a rainstorm's static sound. After days and nights, though, he'd teased out differences. The Foti skar meandered through its whispers, as if casting about and lunging for a phrase only to wait, muttering, till the next idea came into focus. Its Vis counterpart adopted a more pleasant buzz, a continual chatter looping back on itself, a stuttering repeat building, after hours, to a rapid chittering finale.

As to what any of it meant, Wax had no idea. The words weren't in any tongue he'd ever heard, and the cadence, the pauses seemed at odds with any language he knew.

But the skars gave Wax other clues, like the Vis one did right now, skittering as Wax strained to get this next crate up the last ramp to the dock. As it did, Wax felt his tired muscles pick up their energy, a surge like the one he'd felt when swinging through the trees on Vis. A rush, but what the skar provided wouldn't cost him later. When he sat the crate down, the Vis skar receded to quiet, but his legs, arms, felt as strong as ever.

Quik, meanwhile, breathed hard, his arms coated in sweat. He looked Wax over as the Renewal stretched. "Careful. They'll notice."

Wax looked down at himself. The work's smudges were there, but no scratches, little sweat, and certainly no listing exhaustion from a hard day's labor.

"Sorry. It's easy to forget," Wax replied, affecting a slight limp as they went back in for the last crate.

Ever since bandits on Foti had taken Wax and his siblings hostage solely for the skar and its value, keeping the stone a secret had been a priority. The resulting Najahn raid on those same bandits made keeping his Renewal status secret an absolute.

Wax didn't need more deaths on his conscience, no matter how deserved.

"Hey," Quik said after they dropped the last crate near the cart. "Didn't we see that ship when we left Foti?"

The Kance vessel Quik pointed to had an ethereal opulence, as if the ship deigned to dock, to touch the water. The massive intersecting sails caught wind in ways Wax couldn't fathom, bringing the seas to heel as even the Rana couldn't master. Yet, this far away from Kance, even their light ships were rare, an event big enough to draw stares from more than just Wax and his brother.

"The Kance Renewal," Wax said. "She's caught up to us."

"Past you, I think." Quik folded his arms as they watched the boat, the same guard-Renewal-guard order leading the disembarking, though this time a third soldier followed. All clad in regal, silver Kance armor. "She's got to have the Kance skar already."

"You're saying I'm slow?"

"I'm saying you're on your way to better future than she is."

Collect all the skars first, win your short life's imprisonment on Noctia. The Aegis, guarding the land from fiends until they shriveled up. An honor for your isle, for you, though Wax wasn't sure any Aegis would feel proud at the end.

"Maybe," Wax muttered, rubbing his chin and watching the imperious Renewal make her way up the dock. "Or maybe I just need to do some catching up."

"Hard to do that when you can't afford a boat."

The Kance Renewal had a certain grace as the sun set, her loose, silver-blue robes catching a glinting fire as the sky diamonds in their hems embraced the fading orange light. The woman didn't seem to notice, her mouth set straight, her eyes ahead, hands at her sides and tight with poised purpose.

Kance, a land of two Queens. One, so the rumor went, was always chosen for the Renewal. The one, so the rumor continued, who wanted for power, for influence.

"Quik, I bet she's rich," Wax said.

"Not a bet I'm taking, brother."

"No, but one we might be able to use anyway."

Quik shook his head, turned to visit the dockmaster, collect their meager pay in the form of potatoes, grains stacked in sacks behind the man.

From the first, this quest had rewarded ingenuity, risk, invention. Wax had those, and he had a new idea.

As the Vis Renewal took off after the Kance Queen, the Foti skar snapped and churned its whispers in Wax's head. Approving, or so he thought.

CHAPTER 2
THE FROZEN ROAD

Maena, Rana captain, commander of her own ship and leader of sailors by the dozen, wiped her nose on a dirt-covered sleeve as the Whent wind whipped her dry, stringy hair into her face. The rest of her wasn't much better off, the weeks in the caves clinging to her as hard as the ropes binding her wrists, her ankles to metal loops on the rolling wagon.

She shared the rumbling trek across Whent's choppy tundra with the ones who'd followed her down into the Dark Below, or at least the last few who'd remained till the end: Svarde, the hulking Foti Guardian and his loyal Ferrite sat in ponderous thought toward's the wagon's front. Near them, Rasslebeck and Pennifer, two Rana fighters who belonged slitting Whent throats instead of being held by the rockbiters, sat across from one another spitting old stories. Dire laughter seemed their default mode on this fourth day crossing Whent's massive isle.

Several nameless prisoners filled the benches, ones Maena hadn't spoken to, and they shared her lack of interest, spending their time instead picking at lice and lost in their own half-frozen minds.

At least they likely had only one.

Maena shifted her gaze right, out the wagon's scant back. The Whent prison train continued, another four wagons following them and five more in front, all heading towards that Whent dungeon known as the Pits.

Then again, Maena might not even know when she arrived, seeing as she spent so much time locked in a struggle with her own head.

The fiend in the Dark Below had shredded her memory, siphoned away Maena's past like she might eat a snack. What'd been left behind built, in the short time it existed, a version of her. One it fought to keep alive even when Svarde had smashed the original Maena back into being.

Why won't you die?

Because I barely had a chance to live.

The conversations pattered endless through the minutes, the hours, the days. Every thought Maena had would prompt an interjection from her other self, an opinion, a suggestion, a demand.

You'll never take me back.

It happened once. It can happen again. I'll wait.

Maena sniffed. Wiped her nose a second time. Blinked wind-bitten tears away. She wasn't a crier, but with her skin chapped, without shelter from the cutting gales, the occasional snowy blusters, her body adopted other measures.

Can we live with each other?

Not with you at the till.

That was a laugh. A till. Maena had agreed with all the other sailors to give up that life with the expedition, an agreement that frayed soon after the dark grew too deep, the fiend cries too loud. She'd given up what she loved only to fail at what she wanted.

I didn't even have a chance at that.

Roars harkened their arrival before the wagon slowed, the echoes rising over the plains like a waterfall's wail. Soon enough the landscape followed suit, the wagon rolling through a palisade gate, one with the wood stakes pointing inward, the guards in watchtowers angling their eyes the wrong way.

Before the gate, tents sprouted across the landscape, their pitched sites offering fire pits and cheerful fur-clad Whents enjoying their days after the harvest season. Some raised flagons to toast the coming wagons, others raised jeers.

On the gate's other side came what good trading could get you. Real buildings, stacked with Whent logs and buttressed by the rocky isle's stone. Smoke rose high from a hundred chimneys, but the air held none of Foti's mining stink. Maena saw shops, butchers, inns, and restaurants aplenty, all supported by roving livestock and hardy vegetable gardens, most now fallow for winter.

The wagons drew more cheers from passersby as they rolled along. Maena could only shiver in response, the glee in those stares a manic violence justifying all the Rana raids she'd pitted against the Whent barbarians. These people loved their bloodsport, so long as they could watch from their rocky mantels.

When the wagons came to a halt, their destination appeared less a prison cell than another stone hole. Maena's stomach lurched at the downward sloping entry, the torches burning along its walls.

You can't be scared of that now, can you? I lived my whole life in one. Be brave, thief.

Thief? This is my life.

Think what you want.

"Pay attention," some Whent man shouted at her, untying her ropes from the loops and immediately stringing them through another, thinner chain. This one tied her ankles to the prisoner behind her, one in a loping line. "You'll follow me close, mind, or you'll get a beating. They won't hold off your turn either, so if you want a chance to get out of here, best keep your tongue shut and your eyes sharp."

Another man next to him, at the slopes mouth beneath that leering palisade, laughed. In one hand, he flipped a skinning knife.

"Barten," the man said, "You're giving them hope when there is none. Why do you torture them so?"

Barten rolled his eyes, a great thing given their size, nestled back in his wrinkled, bearded face. "They're more fun when they have something to lose, Tross." Barten stepped back off the wagon, tugged Maena upright. "There's a ferrite in this batch too. Damn Foti fire lizard won't leave its master."

"Can't we kill it?"

"Jochi says no, says it'll be an interesting fighter."

Another tug and Maena took a step off the wagon. Farther than she thought, and her legs weren't quite awake yet. She fell forward, only for Barten to catch her with one hand, hoist her back upright.

Tross cursed, slotted his knife away, headed off towards the wagon train's front. Maena's eyes followed him as Barten pulled the others off the wagon.

"He's going to give your train master a talking to," Barten said, answering a question voiced by Rasslebeck. "You're all looking less than ready. The Pits only wants healthy ones, and it's looking like we might have to spend a few days nursing you all back to contesting shape."

Contesting?

The Pits, so Maena knew, offered Whent prisoners, criminals, a chance at justice through prowess. Succeed at this or that contest and you'd get yourself let go. How possible that really was, Maena didn't know.

She'd never met anyone who'd escaped.

Then we could be the first, if you let me handle things.

Maena laughed, a hoarse rasp. There was an idea. In her condition, tired, half-frozen, and with voices talking in her head, Maena would be lucky to survive crossing blades with a baby.

Now, that's an exaggeration, no baby could lift a sword

You don't sound like me, know that?

I am you, so that's an impossibility, Maena.

Barten pulled their prison train down the hole and under the ground. At least, with all the torches, the chill disappeared. Stale air replaced it, but Maena would keep it to feel her fingers and toes.

The guards lumped their wagon into a single cell, one with scattered, moldering straw slats. A hole in the corner served as the latrine.

"Meals will come as we see fit," Barten said. "Best you eat them when they arrive, as you'll need every bit to stay alive." He pulled the rope's end through a gap in the wood door, then tugged once, a single hard jerk. At the pull, all the knots around their wrists and ankles came undone, leaving a slithering cord Barten reeled in.

"Make any fuss, give us any grief, and you'll be dinner for something else," Barten continued, sweeping his scruff gaze among them all. "You're among the damned now, but not yet among the dead. How long that takes is up to you."

A glimmer, a slight upturn among those scraggled curls. "Some lucky few might even make it out alive." That glint faded with a frown. "Not that I see any here."

"Hold, Whent." The growl pulled Maena's attention to her left, to Svarde's figure, still hulking despite losing his armor, his axes. "Where's the ferrite?"

"The lizard's got the same chance as you. If it earns its freedom, we'll send it back to your blasted isle."

With that, Barten twisted a key in the wood gate, locking them into the dirt and dust.

Seven people in a cell big enough for double that meant straw for everyone, though the latrine's smell ruined what little comfort that provided. The first meal came quick enough, at least, and Maena had to stare at it long to understand what she saw.

Better than what we ate down below, tell you that much.

Real meat. Cooked and tossed with potatoes. Carrots alongside. No ale, but a water barrel and earthen cups came with meal. One of the other prisoners started crying at the sight, shoveling the stuff into his mouth with his hands.

"Wash those fingers first," Svarde announced to the room, a little late for the one. "Go to Tamas and they'll tell you. The fastest way to die comes from disease in a place like this."

Another prisoner, a thin lady who bore a thrice-broken nose, laughed, "If you think disease is going to take you before a sword in here, or a beast's maw, then I envy your hope."

But she washed her hands, as did Maena and all the others. Even the first prisoner, once he'd finished stuffing his mouth, cleaned his grubby mitts.

So what are you going to do, thief? Sit here in silence?

After Svarde's warning, the group had settled into their

places. Maena felt the Foti man's eyes cross to her from time to time, looks she ignored. He'd tried to rebuild their relationship on the walk out of the Dark Below, but Svarde had known the old Maena, the one still put together.

That one didn't exist any longer.

What, you have a better idea?

I didn't take charge in that cave, and I died for it. Don't kill me a second time.

Maena stiffened. Her second self had it right. The Pits could be a death sentence, but they could be something greater. If she could muster the energy to try.

Muster? If I'd known the real me was this pathetic, I'd have shot myself instead of that fiend.

Maena snorted a quiet laugh. Again, the second self had a point. How many raids had she led? How many swords had she crossed to earn the medals on her lost armor? This would only be one more challenge in a life filled with them.

Now, that's more like it. Show me who I really am.

Finishing her meal, Maena tossed the bowl against the gate and stood. The clatter drew attention to her, the prisoners watching as her torn, dirty, rag-clothed form found its spine.

"I don't know about any of you," Maena said, the rasp dying as she punched through her tired throat, "but I left a job unfinished back there, and I mean to see it through. That means fighting our way out of here, no matter what these Whent bastards throw at us. Who's with me?"

The prisoner cackled again, opened her mouth, then shut it as Svarde stood, the man glaring at her for a long moment before nodding at Maena.

"To the end, Rana. To the bitter, violent end."

"If I had a saber, you'd have it," Rasslebeck added, standing.

Pennifer stood too, "My fists are yours, though they'd be better with a crossbow in'em."

The other three prisoners eyed the quartet with confused wariness, but under Svarde's glare, they must have found a measure of confidence, because soon they too were on their feet.

Just in time for a bell's clarion ring to sound.

CHAPTER 3

ROOFTOP RIDE

Rana nights gave off a glow Foti never had. The rivers curling about Riroca caught Sichi's pink light and cast it into glass ovals lining the canals, each shaded in different colors so every river painted its route in a unique gold, blue, green or red. The reflections danced on the buildings, glinted off gilded rails, and generally helped Bliss lead their foursome over the rooftops.

Compared to swinging vines, leaping light from one slate roof to the next came about as easy as Bliss could want: stable landings, no slippery leaves, and clear sight lines all the way to her destination?

Yes please.

She'd volunteered to lead after Wax gave out the plan, declaring that it might be better for Bliss to chance any fall, any spying by Rana guards rather than the Renewal himself. With Quik backing her, Wax's usual position at their group's head fell away. Now he sat third, with Torny watching their backs.

Their goal waited several blocks away, resting in the river while its passengers loaded up their gear. While Bliss and Torny suffered through another shift slinging plates and washing the same at a bland inn, Wax and Quik had watched the Kance crew, tracked their intended take-off to tonight, to just ahead.

When Wax had inquired after the Kance departed, the river roller's captain declared no empty rooms would be filled, especially not at a discount rate.

So Wax offered an alternative over their meager dinner: jump on as the roller left, plead for mercy as Renewals, and hope for the best.

As a plan, the other three universally agreed it sucked. Put against another day working a shift in the city, though, suck didn't seem so bad.

"Worst thing," Torny said, "they drop us on the river bank and we're hiking. Not so bad."

With winter on the approach, a foot-by-foot march through Rana's wild lands might not be the best route, but better to try and fail than sit here, wasting day after day for nothing.

Bliss signed as much, and even Quik agreed to give the rogue option a try.

Now Bliss waited on a flat roof's edge, watching a Rana guard trio turn a corner half a block away, disappearing from sight. To get on from here, they'd have to jump a canal, a leap intimidating to anyone without much experience hurling themselves into the void.

Thankfully, Bliss had a staff.

'Watch me,' Bliss signed, backing up several strides.

The other three made room. Torny had worry in her moonlit face. Wax and Quik only bored confidence. Below, golden glows showed the distance, a slight drop to the house on the other side.

Bliss took a slow breath, let the cool air play about,

give her energy. Bounced her feet. Steadied her staff in her right hand with one metal capped end resting on her shoulder.

With an exhale she moved, lifting the staff up on the first step and planting it on the third, its end digging into the roof, running against the shallow lip on its flat side. Bliss pressed off, flew into the air, the trees and canal flying by below her. She tucked up her knees, pitched forward, and rolled as she hit the house on the far side.

The slate hurt more than cozy jungle dirt, but the roll worked just the same, letting Bliss tumble out her momentum on the rooftop. She came to a stop with her back against the ground, looking right up at the sky.

Okay, so not a perfect landing, but she'd lived, she'd proved it could be done.

Now for the next trick.

Standing, heading back to the rooftop's edge, Bliss hefted the staff, took another few strides back, then ran and launched it backward. The light-but-strong bamboo proved as adept in flight as Bliss had, soaring over the gap into Quik's waiting hands.

The next two jumps went as well as the first, Wax and Quik joining their sister across the canal. When Quik went to throw the staff back for Torny, though, the thief shook her head. Held up a single finger, then vanished into the dark.

"What's she doing?" Quik asked. "Finally giving up on this game?"

'She's not leaving,' Bliss signed.

"Would hope not. She's my Guardian now too." Wax plucked the staff from Quik's hands, gave it to Bliss. "Unless she likes breaking oaths."

"Would that really surprise you?" Quik said.

"Know what'd really surprise me? You being anything other than an ass towards Torny."

Quik scowled, looked away. Wax gave Bliss a what-can-you-do glance, then wandered to the rooftop's far side, Bliss following.

"Two more jumps and we're there," Wax said.

'Three. You're forgetting the leap to the roller.'

"That's more a fall."

'Why do you think this'll work, Wax?'

"Because I saw her," Wax replied. "She didn't look happy."

'And that means?'

Wax flashed a grin. "Means a joker like myself can get on her good side. Once that happens, we're in."

Torny appeared two buildings down, signaling the trio by holding up a long knife to catch the moonlight. How she made it that far without getting caught, without suspicion, was anyone's guess, but even Quik couldn't argue with the results.

"Guess we're playing catch-up," Quik muttered when he saw the bandit. "She can move."

The last few jumps went fast with no more canals to cross. The houses, all built to hold Rana families in multitudes, offered landing space aplenty, and soon the group looked into a true Rana river, one wrapping the city's eastern side and continuing on north. A major artery, according to the maps Bliss had spied in the various inns.

"You're sure they wanted to leave now? In the dark?" Torny asked as they looked at the empty, flowing water.

The bank near them lit up in orange, spiral glass lanterns spaced along a metal rail marking the city's edge. Few people walked it, both due to cold and, Bliss figured, the growing fiend threat. Any romantic or peaceful stroll might get interrupted by a spitting horror, something that clamped down on the joy.

"The captain told me I wouldn't be able to harass her tomorrow when I asked," Wax said, then gave a quiet chuckle. "Told her I'd have enough cabbage to buy passage after my next shift. Think that scared her into telling me."

'Bet it wasn't so much the cabbage as the thought of you on her roller,' Bliss signed.

"Since when do Guardians get to give their Renewal crap?"

'Since always.'

Wax's info proved right not many minutes later. A churning rustle broke the river's babling flow, the roller's large wheel scooping through the water. Sticking to the deeper middle channel, the roller rose up above the metal railing, its main deck offering room for scant crew and passengers aplenty. Small lanterns graced the ship's light metal sides, turning the vessel into an orange beacon on its way north.

"Told you," Wax said. "That Queen's not wasting time."

Bliss frowned, reading the distance as the roller churned their way. 'The jump's going to be too far. We won't have time to do the staff again.'

The hope had been the roller's size would keep it near enough to the rail to make a leap viable. From here, though, it'd take all of Bliss's effort just to make the ship's port side. As it was, she'd smack right into the wall, a promise already making her head ache.

"Then we do it my way," Torny said.

The three turned, saw Torny unraveling a thin rope, with one end tied to her long knife. Bliss had noticed the coiled rope earlier, stuffed into Torny's satchel, but the bandit kept all manner of weird things on her person, had a habit of twisting away any questions asked.

"You make the jump," Torny told Bliss. "Stick my knife in the side and we'll slide down the rope to meet you."

"So that's how you did it," Quik said, motioning towards the buildings behind them. "You threw this up and used it to—"

"Nope," Torny shook her head. "These buildings have handholds everywhere. Easy to climb. If you three could sneak worth a damn, I'd have said we could just run all the way here."

Always like Torny to slide an insult into an answer.

"Bliss?" Wax asked. "Think you can do it?"

'Don't have much choice.'

Nobody argued with that, so Bliss set herself up with Torny's satchel, giving her own to the bandit. Again the staff found its way to Bliss's shoulder as she measured the timing, the distance to the roller. Up close the boat loomed larger than before, and Bliss could make out the captain's form in the boat's forward cabin, looking out with one hand on a wheel.

Hopefully the woman wouldn't get so shocked she'd drive the raft aground.

Quik offered up a prayer to Vis as Bliss set herself, those words sounding strange so far from home. Then again, Bliss would take any help their long dead god could offer.

She sprinted forward, slammed the staff down, and flew into space. The familiar rush returned, the weightless burst with nothing around her as Bliss tumbled, the satchel throwing off her weight.

Her weight, but not her distance.

Bliss smacked the roller's port edge, flipping over it to land on the narrow deck. Her left shin exploded with pain, wouldn't let Bliss stand up as shouts broke out on the boat around her.

Time to deal with that later.

Still holding her staff, Bliss leaned on it, planted its end on the roller's deck to get to a shaking stand. The rope bled out from the satchel, Torny and Quik holding its other end back on the rooftop. An end rapidly playing out as the boat shuffled on up-river.

Bliss dug out the dagger, slammed the knife into the deck's floor. The move shook her left leg again, the staff's blunt end slipping and sending Bliss once more to the deck.

Footsteps came her way, Bliss rolling to see a Kance guard approach, rapiers already in both hands. Clad in full armor, looking like walking glass, the guard gave Bliss a narrow glare before tracking to the tightening rope.

Oh no you don't.

With her right hand, Bliss swung her staff. On the ground, with minimal leverage, the weapon did little more than bounce off the Kance man's armored shins. It did, though, get the man's attention, a rapier point leveling at Bliss's face.

"What're you doing?" The guard asked, his voice a feathered growl, as if the man wanted to be menacing but didn't quite know how.

"Hitching a ride," Bliss answered.

The guard blinked at her, then lurched forward with a curse. Bouncing off him, landing butt-first on the deck, was Bliss's older brother and fellow guardian. Quik sprang to his feet, fists rising up--a wise choice to keep his gauntlets off now--and bellowing at the guard to keep his swords to himself.

Not that the guard, and his approaching friends felt like

listening. They did, though, stop and shout as Wax followed Quik, making a smoother entry onto the boat.

"Cut the rope!" came the captain's shout, through an opened window in the roller's forward cabin. "Don't let anymore on!"

The first guard, standing next to Bliss, made good on the order, even as Quik moved to stop him. The rapier cut the rope, and off the boat's side, there in the river's dark waters, a splash sounded above the roller's roiling motion.

Torny.

CHAPTER 4
ADVENTURE'S CALL

Sawi read the design on her hand's back as she reached up and pulled the mango from its branch. Orange lines ran along her veins before spidering out, much like the tree she hung from now. Those lines marked her place in Kitaye, her world. As vivid as ever today. Her rope kept Sawi suspended as she picked the fruit and dropped it into her satchel. A late harvest before winter's onset, one looking to be chilly by the last few nights.

Wax, wherever he was, might even be seeing snow now. Wouldn't that be a thing, an experience. Vis only saw the white fluff on its tallest mountains far away to the east and west, nowhere Sawi would go. Not anymore.

Sawi frowned as her eyes tracked from the tree to the ground, the grove not far from Kitaye's western border, running up along the cliffs overlooking the ocean. Not so long ago, when she'd joined older gatherers to learn the trade, climbing the trees, taking the fruits, was a peaceful exercise. A chance to be at one with the nature Vis fluorished.

Now, hunters roamed the trees with them. They held spears, bows, sharp eyes and tense frames. Soundless save for timed whoops, cries giving the all-clear every so often. The first few days, those cries set Sawi's nerves aflame. She'd dropped fruit. Nearly lost a satchel.

But that's what happens when a fiend nearly kills you, or so her parents said. Or so the village elders pronounced to the city as more and more people straggled in from around the isle.

The fiends had come, and they were making Vis a dangerous place. Maybe Wax had left right on time.

Nonetheless, Kitaye had mouths to feed and brave faces to answer that call. Sawi did so, held herself to the oath the ink on her shoulders and hands demanded. She went out at dawn every morning with a hunter escort, picking fruit, herbs, grain, and mushrooms, stuffing satchel after satchel with what bounty Vis would provide.

The results filled her stomach, brought happiness to plenty more besides, but peace never seemed to come with it.

Then again, how could you find peace when the world seemed to be tearing itself apart around you?

Sawi, her satchel filled and the sun getting low, shifted the satchel to her shoulder and let herself down, one careful foothold at the time—Wax would've just dropped, trusting fate and his instincts to keep him alive—and hit the rain-softened ground with her forage intact.

She put two fingers to her mouth and whistled. Time to go home.

Kitaye buzzed a different tune when Sawi and her several hunter escort returned. Cooking spices, songs, and whoops from returning parties came the same as always, but an excited undercurrent ran beneath the familiar, its explanation lying in looks back towards the inlet.

"A new ship?" Sawi asked a hunter who'd come back with her. The young man—they kept getting younger now, with so many wounded—shook his head. He'd been with her, how would he know?

Yet, what other explanation was there? Kitaye and Vis, for all their soft pleasures, ran a regular routine. The seasons drove hunters and gatherers to rotating responsibilities, while families grew fat creating the next generation. The other Seven Isles did their things, waged their tiny wars and played their political games, leaving Vis and its all-important foods and medicines alone.

So if you wanted to spark excitement in Kitaye, the real verve, you had to bring in something truly new. Like a ship, and not just a trading vessel, flush with Foti metals or Kance jewels.

Even Sawi couldn't believe it at first glance. She'd dropped off her satchels with the gatherers and joined the steady stream making their way to the inlet, many craning their necks to see just what would be coming off the docks.

A Najahn ship, and a big one. A blend of a Foti galleon's size with a Rana sloop's slick lines, the black wood sealed with metal carving an imposing line in the bay. The lone Kance cutter sharing the bay with the big ship looked tiny, if beautiful, but no beauty could compare with a jungle day, so attention due that little ship was scant.

Instead, Sawi watched Najahn soldiers take down the big ship's riggings, tapering the sails, throwing an anchor, and tying off the massive ship. Sawi counted a full four decks from top to bottom, with three monstrous masts spiking as high as a jungle tree into the sky. What would such a ship want with a place like Kitaye?

The answer didn't come with those disembarking, though more questions certainly did. Several guards in full regalia, the curved voulges and bladed rings along their backs complementing the purple, black, and gold armor. Heavy gear, enough that Sawi figured the trio must be sweating despite the cooler evening air. Their deckhand gave way to the ship's star, announced as such by his descent to the dock, followed by several robed scholars carrying books, satchels, and a large trunk.

The guards fanned out at the pier's edge, saying not a word to the Kitaye elders waiting to greet them. Instead they stood silent, imperious and impervious while their leader walked the wood path to land.

The man seemed built for a life of leisure. Despite his robes, Sawi saw little speed in the man's hefty frame. Svarde, the Foti Guardian, had been similarly large, but carried his bulk as if waiting for a chance to strike something with it. This one, this one expected fate to come to him.

When the elders finally had their chance to speak to the man, the Najahn leader brushed them away with mollifying words. A hand on the arm, a polite nod of his head, and the elders stepped back, gave the Najahn man a chance to look at the assembled crowd.

And Sawi, who'd snaked her way closer to the front, hoping, dreading that this Najahn vessel would have some news of Wax, made an adjustment.

This Najahn leader wasn't soft, despite how he might look. The man, his hands clasped before him, his wrinkled eyes hard as he swept his gaze around, was most definitely a hunter, though of a different kind than Sawi knew.

"A great welcome," the man opened, marbling the words as he spoke them, "from a great people. Journeys are tiresome things, and I regret I have no special news to share, only a stop on my trek to our outpost a little farther on. Please, carry on, and let us interfere with your evening no longer."

Disappointed murmurs ran through the crowd, loud enough for the Najahn man to notice, though he gave no sign, only nodding ahead for his guards, his luggage to follow.

No special news? Was that a good thing? Sawi squeezed away from the crowd, buffeted as onlookers returned to their cook fires, closing their trading posts, or to the endless other tasks required to keep a home running in these grim times.

Sawi ditched her own family, eschewed her neighborhood's grove and its dinner to trail the Najahn man. His guards shooed away children and others like Sawi, people lobbing questions or offers of treasures for sale. Their target seemed to take no notice, save to wave the requests away while trudging forward. Past, it seemed, Kitaye's main inns.

Did the man mean to go on foot all the way now, in the dark?

The question slowed Sawi's steps, forced her to consider what she was doing. The man said he had no news, and she had a full harvest day ahead. Trailing the Najahn might get her nothing save less sleep and more frustration. Even if he could say no Renewal had died, news traveled slow between the isles. Anything he offered would be old before it left his tongue.

And yet.

The jungle thickened as the Najahn went deeper into the city, Sawi padded after, mingling with crowds as she went. The great leaves overhead, black shadows on a clouding night, brought with them past questions, past conversations.

How many times had she and Wax talked about adventure up among those leaves, those branches? How many times had they insisted to each other they would go, chase the action and live their days on a vine's swooping curl, leaping into the unknown?

Wax had. Though, Sawi had to remember, he'd been pushed there by Pan. Still, despite the tragedy, Wax continued. He boarded the Kance boat and sailed off, heading to someplace new while Sawi, that morning, learned which fields and trees would be hers to preserve.

What promises mattered more, the ones made to her younger self, or to her city, her tribe?

Fifteen Najahn formed the train, scholars and guards, the latter doubling the knowledge seekers, bubbling and babbling around their leader. The group hit Kitaye's edge, the torchlight's last flickers forcing a halt.

Sawi waited, watched behind a tree. Several other Vis clung nearby too, one continuing to hawk food and water, necessary for the Najahn's journey, and earning herself some trade from the travelers' supplies.

"We camp here," the Najahn leader said, casting his look around. "The fiends make nighttime travel dangerous, and any difficulties tonight will bring us the city's support."

"There were inns not far back?" A scholar voiced. "Surely we—"

"There will be few comforts on the road to our outpost, my friend," the leader replied. "We'll need what we have to make it there. I'll not spend it on needless luxury now."

The scholar spread his arms, "We're the richest isle, surely we can spare--"

"When you rise to my station, Noctia forbid, you can

spend her bounty as you see fit," the leader replied. "Our time here may be short, it may be long. I plan for the latter. If that is too hard for you to understand, I suggest you return to the boat and wait with the sailors."

At that, the scholar quit his argument and began, like the others, unpacking a bedroll. The Najahn soldiers sparked up a cookfire and chased away the remaining traders, leaving Sawi alone watching their party, working up the nerve.

Then again, what was the worst they could do?

She stepped forward, the small camp immersed in its mealtime preparations. A guard saw her first, rose and waved her off, declaring no further deals were to be made this night.

"I'm not interested in trade," Sawi replied. "I have a question."

"Ask it, then."

"Do you have news of the Renewals? My friends represent Vis, and they traveled to Foti weeks ago. I haven't—"

The guard softened, gave her a torchlight smile, "Then rest easy. Only the Tamas Renewal has quit the field so far, and that due to injury, not death, in climbing the Kance ridges. So far as Noctia knows, your friend still lives."

"A lucky thing, isn't it?" The Najahn leader spoke up, looking over from his soup bowl. The scholars followed his look, matching their leader like babies their mothers. "With the fiends as wild as they are, that so many Renewals are still alive."

The tone didn't push a dismissal with it, and the leader's look seemed to search Sawi, as if he saw deep into her heart.

"It is," Sawi said, and lingered. Fruits and grains. Harvest satchels waited for her. And yet, here lay another possibility, another chance at a prior choice. The thought turned her stomach, a cold betrayal even as her voice asked the question. "If you need a guide, I would be at your service."

The Najahn leader chuckled, looked around the fire at the others. "For all the offers we've heard since landing here, not one has been to show us the way. Were I to guess why, it's fear of fiends that holds your people back. Why are you different?"

The curdling anxiety dissipated at the Najahn's question. She'd taken the first step. Now all Sawi needed to do was walk.

"Because I know that fear well enough to face it again."

"Do you?" The Najahn's eyes glittered, black pits against the fire's shadow. "Then I, Gladdring, Tenet of Noctia, would welcome your services. Lead us well, and be rewarded. Fail, and I'm quite certain you won't survive to suffer the consequences."

CHAPTER 5
QUEEN'S GUARDS

As plans went, Wax was beginning to consider the run-and-jump onto the raft among his worst. Sure, there'd been the exhilarating dashes over the rooftops, the jumps, dodging guards, but it was hard to feel good about any of that with Torny flailing in the water while the roller chugged ahead.

Bliss's fingers flew fast, not that her signed words had any impact on the Kance soldiers, so pretty in their armor, so stern in their mood. Hard eyes, hard souls. They ignored Wax's ask too, just standing there with blades drawn waiting for some hidden signal.

In another few seconds, Torny would be too far behind for that signal to matter.

"She's our Renewal," Wax said, nodding towards the splashing form, more a blur now as the light grew distant. "You let her drown, Vis's hopes go with her."

The guard before him twitched, his face shadowed by the sharp helm. Control won out, though, and his rapier stayed steady, its point aiming right at Wax's gut.

"Please," Quik echoed, on the ground near Bliss with

swords at their own chests. His brother's emotion didn't feel quite so genuine as Wax's own, but at least he tried.

"Help the girl."

The command came from below, a stair leading down to the main deck. From it emerged the Kance Renewal, that icy queen looking no less so now, even in thin clothes wrapped by a hasty blue-white robe.

She repeated the words when no guard moved. This time, the one with his rapier at Wax stepped aside, though the blade held ready.

"Do what you can," the guard said, the reedy voice oozing a snide menace. "Make one other move and I'll have your guts staining the deck."

"That'd be a nightmare to clean," Wax muttered, yanking free the rope they'd just used to drop onto the boat and darting towards the roller's rear. As he passed by the Queen, Wax dished out the slightest nod he could muster.

At least, compared to the sea-faring ships, the roller didn't have so much length. A few long strides put Wax at the aft, the rope trailing like a sand-colored snake behind him.

"Catch this!" Wax called, pulling the rope into a sweeping toss and casting it out.

The end vanished beyond the light, but Wax knew ropes, knew his own strength, and braced himself by the time the first hard yank came back.

"She's got it," Wax said, not turning around. "Could use some help reeling her in!"

The roller's speed and Torny's wet weight put Wax's muscles to a difficult task, one a day's labor hauling crates did little to help. His arms burned after a single pull, those fresh callouses threatening to break and bleed.

And they would've if not for a fresh tug behind him.

The rope pulled tight, behind moving through Wax's own fingers. Heavy still, but with the aid, viable. Wax had his feet pressed against the raft's back lip, a sturdy gold-gilded plank, his eyes forward watching, hunting for any sign.

"Thanks," Wax said, trying to throw his voice behind him. "I'm sure it wasn't your idea."

"All my ideas are my own," came the reply, the same measured, utterly steel tone commanding the guards a moment ago. "Hold on, damn you."

Wax clutched back at the rope, the dry fibers almost slipping from his hands after he heard the Queen's voice. What was she doing back here? And how did one ask that?

Better stick with what he knew, who he was.

Vis had no royalty. He'd never been taught how to handle one.

"Sorry, wasn't expecting, you know—"

"Focus on your friend."

Right. Torny. Wax leaned forward, the reel-in going faster now as success boosted their efforts. The bandit emerged in the roller's trailing lamplight after a few more moments, clinging to the rope with her head splashing above and below the surface. Her arms didn't move, she said no words.

"She's there," Wax said. "Though I can't tell if she's alive."

"A question we'll answer in due time."

If Quik had said those words, Wax would've tossed back something sarcastic. Now he swallowed his tongue, focused on pulling. Another body came behind, relieved the Queen with a quiet order, while a second, this one not in Kance armor but looking as angry as the guards, took her place next to Wax at the boat's aft.

"You'll save her," said the roller's captain, "and then I'll be throwing you lot back in the river."

"Makes the whole thing pointless, doesn't it?" Wax said. Snapping back at the jerk of a captain felt much more comfortable. "How about you let us go along for the ride, and nobody finds out you threw a Renewal overboard while fiends devour us all?"

The captain flushed, put her hands on the back board and watched as Torny's form caught up to the roller, started rising from the water.

"Nobody's going to care, because no Renewal that couldn't pay for a ride's ever going to live to the end anyway," the captain said before reaching over the side, grabbing Torny, and, with a curse, lifting the bandit up and dropping her sodden form to the deck.

Torny's eyes fluttered as her four rescuers, Wax and the Queen, her guard and the captain, leaned over the bandit.

"Take it I'm saved, then?" she spluttered, water flicking out her mouth.

"No, you've just found a different problem," the captain replied.

"You'll let them get cleaned up," the Queen said, stating the words as if they were a fact and not a command. "Then bring them back here and we will decide, all of us, on the right course of action."

"Wise words, my queen," muttered the guard as Wax helped Torny to her feet. "I'll have Akido watch them while we discuss."

"Who's Akido?" Wax asked, while Torny coughed.

The Queen only nodded.

Akido turned out to be the first guard who'd found Bliss, and he treated his rapiers less like swords than like his own arms: always out, always ready.

The sneaky foursome reassembled themselves on the raft's bow under Akido's watchful eye. Wax didn't have much to do save confirming his satchel and the Foti blade had made the passage intact. Torny took the most attention, with Bliss helping the bandit change from her soaked clothes to dry linens. A difficult task, Torny said, when your every bone was numb.

'What do you think they'll do?' Quik asked, flashing his fingers at Wax.

'The Queen doesn't seem inclined to kill us,' Wax replied. 'Though the captain wants us in the water.'

"Keep your words in the open where I can hear them," Akido said, pointing a rapier at Wax's fingers. "There'll be no secrets here."

"Oh, we were just calling you ugly," Wax replied.

Those eyes narrowed again. Mere slits now.

"You able to see when you're that angry?" Wax asked, facing Akido full on. "Really, I'm impressed."

"Brother," Quik warned.

"No, I mean it. He's so squinted now," Wax chuckled, pointed at Akido's right hand. "Look, he's trembling too."

With his left, Wax sent a simple message Quik's way.

'Be ready.'

Akido shook his head, leveled the right hand rapier at Wax's chest. Not a tremble in sight any more. "You won't get to me, boy."

"If I'm a boy, someone with your emotional imbalance must be, what, a baby?"

Akido took a step in at Wax, his right hand sweeping up, going for a back-handed strike. The guard's left rapier kept its point on Wax, leaving no opening for a dodge. Torny and Bliss behind blocked a retreat.

Nothing stopped Quik from a free grapple. The Vis

hunter snagged Akido's wrists, pushing the man's right arm up around his neck and pinning the left to Akido's waist. Wax drew his Foti blade, pointed the sapphire sword at the opening in the Kance man's helmet.

"Look at that," Wax said. "Guess the boy's in control."

"You'll be dead in a minute," Akido countered as Quik backed him up against the roller's side.

"How long can you swim in all this gear?" Quik asked. "I hear Kance can float on the wind. I'm eager to see."

Akido stiffened, the man's insults dying on Quik's words. Wax waggled his Foti blade at the guard.

"Drop your rapiers, then we'll have a real negotiation."

"He'll do nothing of the kind."

The Queen, flanked by the remaining two guards and the roller's captain, strode their way. "You'll unhand my man now, Vis."

"What'll that get us save a rapier to the gut?" Wax asked, sneaking in a reply before Quik could bother.

Some people knew how to handle a war with words. Quik, in Wax's experience, preferred his battles in more physical arenas.

"It'll get you passage on this vessel," the Queen said. "Something I was going to grant you anyway. Along with the use of a cabin below. Now, I think you'll spend the journey here on the deck."

Wax threw a glance back at Torny, Bliss. Still pulling themselves together. Not ready for a fight.

"You're aware we still have this guy up against a rail, right?" Wax asked. "We could throw him over."

"Then you would die." The Queen didn't narrow her eyes, didn't flush, did nothing save state the fact and leave it there.

"Not negotiating, are we?"

"Wax," Quik said, "take the damn deal."

"Your friend—"

"Brother," Wax sniped.

"Brother, then," the Queen gave Wax a curt nod. "He's giving you good counsel. Take it."

"You ever don't get what you want?"

There, for the briefest moment in the yellowed lantern light, Wax caught a break in the Queen's iced poise. A quiver on the lips, a shiver in those pupils.

"More than you know," the Queen said. She slipped a hand in her robe. It came out with a single, glittering stiletto. "Unhand him, or your life is at an end."

The diamond point, long and narrow, angled towards the ground, but in her hold Wax saw the Kance Windmaster from his first voyage, the one skilled enough in swordplay to accomplish any kill the man wanted.

Maybe, just maybe, Wax could settle this one, walk away with all of them alive.

"Deal, then," Wax said, taking a step back beyond Quik as his brother released Akido.

The guard, though, didn't seem to agree to the terms. Freed, he angled his rapier at Quik and went for a stab, only to freeze the strike a hair's breadth from Quik's stomach.

The reason shone like a bright line in the dark. The Queen's stiletto, its point leading right up beneath Akido's helm to his neck.

"We have a deal, this fight is over," the Queen said. "Captain, leave them on the bow. We'll bar the door to the lower decks. Should they force it, you have my permission to do with them as you want. Akido, with me."

The Queen withdrew her blade and Akido, with one final spit at Quik's feet, turned and followed her. Only the captain remained, an impressive glower on her features.

"Don't much like stowaways getting a free ride," the captain said once the Queen and her entourage had disappeared. "So here's how you're going to pay for it. Every day, I'll have chores for you, whether it's catching fish or cleaning my roller. Do well enough, I'll let you eat our leftovers. Don't, and damn what she says, you're off this ship the first chance I get."

When the captain finished, Wax shrugged. "You could've given me that offer this afternoon and saved us all a lot of trouble."

"Trouble?" The captain laughed, though there was no mirth in it. "There's a lot worse than trouble coming, boy. The Queen didn't pay for this ride with her satchel. Those guards of hers gave me the same choice you had. A quick death or a journey up north."

"They couldn't pay you?"

The captain threw a look back, made sure the Kance party had gone.

"They could pay plenty, but the rumors coming from where we're going now? They say none of us are coming back. Not a damn soul."

CHAPTER 6

INTO THE PITS

B arten had the grace to look, sound apologetic as he led them from their cell. He'd claimed several days to get them up to health, to speed, but those were claims he had no power to enforce. The Pits, it seemed, needed its newcomers sorted quick.

"That," Barten said, guiding the group through wide torch-lit tunnels, "and the afternoon's main events ended early."

"Why?" Maena, at the front after her little speech, asked.

"The big winner slipped and lost his head after less than a minute." Bergen shook his own. "Disappointing. Had a couple meals wagered on him."

"How'd he lose his head?"

"Oh, you'll find out yourself in due time. If you're lucky."

Beyond the torches, the tunnels gave up their dungeon feel. Occasional cuts in the surface gave windowed looks into the sinking gray afternoon sky, muddy lines running down the walls and the tunnel edges showing crude drain work.

A Rana construct would slip that water off somewhere useful.

Prisoner trains passed them going the other way, some as long as their own, while others held only one or two. Joichi, the warlord who'd been waiting at the Dark Below's exit claimed he'd captured all the Rana leaving their fiend murdering expedition, but Maena had yet to see any old friends here. Then again, most of the passing prisoners seemed so battered, mud-covered, and world-weary as to be unrecognizable.

She'd be like that soon enough.

Like we're not used to it.

There was a time we were clean. On the water.

Never had a chance to find out what that's like.

You might yet.

All the fatalism creeping through Maena on the wagon ride dimmed during the tunnel walk, the meal before. She'd spent days with little to do, little hope, but now action's prospect brought some life into her sore, weak limbs. Maena kept her head high rather than letting it sink into her arms.

That's how I was when we went back for the fiend. Guess how that turned out.

Barten's destination, though, didn't hold any fiends. An arena carved out into the earth, dirt walls smoothed off to make handholds a difficult proposition. Deep red clay covered the whole space. Up the walls and over the lip sat wood benches. A sparse, fur-covered crowd gathered, slopping drink and food into their mouths as the show marched in.

Around the arena's edge sat eight boxes, an equal

number to the prisoners. Each box matched Maena's shoulders in width, stretched up to her shins. No handholds, and their deep impressions in the clay suggested they'd not been moved for some time.

In the pit's center lay a stone pile, each one a rough ball no larger than Maena's head. Gray and black, mottled with dirt and time, the stones had been piled in a loose gathering. Unlike the boxes, none looked well settled.

Maena felt the tug on her hands, the rope tying them again falling away. She rubbed her wrists, easing full feeling to her fingers while Bergen called out the instructions.

"Get yourselves to a box, each of you. No sharing, neither," Barten said, louder than necessary for the prisoners. The audience getting the story too. "You'll stand before it, your heels touching the box's edge. No cheating, now." Barten chuckled, pointed to the man who'd shoveled his meal into his mouth. "I know you've been here before, so no spoiling the surprise."

Someone's smart enough to get out of here, yet dumb enough to get caught again?

The Seven Isles have all kinds.

"With me," Svarde muttered, coming up past Maena, giving her the slightest push. "Place like this, best we stick together."

"I thought you were a loner?" Maena countered, though she went with Svarde to the arena's far side.

"Tried that. Didn't work. My mission isn't over."

Hers wasn't either. Despite the battle waging in her head, Maena could see the fiends all too clearly, the ones who'd taken—

"Here's the game, then," Barten shouted again as they all stood before their boxes, heels up against the soft, rotting wood. "In a minute, I'll whistle. Then it's a free-for-all. First two who get three stones in their boxes get the easy way out. Gets rougher from there." Barten drew his skinning knife, gestured up towards the audience. "Anyone tries to climb out, my friend up there's got a nasty pike to stick you with. Don't try it. Otherwise, do what you have to. It's worth it."

Barten backed up to the arena's edge, slipped the knife into his belt.

"We hit them hard," Svarde said. "I'll knock them aside, you grab your stones."

Barten's hand went to his mouth, two fingers inside. A deep breath.

"You play your game, I'll play mine," Maena replied as the man's whistle sounded high and sharp.

Svarde barreled forward, bellowing out some Foti battle cry and scattering cold clay everywhere with his bare feet. Maena took one step then stopped, stared.

What're you doing? Trying to lose?

Watch.

The other seven, Rasslebeck and Pennifer included, made a frenzied dash to the stones in the middle. They bounded into each other, hands scrabbling, pushing and shoving. Pennifer had her leg kicked out, her head smashing into the dirt. The glutton met Svarde's shoulder in an ill-advised dive towards a stone and sank to the ground, dazed.

Maena kept her eye on the cackling woman, whose box lay to Maena's right, watched as the sneaky lady snared a stone from the pile's edge and started with it back to her box.

We're going to lose if you don't move.

Maena ignored her simpler self. Saw Svarde emerge

from the pile with a stone in either hand. The Foti Guardian muscled free, stomping back slow towards his box. Rasslebeck and the other prisoner Maena didn't know had stones too, one apiece on the way home.

Maena's target reached her box, grunted as she lifted the stone in. The woman turned back to the center and ran, arms flying wild, the familiar cackle rising from her lips.

And now, we go.

The Rana captain kicked into action, heading not to the pile but to the other woman's box. Reaching down with both hands, Maena plucked the stone free, turned and lugged it the short way to her own box. Set it inside.

Oh, that's a dastardly move.

"Where'd you get that?" Svarde asked, and Maena noticed he'd come to her box before his own.

"Put those stones in your own box, Svarde. I don't need your charity."

Svarde looked like he was about to argue, so Maena pushed the man. That gave the Foti fighter a hint, Svarde stumbling along the right way.

Which let Maena survey the field. The cackling woman and Pennifer tangled with one another, an inadvertent mashing as they went for the same stone. Rasslebeck about had his second free from the pile, a move blocked when the glutton, coming back to his senses, dove on Rana fighter. The third prisoner, free to score his second stone, hefted it and went back to his box, two away from Maena's own.

Why're they all fighting instead of just grabbing the stones?

Same reason I stole mine. Slow the competition, save yourself.

Maena sprinted left, cut across Svarde as the lumbering barbarian headed back towards the middle. The prisoner lugging his second stone dumped it in his box, turned at

Maena's approach, and threw up his hands in a coward's defense.

For all her talk about getting out alive, Maena didn't let guilty feelings slow her down. Barten had made clear the Pits weren't a team game.

With a feint towards the prisoner's face, Maena drew the scrawny arms up, leaving a wide open elbow to the man's gut. He bent over, and Maena swept her right arm over the prisoner, pushed him down and across her leg to leave him sprawling in the clay.

Without stopping, she reached into the box, hefted the stone. Heavy enough to require two hands, emptying the man's box entirely wasn't in the offing. Maena spun her heels in the clay, headed back the way she'd come.

Off to the left, Rasslebeck had won his fight, leaving the glutton once again dazed in the dirt. His second stone was about home. Pennifer and the cackling woman had split off, with Pennifer winning the struggle for her first prize. The other woman went deeper, scooped up her stone, and was starting back.

Svarde, ever methodical, again had two stones in his arms, trudging homeward.

Maena flashed by him again, letting the clay's soft surface slide her along as much as run. Bending forward, she dropped the second stone in her box, glanced at Svarde.

"Know what? I've changed my mind. Can I have one?" Maena asked.

Svarde rolled the stone in his left arm, lofted it as his palm found its edge and sent the stone on a short flight to a plop in the clay halfway between their boxes.

A quick trip for a win.

Maena closed the distance as Svarde reached his own box, dumped in the third stone.

"We have the first winner!" Bertan shouted over the continued scuffle. "The Foti Beast claims a victory!"

The Foti Beast? Sounds about right.

Maena reached Svarde's thrown stone, scooped it up. Started back to her box only to hear Svarde call out her name.

The man's tone told Maena's instincts what to do, and she ducked, cradling the stone as the cackling woman, spitting curses now, struck Maena. Crusted fingernails, biting teeth, kicking feet assailed Maena like a rotten whirlwind, one Maena endured long enough to swing the stone.

Sure, the rock balls could be used to win the game, but the things had weight, had bulk, and when Maena's two-handed smash took the attacking woman in the chin, she collapsed in the dirt unmoving.

With bleeding scratches and a bruised shin, Maena stumbled to her box, rolled the third stone in. Sat in the clay.

Noticed, for the first time, the furious yelling from the crowd. Curses, jeers, the angry spittle of bets gone awry at the last minute.

"Hold!" Barten shouted, then whistled again. "Hold, my friends, my spirited competitors. The game is over. The Foti Beast was the first to three, but as to the second, we have a dispute." Barten pointed one hand at Maena, another at Rasslebeck. The other Rana fighter, like Maena, stood over his box, three stones resting within. "We all know how ties are broken in the Pits, do we not?"

The crowd roared in response.

"Exactly, exactly," Barten said. "Always a delight. Everyone else, clear yourselves from the arena. Yes, you too, Foti. This contest no longer concerns you."

Two more Whent guards appeared, ropes in hand, at

the exit. Long knives in their waists made clear what would happen should anyone get the wrong idea. Pennifer and the other three prisoners, with the woman Maena had knocked out getting dragged by Svarde, made their way from the arena.

Rasslebeck gave Maena an almost apologetic look, shrugged.

Oh, this is starting to get interesting.

Maena didn't share the sentiment. The crowd broke into a steady chant, one rising in volume as Barten strode to the arena's center, dodging the stones as he walked. The man held both hands up, wiggling his fingers as if to draw the audience into a frenzy.

"All right, my esteemed friends," Barten said. "It's time to settle our game. As with every contest in the Pits, ties are broken in a match of skill, of physical talent, and mental acuity."

Barten's arm went to his waist, drew the skinning knife sheathed there. He dropped it into the center, its point sticking up from the clay.

You'll have to kill each other, won't you?

Maena swallowed, tempered her breathing. Kept her eyes on Rasslebeck. They'd been through how many raids together, how many seasons sailing the isles?

Now this, this I can get behind. Pure struggle. Let the best one win. Show me what we can do, captain.

Barten then put a hand to his ear, nodded. The crowd grew louder. A new sound slithered beyond them, magnified as something new shoved up against the arena's upper edge. A crate, and within it, a creature.

One Maena knew.

"That's right, a rare find indeed. A ferrite, all the way from Foti!" Barten howled. "Once it's released, whichever one of you deals the killing blow earns your victory." Barten dropped to a chuckle. "Let's hope one of you does."

Barten made another slight wave and the cage's door swung open. Someone lifted the cage's back, dumping the ferrite out the front into a rolling tumble to the arena floor.

Kivi, Svarde's friend and their loyal guide in the dark, shook herself, snorted, and found Maena with her curious sapphire eyes.

CHAPTER 7
THE UNLIKELY PRISONER

Free. If Bliss had one word to describe her life before hopping on this journey, that'd be it. Or close to it. Torny, though, picked at the idea, seeming to delight in showing all the ways Kitaye, her family, her society had kept Bliss tied down.

The two sat against the roller's prow, dominated by the gigantic front wheel as dawn crept up, Sichi's light going orange as it mixed with the day. A cloudless day in the offing, brisk and bright. Around them, Riroca's cityscape had long since bled away to its riverbank wilds. Pines rose up along the banks, needled branches stretching over the rustling waters. Small rodents ran along, harried by cawing black birds. Things the captain called Okam paced their progress, four legged, fat-tailed critters with toothy maws. Every so often one would dart to the water, lunge their pointed mouth in, and emerge with a wriggling fish.

"Stringy and dry," the captain said when she pointed out the first one. "If you're starving, they'll serve. Otherwise anything's better."

"Sounds like you know from experience," Torny had replied.

"Experience you might share soon enough."

The captain offered nothing else, save turning back to her till and the river ahead. Wax and Quik had been called aft, stuck back there to manage the roller's own fishing nets, the poles dredging bait in the water.

According to the captain, they'd not had time to stock up the ship enough for the journey as it was, much less with four more mouths to feed. Scavenging would be in order.

'As if there's not any towns along the way,' Bliss signed.

She and Torny, despite the hour, had their own job: cleaning branches and other crud off that big wheel, churning away up front. Bliss wasn't sure how it worked, what made it move, though Torny said it required a boiler and explained why the captain's two other crew rarely made it up top.

"We stole the best jobs on the ship," Torny said as they used a couple wood poles with sweeps on the end to snag debris. "Bet they're not happy with us."

'Why wouldn't the captain stick us with the worst ones?'

"Because if we botch this, the wheel gets a scratch. You mess up the boiler, the whole roller explodes." Torny, wrapped like Bliss in thick Foti linens, looked a bit like a gray mound with a stick flailing out. "We've been churning all night and day so far too. The captain wouldn't be able to keep moving like that without our help."

In a way, knowing they weren't just leeches on the journey gave Bliss a boost. For all Wax's confidence in their attempted sneaking onto the raft, Bliss hadn't done much thieving in her life.

As the captain said, it worked for survival, but if it wasn't necessary?

"You Vis must really keep yourselves in the dark," Torny continued. "You've never seen steam power? I'll grant it's pretty rare, but hang out on any civilized isle and you'll notice it."

'Are you really calling Vis uncivilized?'

Torny had the grace to scrunch up her face, embarrassed. Her hair, tied back like Bliss's to keep the wind from smacking bangs into their eyes, showcased the bandit's forehead, smooth save for a slight red line running up from an ear to her scalp. Another scar with another story Bliss hadn't earned.

"You know what I meant. Not modern."

'Getting worse.'

Torny sighed, "Look, I've never been to Vis, okay? All I have is rumors. What I've heard. They say your isle's a paradise, but that you're all weird. Not like the rest of us."

'Like the rest how?'

Torny stared hard at the wheel, "They say you don't care about power."

'That makes us strange?'

"You and Tamas, yeah."

'Do *you* care about power?'

Torny nodded, "Not, like, being a queen or anything. But I want to control my life. Protect myself. My friends."

The bandit shot Bliss a certain look as she finished. Not knowing what to do with the sudden silence, the odd glance, Bliss swept her pole to the right, clapped Torny on the shoulder.

"Hey, what?" Torny yelped, dropping her own pole to rub the spot.

'Sorry, I was trying to get a leaf you missed.'

"Thanks, jerk."

By midday the pine forest gave way to rolling thistle-coated hills and twisting waterways, the river joining and splitting off with others. Sometimes it seemed wide enough to swallow Kitaye, other times the raft funneled through such narrow canals Bliss would find her breath holding as the captain maneuvered around a tight curl.

Without the debris clogging the wheel, Bliss and Torny went back to help Quik and Wax manage the food supply, a task Quik attacked with delighted gusto. The hunter had given Wax charge of the poles, choosing to leverage a spear gun for himself.

"Took a few tries, but I've got it now," Quik said. "Watch."

Bliss stood next to Quik as he raised the weapon up to his shoulder, the rope hanging loose yet ordered near his feet. Squinting one eye and placing it near the weapon's barrel, Quik sighted into the dark waters. After nary a few seconds, the hunter pulled the trigger, sending the spear flashing into the water downstream.

Something splashed and wriggled while Quik set the gun down, took up the rope and started to pull.

"Feel free to help if you're just standing there," Quik said, a grin plastered on his face.

Bliss knew why. This was Quik's element, what he loved, what he'd planned to do since he could first walk around the jungle. The two reeled in the fish together, slapping it inside a thick chest near the back, one filled with fresh Rana ice.

That, at least, the captain had been able to score before their departure the day before.

'Feeling better?' Bliss signed as they began resetting the spear gun.

"What?" Quik asked, then saw where Bliss was looking. The spot near his stomach, where Eggrad, the bandit leader, had stabbed Quik not all that long ago. "Yeah. A little line left over, but the skar's been incredible."

'We're lucky,' Bliss signed, then nodded towards Wax. Her brother and Torny were dealing with a line tangle that looked positively nightmarish. 'Without the skar, you—'

"Without it? We wouldn't be here if Wax wasn't trying this."

'I thought you wanted adventure?' Bliss picked up a line, a ruffled feather.

"I do. But this is all so random," Quik replied. "We get to Foti, know nothing, then get kidnapped. Repeat the same thing here, and now we're bottom feeders on a boat hired by another Renewal." Quik sighed. "Maybe I'm just tired of getting thrown around. We're supposed to be saving the world, not spearing fish."

'Follow the tracks, not the dream.'

Quik chuckled, "Okay, elder. I don't think they were talking about Renewals."

'How do you know?'

"Guess I don't. Even so. You remember those Najahn we were with? They understood. They gave us what we needed, helped us out. More, nobody gave them any grief."

'Yeah, because they're Najahn. Everyone's scared of what they could do.'

"Not scared, Bliss. They believe the Najahn are their only hope. That's what we should be. Hope. Strength. The future." Quik, spear gun reloaded, stood up with Bliss and handed her the weapon. "Isn't that what you want to be?"

'I'll settle for getting Wax through this alive. Seems like that might be hard enough.'

"I'm with you there. Now, hold it like this, and you feel the stock here . . . "

Sleep wasn't hard to find that night for most of them. Torny and Wax conked out first. Quik took longer, laying on the deck. The captain gave them a few coarse blankets, suggesting their own satchels as pillows. Bliss, though, lay awake last, watching the stars.

Save the chill, things felt good, and that feeling seemed alien. The last time Bliss could say she'd been at peace was back on Kitaye, before the fiends ever visited. Before the Renewal, Pan, and her own barely-survived attempt to take out those monsters.

But here, with the wheel churning away behind her, its rumble mingling with the river for some good vibrations, Bliss could let her staff go, could stretch out without needing to know who'd been posted on watch. No bandits would attack here, and the captain said they were a couple days away yet from real iffy territory.

Take the moment, then. Let herself relax.

Or she would've, anyway, if not for footsteps on the deck. Quiet ones, but more than two. Heading aft.

Bliss sat up, looked over and saw none of the other three awake. Wax's soft snores lost themselves in the river's noise. Torny had her face mashed into her satchel, while Quik had a hunter's rest, the quick-in, quick-out sleep for someone who needed to snatch what he could from slim slumbers.

A word cut the noise. Not clear enough to make out, but the tone came through. Anger, irritation. Maybe something harsher. The footsteps continued aft.

Leave and let be?

Bliss looked at Torny again. No way the bandit would

take that. She'd say something like any information on the others was useful.

Well, Bliss could be damn quiet if she wanted.

Rolling up onto her bare feet, Bliss kept to a crouch. The front cabin had a lantern burning, the night crewman at the till, but the man had his eyes watching the water, not Bliss as she moved around the corner to the raft's port side.

The narrow walkway along the raft's side didn't give Bliss much cover, so she adopted a different stance. Standing straight, putting a bleary expression on her face. Ready to argue she was just finding a place to pee if someone found her. Still, she kept her walk quiet, noticed the stairway down had its door closed.

But the words came again, cutting, from the aft. And now, with the wheel blunted by distance and the raft's bulk, Bliss could make them out.

"I said I needed air." The Queen's iced tones. Only now, they lacked the iron command Bliss had heard before. More frustrated, uncertain. "You can't keep me down there all day."

"It's for your own safety," a different sort of iron speech here. A mother speaking to a child, tones Bliss knew well enough from growing up. "You'll do as we need, and the Aegis will be yours."

"And Kance will be hers."

Bliss reached the aft, kept herself pressed to the raft's inner wall. Listened.

"Be careful what you speak, highness," the guard said. "You're a long way from home."

"Kill me now, Silvrin, and you'll seal your own fate."

"Then how about we both agree to be nice, and nobody needs to get hurt."

Bliss went back a step. She wouldn't consider herself an

expert on Kance, their politics, or how much of anything off Vis worked, but it seemed strange a guard would talk back to the Queen like that.

And the Queen had said kill? As in, the guard would kill her?

"'Scuse me, Bliss."

Behind her, Wax pushed on past, forcing Bliss around the corner into the open. The Queen and Silvrin turned glares their way, though both ignored Wax as he refreshed his water skin from the barrel, and kept their eyes on Bliss.

"What're you doing over here?" Wax asked her, his skin filled.

'You're an idiot,' Bliss signed, turning on her heel and stalking back up front.

Always account for fools, they said back home. Something Bliss needed to remember anytime Wax was around.

CHAPTER 8
JUNGLE TEETH

Noise: the one thing Sawi could say describing the Najahn after their first morning traveling together. Despite the cleared path south east, a several days journey to the Najahn outpost and the Great Sana, Gladdring's squad packed as if preparing for a months-long expedition, and a dangerous one at that.

Every step blotted out the jungle's song with clinks and clashes, armor and gear bouncing off itself. Najahn conversation contributed too, hard syllables and city slang mashing with the verdant wildlife around them. Sawi winced every time she saw a soldier kick a plant aside or hack away an offending vine.

The gatherers maintaining these routes did so with respect, moving plants to where they could grow without interference, not killing without thought.

The Najahn were all too happy to take as well, accepting Sawi's offered food, fresh-baked fish and fruit for breakfast with barely any thanks and no offer to reply in kind. The children who'd followed Sawi to watch the Najahn leave, hoping for a trinket or two, went away empty-handed.

Gladdring and his scholars did their part to keep her attention, at least. They peppered Sawi with questions about this and that, everything from Vis customs to the names of plants and animals witnessed on their journey. The scholars, with strange paper scrolls, recorded everything she said.

The whole combination cured Sawi of any shyness, spoiled fascination into crass curiosity and acid archness, prompting Sawi, at their lunch break beneath a warm sun in a grove beneath speckled pink and white flowers, to ask Gladdring what they wanted.

"Everyone here has different goals," Gladdring said, more genial now than the night before. Sweat soaked his face, but Gladdring seemed not to mind. His black and purple robes, dirty now, staying on. "Several of these guards are going to reinforce the outpost or trade rotations with ones already there. These scholars belong to different Tenets, some recording information to be shared back home, while others look for ways to use it."

"Use it?"

"Just as you would back in Kitaye, Sawi." Gladdring accepted some cured meat from a guard, offered a piece to Sawi, who refused. "Only one for your own foods?"

"They're what I know."

"And venturing beyond what you know is a frightening thing?"

With Wax, Sawi wouldn't have said so. Together, they'd found the unknown a place to be explored, conquered. Alone?

"I'm here," Sawi said. "Let's leave it at that for now."

"Of course. Though if you find it difficult to try even a little of something new, you're going to find leaving Vis very hard indeed."

"Who says I mean to leave?"

Gladddring chuckled, a frog-like burble. "Perhaps you will surprise me, Sawi, by not showing up at our boat on the day of departure, but I do not think so."

The afternoon played out much the same as the morning, a steady hike slowing as the sun dipped to an early winter rain. The path muddied, the Najahn mood soured. Sawi pointed out the thicker canopies to stay beneath, found most Najahn too stubborn, too dismissive to take her advice.

Gladdring, though, followed her steps exactly.

Evening found the storm letting up, a camp pitched in a gloomy, buggy dark. Fires proved hard to light, smokey spitting things. Sawi would've simply scaled a tree, tied herself to a branch and enjoyed some fruit and an early bedtime. Instead, she helped the intruders find some small comfort on the wet, mossy forest floor.

"What's that, then?" asked a Najahn guard, loud enough to draw everyone's attention.

The man had his voulge unlimbered, pointed the curved spear through the trees. His target: six small flickering orbs spaced well enough as they moved, well back and cloaked in the dark.

Before Sawi could speak, another Najahn soldier gave a sharp whistle, sending the camp into a scramble. Gladdring and the scholars made for the middle, the Najahn guards drawing weapons and forming a ring.

Sawi, eyebrows raising throughout, watched, laughed when the formation finished, leaving her on its outside.

"Get behind our spears, girl," snapped the guard who'd made the order. "We can't protect you from the fiends if you're out there."

"Fiends?" Sawi asked, keeping the laughter in her voice. "Strange, is it not, that the native doesn't seem concerned?"

"Tell us, then," Gladdring announced from the middle. "If we shouldn't be worried, why?"

"Those things won't hurt you," Sawi replied. "Several hanoko. A mother and her kittens. This is their territory, at least through the winter till the kittens go their own way. Hanokos won't hunt a group like us." Sawi let a sly grin slip on. "Though I suggest going in pairs if you need to leave the fire at night."

"If it's dangerous, we ought to chase them away," the Najahn guard said, the words directed at Gladdring. "We can't stay here if there's a chance they'll attack."

"Will these hanokos respond to a threat?" Gladdring asked Sawi.

"This is their home," Sawi replied. She picked up and put down a dozen different ideas, deeming each too far beyond these urban soldiers. "You won't scare them away. You'll more likely frighten them into a fight, which you do not want."

"Then you believe we're safe?"

"There's easier prey out here than us. You'll be fine."

Gladdring, standing tall over his guards, gave Sawi a nod. "We'll trust the native, captain. Relax your arms, though the watchman should be more vigilant."

"I'll take the first shift myself." The captain, who looked like all the others save a gold circular pin on his breastplate, stamped his voulge in the ground as he spoke, as if that made him intimidating.

Sawi tried not to laugh and mostly succeeded.

While the rest of the camp settled in, Gladdring approached Sawi, who was trying to decide which tree would make a more comfortable bed.

"Can you take me to find them?" Gladdring asked. "These hanokos?"

The eyes had vanished soon after the captain's panicked whistle. Finding the large cats' trail in the dark wouldn't be easy, even for a veteran Vis hunter.

"It's not a good idea," Sawi replied. "We'd likely stumble around in the wet until, bored, exhausted, and dirty, we came back here with nothing to show."

Disappointment drained Gladdring's face, the urgent sparkle in his step dying in a sigh. "That's a no, then?"

"We've got a long walk tomorrow, Tenet. And the day after. Better rest while we can."

Gladdring's eyes narrowed, his hands, fingers curled tightly around each other and, if Sawi guessed right, some small object between them.

"You don't trust me out there in the dark," Gladdring said. Not a question. "You don't think me capable."

Sawi blinked. The man spoke the truth, albeit one she'd not put into conscious words till he himself said it.

"You and your people don't belong here," Sawi said. "You're not at home in the jungle. It's not so dangerous to me, who's spent every day of my life in it, but you? A broken ankle, a prick from a poison thorn—"

"Is not your concern," Gladdring said. "Whatever you might think of the Najahn, of me, know we are more than capable of handling your plants and animals."

"Then why take me along at all?"

"For this, right here." Gladdring nodded behind Sawi, into the dark. "Please, if only for a short while. I would very much like to see one of these creatures."

Sawi again started to voice her objection, but found the dissent fading even as it formed in her throat. So the man wanted to take a foolish wander in the dark? What of it?

Getting away from all the Najahn grumbling, their curses and complaints, might be a good thing before a night's rest.

"A short walk," Sawi agreed.

The Najahn captain made his disapproval known, but Gladdring waved it away. Declared he and the Vis could handle themselves, that they would stay close enough for the captain to effect a rescue should any fiends come prowling by.

So, with the rain dripping, armed with her rope and Gladdring's form behind her, Sawi set off into the dark.

A cloudy sky meant Sichi and the stars added little light, making the first moments away from the Najahn fire a tentative exercise. Her feet bare—the climbing shoes tucked away in her satchel—Sawi used her toes, her fingers, her nose to guide her. Gladdring followed, and Sawi found her estimation of the man growing as he matched her walk in near-silence.

No metal jangles, no curses, no loud breaths. Only a quiet confidence coming from the Tenet.

Not all Najahn, then, were alike. Something to remember.

Putting the fire behind them, Sawi and Gladdring ventured to where the Hanoko's flickering eyes had last been seen. The cats could move lightly when they needed to, but Sawi found their paw prints easy enough in the muddy floor. Flattened leaves, ferns, and the sticky scent of hanoko urine marked the trail well enough. With her eyes adjusting, the absolute black became a shadowed world, gray lines mingling with one another. A few insects scurried in to investigate the pair, their numbers shrinking for the coming winter.

"Here," Sawi said, recognizing a weed to her left and reaching to crush its petals in her palms. Tiny pustules in the leaves broke to leave a small slime. "Rub this along your face and you'll be spared the worst bites."

Gladdring didn't protest, accepting the offer and spreading it on.

Another mark in his favor.

The man scored further points by not speaking as Sawi led them along the trail. She stayed low and soft, Gladdring matched, and the two stalked the cats for longer than Sawi intended, the clues too clear to pass up.

"The den," Sawi whispered, almost breathed, when they came upon the huge fallen tree. It'd smashed into another, the two crumpling together to form a shelter, one that would last several seasons or more. "They'll be waiting in there."

"Waiting?" Gladdring asked. "Not sleeping?"

"Hanokos hunt as often at night as during the day," Sawi replied. "The mother might be behind us already, waiting to see if we make a move on her children."

"But you aren't afraid."

Sawi straightened. "If we don't attack them, the hanoko will leave us alone. Again, there's easier prey."

"Unfortunate," Gladdring said. "I would have liked to see one up close."

Now Sawi turned around. "Why?"

In the dark, she couldn't make out the finer contours of Gladdring's face, but read the rebuke in his tone.

"My reasons are my own, Sawi. I appreciate your efforts in bringing me here, but I'm afraid they are not enough."

"I don't—"

"The Isles are in danger. A Renewal has been called, and the Najahn are tasked with keeping us all alive until a new Aegis is earned. " Gladdring put a hand on Sawi's shoulder. Gave the slightest shove back towards the hanoko den. "To do my part, I must see one of these cats of yours up close. Now, if you would."

The arguments against Gladdring's idea were many. They played out, a frantic litany, as Sawi took the first step towards the hanoko den. If the cats found her a threat, they would dive on the pair, they would attack and tear her and Gladdring apart.

Yet, Gladdring had suggested a single provocation, a single hanoko up close could help save the isles. Could give Wax a better chance at success.

How could Sawi say no?

With her second step, she opened her mouth, gave a low hunter's whoop, the classic call when a catch had been found. A sound these hanoko would've heard, would've learned to fear.

So Sawi wasn't surprised at all when the shadows before her moved, fast and quiet, save for a growl, loud and rumbling, from the trees above.

CHAPTER 9
SPEAR GAMES

When Bliss missed the third shot in a row, Quik knew something was up. His sister, who'd burned yesterday with him in the roller's aft becoming experts with the spear gun, didn't botch her aim like that.

Ever since she could lift that staff, blow a puff into a dart gun and send its needle into the tree, Quik's own father riled him by saying Bliss was destined to be the real hunter in the family.

"For all those muscles," his father said, "she'd have you on your back and out in a few seconds time."

As every sibling must, Quik learned to deal with the digs, usually by joining the closest hunting party and taking out the frustration on his next dinner. Soon enough, he started laughing along with his father, both admiring her progress as she came back to Kitaye first with vermin, then game birds, and finally with the prized lumbering beasts ever harder to find on Vis.

'I've got it,' Bliss signed as Quik moved to help her

reload the spear gun. Irritation played into her fingers. 'It's what I deserve.''

That irritation, though, didn't cross to her face, her eyes. Bliss's focus flashed constantly to her left, across the aft landing to the fishing nets manned by Wax and the Kance Queen. One of her guards stood nearby, watching the pair with what seemed like a permanent glare.

The Najahn never looked that angry. Quik had to wonder whether the Queen just chose the most difficult bruisers for the job. Then again, who'd want to coast around all Seven Isles with this bunch of jerks?

Wax didn't seem to mind, his brother doing what he always did: digging into things with plucky aplomb. If Quik's parents declared Bliss the true killer of the group, they didn't know what to do with Wax. He'd been thrown free, left to figure things out as he spent the days swinging from one vine to the next.

Quik gave Bliss space, took a longer look at both his siblings. A quiet smile ticked up. Not so long ago, they'd both been so tiny, Quik carrying them around the tree-house, over to the inlet for a bath. Now here they were, adventuring together.

How lucky could one family get?

"You going to block the whole boat?"

Quik's smile slid to straight nothing as Torny brushed by, a mid-morning snack in her arms. A tray fleshed out with small rice bowls, boiled off the same heat running the roller on its churning journey northward.

"Captain says you each get one, and that you're supposed to be happy about it," Torny continued, holding the tray out to each person in turn. Even the surly guard took one, muttering a snip thank you. Wood spoons, each no larger than Quik's fingers, sufficed to scoop the soft brown grains into his mouth.

The rice matched the day's taste: bland and harmless. Gray clouds that might've uttered snow with harsher weather blotted out the sun, but for once the wind didn't seem inclined to blow them away. Quik pinned that to the broad paddies rising up on either side and farther back.

The makers of the very rice they ate now, and Rana's main crop, to hear the captain tell it. The last bit of good territory they'd be churning through before hitting Rana's northern expanse, its wilder rivers, and, eventually, the Whirlpool.

"Like it?" Wax asked, and Quik thought he was the target, but heard instead the Queen's voice in response.

"Fair," the Queen replied. "I'll not cast a word against the food of the vessel I need, though."

"Scared the captain's going to dump you over the side?" Wax laughed.

"She won't," the guard's interjection landed without humor, without doubt. The man scooped more rice, ground it in his teeth. "She's been paid. She'll deliver."

The Queen looked frozen at the words, a set stare towards her own man, broken only after Wax cracked some bad joke about delivering a Renewal like him to the Whirlpool.

"A regular comedian, that guy," Torny said, finishing her own bowl near Quik. "He's always been that way?"

"As soon as he had a mouth, he used it to make us laugh," Quik said.

'Or groan,' Bliss signed. Done with the speargun, she set it against the boat's back. 'You two have a moment?'

"Where else are we going to go?" Torny asked, and Quik had to agree.

The roller's size remained something of a mystery, as the Queen forbade the Vis group, and Torny, from descending inside. Only luck had kept the weather nice enough to not force the issue, and the beautiful views kept Quik's wanderlust from taking control, but even so, he often lingered by the stair. The old urge to adventure, to explore. The one thing he and Wax had in common.

Bliss shot another look at the guard, munching his rice. The man dined slow given his constant looks towards the Queen. Protective, but then, rumors always said Kance royalty had violent tendencies.

'Last night, they were up here,' Bliss signed, slipping a point towards the Queen, Wax, and the guard.

"Wax?" Quik said, only to catch a glare from his sister.

"Thinking she means this to be a secret," Torny muttered. "Though we'll need to keep up some charade."

'Talk about Foti,' Bliss signed. 'The tolekat and the fiend.'

For a story not all that old, Torny put on quite a spin, dropping into the discovery, the lava pit, the following fight and reunion between brother and sister. Already, Torny twisted in bits of legend, descriptions bending reality and bringing in magic, delight. A natural embellishment.

All the while, Quik watched Bliss's fingers fly, and he matched her with questions of his own. Torny, still a novice at the lingo, mostly focused on her story, occasionally signing to Quik for him to laugh.

Bliss's tale lacked Torny's imagination, the monster, and the murderous triumph, but it had the absolute advantage of being important to their immediate situation.

'You believe the Queen's being held against her will?' Quik signed. 'You're certain?'

'No way. I heard an argument, that's all.'

Back on Foti, when Quik had gone to the Najahn commander with their plight, the purple and black hadn't hesitated for a moment before declaring their intent to rescue Wax. By that night the sloop had been loaded, casting off and risking poor lighting to save his brother's life.

Not because Wax was a Vis in need of help, but because he was a Renewal, and the world needed his chance.

If Bliss had it right, then the Queen might be a hostage, however unbelievable that would seem.

And what, exactly, would they do with that information?

'She's still here,' Quik signed. 'She's not trying to get away.'

'Because those guards are all over her,' Bliss replied. 'What would she do, fight them?'

A mistake that'd be. Quik figured the Queen's robes could hide a knife or two, and Kance had a reputation with small blades, but against her three guards? With no support?

Quik straightened. Torny's tale neared its end, and they'd have to make a choice.

'We don't know enough,' Quik signed. 'The Najahn wouldn't want any Renewal pressed into this.'

Torny snorted mid-line. "The Najahn don't give a damn about any of us," she muttered, before rising her voice back up into the climactic dance with the clam-like fiend.

Quik frowned at the bandit, then pushed it away. Torny didn't matter, was insignificant save for how she could help Wax. And Bliss seemed to enjoy her company, so Quik would put up with her.

For now.

'So can we ask her?' Bliss signed. 'Find a way to know for sure?'

Quik glanced at the guard, the Queen, and Wax, returned now to their fishing nets. The guard's stare didn't seem quite so protective anymore. Instead, he seemed to be expecting the Queen to take a leap, ready on his feet to dive and catch her.

"Distraction," Torny said, putting the bowls back on the tray. "That's what this roller needs. A good old distraction."

The bandit threw Quik a wink as she left, dishes acquired for a washing.

'A distraction?' Bliss asked. 'How?'

Quik, though, had an inkling. 'I've got an idea. When it happens, you get Wax to ask her. You won't have much time.'

'What're you going to do?'

Quik, though, just grinned. Told Bliss to step aside, picked up the spear gun. Held it in on hand. Lighter than the full spears he wielded back home.

Easy.

"See, Bliss, you're holding it wrong," Quik announced. "You've gotta get both hands on the barrel, aim down the sights, and then, no matter where you aim . . . " Quik swept the speargun around, Bliss ducking as the dart went over her.

The roller wasn't an unstable ship, but she roiled and rocked with the river's running course. Rapids, rocks, and the simple churn inherent to every waterway kept the roller at a slight shifting, one Quik leveraged now to set himself off balance.

He pitched back, yelping, and pressed the trigger. The spear gun fired, glanced off the guard's Kance armor and flew off the boat's far side.

"Watch your damn aim," the guard growled as Quik found his feet. "I'm not some fish, you Vis flowerkisser."

The hunter kept the anger down. Bad shot or no, the slur wasn't necessary. Nevertheless, the words gave Quik pep as he ran to the guard, getting up real close and inspecting where the spear had slashed.

Nothing there save a slight dent in the guard's sterling silver shoulderplate, but Quik put on his best headshake anyway.

"Looks bad," Quik said. "We'd better check with the captain to see if she's got something to help you."

The guard tried to resist as Quik clapped his right arm on the guard's left, turning the man toward's the roller's walkway.

"Won't take more'en a minute or two, I'm sure," Quik said. "And of course, I'll pay for it. My fault."

"Absolutely is," the guard said, trying to shrug Quik's arm off. "If you've damaged my mail, I'll-"

The guard kept talking, Quik kept pushing, and Bliss went right by them as Quik guided the guard around the corner.

Hopefully his sister could get some answers.

Quik grinned. Of course she could. Bliss was the best. They'd all known it for so long now.

CHAPTER 10

SAVAGE STONES

A good captain knows her crew's minds without a word passing between their lips. A single look, like the one Maena threw across the arena to Rasslebeck, told her the man didn't plan on skewering her. Told her the ferrite standing between them was safe enough as well. Rasslebeck would, no doubt, see the same in Maena's eyes.

Not that Barten cared. The guard continued hollering his gross accolades, building Kivi up as a man-devouring monster, as liable to leap from the pit and snarf the crowd as eat the two combatants. With only Barten's old knife in the pit's center, what chance did these two really have?

Left out were the odds Barten himself, strolling the arena's edges with waving arms, might prove a snack.

If it would shut him up, I'd be in favor.

Maena broke forward, sprinting across the arena towards the fallen knife. Dust blew up as she slid to a stop near the blade. Kivi seemed not the least perturbed, snorting once and taking a bite from one of the stone balls remaining in the arena's middle. Rasslebeck remained where he was near the arena's lone exit, with his arms at his sides, face narrowed and wincing.

"A bold risk, leaving the weapon to your enemy," Bergen cried as Maena scooped up the knife, flipped it to a right-handed grip. "Perhaps he thinks the lizard might eat her now?"

"Stay with me," Maena muttered to Kivi. "I've a plan."

Kivi snorted. Rasslebeck read her flicking knife and edged closer to the arena door.

"The lizard seems placid," Barten said. "Perhaps now's the chance for a killing blow!"

"Chase me," Maena muttered.

Kivi cocked her head, stuck her forked tongue out to taste the air.

"Now." Maena snapped forward again, rushing Rasslebeck and throwing on the angriest scowl she could muster.

Kivi read the intentions right, broke after Maena, scampering along the dirt floor. Rasslebeck proved he was no fool, sidestepped right against the door.

Barten, proving he was, called out that there would be no escape, the door would not be opening save to let the victor out.

Gutting him already? Seems cruel, for all the help he gave us.

You don't know what you're talking about.

Hey, I've only been alive a few weeks.

Maena barreled into Rasslebeck, the man's eyes going wide as he realized she wasn't going to stop. The two fell to the ground, leaning up against that grated exit. Kivi caught up with them, stopping short of the pile.

"Break the bars," Maena snapped at the ferrite.

"That's what you're thinking?" Rasslebeck whispered while Bergan shouted out an imaginary stabbing, a fight for their lives. "Ferrite's eat rock, not iron."

Kivi, though, seemed determined to prove Rasslebeck wrong. She went around their feet, towards the grated gate's corner, opened her maw, and took a snapping bite at the black wrought metal. Her rock teeth threw sparks when they collided, and the gate shook.

"We've got to keep them distracted," Maena said, twisting and throwing Rasslebeck off her, back into the arena. "Come at me."

"Captain, time was I'd be down for a brawl," Rasslebeck rose, brought up his fists. "Not feeling it now."

"Damn your feelings." Maena brought up the knife, pointed it Rasslebeck's way. Barten howled a stabbing doom was near. "Make it real, or we both die today."

Behind her, another crunch. Something hard snapped. A chance, then.

She dove in at Rasslebeck, leading with the knife, sending its point just wide of the man's waist while Rasslebeck grabbed her shoulders, pushed her back into the gate.

The iron dug in, rough screws scratching Maena's back. Kivi put in another bite, a slight look confirming the corner falling away. Much more work needed to make enough room for an escape, unless either one planned to crawl free.

Rasslebeck relaxed his grip upon impact, perhaps wondering if he'd actually hurt his captain. Instead, Maena took the opening, plunged her left, free fist into Rasslebeck's stomach, doubling him over.

"Pretend you've been stabbed," Maena said, slipping the knife into Rasslebeck's ratty tunic, cutting into the fabric and maybe, just maybe, scraping his skin.

The Rana raider knew his role, though, and played it well, pinning the blade to his side and stumbling back a step.

Kivi crunched through another grate.

"What's this? A gutting blow for the finish?" Barten crowed. "A surprise turn, the stab not of the creature, but of her former friend!" Barten waved Maena forward, the captain accepting the offer for a slow walk. "Yes, you heard me right. She was her victim's leader, a Rana captain, now a lowly murderer for your entertainment. Yet, such things we must become if we are to win freedom in the Pits."

Maena slowed at Barten's haphazard biography. Their Whent captors had forced out cursory conversations with them all at the nights en route to the Pits, bits of background that seemed innocuous enough. Almost pleasant, the interest those scribes had taken in the dirty prisoners.

Of course, it all led back to profit, to the show.

"Come on, come on," Barten continued beseeching Maena. "Accept your glory, captain, for you've earned it. Bittersweet though it may be, it surely beats lying in the dust, your guts bleeding into the dirt?"

Another crunch, another snap. Kivi munching away. Barten, for the first time, frowned at the ferrite.

"It seems the lizard has a taste for our metal," Barten said, then waved a sharper cut to the guards up at the arena's edge. "Best put the ferrite back in her box, my friends, lest we have to shut this pit down for repairs." Barten put on a showy wink to the crowd, who laughed. "As if we would ever. A gate can easily be replaced with spears. We have enough guards to wield them, and if we ever ran out, surely any of you would jump at the chance!"

Maena reached his side, accepted Barten's hand as he

held her wrist up high. The crowd responded with a mix of claps, groans, insults and compliments. Spittle and ale flew, some landing on the pair. Barten took it all with a grin. Maena closed her eyes, looked away.

You came back for all this. Aren't you happy?

I didn't choose to come back.

Maena's other side didn't have a response to that. Instead, another snap drew Maena's look away from the offal rain, back to the gate. Another slot gone, the opening big enough now to get through at a crouch. Rasslebeck laid still.

Move. Maena tried to send the order, pass it along through some ethereal tie to Rasslebeck, but the man didn't budge. Waiting for some signal, then. Some permission to abandon his captain and run.

She could give him that.

Mustering up her breath, Maena put her fingers to her mouth and whistled. Sharp and loud, the command rose above the noise. To the crowd, it seemed a victory sign. To Rasslebeck, lying in the dust, the whistle would've meant one thing: attack.

The raider rolled forward, off the floor and dove through Kivi's opening. Maena watched as Kivi threw one look back her way before breaking off after Rasslebeck, the two vanishing into the halls beneath the Pits.

The crowd broke out into different shouting then, Barten turning to follow their points and catching the last moments of Rasslebeck's flight.

"A strong man, that one!" Barten cried. "Feigning death only to make an escape." A loud, forced chuckle, all the while his grip on Maena's wrist remained tight. "Not that it'll matter. Nobody escapes the Pits." A deep breath.

"That'll be all for this session, and for the day in this arena. Enjoy your time at the Pits, and may the blood be ever thick!"

With one last wave, the crowd bustling away to find new events, new drinks, and new stones to throw, Barten wrenched Maena to the side.

Up close, Maena counted the man's gnarled, chipped teeth. His broken nose. Breath liable to kill someone just with its stench. Yet Barten's dried eyes held a wary menace.

"Don't think we don't know what you did there, captain," Barten said, the jester's lilt gone. "Your friend's going to be stuck, either by a guard's spear or another prisoner's knife. Attempting escape puts you on a path there's no running from."

"We were dead anyway. At least now he has a chance."

"A chance?" Barten shook his head, faux mourning in the motion. "You had a chance. You both did right here. The Pits are not some dungeon where death awaits everyone, captain. There is hope here. Real opportunity to break free and give yourself another life." Barten shoved Maena away, back towards the gate. Followed, still talking. "I'm not some monster looking to damn others to misery. This is justice, plain and simple. Those who want to prove their innocence can do so. Now, you've dug your friend a hole he'll never escape."

Nice work.

Didn't hear you coming up with any ideas.

I have one now. Do you have the guts for it?

"And me, Barten? Do I get the winner's prize?" Maena asked, turning again to face the man.

"The winner's prize? To do that, you'd need to have won. Neither the beast nor your opponent is dead." Barten reached, pushed Maena back again. The captain didn't stumble, let the steps come. Stood still. "What you get is a failure's sentence. The harshest punishment I can give. The one we reserve for those who won't try, who have already given up so much of themselves they won't attempt to recover."

Barten closed again, aimed to give Maena another shove. Maena waited for the arms to close, then swept forward, beneath the reach. She jerked her head up, slammed its roof into Barten's chin. His jaw clacked hard, the man rocking back. Maena snapped a kick with her right foot, catching Barten's ankle and sending him sprawling to the ground.

Not a soul cried out, not a spear nor an arrow flew her way. The guards standing watch had gone with the crowd.

Barten sputtered something as Maena closed, delivered another kick to the man, leaving him crumpled. Several steps past him, Maena bent down, picked up a stone ball.

Do it. Now.

Maena turned around, holding the ball in both hands. Heavy. Barten moaned.

Be quiet. You know nothing.

The one thing I do know is that letting your enemies live will cost you.

She lifted the stone. Barten rolled, put his hands on the ground, moved his knees under him. In another moment, he'd be up.

Don't be merciful now. You weren't with me. Finish it, for once.

WHEN MAENA LEFT, crouching through the same hole Kivi had chewed minutes earlier, she left behind a silent arena. Her hands dusty, her feet red and wet.

She looked right, looked left. Listened, heard footsteps and curses coming the leftward way. So Maena, unarmed, wearing nothing save some linen scraps, broke right instead, listening to her instinct and that alone.

For once, the voice in her head had fallen silent.

CHAPTER II
THE NIGHT WHISPERS

The Queen grabbed Wax's arm when the speargun went off. Good thing too: the sudden sound, the bright flash as the spear went flying by, bouncing off the guard's shoulder, had Wax stepping back into the roller's aft edge. He over-balanced, would've fallen over if not for the Queen's quick hand, its surprising strength as she pulled him back onto the boat.

"Keep your cool," she said as Wax steadied himself, motion erupting behind them. "I'm not your minder."

"My minder?"

Quik interrupted the question with an absurd line to the guard about his shoulder, some potential wound. In all his years, Wax knew Quik to be a caring man, but in a gruff distant sense. No way he'd give a damn about some random Kance guard.

No way, as Wax traced what'd just happened, Quik would misfire so bad either.

"You're not listening, are you?" the Queen said, sharpening her tone enough to cut through.

"Sorry," Wax said, still watching as his brother dragged the grumbling guard away. "I'm trying to figure out—"

Bliss popped between the two, her fingers flashing. Wax refocused, caught the symbols while the Queen, her composure finally breaking, narrowed her eyes, creased her mouth.

'I heard a guard last night, her guard, threatening her,' Bliss signed Wax's way. 'You have to ask her if she's all right.'

A question. All morning, Wax had been lobbing them at the Queen and receiving little more than dismissals in return. She'd either go silent or rebound with a question of her own, avoiding an answer and replacing it with some mild inquiry about Vis, about Wax's home, what food he liked best. Wax parried these with genial replies, always trying to steer the conversation back to his probing, but the Queen thus far proved better at wordplay, leaving Wax seeing Bliss's instruction less as an option and more as a desperate opening.

Without the guard here, with something so direct, maybe the Queen couldn't hide.

"Are you a hostage?" Wax asked, dropping his voice.

The waters, the cloudy morning wind flush with bird calls, and the roller's engine gave enough burbling noise to stall out eavesdroppers, but Wax saw little sense in being boisterous.

After Sledge, after Foti, the group had adopted a new philosophy: enemies were everywhere.

The Queen took the question like Wax took to his fourth ale of the night, with a sort of soft stupor, as though being confronted with this reality had no ready comeback, no skilled repartee.

She said nothing.

Bliss, frowning, signed to Wax again.

"My sister says she heard you, last night," Wax said, then blinked. "Wait, Bliss, is that what you were doing when I stumbled into you?"

Bliss rolled her eyes. 'Stop being an idiot, Wax, and focus.'

"I'm not a hostage," the Queen replied, thawing from her stunned cell. "I'm a Kance Queen. My guards are merely looking out for me. That's all."

Wax glanced at Bliss, whose frown only deepened. 'She's lying.'

"Don't mean to insult you, uh . . ."

"Your majesty will do," the Queen said, backing off a step, a solid scowl breaking over her face. "And I'll accept one nasty remark, but not two. Keep your suspicions to yourselves. Stowaways, no matter who they might be, don't get to disrupt my ship. Ask again, and I'll have my guards throw you overboard."

With a rigid turn, one nonetheless perfect despite the ship rocking on the river's churn, the Queen stomped away, vanishing around the boat's corner.

'Well that didn't go so well,' Bliss signed, pursing her lips. 'Quik played his part perfectly, too.'

"I was impressed," Wax muttered, watching where the Queen had been, trying to put her puzzle together and failing.

All that morning, while she'd dodged his questions, she'd been casting the poles and nets like a fisherwoman who'd spent a life in the boats. Without her robe on, replaced with clean Kance trousers and a working shirt, she'd shown off muscles honed not in any royal court Wax had ever heard of.

So the Vis sayings went, the more puffed up your title, the more air lay inside. The Queen defied all that.

And more, she'd shown real smiles while hauling in the catch, pulling tight the lines and seeing their rewards. As if the Queen relished the simple task, despite the many grumbles from her guard that she should go back below, leave the duties to those meant to work them.

'You losing it, brother?' Bliss signed, then snapped her fingers before his face. 'Is the sun getting to you?'

"It's cloudy," Wax said, twiching back.

'Yeah, but knowing you, I wouldn't be surprised.'

Wax shook his head. Felt the pull as a pole announced it found another catch. No matter how much he might wish, the roller gave little time to musing.

The afternoon marked a change. Not in the weather, which remained a gloomy chill, and not in the waters, which continued their ceaseless flow. The land around them, though, broke up its careful manicured paddies. The hills flattened out into clogged marshland, with short trees jutting up and spreading vast, spindly branches out in all directions. Like stubbled mushrooms. Those branches gave shelter to all manner of strange plants, their dried stalks and bulbs giving hints to what a wild place this might be in spring and summer.

"Better now," the captain muttered, joining Wax and Torny up near the roller's forward wheel.

Once again, two needed to stay at all times near the churning beast, clearing gunk off as it rolled forward. The captain looked as nerve-bitten as ever, though Wax noticed she'd changed her gear. No longer just warm clothing, but Rana leathers. A saber rested on her belt.

"Come here a few months back and you'd have a head clouded with insects, then harassed by the birds chasing'em," the captain continued, not focusing on either Wax or Torny, just talking into the wind. "More ship traffic too. Fishers, divers, harvesters making their runs. All done now, won't start again till we've got a new Aegis, summer or no."

"Too scared?" Torny offered, the question drawing a grimace from its target.

"Too sensible, more like. The Whirpool's a gate. Goes as far down as anywhere on the Isles, and it scoops up as much as it drowns. When the fiends start coming, it's around the Whirlpool that they'll be."

"Wait," Wax said. "Isn't the Whirlpool where the skars are?"

The captain nodded, "Every isle has its challenge, or so I've heard. Rana, you've got to get into that beast and come out with your jewel. The hardest one, I bet."

"Don't the Najahn keep it protected?"

"That's where we're going, Vis." The captain pointed towards the horizon. "Another day and we'll be there. Though we'll not be moving overnight, not here. Too much in the way."

"So the Najahn are here?"

The captain laughed, as ever putting her grim spin on the chuckle. "You'd better hope they're not all dead already."

The dire mood seemed to shroud the roller as the sun, always hidden, let the world fade to dark. An anchor dropped, the engine turned off, and for the first time in days Wax didn't feel, didn't hear, a roller's rumble. Everyone seemed to go quiet in response. The Queen and her guards made no appearances, stuck below. The captain only opened the doors inside to dish out dinner.

"Keep your weapons handy tonight," the captain warned. "And set a watch."

"You're not helping?" Quik asked.

"You let this ship sink, you're not getting where you want either. Don't let any harm come to her, and you'll get off alive tomorrow."

Wax offered to take the first shift, settling in with his Foti blade. He missed the knife, unseen since the battle with the ferrites on Foti's lava floes. The two weapons had complemented each other. Now, in the ship's lantern glow, Wax turned his blue blade and watched the light.

He'd barely used the sword since trading for it back on Vis. What an idea that'd been. Protection. He'd managed one strike with it, the beetle in the Foti lava tube. All the rest, failures.

Wax grinned. Not failures, no, just missed opportunities. Maybe Rana would give him a chance. Though how could one stab a whirlpool?

The marsh didn't hold answers. Without the rumble, the few bugs couldn't compensate, leaving Wax largely in quiet. The clouds stuck around too, giving the night a closed-in feel. If Wax was one for ghosts, he might've claimed to see them drifting in the dark.

Instead, he dangled his legs over the roller's edge, the blade resting in his lap. Turned his attention to the two skars, listened to their whispers. They grew as Wax focused, like a conversation turning to include him. Vis's skar spoke in quiet, calm tones, while Foti's, in a manner like its birthplace, declared its thoughts in hard, short lines.

What those thoughts were, Wax didn't know. But maybe, tonight, he could try to tease them out.

Start with home first.

If Wax wanted a speech, the Vis skar didn't give him one. Instead, it spoke in repeated lines, the same two or three phrases over and over again in a language Wax didn't know. At first Wax assumed the words were random, his hands resting on the Foti blade. He listened, found nothing to grab on to.

Until some insect found its dinner on his ear. When Wax moved his left hand up, brushed the bug away, the skar changed its song, lighting itself up. The skar grew louder, more excited, like Sawi telling Wax she'd found a new sana to climb.

And with its thrill, the skar seemed to work its strange magic, winnowing away the bite's pain, though the mark itself would take time.

Different words, emotions when the skar found its purpose. It made a certain sense, though Wax wasn't sure what he could do with that knowledge.

Store it away for later. Maybe if he ever became the Aegis, someone could use it.

Until then, he would listen to the skars chatter, watch the clouds, and wait for the chance to dream on the roller's hard deck.

CHAPTER 12

KNIVES AMONG FRIENDS

Sawi threw her arms out, gave a shout, not a scream. Determined, confident despite Gladdring's idiocy. She took not one single step closer to the hanoko den, and the big cats came no closer to her. Those glittering orbs stayed within their tree-covered shelter, the mother also keeping her distance.

Don't project weakness, don't provoke a threat, and the hanokos would leave her alone.

"Calm in the face of disaster," Gladdring muttered. "Are all Vis like you?"

"If you don't turn around and head back to the camp, I'll leave you out here," Sawi said without turning around.

"And willing to threaten me. Well, this wasn't what I was trying to learn, but I will walk away happy regardless. Apologies for the ambush, Sawi, but I had to know."

"Had to know what?" Sawi asked, stepping backward once she heard Gladdring's rustle through the ferns, the mud.

"Whether you were a spy."

Sawi tried to get Gladdring to elaborate, but the Tenet refused, saying only that Sawi had passed. The response did nothing to diffuse Sawi's rising anger, damn justified after being thrown to the cat's mercy. She stewed in it the entire walk back to the camp, whereupon she scaled her chosen tree, a high, sturdy branch.

As cozy as the soft ground? Likely not, but Sawi wouldn't find a knife in her back up here.

The branch had another bonus: its knotted gnarls lacked enough comfort to wake Sawi before most of the Najahn, giving her a chance to do exactly what Gladdring said she wasn't: spy.

The Tenet, despite the sun's early light, had his scholars up and circled. He seemed to be leading them in some animated discussion, his arms blowing wide, pointing this way and that. At one point a scholar raised their voice— Sawi hooked on the word 'skar'—only for Gladdring to shut the man down with a violent denial.

"This trip is only for research," Gladdring said, his voice raising clear enough for Sawi to hear. "We want to know whether the fiends are congregating on Vis, whether they are making for the Great Sana. You all have your assigned studies. Beyond that, concern yourselves with nothing save your own survival."

As he finished, Gladdring looked up, noticed Sawi, and curled his hand into a summons.

"Good to see you awake, Sawi. Another day's travel and I believe we'll arrive, yes?"

"If you keep up a good pace," Sawi shouted down, untangling her rope.

"Then I rely upon you to keep it," Gladdring replied. "Lead on."

Despite Gladdring's words, the Najahn didn't look to or listen to Sawi as they continued down the road leading towards the Great Sana. Gladdring's estimations of their progress also proved off, with another night on the road likely despite the hard-pressed pace. It'd taken Wax and Pan a couple days swinging through the jungle, and no marching group could match a pair of Vis for speed.

Sawi, though, kept that opinion to herself. Kept her words, her thoughts to herself too, and Gladdring's band seemed fine letting her stew. At least until the lunch break, when again Gladdring abandoned his followers to find Sawi sitting alone in the sunny grove just off the road.

"You don't care to join us? Tell us more about your isle?" Gladdring asked before pulling out some strange cracker and handing it to her. "A cinnamon cookie. Baked on Noctia, but, I swear, the recipe is from home."

Sawi eyed the cookie. A hard white, covered in brown dust. Cinnamon wasn't a word she knew, but Gladdring wouldn't catch her afraid, wouldn't catch her tentative. She took it, ate a big bite, and had to lunge for her water skin to keep from coughing.

The cinnamon meshed with the cookie in a burning sweet way, a nutty warmth blooming as the cookie dissolved in her mouth.

"I'll admit," Gladdring said, reading Sawi's expression and coming to the wrong conclusion, "these are better suited to the colder climes."

"The cookie is fine," Sawi said, the hasty water drippiing off her chin. "What's not is you trying to get me killed."

"As I said—"

"You're not the first person I've met with secrets," Sawi said, recalling Svarde and the Foti man's many half-answers. "You're not the first to look at me, at my friends and think we're simple people with nothing to offer save some fruit and a warm sun." Sawi stood, brushed off the cookie's crumbs. "I don't have to prove anything to you. I came because I was curious, and I'm staying because I said I'd help guide you, but I'm not your plaything. I'm not your example, your subject."

Gladdring seemed to shrivel up as Sawi spoke, the man's warmth fading to a stiff regard. She went from insect to enemy, and for a moment Sawi wondered if Gladdring would order the Najahn to cut her apart.

Instead, Gladdring reached out, took Sawi's hand with a swiftness she didn't expect. The grip wasn't aggressive, but soft, a friend's clasp.

"My world is one of agendas, motives, and maledicts, Sawi," Gladdring said, bowing his head just enough to add sincerity. "Immersed in such things for so long, one begins to see schemes everywhere, even in places where they make no sense at all." Gladdring nodded to the clearing's opposite end, farther away again from the Najahn. "Please, I would share somethig with you."

Sawi crinkled up her face, was about to ask what required the slight walk, only for Gladdring's eyes to tell a different story. Speak not, they said, and follow.

Kitaye and Vis, so far as Sawi knew, didn't deal in deception. Back-biting, schemes, undercutting and overwhelming your enemies with lies and surprise just . . . didn't happen. The elders ran the isle's towns and cities through experience and will. No elections, just a desire to show up and help. No rulers, just reasonable people. So when Gladdring intimated something secret was going on, Sawi took to it with a neophyte's naivety.

She spent the strides crossing the clearing looking back

at the Najahn group, trying to identify . . . what, exactly? An enemy? But wasn't Gladdring the one who'd tried to get her killed?

What she wouldn't give to be back among her sanas, the fruits and grasses.

"Have you ever taken a journey?" Gladdring asked when they settled against another tree, its bark an earthy brown, the crevasses cluttered with scuttling ants.

"Not the kind you mean."

Gladdring slid up a smile, "I'm here for a specific reason, and I chose to bring several of those scholars with me. Yet, after I invited them along, I found double their number waiting at the boat to cast off. And more Najahn soldiers besides."

Gladdring waited and Sawi felt she was supposed to infer something from his words.

"What, that's not supposed to happen?" She asked.

The obvious, and even Sawi's fresh exposure to spycraft made it so, thing was that some of these hangers-ons had goals anathema to Gladdring's own. What Sawi was supposed to do about that remained unclear.

"The Najahn, even scholars, but especially soldiers, do not travel for nothing," Gladdring said. "Their voulges, their loyalty, is for hire. And there are some who would very much like me removed."

Several options presented themselves. Sawi chose none, instead going to the point. She'd had to do that so often with Wax, a man prone to wild dalliances from his goals. If you wanted to be done talking to Wax before sundown, you had to steer him right.

Gladdring, it seemed, was no different, if perhaps less innocent in his motives.

"Why are you bringing this to me?" Sawi asked. "You said you have friends there?"

Gladdring shrugged, "Friends? For a time, at a time, perhaps. Noctia is built on shifting stones, Sawi. Now, I think, it is time leave them behind."

"What do you mean?"

When Gladdring told her, his eyes took on a familiar sparkle. The man loomed, but not in a dangerous way, eagerness and adventure pouring off his words, possibilities and potential echoing in his promises.

Do these things and Sawi could find her life transformed. Do them well, and she would once again find herself at odds with her obligations: to choose Vis, or a more dangerous path?

When they set up camp again, Sawi directed the Najahn off the roadside to a more crowded grove. Stumps and fallen trees marked this one, enough damaged foliage to show something rough had happened here not too long ago.

Sawi saw the red marks, the splatters hidden beneath leaves and ferns. A trail she'd picked up some time ago, followed along the path all the way here.

A traveler or some animal, captured, dragged, and devoured. The Najahn, not a hunter among them, didn't see the signs. Noted, yes, the scraped bark, the trampled leaves, but when Sawi said this was a frequent stopping point, the troop didn't question her. They lit fires, spread their rolls, and batted away curious bugs.

Gladdring didn't look her way once.

Sichi came out early, the pink glow smattering among them when it could dodge the leaves overhead. As the Najahn ate their dinners, Sawi slipped away, following yet more marks, knowing what she tracked and suppressing her fears.

No predator native to Vis would leave such a trail.

Gladdring asked for a distraction, and he would get it. Otherwise, so he said, so Sawi surmised, the Najahn would give chase.

As she walked, weaving between trees and ferns, Sawi played with another idea, a possibility at first disgusting in its brutality, but attractive as she stalked deeper and deeper into the forest: if the trap wound up killing Gladdring, then Sawi might be able to reap a different reward in returning his belongings, proof of what happened to the Najahn outpost. More favor for Kitaye, for her, and no need to risk her life.

Too dark? Sawi glanced up at the shadowed canopy. The Isles didn't allow for innocence these days. Not since Pan. Not since Wax and Bliss left, unlikely to come back.

She'd made one choice to come this way, to follow Gladdring. What happened next, well, she would see how Vis wanted it to go.

The Isle didn't keep Sawi waiting long. Beyond the jungle's nighttime music, a hard gnashing grind interrupted Sawi's flow. She crouched, every footfall a ginger thing, her fingers guiding leaves and branches away with nary a sound. Her breath came and went slow, blinks a rare thing until she caught it.

The fiend offered arms aplenty, mouths to match on a long and thin body. A centipede, save with fingers and thumbs instead of its gripping feet. Bulbous eyes dangled along its body from springing antennae, each one glinting whenever they caught Sichi's light. The fiend lay in the pool, its hands scooping water up into the mouths lining its underside. As large as two men put side-by-side, the fiend wasn't as scary as some Sawi had seen—that honor would forever remain with the giant beast that'd assaulted Kitaye —but should, would give Gladdring what he wanted.

With her right hand, Sawi felt around, found a stone. Lives balanced on pivotal moments. She'd let hers fall one way when she told Wax no and let him leave.

This time, Sawi chose the chase.

CHAPTER 13

VINE BITE

The marsh was kind enough to wait until Wax had traded off his shift, had fallen into a deep and pleasant dream concerning vines and swinging on them. At that point, or so Wax figured in the panicked first moments when screams and shouts broke him open, the marsh decided he'd had enough of a break.

Torny's voice broke Wax's sleep shell first, a true scorching curse litany that Wax shot up wondering, and pitying, whomever could've earned such a tongue lashing.

The target wasn't hard to find. The question, though, was whether it was even one target at all.

"The weeds are attacking us?" Wax said, his question immediately lost in the fray.

To his left, Torny and Bliss, beating Wax from their blankets by several seconds, hacked and bashed away at splitting deep green strands. As thick as branches and seeming to defy the common pull yanking things in the air to the ground, the tendrils rose up over the roller's edge and swept, seemingly suspended, towards them. A spiderweb spawning in real-time, each thread coated in fine bristles.

He'd be damned if one would touch him. A sword-fighter, Wax might not be, but he could cut a few plants.

Wax swept a slash through the nearest cluster, the bits falling to the boat's deck while the remainder, spreading away from Wax and over the roller's bow, began its regrowth.

"This thing's stubborn," Quik snarled to Wax's left, those gauntlets on and slashing back and forth.

Every swing delayed the growth only a moment or two.

"Not a fight we're going to win," Wax said, looking left as he cleaved more plants away. "Where's the captain?"

"Asking the wrong guy," Quik replied.

Torny and Bliss curled in behind Wax, putting their backs to the boat's middle cabin. The encroaching fiend snarled up the sides, the floor, threatening to push Quik and Wax in alongside the pair. Once there, they'd be trapped, maybe able to keep the growths at bay till their energy out.

Not the way Wax wanted to die.

"Cover me," Wax said, snapping left behind Quik, along the roller's overgrown side rail.

"Cover you how?" Quik shouted. "I can't cover myself!"

Wax didn't reply, his attention taken up with broad cuts through the plants before him. Two swings with the Foti blade brought Wax to the door leading down. Ahead, the roller's aft looked lost, already coated with tendrils. Behind Wax, soon enough, his way back would be the same.

There would be no saving the roller. Escape, though?

There, possibility lay.

"Quik," Wax called, his brother's working gauntlets visible. "Get Torny and Bliss off the boat. Make for the shallows off the port side."

"What about you?"

"I'll meet you there."

Wax wanted to drum up something more inspiring, but the encroaching vines didn't give him much time. More pressing, really, was why nobody had come dashing up the roller's steps. Surely, with all the noise, all the shouting, the captain, her couple crew, and the Kance party would know disaster had found them.

So why were they all still below deck?

Then again, why would Wax care? He could turn back, dash off over the plants with his Guardians. Let this fiend take one Renewal off Wax's list, especially one beating him in the skar collection race.

Oh, right. Being the Aegis was a crap prize. Letting the Queen win meant keeping himself off that awful stone throne.

"Wake up!" Wax yelled as he went through the narrow door.

To his left, the captain's cabin lay empty. Its globe lantern was dark, but the glow from outside showed a disheveled cot. The roller's engine off, the till still. To Wax's right, the crew quarters appeared similarly empty, two bunks deserted, but satchels and gear still stuffed in the cubbies.

So they'd woken up, decided to go down?

The stairs sat before Wax, polished wood steps heading towards pure dark. No lamps glowing down there, few sounds either. Just ominous creaking, cracking as boards sought to stay whole.

Wax, keeping his blade before him, went down slow, giving his eyes time to adjust, to soak up as much as they could from the brave light making its way this far. At its bottom, the stair ended against the roller's starboard side, a T-shaped split.

Bare feet gave Wax the first clue when his toes touched something decidedly not wood. He saw only shadows, heard only creaks, but the tendrils quivered at Wax's touch. New growths spurred out, testing Wax's feet for a suitable surface.

Picking a direction quick to keep from being swallowed, Wax lunged right, towards the aft end. The narrow hallway turned hard after a stride, Wax's Foti blade sweeping before him in tentative cuts. Tendrils hung from the ceiling, reached out from the walls, tugged at his toes. Wax called out, heard no reply.

Yet he couldn't slash with abandon, for fear he'd strike some wayward guard, some roller crew.

A signal, if it could be called that, came from the first room Wax passed on his left. Wax couldn't tell worth a damn where he was, save the Foti blade didn't hit a wall on a cross-cut, cluing Wax into the doorway. A turn, a listen, and a muffled struggle emerged, blending into the roller's cracks as it died.

"Who's in here?" Wax asked, stepping forward.

His feet landed in more tendrils, but water too, the brackish swamp cold and slimy to the touch.

So the fiend had broken up through the roller's hull. Wonderful.

The struggle increased, and Wax traced the tendrils to the room's middle, near the thin bed.

"I can't see, so sorry if I cut you," Wax muttered, keeping his feet shuffling while he felt out the first form.

The legs, arms, and armor declared the captive to be one of the Queen's guards, and Wax might've left the man there save the situation required allies, required desperation.

The Foti blade cut clean and close, delivering an angled

swipe up the guard's leg, near the man's chest, and Wax would've cut further save for more movement to his right. A second, maybe a third body, all together, clustered around the bed.

Guards protecting their Queen, or killing her?

The man he'd cut made use of the assist, surging up with enough strength to snap the tendrils cloaking him.

"Cut them free," the guard rasped as Wax made to do just that. "There's no time."

"Well aware," Wax said. "Don't have a light, do you?"

"The lanterns are all broken."

Nevertheless, working blind, the pair freed a second guard, followed by, yes, the Queen last among them. Tendrils closed in from outside, from below, but the guards found their form, swapping their rapiers for more precise knives and using them to keep an opening, work their way towards the room's exit.

"Stay with the Queen behind us," said Akido, the second guard freed. "We've one more of our own to save."

"We'll be going to the exit, thank you very much," Wax replied as the foursome hacked, tripped, and felt their way from the room.

"You'll come with us—" the guard started.

"He'll do as he pleases, and I'll go with him," the Queen said. "Save the crew and follow us."

In another situation, without the dark tendrils snatching and grasping, without the boards breaking beneath their feet, Wax bet Akido would've overruled the Queen. His sharp breath said as much, but any rebuttal died as the other guard cursed the tendril's growing progress, their thickness.

"C'mon," Wax said, tugging the Queen back towards the stair. Just enough light, a single pink beam from Sichi, gave them the direction. "They'll be fine."

"Of that, I have no doubt."

Getting to the stair proved easy enough. Climbing it, though, wouldn't be possible. The tendrils had scaled the steps from inside and out, the vines bursting through and breaking the wood apart, leaving nothing more than a fractured tendril forest before them.

"We're trapped," the Queen muttered.

"Not with a Vis," Wax countered, then flipped the Foti blade's hilt towards the Queen. They both bobbed there, keeping their feet moving so the tendrils couldn't find a hold. "You cut, I run."

Wax wished there'd been enough light to see the Queen's face at his comment, but the shadows didn't give him that much. He did, though, feel her take the sword.

"And after?" the Queen asked.

"Just keep cutting. Now."

The Queen swung the blade before them, slicing tendrils away from their face, opening a dire path forward. Wax reached, took the Queen, and lifted her. Not a full carry —the stairwell didn't have the room for that, even without plants clogging the way—but Wax kept her feet off the floor, the Queen at a slight forward lean so she could keep the blade working.

"Here we go," Wax said, and the Vis climbed.

The Queen sliced away hanging tendrils and Wax followed, trusting his feet to land and keep their balance from one broken step to the next, just like hopping branches back home. With every lurch, the Queen muttered curses, but up they went, one lunge at a time.

Until the roller split in two.

The aft and bow sides nearest the climbing pair tore

away, angling at the sky and plunging their makeshift progress into the swampy sea. Tendrils fell and flailed around them, snaring Wax's hair, pulling at his clothes.

"Swim," the Queen snapped as they hit the water, its chill seeping right to Wax's bones.

The beach, the Foti beach. The last time he'd felt such horrible cold, such muscle numbing ice. Wax froze, his mind reeling back to that moment, those minutes suffering in such blank agony.

Something slapped him. Splashed him. Sichi's light poured around Wax, the roller gone. Before him, Foti blade in one hand and her eyes a pink-lit green fire, was the Queen.

"I said swim, Wax," the Queen repeated, her voice colder still than the water. "Now."

His legs found their surge, peddling after the Queen as the tendrils beneath and around them struggled to keep their grip. Clothing tore, some plants left scrapes and marks on his arms, but together the two headed across the slime.

No words, nothing save breathing, their arms and legs kicking. Ahead, grass and muddy mounds rose free from the water. Forms moved on them, a trio Wax recognized, that gave him further hope.

"Here," Quik called when they neared, the chill in Wax's bones blending with a low fire as his body strained to keep him moving. "Got you."

The rope came out. Scavenged with their satchels from the roller, and both Wax and the Queen rode it the last few lengths before climbing onto the muddy banks.

Torny and Bliss, scooping dried grasses, leaves, and twigs into a pile had a small fire already growing, one Wax and the Queen planted themselves near. Together, the whole band watched as the roller finished its life, the tendrils rising, encasing the whole ship in a plant lattice. The lit lanterns on the ship's sides burst into smoking sparks one by one, before the whole thing descended into the water.

"Your guards," Wax said. "I don't see them."

"Never count out a Kance Queensguard," the Queen replied, her steel features giving no hint to mourning. "It's the captain and her crew I'd grieve instead."

True enough. Wax gave a slow nod. Behind them, he heard Quik, Bliss, and Torny plotting their next moves. Something he'd concern himself with after a bit more time in the fire's warmth. Until then, Wax reached over, took back his Foti blade from the Queen's side. She watched him.

"Thanks for saving this," Wax said, then hesitated. Could he really call her 'Queen' after all this? Was there such a thing as nobility when they were soaked in muddy water, with little to their names save a few skars?

"You can call me Eujo," the Queen said, seeming to recognize his struggle.

The smile then, as small as it was, did more than her words to make Eujo real.

CHAPTER 14
VICTOR'S PRICE

Maena didn't have an objective, didn't have a focus after she left Bertan's body behind in the empty arena. Some dim part of her played at escaping, at attempting flight from these tunnels and, after mingling with the degenerates gambling on the miserable lives here, walking into the Whent tundra free.

Free and alone.

She'd turned right. Behind her, around the tunnel's curl, Rasslebeck and Kivi would be making their own try. The guards chasing them would no doubt surround the pair, drive them back at spear point to the dirty cell even now approaching on Maena's left, her feet carrying the Rana captain on a slow walk ahead. Pennifer and Svarde might already be there, huddled against the dirt waiting for another meal, another challenge. The others who'd shared their wagon ride, who'd been thrown into the contest?

Dead, maybe, or ditched into some even worse game.

Is that what has you so muddled?

No. The Whent Pits were known. Nothing here surprised Maena. But . . .

You didn't think you'd end up here? Welcome to my little party.

She'd spent so many seasons finding willing raiders, pulled them from their ships, rarely from their families—the types to go into the Dark Below weren't ones with deep connections—and wound up with nothing. Most of her crew was likely here, stuffed in amid Whent criminals and other captives, slinging mud at one another until they drowned in it.

How could Maena have failed so badly?

Not all bad, right? I'm here now, and full of ideas.

A voice in her head. Herself carved different.

Maena stopped. To her left, a split in the tunnel marched upward towards the surface. A gate there would be the only barrier between her and possible freedom. In her rags, Maena wouldn't get far before someone would take an interest, but even so . . .

Look. I didn't let you come back to suffer all this self-pity.

You didn't have a choice.

I could've fought harder. You're a Rana captain, Maena. Act like it.

That simple, right? Get over the grittiness in her stomach and push forward, find the saber's hilt and swing it. Metaphorically, anyway.

Now you're getting it. A little more spilled blood and you'll be fine.

To do that, Maena had to find a different plan. No huddled masses, no simpering escape. A breakout, with weapons and people. Overthrowing the Pits. There'd be guards, but they'd be fat and lazy on their privilege, simple to push over, just like Bertan. They'd—

"Rana," bellowed a thick voice, pouring off the tunnel's

walls. Maena half-turned, tensing her legs in case she needed to run. "It's time we had a word."

The man requesting the meeting stood with two guards behind him. Trailing those were Rasslebeck and Kivi, another militant duo with spearpoints at their necks.

Warlord Jochi, the one who'd rounded them up upon their return to the surface. Maena remembered the name from the man's aggrandizing speech, his layered animal skins coating every surface a glowering dark face. Near-black eyes, veering between slits and circles. A heat came off the man, the same sort Maena had seen in the most brutal warriors on her journeys.

A body born for conquest.

A tough time for him, then. With the Renewal, the Najahn forcing a peace.

"You killed Bertan," Jochi continued, approaching. The guards flanking him raised their spears, pointed them at Maena, but without malice. "A clever ploy. I'll miss his gamesmanship, but he should never have let you get so close."

"No," Maena replied.

"I won't make the same mistake." Jochi folded his arms, showing off various bracelets inset with gemstones. "Do you see these, Rana? Do you know what they are?"

Maena spat at Jochi's feet. She knew damn well what those were.

"Good, some spirit's left in you," Jochi said. "I would've been disappointed if you'd left it all with Bertan. You'll need it where you're going."

"I'm not playing another game," Maena said, giving up on her half-turn and facing Jochi square. If they were going to stab her here, then she'd die with dignity. Behind Jochi, she caught Rasslebeck's eye, saw they'd done a number on his face. The older man managed a nod, the swelling mess not able to do anything more.

"No games. Instead, redemption," Jochi said. "A chance to pay back this isle for all it's suffered at your hands."

Oh, this is going to be awful, isn't it? Or delicious?

"You don't deserve any payback."

"You'll give it to me anyway," Jochi replied. "Because I know you Rana captains. All speed and finesse on your ships. Galavanting around, costing lives and laughing all along the way. But when it comes down to the terrible pain, you're all cowards."

Maena's eyes narrowed. "Those bracelets."

Jochi didn't so much grin as give Maena a knowing nod. "Awarded for kills, captain. Most of them slow. Agonizing." A heavy sigh. Those guards kept their spears level. "Not because I like it. No. That would be sadistic. But because I owe it to my people to protect them from you."

"By torturing us? No Rana would do the same—"

Jochi raised a single finger. The guard to his left stepped forward, seemed about to stab Maena until the man flipped the spear haft over his wrist, instead jutting the blunt end into Maena's shoulder and knocking her back.

A bruise, nothing more. She gave them no satisfaction.

"Instead, I'll give you want you wanted," Jochi said. "Just what you were looking for down in those caves." He nodded over Maena's shoulder. "Back to your cell with the others now. Go, or they'll have to face these trials without you, and that wouldn't be very fair, now would it?"

"Fair isn't a concept you'd know, rockbiter."

"Witness how she insults me and I, in my humble restraint, do nothing?" Jochi said, his look flicking to each guard in turn, drawing grins from both. "Why should the fly bother the beast?"

This time, when the guard pushed Maena forward, he had the point against her skin. When she moved, when she gave in, the only one happy about it was the voice in her head, claiming sacrifice now would pay grim dividends in the future.

Svarde and Pennifer waited in the cell. Their mates, the group that'd failed the trial, had disappeared off to some other home, no doubt as decrepit and filth-ridden. Fresh slop waited for them, already attracting flies, though its contents seemed a greenish gray too gross even for the insects.

The Foti Guardian stood as Maena stumbled in. He took a slow look at her blood spattered clothes, a body beginning to smell as rancid as she felt. Rather than question it, Svarde only gave her a slow nod as Maena walked past him, sat on the cell's far side. The man did, though, find some affection for Kivi, a close hug the ferrite matched as it loped in behind Rasslebeck.

The two Rana raiders fell into their own conversation, leaving Maena to sit alone, with nothing but her other half ever-present in her head.

Am I that bad? I'm you, aren't I?

Me as I used to be, maybe. Ready with a quip and a cutting word. A vicious heart.

No more?

Look where we are. What spirit does that encourage?

You won. You should be happy.

Svarde came over, holding a filled water basin. "I asked the guard before they left. Said we'd all be vomiting if we didn't get those guts off of you."

Maena blinked, studied herself. An exercise in the visceral arts, she was. Back on a Rana raider, they'd have thrown her into the sea for an hour to wash up.

"I guess it did get a little messy. Did they give you a cloth?"

"That they didn't, but Jochi promised new rags were on the way."

"How nice."

Svarde sniffed, tore off part of his gray shirt. Dipped it in the water. Maena held out an arm. The cool liquid came almost as a shock, running against her skin, sloughing off dirt and worse. Svarde could've used a bath, but the man spared not a drop for himself.

"You've never seen the Pits, then?" Svarde asked, getting between her fingers.

"I'd never set foot on Whent till our expedition."

"Not with all your raids?"

Maena shook her head. "Sea-going, remember? The water's my home. Only when there wasn't any other way."

The cloth torn up, Svarde ripped off another sleeve, moved on to Maena's other arm. Gentle, yet thorough. A strange quality for a rough Foti fighter. Svarde noticed her unasked question.

"Ami, Catya, and I walked a long, hard rode. More than once we had to help each other through a hard spot. More than once, I couldn't use my axes to solve the problem."

"Even if you wanted to."

Svarde stopped for a moment, the dripping, dirty sleeve in his hands. His eyes went unfocused, then he returned to the scrubbing.

"No, there were many times the axes left my mind," Svarde said, quieter now.

"You don't take a journey like that without becoming close friends or bitter enemies."

Svarde didn't reply. Finished the sleeve and tossed it

with the other rag. He reached for his shirt, but Maena ripped off her own sleeve first.

"Already ruined, I know, but you might get more out of it," Maena said.

Svarde nodded, dipped it, moved to her legs. Maena could've done this, and just a scant few weeks ago would've had Svarde spitted on her saber for assuming she couldn't keep herself clean. But maybe, just maybe, after so much trauma, after so much injury, death, and dirt, a little caring would help them both.

The guard came with the promised clothes not much later. Svarde and Maena had little more than scraps left, ones they exchanged readily along with Rasslebeck and Pennifer. The guard, after returning with another requested water basin, stamped his spear on the ground to grab their attention.

"There's a reason Jochi is giving you all these favors," the guard said, practically shivering in excitement as he spoke. "When the sun is at its midpoint tomorrow, you will share the arena with another quintet. It will be a contest before our best audience, one as worthy of your reputation as it is those you will be competing against. The winner will earn their freedom. Be grateful, get clean, and eat well." The guard chirped a chuckle. "It might be your last dinner."

Rasslebeck flung a Rana slur at the man and the guard only grinned in reply, before stomping off to find some other poor soul to harass.

"Another contest?" Pennifer said, taking to the new basin to scrub her own scruffy self. "What, more stones to stack?"

"I bet they'll have us running races," Rasslebeck said. "Kivi'll win it for us."

The ferrite snorted, want over to the rock wall and took a bite.

"Your stubby legs won't do us any favors if that's the line," Maena said. The clean-up job, her other half's continual prodding to lighten up, enjoy the violent life she could get, was nudging Maena from the darkness. "Maybe Svarde can carry you."

"Won't be carrying anyone." Svarde stared at the ground, kneaded his hands together, though not of nerves. A warrior sharpening his weapons. "The guard's not telling the whole truth. Tomorrow's not a contest for freedom. It'll be a fight for our deaths. Only question is how."

CHAPTER 15

SWAMP WALK

The marsh felt like home. Bliss repeated the thought to herself as she lay amid the mud, watching the small creature trundle through the reeds, the pools.

The fen back on Vis hadn't been one of her favorite spots, what with its stifling heat and infinite insects. But it had the same life, the loamy scents and sounds belonging to a natural place. Something Foti damn sure hadn't had, and Rana had evaded up till now, up til the point when the five of them had been cast off the roller and forced to make their way northward with only their guts, gumption, and good luck.

At least, that's what Torny called it. Everything seemed to come back to luck with the bandit. As though skill and tenacity were just accidents, and fortune fate's true arbiter.

Well, Torny would have to think differently after this one.

The creature, about as long as Bliss's arms placed end to end and dominated by a furry snout, scuffled through the plants, occasionally stopping to dig at some mud here, a grassy pile there. Searching for bugs.

Unfortunately for the beast, it didn't seem to have any suspicions that it might be the subject of a hunt. So innocent that, for a moment, Bliss felt sorry for the thing.

But only a moment. A hunter, especially one needing a meal to make it through the next day's hard work—and a marsh march had a way of making the legs burn, the mind fog with effort—couldn't let compassion doom herself to an empty stomach.

Bliss tensed. Brought one foot up near her waist and pressed it into the shallow mud, feeling it well up beneath her toes. Not much grip there, but enough, enough for a flight forward.

The creature closed within her staff's range and Bliss launched, jabbing out with the metal end. A hit to the head ought to knock the beast out, give a simple success to the hunt.

Instead, the mud failed her. Bliss's right foot slipped too far on the kick, letting her staff's swing land woefully short of a killer jab, petering out instead into the grass. The creature jumped, flung out its legs and actually flopped into the air. Four legs kicked, buttressed by webbed feet, and upon returning to earth, the meal scurried away from Bliss.

And right into Quik's gauntlets.

Another rule of the hunt: if you could, set up an ambush.

"Believe we're even now," Quik said as they returned to the camp, filthy but happy with their catch, a satchel loaded with several prizes.

Not all animals either. Mushrooms still rose in the marsh, though winter had robbed any fruits and other snacks from the reeds.

'Only because I let you get that last one.'

"Let? You missed."

Bliss shrugged, 'Maybe I did, maybe I didn't.'

Quik laughed. A good sound. One Bliss had been hearing more often in the couple days since the roller disaster. As if walking through the wilds restored the group, jokes cracked up more than they had on the boat, and definitely more than back in Riroco. Smiles came, even on Eujo's face, confirming Bliss's suspicion that she held no love for her missing guards.

The morning after the roller's sinking, Quik had led a short prayer to Vis for the apparently-drowned crew and captain. He'd thrown the Kance in there too, only for Eujo to once again warn that they weren't likely dead. Wax pressed her on that score, but Eujo wouldn't elaborate, saying only that it took a lot to kill a Kance Queensguard.

But those mythical menaces hadn't shown up yet. Instead, it'd been gray days, chill wind, and hearty hikes filling the hours. North, across a marsh thankfully at its lowest point of the season. They didn't have anyone from Rana with them to say for sure, but the rains on Vis tended to the spring, so if Rana matched, then the slushy walkways they used now would've been underwater any other time.

The land also gave them a chance to build fires with struck flint. The mounds offered little room for bedrolls, but the Vis crew could sleep on soft ground without issue. Torny adapted, though her grumbling rose up every night as she curled into a slumber between the weeds.

Eujo, in Bliss's opinion, had barely slept. She always volunteered for first watch, and more than once, on her own shift, Bliss had caught the Queen awake and staring off into the sky, the horizon, as if some answer lay in the fogged dark.

Not that it mattered. The Queen was a rival, and while Bliss wouldn't mind her getting free from the guard's harassment, ditching Eujo off to deal with her own crises at the next town seemed like the best plan.

Which was why Bliss frowned when, yet again, she and Quik came back to camp to find Wax and Eujo, heads together, going over how to keep the fire lit.

"Whoa, that looks good," Torny said, jumping up from sharpening her long knife. "Can I eat any of it now? I'm starving."

"Better cook it first," Quik replied, setting the satchel down. "No telling what these things have been around."

"Good work, you two," Wax added, looking up as Eujo struck some feeble sparks into the fire pit. "True Guardians."

"Didn't think being a Guardian meant making you dinner," Quik said.

"Guess you thought wrong."

Bliss let Quik prep the meat for roasting and went over by Wax and Eujo. The Queen seemed focused on perfecting her flint work, so Wax gave Bliss his attention when she poked him.

'Are you best friends now?' Bliss signed, nodding past Wax to Eujo.

'She's trying to live, same as us.' Wax frowned as he signed. 'What's the problem?'

'She's your rival, that's what.'

'You're the one who pointed out her trouble with the guards.'

'I didn't mean to have her join up with us.'

Wax started to reply, but Eujo coughed, drew their attention.

"If you're talking about me, I would hear it," Eujo said, setting the flint aside.

'Nice work,' Wax flashed at Bliss, as if this whole thing was her fault. "Sorry, Bliss is trying to tell me that we should be bitter rivals or something."

"The skars? The Aegis? Is that what you're concerned about?" Eujo asked.

Again Bliss found herself starting to shrug but stopped it. No. This wasn't a time, out here in this swamped crap, to go halfway. Instead, she nodded, sharpened her look.

"It will be mine," Eujo said, as flat and certain as if she was describing the weather. "I have the lead, according to my informants—"

"Informants?" Torny asked from across the budding fire. "You have informants?"

"From your own group, if I'm not mistaking you," Eujo replied. "Though why one of you is out here with these three deserves an answer of its own."

Torny's glib questioning burned at Eujo's words, a scowl as scathing as Bliss had ever seen coming across the bandit's face.

'What is she talking about?' Bliss flashed the signs at Torny. Quik, beside the bandit, wore his own skepticism, but the hunter turned back to the meal after seeing Bliss's signs.

That's right, let the sister do the talking. She could get answers from Torny without getting stabbed, which her brother couldn't do.

"We've all got pasts," Torny replied, slipping a three-fingered slash Bliss's way. Not answering that question. "I'm talking about the future. You think you'll win without any guardians?"

"Once Kance hears about their loss, another group will

be sent," Eujo said, no sadness in those words. "If they're gone."

"And then what, you get to continue on your merry way, snapping up skars without any effort?" Torny asked.

"Hey," Wax interjected. "She's trying. She's here with us."

"By chance," Torny snapped. "Without that fiend attacking, she would've just rode the roller right to the skar, had one of her guards pick it up, and flounce on to the next."

"You talk like you know me," Eujo said, that ice turning to steel. "You, thief, do not. Spit more slander and I'll have it out with you. Right here."

"Royalty against a ruffian?" Torny grinned. "I like those odds."

"But I don't," Wax said.

Her brother was ever the peacemaker. He'd often be the feud starter too, but Wax seemed to avoid violence as much as possible. The guy always joked about being a hunter, but, alone, Quik and Bliss figured the gatherers would be as likely to take him.

Not that such things mattered now.

"You should be all about it, Wax," Torny said. "That's part of the Renewal game. Get the others out of your way. I'm your Guardian, let me do it for you."

Bliss moved before Wax could react. She stood, pulled Torny up with her and marched the bandit, protesting, away from the fire and into the shallow waters beyond. Far enough where the few buzzing insects, the water's lapping noise brought a measure of privacy.

'What're you doing?' Bliss signed, the two facing each other, chilly water soaking up to their shins.

'First, I was drying out, but that's ruined," Torny said.

Bliss glanced at Torny's hands. The bandit knew enough signing to use it. Torny, though, didn't seem to care.

"She's picking at me," Torny continued, folding her arms, looking away. "Like she gets to do whatever her highness wants."

'She doesn't. You're being a child.'

"Yeah, well, so what if I am?" Torny asked, still refusing to look Bliss in the eye. "That's me. That's who I am."

'Is it?'

Torny faltered at the simple reply. Bliss wanted to sigh. The bandit seemed so fragile, paper thin, despite her ideas, her gadgets, her wide array of skills that'd all be near useless back on Vis.

Wait.

"Look," Torny said, letting her hands fall to her waist. "I'll go apologize. Smooth things over. Let Eujo carry on being herself. No more sassy me, okay?"

'I don't care about Eujo,' Bliss signed. 'I'm asking you if you're all right?'

Torny hesitated, then curled up a slapdash grin. "Of course I'm all right. You smell what Quik's cooking up? Seems better than that toleket."

'Then what about the other thing, that Eujo mentioned?'

Another falter, but Torny found her poise after this one. Those arms came up, planted on Bliss's shoulders.

"You want to know who I was, Bliss, I'll tell you. But not now, not without some ale, some real food, and some dry shoes."

'Promise?'

"Promise," Torny said. "And hey, it might not be that long."

At Bliss's questioning look, Torny pointed to the north, where the sky darkened but not so much along one crescent line.

"That's not a natural glow, if I make my guess," Torny said. "Bet you a whole night's rounds there's a town and a tavern there, ripe for our patronage. How about we get the others onboard. Bet it's only a few hours walk."

In the dark, through a marsh known to have at least one nasty fiend in it. Bliss told Torny as much, broke the thief down, and together the two returned to the campfire, to Quik's delicious meal, and made no mention of the town.

They'd come to it soon enough, and until they did, Bliss would listen to the frongs, to the wind rustling the grasses, and breathe in the campfire's smell with a smile.

They were a long way from home, but sometimes, just a little piece of Vis might show up anyway.

CHAPTER 16

TRICK TRUTH

Oh, what one rock could do.

The stone, small and rugged, smacked the fiend as it splashed into the pond, an insignificant bump to a thing so large, but some animals didn't take lightly to an insult. Some went berzerk, some made noise, some charged after their attacker.

This fiend did all three and more besides.

Its centipede form erupted from the water when Sawi's stone hit, wrapping towards her with its antenna eyes finding her in a snap. Sawi gave the monster a slight wave before spinning on her heels and dashing back through the grass. She waited till she heard the telltale swishes, the splatters, the snarls behind her before calling out a warning.

Simple words: fiend incoming, yelled high and bright into the evening.

Hopefully the Najahn were listening. Hopefully, Gladdring understood.

The sprint in the cave rose back as Sawi ducked under branches, slid past tree trunks, jumped over fallen logs and sprawling brambles. Back then she'd gone by torchlight, a haphazard rush up rocks without any idea of what lay behind, terror clutching at her throat, her hands and feet numb with the knowledge her death was imminent.

Now, now Sawi ran with determination, a stone certainty that she'd picked her course. She'd not deviate now, no matter what came next. Though she hoped the Najahn could comport themselves well enough not to die.

And if they didn't?

Sawi broke through into the chosen grove, saw a voulge wall before her as the guards stared stern towards the woods. Behind them the scholars stood, more than a few with flimsy knives. One held a crossbow, fiddling with the loading mechanism. Behind them all, the person Sawi sought, no fear on his face, only expectation.

Gladdring was ready.

"It's right behind me!" Sawi shouted, cutting left towards the protection's outer edge. "A snake thing!"

"Just get behind us," the Najahn captain snarled.

That, she could do.

Without drawing so much as another stare, Sawi curled behind the Najahn formation, slipped past the scholars to Gladdring's side. As she slowed, catching her breath, the fiend pushed through into the grove, leaves and brush flying with it.

"Now," Gladdring said, turning away as the Najahn captain bellowed out a charge.

The scholar's crossbow punctuated the order with a click. The fiend roared. Gladdring pushed Sawi to the side, stepping off after her. Their satchels, Sawi noticed, lay right in their path, an easy grab on their way out.

Gladdring again proved his agility, matching Sawi stride for stride, his robes snapping in the cool evening as they hit the path. Behind them, the fiend's gurgling roars continued, and while Sawi listened for cries of pain, none echoed after them.

"Your soldiers are good," Sawi said after a couple padding breaths, the light beginning to dwindle around them.

"The very best," Gladdring replied, sweat running through the lines on his face. "Najahn deserve their reputation."

"You're sure they won't find us?"

"They'll head to the outpost and assume I've gone there."

"Isn't that where we're going?"

"Not anymore."

Deception, according to Gladdring, came in layers. Every one meant to test the target, see how much farther they could go. First, Gladdring had to know whether Sawi was at all competent, whether she could guide them, or if she just wanted to hang on and see a Najahn patrol in action.

Then came the reflex test, whether Sawi could make it in the wild, what she really wanted. Sawi wasn't quite sure how Gladdring figured on that last part, but whatever his reasoning, she'd passed, which pushed her to the next step: the escape.

"Who did you trust," Gladdring said as they sat, fireless, for a short break off the path. True night landed now, scattered clouds and a thick canopy making everything a muddled gray and black. Gladdring forbade any torches, trusting instead in Sawi's nocturnal navigation. "Was it me, or my guards, one of the scholars?"

"If I went to them, you mean?"

"I'd disavow the plan, of course. Accuse you of

attempting to kidnap me, or something equally foolish. You would have been killed on the spot."

Gladdring's face was little more than a smear as he said the words, a shadow within Sawi's reach, but the bloodless fact chilled her all the same. Never, Sawi had to remind herself, could she really trust this man, no matter what he said.

Schemes within schemes, and most seemed to have her death as an early out.

Was this what adventure really was? Had Wax found himself similarly trapped, running along an edge every second since he'd left home?

"But again you acquitted yourself with aplomb. That fiend, what a brilliant find. Not a one will doubt why we might have run off, a safe escape in the face of disaster." Gladdring chuckled, a deep rolling sound. "And when we don't arrive at the outpost before them, they'll assume we've died or been lost."

"They'll search for you."

"Of course, and even find us, when the time is right." Gladdring stretched, massaged his legs. "I must admit, the flight was one thing, but the prospect of an all-night's march is something I don't look forward to."

"We could try scaling a tree to sleep."

"No." Finality there. No negotiation in the man's tone. "A chance discovery by my old friends and this is all ruined. If one sleepless night is what it takes for this to work, then that's what we'll do."

"For what to work?"

"Ah, Sawi. For once, you dig for better answers, and I regret that I cannot give them to you. Not yet. Layers, you remember?" Gladdring must've been smiling, though Sawi couldn't see it. "I can, though, give you our next goal. Mottilan. Your eastern city. Take me there."

More whys erupted, though Sawi shut them up before they left her mouth. Gladdring could've sailed right to Mottilan. Going over land from Kitaye would take several more days, would stress their gear in colder mountains near winter's onset. A thousand other objections rose, killed by Gladdring's next words.

"If you object, Sawi, you are too late," Gladdring said. "I have no doubt you could abandon me here in the dark, but if I lived, I would send the Najahn to find and destroy you. If they find my body instead, they will do the same. There is no escape, save doing what I ask." Another breath. "This will all be worth it in the end, I promise you. A Najahn Tenet does not make requests idly, and does not do so without adequate remedy for those who help him. You will be rewarded, and well."

"With what?" Sawi asked. "What could I want that you could give me? I have—"

"You already know, or at least have an idea, else you would not have joined us." Gladdring stood, at least one knee snapping with the effort. Getting to Mottilan was one thing, whether Gladdring would survive that long was another. "Come, I'm ready for another leg."

THEY PUSHED on another two hours. A fast walk, sticking to the path. At the right junction, a larger clearing where the Kitaye road met another, Sawi asked Gladdring whether he was sure what he wanted.

"We go left here, it's a long way," Sawi said. "I've only gone once, when I was much younger. A trading trip."

"You remember it well enough?"

"It's a road. I don't have to remember." Sticking a little venom in her words felt good. Gladdring's commands, his manipulation had begun to feel stifling, like she'd been put in some cage with no way out. "It won't be an easy one, and there won't be travelers this time of year to help us."

"All the better. Secrecy is our friend, Sawi."

She led him, going west and heading towards the jungle's edge, a steady rise to Vis's eastern mountains. More tame than the west, but still a wild place.

Sawi tried to pull the isle's map up in her mind, the scattered dots marking the few towns beyond the isle's two cities. Most lay west and south of Kitaye, where the jungle grew dense and flush with fruits, medicinal plants, and more. Some scattered along the northern coast, fish and the isle's few field-worthy plains making for viable homes.

But along this road? Little to offer. Mountain run-off made the soil soft, not quite a marsh but not far from it. Creeks broke over the path often, dry now or the route would've been all but impassable on their feet alone. Hanoko tracks paced after smaller game, and Sawi felt eyes on them often, creatures making bets on whether the pair would live or die.

"What could be worth it?" Sawi asked aloud as night veered into early morning. Sichi held more sway now, dominating the sky and blasting its pink along their road. "All this effort?"

"Power," Gladdring replied. "Simply power, Sawi. Both acquiring it, and keeping it from those who would wield it poorly."

"Power to do what?"

"Shape the future. End the fiend scourge. Bring about a time of plenty, of happiness, of joy and peace."

"You don't seem like a man who wants peace."

"Judging me already, are you?" Gladdring laughed, louder this time, though tinged with the same exhaustion that'd slowed their pace of late. "Wait until the end, Sawi, and then decide. There are many out there more sinister than I, be assured."

"I'm not."

"Then you are wise," Gladdring said. He stopped, Sawi glancing back. "Do you think we've made it far enough for the night?"

"Depends on how vigorous your soldiers are."

"They'll deposit the scholars first. No love lost between a soldier and the people they're supposed to protect."

Sawi scrunched up her face. Gladdring had a habit of these pronouncements, decrees as if he knew such things with certainty.

"Then we'll have some time," Sawi said. "Rest for a few hours off to the side, then begin again."

"When the day's at its hottest point, no doubt."

"Not this time of year. It'll be cool enough."

"For your warm blood, perhaps. Some of us prefer true cold."

"You came to the wrong isle, Gladdring."

"No, no, Sawi. I'm exactly where I want to be." Gladdring settled in near Sawi in a haphazard fern collection off the road's side. Soft enough to lay down, the fronds doing well enough to hide them from passing glances. "And, unless I miss my guess, so too are you."

Sawi spent hours after lying there, staring up into the sky, knowing Gladdring was right.

CHAPTER 17

SHATTERED RAFTS

Stay away and smile. Don't ask questions. Don't refuse. Respect them, but most of all, stay away.

A mother's words to Wax about the Najahn. Repeated every time one of their ships docked on Kitaye's shores. Their purple-black armor at odds with the Vis green vibrance. Their scowls a poor match for the whooping song in the isle's air.

He and Pan would laugh often enough about the warnings, writing the Najahn off as armed arrogance and little more. And yet, you couldn't remove the mystery. All that polish, all that gleam. An order so far removed from Wax's own life as to be tantalizing in its fashion.

A different version of perfect.

So Wax found his legs going a bit weak, his mouth stumbling open as the group closed in on the Najahn outpost. Like them all, this one supposedly kept watch over Rana's skars, providing a haven for Renewals, assurance that skars would be there when a new Aegis needed nominating.

This one, if it kept any watch at all, would be missing much.

They neared the outpost by mid-morning on a crisp blue day, cheery enough weather for a marsh. Wax hated waking up, finding the fire dwindled and a chill setting into his bones, but such mornings seemed to be the pace in the North. Eujo, nearby, put on a stoic air as she rose and readied herself, so Wax did his best to match.

Renewals had to keep pace with each other.

But not even the Queen could hide her confusion at the tilting, broken, and outright sinking raft collection making up the Najahn base. Huge squares tied together with thick ropes and chains bobbed against one another at the marsh's northern fringe, steady waves lapping against their sides. Smaller than the outpost on Vis, the Najahn gave this one more pop, decorating their various cabins with Rana's flowing, gilded artwork. Purple black flags flew, though some had snapped poles or seemed missing altogether. Some raft huts drifted, clinging to the main base with only a single scant rope.

Worse yet, few people ran around tending to the obvious disaster. Instead, yelling, cursing in different tongues poured forth from the small cluster's middle, where several rafts tied together merged their cabins into what looked like a bedraggled barn.

"This place is an insult," Quik said as they reached a shallow walkway leading from the nearest grassy mound onto the rafts. "Whomever's running it should be kicked out. The Najahn should be better."

"I'm sure they'll let you take over if you ask," Torny said. "You've certainly got the attitude."

"Quik's right, though," Eujo said as the quintet, with Bliss dropping to the rear, climbed the ramp. As good a scout as she was, most people they met would start with a hail, one Bliss couldn't answer. "This isn't how a Najahn outpost should look. They're hurting."

Nobody needed to ask what could cause this kind of damage, so nobody did. Instead, with the continued yelling, now drawing in a whole crowd, they walked on in quiet, stepping along soaked boards with rusted bolts, past battered homes and makeshift smithies, tool sheds, and growing huts. All the things you'd need to make a lively town, all looking one good push away from crumbling.

If Wax wanted to tie what he saw to anything, the floating disaster resembled Kitaye after the fiend's attack. When the city seemed one bad storm, one broken will away from collapse.

"Not exactly comforting," Wax said as they neared the center, still not a soul in sight. "What happens if a fiend attacks while they're all meeting?"

"Guessing they've decided they have bigger problems," Quik murmured. "Either way, how about you and Eujo take the lead? We'll keep an eye out."

"Don't want to get your hands dirty?"

"He's being smart," Eujo said. "The goal is the skar. If these people can't help us, then we take what we can and push on to the Whirlpool."

Wax laughed, "Right, because we all know what to do there. Unless you have some secret knowledge that I don't, Eujo?"

"Maybe I do."

Wax threw the Queen a questioning look, one that went unanswered as they came to the askew doorway leading into the central building. A large rounded-roof structure, walls buttressed by mud on floating slates, its roof one of thatching and wound rope, the place, like the rest of the outpost, grasped for glittering Rana glamour and fell short.

A single, weak Najahn flag fluttered up on the roof's top, purple and black a poor contrast to the icy blue sky.

Heat poured from the open door, not in temperature but in conversation, spitted voices resuming their arguing. Wax and Eujo, following Quik's guidance, placed themselves at the group's head and led the first steps inside.

What'd clearly been an inn's common room had been reshuffled, tables and chairs bundled together towards the center where the outposts's scant occupants—Wax counted no more than twenty—sat or stood around a center ring. There, over a raised metal oven wherein hot coals radiated an orange glow, argued a man and a woman, both in Najahn purple and black armor. Weapons lay strewn about the building's curling outer walls, some stacked with care and others tossed without regard. At the building's back, rickety shelves sat full, stocked with jars and sacks. Several hanging lines showed off smoked fish.

"Apparently they're not lacking for food," Eujo muttered.

Whether the pair in the middle heard Eujo or simply noticed the new arrivals, Wax couldn't be sure, but their argument broke off quick, their eyes and, following them, the crowd's glancing at first with fear then sustained suspicion towards the duo and the shadows behind them.

"Who're you?" called the man, dropping his hands to his waist, where some simple dirk or other lurked.

"Renewals," Eujo answered before Wax, throwing on her regal tone, brooking no insults or counters. "We've come to do what we must. Get passage to the Whirlpool and guidance on its navigation, so we can get our skars and continue on."

The two centers glanced at each other before the man turned back to them.

"And you have Guardians? How many?"

His voice leaked desperate hope, enough to put Wax on edge. He'd heard that hope before, back among the bandits on Foti.

"Enough to keep us safe," Eujo replied, walking further into the space.

"Enough, perhaps, to help us?" the woman asked. "If you haven't noticed, these are dark times."

"Dark times everywhere," Eujo replied. "Can't you send word back to Noctia, if you need help?"

"By the time it arrives, if it gets—" the woman cut off her speech, pointed at the Wax, Eujo, and their group. "How did you arrive? We would've seen a roller coming into port."

"Not if you were all sitting in here," Quik muttered behind Wax.

"Our roller sank. A fiend attacked and brought it down. We escaped." Eujo, though she wasn't tall, put on her imperious look and cast it about the room. "You won't aid us, then? Even though our success would save you from your own struggles?"

"Not a damn soul here'll live long enough for you to cross the other isles," the man said. "My names Castilan, she's Reathe. We're all that's left of the Najahn. Everyone else you're looking at are Rana locals, farmers and fishermen who either lived here or came running for shelter." Now eyes shifted away, to the floor, the walls, the hot coals. Everyone in their own memories. "You've come at our lowest, it's true. But Reathe and I will hold to our oaths if you press us. We can guide you, though it'll mean the deaths of everyone here."

"Okay," Wax interrupted, as Castilan had his arms up as if he was about to continue jabbering on. "Time's burning away, we're all hungry. I'm as interested in hearing the story as anyone, but how about we break out lunch and then you tell us what's up?"

Behind him, Torny laughed.

THE SALTED fish proved as tasty as they looked, especially when mixed with rice and delicious roasted reeds. The group gathered in the building seemed a tad relieved at Wax's suggestion, most taking the chance to break off, grab their gear and filter out. A days' work still needed doing, said Castilan, and the morning's meeting had gone well over time.

"Everyone wants their say when it's their lives on the table," Reathe said, the seven of them sitting on chairs around the smoldering coals. "They were content enough to let us Najahn throw our lives away to keep them safe, but now when we're asking them to do the same, they protest."

"You're asking them to throw their lives away?" Quik said. "I'd protest too."

"She's speaking harshly." Castilan put a hand on Reathe's arm, a tender grasp that drew a sigh. "What we're saying is what plagues us doesn't seem to have a weakness. The fiend harasses and breaks our spirits, resists our every attempt to hurt it, and when more bodies come back floating face down, you can imagine the response."

"For how long?" Eujo asked.

"Nearly a month," Castilan replied. "The Rana Renewal came through, achieved their skar without issue. The Foti one followed not long after, barely made it out alive. If he's still living, I suspect they've not left our isle." He glowered at the coals. "Since then, the fiend's only become more aggressive. I think the Renewals taking the skars aggravated it, and as more of you arrive, it'll only become more dangerous."

"You seem to know a lot about this fiend," Wax said.

"Of course we do," Reathe replied. "It's lived in the Whirlpool since the last Renewal, largely leaving us alone."

"Then it's time to deal with it." Eujo announced. "The question is, how?"

Reathe blinked at the Queen, "You think we've not had the same realization?"

Eujo, for once, didn't have a ready reply. Flushed, turned back to her fish without a word.

"In any case, the fiend's moved between here and the Whirlpool. You want the skar, you'll have to go through it," Castilan said. "We've tried all manner of attacks, from straight on rushes to gentle prods. All we've earned is death."

"It's not waiting anymore," Wax said, nodding.

"No." Castilan said, and as he spoke, a bell began to ring, sharp and clear. "And there it is. Someone's sighted the fiend. Perhaps this time it will put us all out of our misery." Castilan cast a wan smile about the room. "I'm sorry, Guardians, Renewals, that you have come to this doomed place. But I will not deny that you give me some hope. Maybe there is one among you with the ability, the genius to see our way free from this horror." Castilan rose, matching Reathe. "Or we will find ourselves at the water's bottom, where none of these worries need concern us again."

The bell's ringing grew faster, and once again, Wax heard screams and shouts rise on the air.

CHAPTER 18
BUG BASHING

A cold day. A blizzard day. Not that Maena and the others, fattened by an oat cake and warm goat's milk breakfast knew it until they left the tunnel's torch-lit warmth for their arena's blistering chill.

Like the one with the stones, the wide circle left itself open to the air, its boundaries raised higher by the packed stands circling its sides. A difference played out opposite their entry gate, where a sealed black barrier looked to bridge two sections of smoothed earthen wall. The stands near the area, too, stopped their curving build to extend straight beyond their sightline. Audiences, to Maena's eye, looked back and forth.

Multiple games to watch then.

To their left waited a second gate, smaller and grated like the one they'd walked through. Before it waited a guard, armored with more layers than Bertan and with a smile no less leering. The joy of bloodlust infected everyone around here.

Ale splashed around Maena's head as she and Svarde led their group out into the pit. The honeyed warmth stuck to her hair, steamed where it hit the snow-coated ground. At least they had shoes now, patched sandals really, to keep their toes from going numb.

Bit early for a drink, isn't it?

Winter in Whent. No crops to farm. Only entertainment from sun-up till, well, till the next sun-up.

And you raided this isle instead of joining it?

If you haven't already seen why, today might convince you.

The leering guard, at their entry, with the gate out latching shut behind them, launched into the day's event. It matched, at first, Jochi's description.

The warlord pitched them a contest, one for freedom against another group who'd earned their way to this point. The discord began at that mention, one that seemed without evidence, as no other group stood before the five. Yet the guard proclaimed they were there, and the crowd roared as if such a match was in the offing.

Not that Maena and the others weren't prepared.

They'd spent the night around their low fire discussing tactics, Svarde and Rasslebeck at first leading the dialog before Maena found herself unable to resist. The Rana captain in her took the bait and ran with it, isolating their group's strengths and assigning roles. Svarde and Rasslebeck on the front lines, handling the first fiends through while Maena and Pennifer would scout out, look for opportunities to snipe.

Kivi would roam, rescue anyone in trouble before backing off and repeating the same. Simple enough, but without more details, that was the best the group could come up with. After some fine-tuning—Svarde the true front, Rasslebeck staying back to watch for surprises—Maena urged them all to get what sleep they could.

She had, in fact, slept soundly, save for the every-so-often replay of Bertan's end filtering through Maena's dreams.

Brutality's true cost.

The pit offered them few weapons. Stones in the middle, several crude staves long since retired from more active use. One weathered sling and a rock pile to go with it.

"Yours," Maena said to Pennifer while the guard continued on, preaching about odds, where bets could be placed, and the assuredly cheap price of more ale.

"What'll you have, then?" Pennifer asked.

"A staff will serve to start," Maena replied. "Then I'll take the first tooth I knock out."

"Captain, it's good to have you back."

Are you back?

Maena only grinned, forced but real enough for Pennifer to lope across the pit and grab her sling. Svarde and Rasslebeck each took a stone, the big Foti Guardian picking one for each hand. The staff's grips were so icy Maena nearly dropped the thing at first touch before swallowing her pain and letting the numbness coat her palms.

A little cold was nothing next to death's long chill.

He's done talking.

The guard had indeed wrapped his speech, retreated over to the gate Maena and the others had entered through. The man's grin slipped now into a focused frown, one answered by a bell ringing somewhere nearby. At its noise, both gates opened.

The guard slipped out the one, his exit replaced by several more appearing on the pit's upper edge, each armed with crossbows. Security, then, for both the prisoners and the fiends.

"Here they come," Svarde warned. Kivi snorted, the ferrite making her way to the pit's left side. "Stand ready."

The crowd, those delirious, drunk, dazzled people, roared overhead. Someone threw a half-chewed mutton leg into their pit, marring the snow with its first red.

The fiends followed.

Four, and fast. Like skittering, wingless wasps. Six skeletal legs, a deep ruby red and connecting to sectioned bodies. Twin stingers rose off the monster's back ends, soaring up into the sky as the creatures left their tunnel at the hands of some chasing fire.

Each one stood near Svarde's height, and all four sighted on the Foti man, stacked mandibles surrounded by beady eyes snapping towards the Guardian.

Pennifer's sling fired first, a stone launching past Maena's shoulder and slapping into the first fiend as it sprang into the pit. The rock bashed against the bug's carapace, making not a dent, but driving the creature's attention away from Svarde, the Foti man belting out some chant about iron and stone.

First play of the day.

Since when are you so cheery?

After you've died once, doing it again doesn't faze you.

Maena gripped the staff in both hands as Pennifer's victim threw up snow in its path around Svarde. The fiend seemed not to notice Maena, at least not until the Rana captain swung the staff in a wide, hammering arc right into the big bug's mandibles.

If the carapace on its legs and body could take a hit, the mandibles proved less fortified. Maena's strike, a vibrating one rumbling up the staff through her arms, shoulders, legs, knocked the crescent spike clean off the insect's face, throwing it to the snow where it quivered, black and seeping.

The fiend cooed, a fluttering noise like a bird in the midst of a heart attack, and rose up on its hind legs.

"Go for the mouth!" Maena yelled, Pennifer's second stone flying in and nailing the fiend's face, right where Maena's staff had struck a second ago.

Amazing shot.

It's what she does.

The fiend reeled, stumbling over its legs towards the pit's far side, unknown ichor flying from the stone's impact.

"Kivi, that one's yours," Maena said, rotating to her right, seeing the three-on-two battle between Svarde, Rasslebeck, and the other bugs.

Svarde himself had seen better fights. The man used his stones to block, batter, and drive away two fiends while Rasslebeck ran, slipped, and stumbled around a chasing third. Svarde's success seemed soft, as the man bled already from several stings. As Maena started his way, Svarde, lunging in at the one on his left and delivering a wallop, took another gashing slice from the fiend to his right.

Whether those stings held venom, Maena didn't know. Didn't want to guess.

Svarde stumbled, his target recovering from the man's strike to make a mandible-led bite at Svarde's gut.

Thankfully, staffs had a long reach.

Maena lunged, slipping her grip to the staff's butt end to give it the farthest push forward. The bug's bite hit the staff first, crunched into its leading wood and snapped it apart, leaving Maena with a shorter, but much sharper, stake.

The bug sputtered, shook off the wood bits. Sighted its too-many eyes on Maena, and—

"Watch out, captain!" Pennifer's call, and Maena rolled left, drenching her outfit in snow.

The rightward fiend, the one who'd lanced Svarde a moment ago, jabbed both stingers into the ground where Maena had been. Its reward, instead of a punctured captain, was another Pennifer-flung stone into its crunchy eyes.

The crowd roared.

Maena planted her hands on the ground, brought a knee up as the fiend flung its stingers back and broke towards Pennifer. Too fast for the slinger to reload. Too fast for anyone to get there.

Maena threw her shard. Leaned into the launch as she rose, the splintered end flying right into the biggest spot she could target: the fat stingers on the bug's back. The speckled fat sacs rose up bulbous from the bug's butt, making an appealing, easy-to-hit spot that took Maena's dart like soft cheese might a toothpick.

The right stinger sac broke, a pressure pop blowing open and sending the fiend into a leftward stagger. The blown stinger limped to the ground, while Pennifer backpedaled, slotting another stone into her sling.

Worry about yourself for a second.

True, Maena had no weapon. Svarde bumbled by on her right, bleeding from yet more cuts, though his hands still held both stones, their ends raw with won strikes. On her left, Rasslebeck seemed to be playing a losing game of tag with his own bug, the insect backing him into a corner with little damage to show for it.

The only outright winner seemed to be Kivi, whose one-on-one contest looked to be in the ferrite's favor: both the bug's stinger points lay bent and broken after failed attempts to pierce the ferrite's rocky shell, and now the fiend retreated, trapped against the pit's wall as the ferrite used its claws and jaws to take the fight to a certain end.

"Go left," Svarde growled, catching his footing and barreling back towards Maena, towards the bug behind her.

Maena kicked off that way, turning around as she did so. Svarde slammed into the bug, closing quick enough for the stings to glaze over his shoulders, letting the Foti barbarian ram the stones into an already mashed mandible mass.

Again that fluttering sound.

Maena's foot struck another staff, one of three remaining. She scooped it up in one motion, went after Rasslebeck and his winning bug.

The big fiend, an ugly brown, red, and mossy green, backed Rasslebeck down. It bit and kicked with its front legs, drawing blood along Rasslebeck's arms, his thighs, while the Rana raider tried to bash back with the rock. Rasslebeck didn't have Svarde's strength or the man's blind courage, making his swings an annoyance at best.

But they kept the bug's attention, and that was enough.

Maena raised the staff over her shoulder as she charged, before bringing it down with all her momentum on the bug's left stinger sac. The carapace squished in, bending with the blow.

Not breaking.

The bug whirled, those stingers jutting in at Maena as she bounced back from her swing. She went into a roll, slipping some on the snow and landing on her back. The bug raised its forelegs, stamped them on Maena's own, its weight pressing her into the snow. The stingers came down.

White hot pain flared in Maena's right shoulder. The left should've been the same, but the stinger never hit.

Instead, just like the one chasing Pennifer, the stinger sac broke, the reason clear enough as the bug fell away.

Behind it, covered in a greenish-clear liquid, stood Rasslebeck, sharp stone in hand.

"Don't let it recover," Maena said, pushing away the pain.

Her left arm didn't want to let her, a burning bloom spreading from the clear hole where the stinger had found its purchase.

Are we dead now? Am I dead again, so quickly?

Don't count us out.

The crowd didn't either, the cheers growing louder. More trash flew into the arena, finished food, earthen mugs shattering on impact. Above, the archers remained stoic, watching without emotion.

Maena found her feet, found too that Kivi had finished its meal, the fiend twitching idly in the corner. The ferrite went to Svarde next, leaping on the bug as it engaged Svarde in an awful, up-close fight. Mandibles and mitts flew fast, bits and blood ruining the snowfall.

The stinger sacs, though, seemed to be the key. Shaking, trying to blink away the venom, Maena saw Pennifer close on the bug wounded by Maena's staff. The fiend couldn't stand straight, could do little more than lash out with a leg or two. Pennifer dodged those, spun up her sling, and dealt a fatal strike at near point-blank range.

Rasslebeck's own victorious cry came behind her. Svarde's followed moments later, as Maena found her breathing hard to continue, air unable to get through a throat suddenly prone to twitching closed.

She lay on her knees now, hands planted in the snow. Her left arm faltered, Maena rolling to her side, looking now at the great black divide in the earth.

A bell rang, loud and shining. The crowd roared, somehow still louder, or perhaps that was a wailing in Maena's own mind, her other self dying a second time.

Two crossbowmen let their weapons hang, reaching that great divide and pulling on some unseen ties. The sheet fell away, a great curtain, hiding a second arena, and in it, split from them by another grated gate, lay another battle.

One also concluded.

Maena felt hands land beneath her head, lift her up, turn her eyes away from the fiends and their meal, those fighters so close to freedom.

CHAPTER 19

BUBBLE

While Bliss would never say she preferred fighting at night to the day, the darkness did have one advantage woefully missing beneath that clear Rana sky: keeping things black meant she didn't have to see the whole monster all at once.

Bliss, followed by everyone else, left the warehouse with her staff in hand. Where to go wasn't hard to parse as the shouts came from one direction: north. Wheeling that way, stumbling on the rocking raft, Bliss slapped her staff into both palms. Ready to strike, to guard, to do what needed doing.

What that was, according to what she saw, was finding a way to get about a thousand more people here. Preferably armed and ready to fire.

The fiend rose up before the raft outpost like a wave, a gelatinous form whose skin, so far as Bliss could tell, resembled the sheen of a drifting bubble, radiant in the light and casting its blinding prisms everywhere. Looking away quickly became a poor solution, as the squelching fiend, with the hissing of a thousand snakes, launched watery sprays out onto the buildings with the enthusiasm of a Vis child playing in the beach surf. The fountains struck and splattered, the film catching the sun's light and shining it, seemingly, right into Bliss's eyes.

Torny's colorful curses, shouted as the bandit retreated back into the warehouse, described the situation pretty damn well. Torny could run if she wanted, though. Bliss was a Lira, and Lira didn't flee, especially not from fiends.

Instead, slipping the staff into its back holster, Bliss made her way towards the monster. She used the buildings as cover, ducking behind flimsy walls and stacked crates whenever the fiend sprayed anything near her. The water gouts simply rose and blasted from the water's surface, without showing any targets.

Though that didn't mean the people here didn't try. Arrows and darts, rocks and random debris flew out at the fiend from the defenders and the desperate. Most bounced off. Some arrows, sharp enough, pierced the film only to lodge there, wiggling brown errors in the fiend's otherwise perfect picture.

"How do we hurt it?" Quik asked, surprising Bliss by keeping to her heels.

She glanced back, saw the two of them were alone, having outpaced the others. Wax and Eujo, along with Torny, looked to have gone back inside. The Renewals not risking themselves made sense, though Bliss wasn't sure what good hiding would do: if this fiend wanted to destroy the town, it definitely could.

'We've gotta get a closer look,' Bliss signed.

"Okay," Quik said as another rattling spray struck the shack they hid behind, "I see what you're saying, but that's not going to work."

'Be creative.'

Quik gave her a frown. Bliss rolled away, dashing along the shack, thin boards ending in water a few steps to her left. Ahead this raft ended in a jutting pier, a lone fishing boat struggling to keep tied to the roiling dock. Beyond it, many boat lengths more, lay the fiend's sweeping bulk.

Could she leap that far?

Bliss's calculation ended as a rounded, muddy red flap crested the water before her, the thing scooping the water back towards the fiend's body. As it did, the liquid mashed against the filament before, as the flap squeezed tight, launching out an arcing spray towards the outpost.

The film landed and Bliss heard a cry to her left, saw an archer covered in the stuff. It bore the man to the ground, the film sealing around him, making its way in his throat, his nose.

The way this monster killed became all too clear.

"I'm on him," Quik shouted as Bliss started back to the downed man. "You worry about the monster."

Oh, she would. She was. Switching back to the task at hand, Bliss again kicked into a run, veering left and right with the raft's rocking.

As she sprinted across the final portion, littered with toppled tools, sprawling rope, and other nonsense forcing careful steps, the fiend again squeezed the water into a spray, this one a short arc aiming right for her.

Bliss flipped her staff to her left hand and leapt, her jump carrying her past the raft's end and into the roiling, cold green-blue waters. She struck and dove beneath the surface as the fiend's spray splattered the water above her. Bliss kept her eyes open, saw the fiend's film sink, the heavy bubbles descending towards the marsh's floor.

A current found Bliss and yanked her with it, pulling her into the fiend, a vacuum Bliss couldn't hope to compete with. She clamped her mouth shut, tried to hold in air, and looked towards the thing sucking her in.

Wider than the raft's main building, the huge fiend had a body going well beneath the water's surface. The curves above extended down below, save the sections separating into those water pushing fins. The monster's underside curled up into itself, pulsing like the jellyfish sometimes washing up in Kitaye's inlet. That pulsing must generate the current, the one continuing to drag Bliss down, down, and deeper still till the sunny day up above appeared as nothing more than dim light shafts cast through a miserable swirling dark.

Her lungs ached as Bliss felt the current change its tack, sending her not down, now, but up. She'd crossed beneath the fiend's outer bulb, and now the monster was bringing her to whatever end awaited in its center.

From what Bliss could tell, her vision smearing with a water now muddy as the fiend's pulsing sucked up all the dirt below, her destination looked an awful lot like a berry bush beginning to rot.

But given her options seemed a choice between that rotting berry bush and drowning, Bliss kicked her feet hard for the surface. She broke the water into a stifling bubble, one filled by dripping, floating red. Apple-colored balls and strings clustered and broke, drifting together on long threads attached to the fiend's bubble shell, the ends spidering out against the skin.

Around her, Bliss felt the water congealing, drawing up into those tethered masses. Was that how the fiend ate? Somehow drinking--

The burn came quick, sudden, and all over. Vis had more than a few stinging insects, some wildlife that could, if pestered, spit a nasty acid onto your skin, and Bliss felt that now. Everywhere.

She sighted the closest red mass, cherry-like balls clustered together in a beating organ, and kicked towards it. Her hair started to disintegrate, her nose screamed as water splashed up inside, thick and hot. Bliss kept her mouth closed, not knowing, not wanting to know what might happen if the stuff made its way down her throat.

The staff gave her a path. She reached out with its metal end, plunged it into the red mass and felt the soft stuff give way. The staff lodged in, the organ—if that's what it was— bending around it. With one hand, Bliss pulled herself up the staff's length, reaching with the other to grab a cherry. Warm to the touch, soft and slippery, Bliss dug in her grip. Found the same mess dissolving her skin worked well enough to stick her to the organ.

Another lift, and Bliss found herself clinging a length or two over the deadly water, dripping her own death.

A caustic chill followed, Bliss holding to her rescue and breathing, just breathing. Her skin flared over with angry welts and worse, veiny ribbons running across every exposed patch and, Bliss figured, everywhere beneath too.

Her eyes, her mouth worked. Her arms and legs could move, though their every motion brought a scalding ache. Such was life for a Lira.

Yet life she had, and Bliss meant to use it.

Inside the fiend, sound took on an echo. Water's splash, the occasional shout from outside, the burble and churn of the thing's innards all bounced around in a sonic smear. The light outside plastered everything in an odd glow.

If life back on Vis had been a pleasant calm, her days since leaving the isle competed with each other for most absurd. So far, this one was winning.

Okay. Think like a hunter. Needing to kill a beast bigger and stronger than herself meant finding its weakness. Finding that fatal spot might take out Bliss in the process— the great bubble collapsing on her prompted a tight wince —but that would mean saving Wax, saving Quik, saving Torny.

The quivering red she clung to now seemed focused on the water below, dipping down into it to suck up stuff dissolved by the fiend's acid self. Tubes, orange-yellow things branching out from the organ she was on to several others, strung out in various directions.

Like her own stomach, sending its prizes all over the body. Bliss traced the veins, found two leading to smaller pulsing pieces, ones sharing shape and size and color. Destroying one, then, might not be the killing blow she wanted.

Up above, though, waited a much larger, almost cube-like organ. Suspended in the bubble's center, kept there by stringing veins, coated in odd growths, like a log overtaken by mushrooms and moss, the organ seemed like the fiend's centerpiece. Get up there, give it a good hit, and the fiend would feel it.

Who knew whether the monster would die, but if Bliss had only one option—and she definitely did—then this was going to be the one.

The hunter moved with her hand and staff, driving the latter into the organ every time she wanted a better foothold, a chance to get her breath back. Reaching the upward vein took minutes, filled with breaks Bliss had to spend closing her eyes, breathing slow, finding the strength for the next climb.

She looped the staff onto her back, nearly lost it when

the weapon slipped through a holster no longer there. Only in weak strands did the leather survive, dissolved by acid.

New tactic then.

Bliss tried jamming the staff into the vein. Unlike the organ, the stiffer skin didn't give, the staff bouncing off. Striking harder might cause the vessel to burst, and Bliss didn't want her only way up to get destroyed, much less some explosion drive her back into the deadly water.

If she couldn't use both her hands, then, her feet would have to suffice. Bliss kicked off her ruined shoes, wiggling her scalded toes, and made the first jump. The vein wasn't smooth, but, like everything else in the fiend, had its surface coated in ridges and odd growths. The handholds helped, gave her toes something to wrap around. With her left hand, Bliss pressed the staff against the vein, used what leverage she could find, and climbed.

One foot, one hand after the next, heading towards the giant organ in the fiend's center, heading for hope.

CHAPTER 20

CLIFF DEALS

The pass and the bitter cold died away together as Mottilan came into view. Shaggy cliffs, forested up where Sawi stood and thawing to messy vines, grasses, and trees descended before them to the ocean's shore, a broad rocky beach overrun with fishing boats thrust upon the shoals, though soon they'd be embarking for the morning's catch.

Gladdring insisted on moving early, claiming his own stamina faded as the sun wore him down, and preferring late afternoons and evenings for conversation. Those words, shared over campfires and what food Sawi could forage from the forests, from the nooks, from the sparse towns they passed in the days it took them to get over the mountains, covered things Sawi never knew, never questioned, never wondered.

By the time they reached the overlook, Sawi figured she must've been as much an expert on Noctia and Najahn politics as anyone on the isle. More than that, she knew Gladdring considered her bound to him, in some way she hadn't yet discovered.

That debt, that tie kept him close to her, the Tenet's looming form drawing in the view, sparkling with the rising sun.

"I've never seen it from this angle before," Gladdring murmured. "Your isle is truly a delight for the eyes."

"They have this, and little else," Sawi replied.

"Still with the casual dislike of your sister city. Is everyone in Kitaye so dismissive of their brethren?"

"They are as dismissive as we are."

"So you are spoiled children, then. Not willing to come to terms?"

Sawi bit off a more cutting remark. Wax and her friends would've understood without saying. Gladdring might, if she brought up Pan's death at the hands of these sea-faring brutes. Thus far, though, she'd kept that part a secret, allowing Gladdring to dominate with stories of his own. Better, according to the man's own words, to listen rather than feed opportunities to others.

How would Pan's death be used against her? Sawi wasn't sure, but if she'd learned anything from the walks with Gladdring, it was that everything could be used, somehow.

"It's a long trek yet down to the city," Sawi said. "We should get moving."

"If only to be where it is warmer," Gladdring replied. "Winters are always my least favorite time. Which is why, of course, I chose now to come to your beautiful isle . . . "

The man's words flowed out as they walked, ceaseless in their sound, spreading out over one topic and the next as Sawi watched her feet, the path, and wondered what Gladdring wanted with this fishing city.

At least it was easy to see what the city wanted with Gladdring. While Sawi herself drew little more than glares

—her weave and ink made it clear she'd come from Kitaye —Gladdring earned offers for trade, for tales, for opportunities. The Tenet, much as he had in Kitaye, waved off the requests with polite replies, yet still drew a following, one that spread out and watched from stone-and-stick buildings as the pair reached Mottilan's center.

"Now," Gladdring said, "I believe I've drawn the attention of the entire village."

"Probably." Sawi nodded at the man. "You're not inconspicuous. Nobody wears robes like that, no matter the season."

"Fashion is one thing Noctia could stand to export," Gladdring tugged at his wide purple-black hems. "These truly are comfortable, and easy to move in a pinch."

"You think we'll be running?"

"Sawi, let us say, my business here is of a delicate sort. I would keep your eyes open."

Yet, for all that, the first thing Gladdring wanted to do was find a fresh meal and a place to park their satchels. Have a bath. Those errands bled away the morning, after which Gladdring told Sawi to amuse herself till later that evening while he went about looking for this so-called business.

With hours before her, Sawi looked at the prospect of remaining in Motillan and shivered. The hostile eyes had already told her to leave, so, at least for a little bit, she did. Went to that rocky beach and wandered along it up the coast, feeling the occasional warm brush from the water.

How odd it was to go from the chill just up there to something so pleasant down here.

Seagulls marked her progress in the air, while crabs and other critters dashed away from Sawi's approach, her feet, bare, treasuring soft stones and sand. Coarser than Kitaye's inlet, but less crowded.

Back home, there'd be children aplenty out here on a blue day like this one. Adults too, taking their relaxation out to the beach. Motillan, though, rang with effort's noise. Fishermen calling out to one another or coming back with catch that needed filleting, the port buzzing as Kance ships came and went. A single Tamas vessel, its broad base and dyed sails offering a chromatic bent to the traffic, stood out.

Sawi watched it all. Tried to find that spark, the one that must've drove Wax and Quik to embark away. Gladdring stirred something, with all his talk, though Sawi had yet to find a sentence, a description, a suggestion that truly pulled her from Vis.

All of it sounded more grim, more gray, more liable to end up face down with a knife in your back or destitute, one bad day away from the gutter.

Her eyes drifted to the mountain pass. A long way to go alone, but she could leave now. Be back to the last little inn not long after sunset, trade away her remaining forages for a night by the fire, and then on. Back home.

"Strange to see a Kitaye here not hawking their wares."

The rail-thin woman, hair riffled with glimmering shells, approached from the port's side. She offered Sawi a pleasant smile, revealing teeth inked over in the way Mottilan marked their elders.

"I wouldn't be here save for a job," Sawi replied.

"The Noctia man."

Sawi let any surprise drain out into the surf tickling her toes. Mottilan had size, true, but it didn't sprawl like Kitaye. Word would travel fast here, and anyone caring enough to come out all this way and talk to her would want something, would know most everything there was to know.

"Do you understand who he is?" the woman asked after Sawi didn't reply.

"He's told me."

The woman laughed, as tired and ancient as the waves crashing around them.

"So suspicious of us. As if Mottilan has done anything to you."

"Your people killed my friend."

Hah. Sawi treasured that little satisfied bloom as the woman's eyes widened.

"There've been deaths aplenty with the fiends," the woman said, caution creeping in, "yet I don't recall any fights between Vis's people. Nor should there be."

"I would've said the same."

"Close to your heart, then."

Sawi nodded, kept her eyes out to sea. The sun behind her now, casting golden shadows off the mountain onto the water.

"What do you want?" Sawi asked.

"Has he made a deal with you? With Kitaye?"

"I'm his guide, nothing else."

"Guide to here? No further?"

"That's for him to decide."

"He owns you then?"

Sawi whirled, planted her hand on the rocks, "He doesn't own me."

"Sounds like he does, girl, from your talk," the woman said, baring those teeth again. "Or do you have some say in the matter?"

"Why do you care?"

A sniff. "Because my city needs this man, however much it hurts me to say so."

Sawi hesitated. Not the words she expected.

"The Najahn ignored us. Noctia didn't care," the woman continued, "until he showed up. Now, we're visited. Not often, but more, much more, and the trade is bringing a new life to this coast."

"Sounds great."

"It is essential," the woman continued. "But not everyone sees it that way. There are those that look at a debt to the Najahn and feel trapped, feel they must be free no matter what the cost."

"Any prisoner would feel that way. I would."

"Yet, Gladdring is worth protecting."

"From who, these people?"

A faint smile, "Nobody watches the old ladies, girl. Nobody cares where we walk. I'm telling you, Gladdring has made a mistake coming back here. If you want him to survive, get him out of the city. Tonight. Now."

Sawi started a shrug. The woman stopped it with a cold hand on her shoulder.

"It's not your business, is it, what the man chooses to do with his time, with his deals?" the woman asked. "You are just his guide, and so be it?"

What sort of answer could Sawi give to that? In any case, the woman didn't seem interested in one, again drawing in her breath to speak.

"Then consider your isle and Kitaye. Consider what he means to it. Don't let the brash actions of a fearful few turn us into ashes. The Najahn won't take a Tenet's fall lightly."

"Then why aren't you stopping them?"

"Because I am one voice against many. Too many who can't see our only way lies at Gladdring's feet, however much it pains us to be there."

Sawi laughed. "So I'm your only hope?"

"The only one Gladdring will trust."

Gladdring, though, wasn't anywhere to be found. Mottilan lit its streets with oiled torches when night fell, yet Sawi failed to find the Najahn Tenet in the shadows around their chosen inn. Neither was he inside, grabbing dinner and regaling the guests, an activity Gladdring had seemed to enjoy at the small towns along the way. Nobody had seen him either, when Sawi put the discrete whisper around.

Which led her, with a slip and a climb, to the inn's roof. She perched on the strong wood, a frame covering carved stone walls, and looked.

The first surprise came when she realized she wasn't alone. On the inn's roof, yes, but around her, on rooftops spread throughout the town, Mottilan's residents took to their tops to watch the stars emerge. Many rested on blankets, picked up glasses and fruited desserts. A cool breeze carried away the day's warmth, and those stars did indeed capture the night in a way Kitaye and its jungle didn't allow.

Hard to enjoy something beautiful when you had to find someone, though.

Sawi's clue came through sound. Sneaking in behind the mashing surf, above a few instruments and beneath the rustled conversation from the inn below her were cracks, vocal ones. A voice rising, and falling, as if delivering a speech.

Sawi turned, looked up the cliff. Mottilan's bulk lay near the port, before giving way to wealthier dwellings further up the cliffside. One of those seemed brighter lit than the others, the walkway up from the main cliff path lined with glowing fire. Expecting guests, perhaps.

Sawi slipped off the inn's roof, made her way back through a quieting town and up the cliff. She still felt eyes on her the whole way, both hostile and curious, but trying to catch them out only had her looking at shadows.

She'd have to treat them like hanoko. Always there, but rarely a danger unless she did something stupid.

Getting up near the large home took time, and the voices changed, disappeared and returned in differing tones, colors. Some heated, others not. Arguments, then. Discussions. And mixed in them, every so often, yet more clear as Sawi approached and deciphered the honeyed words, a certain Noctia diction.

She skipped the lit path, instead darting onto the rocks, letting her hands pick out every move with leading reaches, testing toes. The route took her beneath the house, and she rose to its level only when no torch seemed near enough to break the night's shroud.

Sichi, either absent or blocked by the cliff, did everything to help her.

Everyone on Vis learned how to sneak, to catch up on unsuspecting game or escape from a feisty predator. Those instincts settled Sawi as she came up on the loose grass patch, nary more than a few strides before the house. Windows, open to the air, looked back her way and for a moment Sawi thought she was caught.

A moment passed in silence as she realized the voices, the lit inside, came from the house's other end. The side facing the rock, from where nobody could see in.

"Gladdring," grumbled a man, sounding enough like Sawi's father, but not quite his age, "you've spent hours now trying to spin you way free. We've listened, but not a one of us agrees with you. Your word means nothing. Your death, or perhaps your traded life, could give us everything."

CHAPTER 21
FOTI'S GIFT

Quik and Bliss burst out the warehouse door, cutting right towards the massive bubble fiend. Torny went behind, her feet dragging, eyes searching. A thief looking for a sneak attack, some way to keep herself alive.

At least, that's how Wax, fourth in line, saw it. He would've moved faster, too, if not for Eujo reaching out and snagging his clothes from behind. Giving him a gentle tug, delaying even more till Castilan and Reathe muscled past.

"You're the Renewal. Let your Guardians do their job," Eujo said.

"They're my family, not just my Guardians." Wax worked himself off her grip, went to the door. Realized Eujo wasn't following. "You're going to stay here? Really?"

"You said it yourself, Wax. What's more important? Us, or a single fiend?"

Wax wanted to throw up his hands, announce that it's damn likely neither one of them would be the Aegis anyway. That he didn't want to sit on a stone throne for years regretting he hadn't helped save a life now, today.

Instead, he said nothing, because Eujo didn't look like someone who could be moved. Her hands sat at her sides, her feet dug in strong to the wood boards, her face the icy glare she did so well. Even her hair, messed up and tangled like everyone's seemed to frame her like a thorny wall.

"You know I'm right," Eujo repeated.

"I'm not going to stay here," Wax replied, trying to find an idea. "Right or no. I'm going out there to help. Damn your purpose."

Before she could say something more, Wax spun and dashed out the door. Stopped nary a meter outside as filmy spray hammered the ground ahead, catching the slow-moving Reathe. The greasy liquid dragged Reathe to the ground, where it seemed to fold around her, trapping the Najahn.

By her face, the woman screamed. By her sound, nothing escaped the bubble.

Wax drew the Foti blade, cut across the raft to Reathe's side and swept the blade's edge through the bubble. Like a fruit peeling back, the bubble opened, deflated into a sticky mess clinging to Reathe.

"It's burning me," Reathe gasped, changing up her shouts for something more useful. "Get it off!"

Wax looked around, saw a rag pile meant for fish guts and worse. Took one of the awful things and started smearing it across Reathe while she brushed at herself with gloved hands. Reathe's efforts proved pointless, her gloves disintegrating as she rubbed them. Wax's rag, perhaps protected by the same fish guts it'd claimed before, did better, sucking up the bubble.

"Here," Wax said, handing the rag to Reathe and grabbing a second one.

Together the two kept at it, wiping Reathe clear enough

to stand. She had her head shaking, skin lined with burn marks.

"It should've hit us again," Reathe said, drawing both her and Wax's looks out towards the fiend.

The bubbling mass stood there still, fins moving to spray again and again, but the arcs chased someone else now, a larger form cutting between cover, making his way ever nearer.

"Quik," Wax muttered. "Though what he's going to do when he gets close . . . "

Though he searched, Wax couldn't spot Bliss anywhere. Castilan claimed a rooftop and a crossbow, launching the occasional bolt towards the immense fiend. As pointless a move as anything.

"What else do you have here?" Wax asked Reathe as they huddled behind battered crates. "We don't have a weapon that'll hurt that thing."

"We're a fishing outpost, a waypoint for Renewals, not a military base," Reathe countered. "Noctia barely remembers we exist between Renewals."

"Nothing? You've had the fiend living nearby for years and you've never thought about how to kill it?"

Reathe sighed. "Okay, not true. We've gathered oil, made it from fat, and it's all in that building." Reathe pointed south, near the town's edge. "Where it won't damage much if it catches fire. The idea was we'd spread it over the fiend, trap it beneath the oil, throw on a torch."

"And you didn't try that, why?"

"Because the people who kept wanting to do it are all dead now, that's why." More spray hit close, sizzling as it smacked the crates. Reathe cursed. "They took some and tried, days ago after the Foti Renewal got hurt. Now the fiend's coming to get its revenge."

"Fiends are dumb. They don't think like that," Wax countered. "Now that it's here, though, how about we give your oil a try?"

Reathe laughed, hunched back further against the crates. "Better to wait till it leaves. Live another day."

"Wax," Eujo said, standing in the warehouse doorway. "I'm with you."

The pair made it to Reathe's chosen building quick, pushed open the unbarred door to find a sparse room, empty save for ten or eleven squat barrels. Someone had painted a black drop, an outline of a fire on the sides.

"So here they are," Wax said. "Now what?"

"I thought you had an idea?"

"Well, I'm more of an on-the-fly guy," Wax replied, frowning. "How heavy are they?"

A single lift, Eujo giving a skeptical eye, showed Wax alone would exhaust himself trying to get one of these all the way to the fiend, much less the whole number.

"Okay, new plan," Wax muttered, going back to the door, spying his solution resting nearby in the canal. A fishing boat, bobbing in the waves. "There we go."

"You're going to, what, load this up with oil and ram it into the fiend?"

"It's not that complicated." Wax hefted the first barrel, carried it from the house and set it in the boat. "Don't even need'em all."

"And how are you going to light it up? Assuming you even get all the way to the fiend."

"You're going to tell Castilan to do it with his crossbow. I'll jump into the water, swim away. Easy."

"Your confidence is surreal."

"Your lack of help with the barrels isn't."

Eujo took the point, and together the pair lugged five

barrels into the boat, nestling them next to one another. As they worked, Wax kept looking back to the fiend, watching its spray and Castilian's continuing fire.

Quik and Bliss seemed nowhere. Some townsfolk ran around, carrying rags and wiping off others caught by the spray. Maybe Reathe spread the word. Still, the raft outpost continued to shake with every slamming gout. More than one building had already collapsed as the acid slime ate through wood, and the fiend showed no sign of leaving.

Maybe it wouldn't tire till everything here was dust.

"You know what to do?" Wax asked.

"Castilan. Shoot the boat with some fire," Eujo said. "Got it."

"See?" Wax pushed the oiled boat off its tie, down the canal towards the fiend. "Isn't this more fun?"

"Just don't die, Wax."

"That'd just give you better odds."

Eujo only frowned at that, then took off running. Wax hefted a single oar, stuck its paddle against the canal's edge, and pushed. He'd need speed, every second he could spare to get this thing to the fiend and live.

The monster, at least, seemed preoccupied. Wax caught the reason as his oil-laden boat neared the raft city's northern edge. Quik, dancing along the dock, lifting and throwing what he could grab at the fiend. Hefting crates and using them to deflect the fiend's spray. A distracting game, but one with a definite clock: the wide dock Quik ran on was nearing empty.

"Wax!" Quik shouted. "What're you doing?"

"Secret plan," Wax called back. "Keep its attention."

"Have you seen Bliss?"

"Haven't you?"

Wax turned back to the fiend. Pushed the boat off the

dock's end. Clear in the water now, swirling waves and scattered weeds between him and the giant bubble monster. The fiend really was huge, reaching up taller than a Kitaye treehouse. And yet, Wax felt none of the fear that'd curled inside him back in Kitaye during that momentous assault.

Was he just that much more brave, now?

Or was it the Foti skar on his necklace, humming with hungry energy, pushing Wax forward with its nonsense words?

Water lapped over the small boat's sides as it careened into the fiend's wave-making wilds. Wax, who'd never in his life wielded an ore—Kitaye's lily pads ran on long poles to push them around the inlet—flailed, trying to keep the boat on course.

Not all that difficult when the target covered the entire horizon.

A massive fin swept by on Wax's right, bucking the boat to his left. When the limb mashed the water against the fiend's side, the spray arced up, high and short. Right at him.

"So you've noticed me now," Wax muttered, then leapt.

Hitting the cold water brought a clarion rush, one propelling Wax to the surface. The fiend's spray crashed around him, forcing Wax to duck beneath the waves. Light filtering beneath showed where, in its bending, the fiend's spray clung to the surface. Wax kicked away from it, following the boat, and hoped, hoped Castilan wasn't quick on the trigger.

A broad stroke brought Wax up to the surface again, near enough to put his hand on the boat, now coasting towards the fiend of its own accord as the monster's motions drew the current inward.

Wax risked a look back at the roof where Castilan was supposed to be and saw nobody. Not a damn soul.

What was Eujo doing?

The boat rocked, driving Wax beneath the water. He kicked, pushed himself to the boat's port side, again rising and hooking his arm over one side. His head followed, though Wax found himself regretting the view.

The fiend's bubbling mass dominated, so close now that behind the rainbow shimmer of its skin, Wax could make out a red forest, strange things looping and tied to one another. And, in that forest, a darker smudged shape on the move.

One monster inside another?

Didn't matter. The boat was about to hit, and Castilan hadn't received the word. Time to, what, abandon the plan?

As Wax scrambled, the skars whispering in his head grew to a roar. The Foti one ran roughshod over Wax's mind, urging him to go, to kick forward, to drive the boat into the creature. What would happen then descended into animal urges, a desire Wax only felt at dinner after a day swinging through the trees. A mad hunger, one needing to be satiated.

Now.

The boat struck the fiend's side, pressing into the bubble in what looked to be an ineffective bounce. A perfect bounce, though, if Castilian's fire-lined bolt hit now, if the boat could catch fire, if—

The necklace burned, even as it dipped in and out of the water. Wax's chest grew hot, so hot he started a curse only to clamp it off as the heat spread, shooting through his body, his arms, his fingers, and into the wood.

Like a sunrise, the boat blew into fantastic flame. The light bright enough, the force following as those flames found the oil barrels, blew Wax across the water, churning him over the surface.

Someone—Quik?—shouted, a voice cutting through the skar's roar, his body's blinding ache and confusion. Water lapped Wax from all sides, turning him over and over, the current tugging him down.

Kick. That's what he had to do, kick. Pedal his arms. Breathe when he found air. Wax repeated the mantra, the simple motions, connecting them through torched muscles into action, rolling as he found the surface and stared at a sudden sky.

No fiend. No bubble. Only screams.

No, not screams. Cheers.

Quik found him, scooped Wax into his arms and started kicking back to the rafts. Castilan, in a different fishing boat, picked them up halfway, helping Wax over and into the hard wood. The fiend, seemingly dead, continued collapsing in on itself, the fire burning up the filament and everything inside, like a lantern losing its glass.

Wax watched it all, wondering at the whispers in his mind. The Foti skar had gone quiet now, replaced by the Vis's active mutterings. His home skar did its work, slow and steady repairing Wax's broken skin, his charred hands and hair.

"Bliss?" Wax asked when the boat nudged against the raft city. "Eujo? Where are they?"

Quik, first off and turning around to offer a hand, took a deep breath.

"Lost, Wax. Or dead."

CHAPTER 22
WARLORD'S WORD

The hustle came quick. Arrows flew down, striking the fiends where they twitched, ending the bugs. Jochi, a full retinue with him, marched into the arena, took Svarde's bloody arm and raised it high so the crowd could cheer once again.

Through it all, Maena laid in the dirt. She had an armor for this, a defense ready to block away all horrors under the auspice of a job necessarily done. A requirement to be a Rana captain, to understand your mission capturing wealth for your home isle, for keeping the Rana reputation alive against other isles with more people, more land. WIth bad odds, you had to be vicious, uncompromising, a terror.

Three Rana had entered the arena, and with a Foti and a ferrite for help, they'd won, dammit. They'd won.

But you're not happy.

How could she be? The fools on the other side of the gate, those poor prisoners who'd been told they were fighting for freedom had been massacred. Would Jochi have done the same with Maena murdering Bertan?

Now that's a trap. Even I know not to go digging that deep.

Then she needed somewhere else to turn. If you didn't want to get stuck in the shallows, you had to keep up your speed. Raise the sails.

"Stand up," snarled a guard, breaking Maena's concentration as he put an arm beneath hers, hefted Maena to her feet. "You won, now act like it."

Maena would've spat at the man, but her mouth ran dry. So she did as the guard forced, stood there and took the cheers. The crowd stayed, clapping and collecting their winnings, until a distant bell signaled another match. The benches emptied quick, then. Spent lives forgotten.

But not for Jochi.

The warlord collected the five, seemed to catalog their various wounds with his eyes. The man's beard looked freshly oiled, the snow melting in among its straightened hair.

"Congratulations on your victory," Jochi said. "I think you'd like a wash, some cleaning for those cuts , and a moment's peace. You'll get those, but not here." Jochi crossed his arms, and for the first time, Maena glimpsed uncertainty in the solid man. "You've done your time in the Pits, damn it all, and I have an offer for you."

"What could meat like you have to offer?" Svarde rumbled. Kivi snorted her back-up.

"Meat like me can offer plenty," Jochi replied, no laughter this time. "Word's spreading about an enemy on the way to a place we can't afford to lose. Whent's thin. You're fat enough to help."

"Why's Whent struggling?" Rasslebeck asked. "Too many getting drunk here, watching people die for laughs?"

"Farmers and wrecked folk are here, finding their sanity in a flagon or two," Jochi replied. "The real reason's not your concern, Rana. What is, is if you help me here, I'll let you walk free."

Now it was Maena's turn to scoff, "There's only five of us? What difference will we make?"

"But you're not just any five, are you?" Jochi said. "Champions, fiend killers. You'll hold up my flag and others will fight. They'll think they have a damn chance. Maybe, with you, they might."

"And if we say no?" Svarde asked.

"You'll die here one by one. No more fair contests. Just bloody sacrifice. The last thing you'll see is spit and old beer from a crowd too happy to see your insides fall out." Jochi spoke without a grin, without a boast.

"The man's serious," Maena said. "We should accept."

"Aiding our captors seems wrong," Rasslebeck kicked at the dirt. "Then, so does dying for nothing."

"I'm a fan of living, speaking personally," Pennifer interjected.

She's not the only one.

"We'll go, then," Svarde announced after drawing nods from the group. "Save your town." When Jochi nodded, though, Svarde continued. "Your scouts say an attack is coming. What kind?"

"Fiends. What other evil's worth fearing?"

They traveled by wagon again, rolling over the tundra. This time, Maena's hands weren't tied and they could move freely about their canvas covered ride. Anyone trying to make a dash out the back, though, would find archers willing to shoot them down.

Not that running away would get you anything save a slow, icy demise amid the isle's frosted plains.

More wagons joined up as they went, intersecting with the train from passing towns, or catching up with further converts from the Pits. Jochi had been right on that score: however the man phrased it, their legend drew more swords, fists, and bodies.

As for her own body, Maena's healed slow, as did the others. Bandages changed, and the stories of how each of them had fared among the bugs started strong and gave way to further horrors, the desperation, the fear. Rasslebeck claimed he couldn't move so well anymore, that whatever had been in the fiend's stinger sac had sapped his muscles of their burst. Svarde's new scars lit up in angry whites along his hands and arms, the man spending more time in stoic silence.

Nothing, then, of the calm and caring Foti who'd helped Maena clean her own wounds before.

Only Pennifer and Kivi seemed inspired to, well, inspire. The Rana sniper ran her words into songs more often than not, slinging out a gamut of sea shanties and drinking tunes, while Kivi scurried among them, venting her scales to keep them warm. She seemed the healthiest, with stones in good supply on the road.

And what about you? Am I driving you insane yet, thief?

What part of me did you come from?

Part? I'm all you.

Then you would know when to stay quiet.

For once, the voice did. For once, Maena could shut her eyes and let the minutes, the hours pass in peace. Or, at least, as much as possible, with those invisible eyes always on her, watching, waiting, judging.

Tallwren's Hearth waited on Whent's southern coast. Nestled in among rolling hills coated with shaggy sheep, the city teemed with brisk industry. Not only the furs and meats from the animals, but, so Jochi said, technology.

The warlord moved between the wagons on the journey, taking time in each one to, so he said, inspire the prisoners for their coming mission.

"This isn't about saving some farmers," Jochi said, "though that ought to be enough. Tallwren's Hearth is Whent's best, our heart, our mind, our might. Take notice."

Maena had heard of the university, second only to the Najahn's secretive palace on Noctia for true scholarship. Rana and the other isles had trade schools, of course. Places to learn truly useful talents. Only isles with too many people and too few opportunities could bother with something like this, a place to ponder what anyone with half a mind could decide for themselves.

As Jochi continued on, blustering through innovations made and honors dubiously earned, the sheep gave way to ridged housing, earthen dwellings built into the hillsides and buttressed with rock. Those in turn shifted to stonework homes, stacked and mortared with some skill, as their train reached the city proper. Still, few offered a second story, and the streets, so far as Maena could tell, remained hard-packed dirt.

Modern smells, at least, mingled on the breeze. Fires burning more than food. The sea's chill tang. A stinking undercurrent that'd only grow as frozen ground led to fewer places to dispose of what humans left behind.

Problems Rana had solved with decidedly better plumbing, washing away to the deep oceans what couldn't be used as fertilizer.

Whent, apparently, kept it as fire fuel should more appealing sources dwindle too far in the long winter.

That admission at least made Jochi frown. Not much 'honor' in that.

"We'll solve it soon," Jochi said. "You can see it now. To our left." The warlord, standing on the wagon's rear flat, pointed and everyone, Maena included, looked.

The flagship of Tallwren's Hearth hardly earned the name. Ringed with a stone wall barely taller than Maena herself, the University scaled up a hill and, with sloping thatched roofs, made clear its bulk lay inside the earth and not above it. As if mice had burrowed large holes into the ground.

"It's better inside," Svarde grumbled at the unimpressive sight. "Whatever you think about Jochi, the school is worth saving."

"So I'm not surrounded by morons. Not entirely."

"Wish I could say the same."

Jochi just laughed.

The prison train disembarked not at the university, but at the docks. A commercial port, but a fortified one. Piers emptied of most ships, save a couple Whent galleons prepping for an end-of-season run to Noctia. Three stone towers watched over the loading, their tops crowned with hefty ballistae. Those Whent crossbows finding their giant brethren here.

"Always wondered why we never raided this city," Rasslebeck said as their Whent guards lined the wagon riders up in a long line. "Guess I know now."

"Easier prey out on the seas," Maena agreed. To her left, Svarde and Kivi aligned, while Pennifer and Rasslebeck waited to her right. "Whent's always obsessed with big and strong, they tend to miss fast and clever."

"That's okay by me."

Jochi's planned defense seemed simple enough. The

Whent soldiers still in town would man the towers, using the artillery to slow down or destroy the incoming fiends. Any remaining that made it to shore would be cut down by the prisoners.

"Any get past you, we'll handle them," Jochi said, waling the line. "Any of you get a coward's belly, we'll handle you too. This isn't a choice. This is your freedom, what you're living for. Save the city, you'll earn yourselves an exile, free from our whips, our swords. Fail," Jochi grinned his murderous leer, "and you'll be too dead to care."

The prisoners would have no shelter while they waited, though the dunes proved bulwark enough from the outside storms. Scrub brush and the debris from several ruined ships gave wood for fires, with Whent-supplied mutton and carrots, potatoes and crab. A fine feast devoured with hands and daggers as the water sloshed nearby.

Jochi's line buttressed themselves beyond the docks, dragging bags of sand meant to staunch floodwaters into the streets, blocking easy travel and ensuring his small crossbowmen corp would be able to cut down any advancing, or fleeing, fools.

Once the fortifications blocked the pathways, Jochi roared some signal and a metal rain began, tossed from those towers to land among the sand. Maena didn't flinch like Rasslebeck, like so many others. She'd caught the glint in the fading light and understood.

"Weapons," Rasslebeck called, the first in their group to reach the treasure sticking out from the coarse pebble-filled grains. "Seems they're not lying afterall."

"So we do their job," Svarde said, staying next to Maena, finishing his roasted mutton. "Get freedom. A fair trade?"

"It's a lie," Maena countered. "Or they'll twist it some-how. Whent doesn't forget. They won't let us go."

"When I came through here with Catya and Ami, we were treated with kindness."

Maena bit into a crab leg, sucked out the soft meat and spat the shell into the sand. Rasslebeck scrounged up several mottled blades, ones that needed a good cleaning, sharpening before they'd be much use. Not that Jochi would provide such a thing.

"You had Noctia behind you, and without Noctia's trade, without the Najahn helping them, Whent would die," Maena replied. "We have nothing now. We're Jochi's playthings, and he won't let us go."

"Then we'll make him," Svarde said, accepting a battered blade. "When this fight is over, Maena, we'll get back to what matters."

"You still think we can do it, Svarde? Even after all this?"

"There is nothing else, Maena. We destroy the fiends, or this world is doomed."

And yet, as Maena looked over the ragged line scrambling to arm themselves with Whent scraps, it wasn't hard to wonder if it wasn't doomed anyway.

Pick up that sword, coward. Remember who you're fighting for.

You?

Right. Don't forget it.

Maena laughed. Drew eyes from her team and shook them off.

"Come on." Maena stood. "Let's see if Jochi will give us a few whetstones before the monsters arrive. I don't plan on dying here."

CHAPTER 23

FLOATING BLADES

Bliss didn't see the fire before it found her. A sudden flash, a bright spot illuminating on the fiend's domed skin before her eyes, almost out of view as she tried to find a weak spot on the boxy, red flesh before her. She'd made the climb with the staff, clambored up and stared at the mass, feeling its vibration in her heels, and tried to see some obvious clue, some clear vulnerability.

Lacking any, she hit it once. Drove the staff right in hard, the blunt metal edge pushing into the flesh, bending and warping it but not breaking through. A tension too strong for her to pierce.

The bright light signaled something new, though, as did the fiend's sudden vibration, a rushing gale as the dead air inside the fiend made a move. The wind blew Bliss off her climb, sucked her back and down as flames burst through behind her, over her, the fires eating up the fiend's bubble skin like it would dry grass.

She held the staff. Held it tight as she fell because there was nothing else to do.

Why had the fiend exploded, what'd hit it, these were

momentary flickers and nothing more. When Bliss struck the water, hard enough with the film to drive the air from her, the first ash and embers as the fiend's insides caught flame fluttered along with her. The water lit up where they touched, the greasy film proving as flammable as it was sticky, slimy, and altogether awful.

Trying to gasp, to draw in something, Bliss scrambled, splashed, as flames grew around her in a sickening version of what might've happened had she misstepped in Foti's Grand Forge. Not lava, here, but nearly as bad, thick and hot and close, oh so close.

The staff, unable to get through the fiend's skin, found a target it could break. Bliss flailed, sent its metal end swiping through the liquid around her. The mottled gray iron broke the film, revealing the lake's thick green brack beneath, and Bliss rolled for it, those flames licking her as she dove.

Submerged, Bliss's lungs reminded her she'd not yet recovered from the fall. Precious little air remained, her legs and arms using too much of it in panicked motion back towards the raft city. Or was she paddling farther away? Directions seemed impossible, the current pulled by the fiend's gyrations a rapid, unceasing top as the creature undulated in its dying moments. Bliss found herself pulled one way, her toes and fingers sucked, only to be socked in the stomach by a rush back the way she'd gone. Somewhere in the mix, the staff blew away, torn from her grip as her fingers lost their strength, her eyes burning, her body beginning to seize.

Up. That, that way she knew, if only because it bloomed like a glorious yellow rose overhead. The fire's work, and one she kicked towards in her last.

A breach, a clarity as water ran off her cheeks, her eyes,

her mouth. A breath, finally, albeit one coated with smoke. But not more, not much more than air beyond. Around her, the film burned, and as it went, the fire followed, dying everywhere soon after its purchase achieved the inferno's desire. Overhead, the bubble skin peeled back to the north, a blazing line clearing the fiend away like the sun chasing the night's sky. As it went, the fire found those same veins Bliss had climbed, consuming them much as it did everything else, the black ashes fluttering down.

All Bliss did, though, was breathe. Breathe, paddle her feet, and watch the fiend die.

TORNY FOUND HER FIRST. She came on a simple cutter, a two-person canoe meant to ferry goods from one part of the city to another, propelled by oars pulled by her arms alone.

The bandit screamed Bliss's name time and time again, there in the floating, smoldering ruins, until she found Bliss's splashes. Her hoarse cries.

"You damn idiot," Torny said, bracing Bliss against the canoe and helping her inside. "What were you thinking?"

Bliss leaned back against the canoe, the rough wood dry and, for once, free of the lake's slime, the fiend's film. Her skin almost glowed, such an angry red, those lines criss-crossing her every surface.

"I'm asking you a question here," Torny said, the bandit leaning over Bliss, close enough for her sharp eyes, her wild cropped hair to cut out the sky. "Why. Did. You. Go. Alone?"

Sensing this was one of those moments that demanded a response, that Bliss couldn't fake herself free of with a sleepy sneak away, she tried to respond. Went for a twitching signal with her left hand and found her arm dead. Not gone, no, but too tired, too shattered to make anything.

So Bliss went with a confused, pained smile.

Torny cursed and sat back, picked up the oars and started to row. Bliss listened to the birds, to the shouts coming from the city.

Not anger, not panic, not desperation, those. Not anymore.

The skar saved them, so Wax said, but her brother couldn't keep his focus. A shouted joy at Bliss's return, followed by a handover of the Vis skar to Bliss's palms.

"Listen to it," Wax said. "It'll help you."

Quik recommended the same, said he'd spent the nights after Eggrad's stabbing simply letting the skar whisper him to sleep. "Felt like it wanted to tell me about every little injury I had. As it did, the wounds stopped hurting."

Beyond that, as Torny helped get Bliss set up in the outpost's lone inn, a place largely converted to a shelter in light of the fiend's increasing attacks, Wax and Quik didn't bother sticking around.

"Eujo's missing," Torny explained when Bliss finally managed to get the question across. "She disappeared while the fiend attacked. Apparently she was right with Wax, but didn't come with him on the boat to blow up the monster."

Bliss tilted her head and tried to ask more with her eyes.

Torny, with a mug of ale in each hand—Bliss had motioned for one and Torny refused, declaring she needed both. Bliss could have water, and water alone.

"What was I doing?" Torny said in response. "The only damn responsible thing to do: chase after you and your crazy self. I saw you go under and went hunting for a boat.

By the time I found one, figured out how to use the oars . . . " Torny glanced around, confirmed that while the inn had a few displaced people inside, none looked to be listening, she leaned in, "Bliss, I think I spun that ship in circles for like ten minutes trying to figure out how the oars worked."

'You didn't know?' The signs were awkward, but Bliss found her right hand could make them, if she pushed through. 'Never before?'

"Hello? I'm a bandit, not a ferryman. What's the point in me learning how to use an oar?" Torny scowled as Bliss tried a grin. "If you say it's to help you, I'll dump this ale on you right now."

'Am I wrong?'

"Look, that's not the lesson. Me learning how to pilot a fishing boat isn't our takeaway." Torny sighed, the both of them laying on the ramshackle cot they'd managed to claim. Bliss lay beneath the covers, a warm straw blanket, while Torny stayed above with her ales. "No, no, the lesson here is that you take me with you when you go."

'Why?'

"So I can protect you, dummy." Another dramatic sigh, long drinks from both cups. "You're a Vis, Bliss. You've seen nothing. I need to keep you from making dumb mistakes, like going after a giant fiend with nothing more than your staff."

That'd been found too, floating near the city. Scooped up and handed over to Castilan, and now resting, drying beneath Bliss's bed.

'I don't need—'

Torny knocked Bliss's hand with an ale mug. "Quit it. You do. Clearly. Because your own brother about turned you into a crispy fritter back there. So next time you get these kinds of notions, you give me a heads-up and we'll tackle it together. Or, better yet, I'll tell you to sit yourself down and stop being stupid."

Bliss leaned back into the pillow. Scratchy, but dry. As much as anything she could want in that moment. Torny flipped her babbling, went on to the aftermath, how they'd be cleaning up, finding out how to get to the Whirlpool in a couple days. Get the adventure on the road again.

'When Wax gets back, you mean?' Bliss signed, her eyes half-closed.

"Well, yeah. He's not going anywhere," Torny said. "Eujo probably slipped, knocked herself silly and fell in a barrel. She'll turn up." Torny sniffed. "Then again, might be good if she doesn't. Maybe the fiend took her out. Leaves us with one less rival, know what I'm saying?"

Bliss opened her eyes, gave Torny the look she deserved for a comment like that.

"Oh, don't get soft on me," Torny said. "Eujo's beating us right now. We're not her Guardians."

'Still. She was nice.'

"Was she?"

Torny's answer earned a punctuation from the building's other side, a bang as the inn's door, a rickety wooden thing, banged open. Castilan came through at a lurch, Quik in his arms. Bliss sat up as Torny swore, saw Quik's bruised and battered body get passed along to the Najahn acting as the town's only healer. The man eased Quik onto a dried weed pile as Bliss and Torny came over, Torny giving up an ale mug to let Bliss hold her arm.

Quik's eyes fluttered, a puffy cheek. His hands held his gauntlets, the sharp wood fingers wet with red. Red Quik himself wore, with cuts along his arms, chest, legs. Cuts too clean and sharp to come from a fiend's claw.

"That's not good," Torny muttered as Bliss knelt beside her brother.

While the healer barked for ointments, for bandages, Bliss took the Viss skar from her own hand, put it in her brother's. Watched his breath ease quick, the flush around his features cool. Her own pain came back, the fading lines along her skin finding their burn.

She could stand that, though. Could endure.

'Give me that,' Bliss signed to Torny, who watched while chewing her bottom lip. 'The ale.'

Torny handed the mug down, probably expecting Bliss to take a drink. Instead, the Vis set the cold mug against her brother's temple, its chill meeting what otherwise felt like a fever's rapid onset.

Quik's eyes shot open, found Bliss's fast.

"Wax," Quik said, "they took him. East, Bliss. You've got to find them."

'Find who?'

"The Queen's guards," Quik said, the words a rattle. "They're back."

CHAPTER 24

ROCK RUN

Like any kids, Sawi, Wax and the others had played games among the trees. Sneaking up on one another in the brush, swinging by on a vine and giving a tap to a shoulder before dashing off, the fun melted days away. They all had their specialties too: Sawi's being speed. She could move between those trees, those vines with an alacrity none of the others could match. Wax, sometimes, could pull out a clever route that'd get him ahead, let him make the hidden scare, but put Sawi on a path between two points and she'd be there before anyone else.

Not that speed helped her as she climbed inside the large Mottilan house, nestled back against the cliff with its grassy lawn stretching towards a steep drop. The speed didn't help, no, but the quiet did. Placing her feet with the toes down first, so they didn't make the slightest sound coming into contact with the rock floors. The cool, rough-cut stone, hammered out with the blunt instruments Vis was known for, had enough texture to give Sawi stability, so when she leaned in, ears listening out for discovery, she kept her balance. Planted both feet, her arms, her body inside a small room.

An empty mossy bed lay to her right, stitched up on boards. Not the hammocks back in Kitaye. Maybe too windy, too hard to make here. Random satchels, little crafts littered the space, including some hung on the thatched bamboo walls. Stone for the outer shell, easier things for the inside. Too many projects, too few completed.

Just like Mottilan to quit the effort halfway.

The voices grew louder again. Gladdring's among them, protesting the argument Sawi had heard. Counters flew fast, followed by a scraping noise. Something heavy being dragged across the floor. Sawi went to the room's sole exit, snuck an eye around the doorway. A central hall ran right and left, thin and stuffed with satchels, loose crates flush with fruits, vegetables, forage. to the right, the house's front door lay almost within Sawi's reach. Closed, the wood an irregular fit to the square stone frame. Across the way waited a glow, the only one in the building, where the noises came from.

What was she doing?

The thought stopped Sawi cold, even as a different sound popped from the next room. A thud, hard and fast, followed by a spat curse from Gladdring's mouth. What was she doing here in this Mottilan mansion? Risking what would surely be a beating, possibly worse if some Mottilan law forbade her sneaking. Vis custom didn't take all too kindly to criminals: easier to toss them off a cliff or feed them to some hanoko than deal with jailing them away. And nobody from Kitaye would get favorable treatment here.

Another punch. Another curse from Gladdring. This one wetter.

She wasn't a fighter. Not one to pick up a sword and go charging in, like Wax with that Foti blade. He didn't know what to do with that thing, but Sawi saw the confidence it gave him. The possibility of defense. Here, they had what, her hands? Her rope?

Sawi cast 'round, found nothing among the junk near her feet that'd serve. Best, then, to keep her hands free, ready to respond to anything that rose up.

Rose up like her, now. Courage, Sawi. That's why she was here. Because she'd ditched out the last time Wax and Pan needed her help, and look what'd happened. Not again, not again. Not now.

She quick-stepped across the hall. Nobody there, not a soul watching. So sure of themselves and their security, or that nobody would dare interrupt.

Sawi hit the next room, plastered herself to the near wall. Crouched and bled a look around the corner, following the glow. The nicest room she'd seen thus far awaited her, for once arranged like someone with a soul lived there. Wood furniture, nicer than anything Sawi had yet seen in Mottilan, nicer too than most of what she'd seen in Kitaye, splayed out around the home's largest room. Several chairs, a teak table, and a fireplace built into a stone alcove. Stuffed cushions—likely Kance-made—splashed around the space, providing platforms for the crowd within to park themselves.

At least six people, all with their eyes locked on Glad-dring. A seventh, a large man with a weathered look to him, loomed over the Tenet. The man had a hook in his hand, the curved metal meant for a fish. The lit fire bounced off it like a star among a dim sky. Beneath it, the man's knuckles bore a bloody hue, one matched by stains across Gladdring's face, his snarled robes. The Tenet looked to have seen better days, his body bunched up in pain, his clothes torn. Red beads dripped from cuts along his arms, and welts rose around the man's eyes. Ones that could've seen Sawi had they looked across the room, but instead held their hurting, squinting gaze on the man.

"—in your death, and nothing else, Korrus," Gladdring was saying as Sawi tuned in. "My friends back on Noctia would like nothing more than to hear I'm dead, but because Noctia cannot be seen to be weak, they will send Najahn here to destroy you and your city."

"So you say," Korrus said. "So you've been saying, Gladdring. Knots are all around us. Everything we do binds us to you and your schemes. You benefit, we lose." Korrus flung a hand back at the crowd, the rope whipping through the air. Several ducked or rocked back on their chairs to dodge the swing. "We were supposed to get the Renewal, and we wound up with nothing. We were supposed to get Noctia's trade, but it went to Kitaye instead. Even Kance sends ships to that cursed city now."

"Not my doing, Korrus."

"Well, that's a shame, because it'd make this even easier."

Korrus wheeled his hand back again. Sawi coughed.

She didn't have to. The breath wasn't biting at her throat, nor was the soot from the fireplace. No, Sawi did it because she didn't know what else to do and faltered halfway between a coward's silence and a martyr's scream.

The cough caught the wrong attention.

Faces, bodies turned as one to regard her, still in a crouch halfway around the door. Mouths opened, heads tilted as their minds tried to find a rationale, a reason for someone they didn't know to be there. Until one provided an answer.

"It's the Kitaye girl," said a swarthy woman near Gladdring's chair. "She came in with him today!"

"So you're not alone," Korrus announced as Sawi stood, kept her legs tensed. "Gladdring, if you ever wanted better evidence for your betrayal, a Kitaye woman is the perfect choice." He nodded towards her. "Take her. Another Noctia pet to ransom."

Sawi spun, kicked off the stone wall as chairs creaked and boots hit the floor. She burst through the bedroom, a spare hand catching the door on the way through and swinging it shut. The window became a narrow path through the trees, one Sawi dove through, dodging the walls and hitting the grass with a forward roll as she might a giant frond. Keep the momentum, keep moving, because to slow, to fall was to die.

A law of the jungle, a law of Vis.

The cool grass gave Sawi traction and she broke forward straight across the yard, right to the cliff. Behind her, shouts grew pointed as the pursuit saw her exit, her path.

What they didn't expect, going by their exclamations, was Sawi's dive off the cliffside.

Starlight coated her fall, air rushing around her as Sawi, hands moving before she hit the cliff's edge, unwound her rope. When Sawi hit space, the rope trailed beneath her, waiting for a snap. One Sawi gave as she dropped, snarling the rope towards a narrow tree sprawling out from a lower ledge, one seemingly trying to reach the horizon rather than the sky. A path plotted on her way in and now taken, the rope making its catch and looping Sawi hard to the right. A swing that'd end with her smacking back into the cliffside if not for her second yank, a slight upward tug on the rope that released the sticking hooks on its end.

Now she truly flew, whipping both down right, a

speeding dart heading towards Mottilan proper, crowded buildings and few trees to make for a rescue. Nevertheless, Sawi didn't panic, couldn't freeze up. To do that was to die, and not in proper fashion. Instead, Sawi snapped her rope again, this time flinging it against the wall to her right as she tumbled. The rope bit into the rock, scraped it, jerking hard enough against her that Sawi felt her shoulder pop, its pain blending with the burn on her skin from the rope's hard brush. The pain found a partner when the rope's pull, slowing her, brought Sawi into a scraping run along the cliff wall. Her skin turned to fire, Sawi's right arm went numb, but she struck the next roof slow enough to avoid death.

Only a bounce along the thatching, only a roll across sticks and leaves, only another fall to a narrow ledge past it. Sawi's rope left her battered hands as she struck, lying there in dusty dirt, a harvested garden. With her face pressed against the hard soil, Sawi sought to breathe, to see if there was a part of herself not yet bruised.

Her feet. Her legs. Scraped, yes, but not destroyed. Her left arm, too, seemed viable enough to push Sawi to a stand. The move brought with it a dizzy wave, Sawi's head suffering its own smack in the wild descent. Still, she sighted her rope, its end hanging over the roof. Her landing spot was little more than a shack, matching the smallest Kitaye treehouses in size and not at all for style. A sole window. No outlet for a fire. And dark inside.

If the owner was gone, then that made at least a small mercy.

Sawi tugged down her rope. Tried to wrap it with her right hand around her waist only for her shoulder to erupt in splintering, breath-stealing pain. Went with a crude left-guided wrap instead. Took a deep breath at the end, tried to find a note of hope in her survival. Gladdring, taken. Likely a hostage or worse.

What would she do now?

Sawi's question took on a more immediate turn quick, as voices carried over the cliffside, ones coming closer. The pursuit hadn't quit, and they were near. Sawi flung a look behind her, to the ledge. Another steep drop with few options for a swing. This wasn't Kitaye. Mottilan wasn't built for her skills. But she had two feet. She could run.

And Sawi, even wounded, even exhausted and scared, had speed.

CHAPTER 25

CAUGHT

The trail wasn't hard to find. A walk back to where Wax had left Eujo when casting off the oil boat and there, breaking back into the marshes south of the city: bent reeds and lines in the mud. Bootprints leading from the abduction into the murk. A question presented itself then, with the light fading fast.

"Going after her now's going to be dangerous," Quik said, already slipping the gauntlets onto his hands.

Wax noticed, nodded at the arms. "But you've made your choice."

"I just know what you're going to do."

Wax flicked a grateful grin. "You think I can't walk away from a fight?"

"Not if you think you're responsible."

Ah, Quik. Like his sister, good and ready to cut to the heart of things when he wanted to. Wax suspected, no, knew his siblings understood Wax better than he did himself. Good thing, then, they were his guardians and not his enemies.

"Then what are we waiting for?"

Quik pointed, those deadly wood gloves on and secure, at the marsh. "We go slow, quiet. A hunt, Wax. These guards aren't stupid, wouldn't be responsible for the Queen if they were. Which means they left those prints on purpose, or didn't have time to clear 'em."

Whether the guards were moving fast or setting an ambush, Quik and Wax took a measured pace, slipping into the reeds and staying low. Wax had his Foti blade ready, still hurting some from the fire around the fiend, but stable enough thanks to the Vis skar. That and the lightning urge to keep moving, keep striking after Eujo. Because Quik had it right: Wax had left her there alone, and while Eujo seemed nothing if not capable, he shouldn't have been that careless.

If that'd even been his decision to make in the first place.

Damn, this was turning out just like Pan. His friend had made the call to catch the skar after Wax threw it, to run away down the Great Sana with it and risk the injury in the chase. Eujo had made her own choice not to go with Wax, to—

"There," Quik whispered, tapping Wax's shoulder. "You can see the armor."

Those Kance plates, so glass-like and beautiful as they moved, had a nasty habit of catching the light, sparkling it like a diamond. Wax couldn't call himself an expert in warfare, but as a hunter, anything giving yourself away like that had no purpose. Well, no purpose save one: warning everything else to stay away.

"Circle them?" Wax whispered.

"We need to make sure they're all around first."

Quik's suggestion came to prescience moments later, as the pair slogged through waist deep water—odd things brushed up again and again on Wax's legs, his waist, and he refused to think about what they were— and neared enough to see Blinth and Silvrin, the guard commander, pulling a struggling Eujo between them. The Queen, blossoming up a wild grin on Wax's face, undercut their every stride. She slipped in the mud, grappled with the guarding pair at every opportunity. The two Kance soldiers snapped demands at her to cooperate, to act her station, only to earn curses from Eujo in return. The Queen herself was coated in mud, plants and dirt in her clothes, her hair, and everything else.

In short, she looked like a Vis hunter after a week in the jungle.

"She's got spirit," Wax whispered. "Gotta admit that."

Quik didn't reply. When Wax looked to his right, expecting to see his brother there, he saw nothing instead. Just the marsh water, always moving with creatures above and below guiding the flow.

"Quik?"

Wax did a full circle. Still no sign. He drew the Foti blade. Looked back towards where Eujo and her guards had been struggling. Saw nothing. Vanished? No. Not even a Kance Windmaster could disappear into thin air. Which meant something worse.

Sinking to his chest into the water, Wax sniffed, listened. Heard only the marsh's drips and drabs, a few distant frogs croaking out a futile search for bugs in the cold air. The water itself bore a chill too, though nothing compared to the icy Foti sea. Wax ignored it, stepped slow onto the low rise where Eujo had been a moment before. Pushed through several reeds. On the other side lay Eujo, back down in the mud and looking unconscious, eyes closed and unmoving. A mark along her face, near her temple.

The monsters.

"I would say you have a choice," Blinth spoke, Wax whirling back to find the third guard rising up from the marsh water behind him. Had the man been submerged in there all along? Or was he simply a phantom? "But you do not. Your outcome is the same, as is your Guardian's."

"What'd you do with Quik?"

In the day's draining pale, Wax's sapphire sword more than matched the muck-covered Kance armor, though Blinth wore it well and tall. Gauntleted hands rested near dual rapiers at the man's waist, each slotted into a slim sheathe and ready for a quick draw. The Windmaster had shown Wax how quick a Kance could go from nothing to deadly threat, timing Wax couldn't beat even if he ran straight at Blinth now, point forward.

"He'll live," Blinth replied. "A warning to your other friends not to follow us, or you." The man kept any expression from his face. No gloating, no irritation. This was a duty performed. Wax had seen the same in the Najahn back home. "Drop the blade, Vis, or I will take it from you."

"Know what? I've lost this blade enough times, thanks."

Blinth gave a slight nod. "Brave, as a Renewal should be. Stupid, as every Vis must be."

A younger, dumber Wax might've jumped at the insult. Might've taken his Foti blade in a big, winner-take-all swing at Blinth's face. Instead, Wax went for the mud. He kicked a foot, flung the wet earth up at the Kance, followed with a winner-take-all swing. A younger Wax might've, too, thought he had a chance to win an out-and-out duel.

The wiser, older Renewal making his gambit knew he had no other choice.

Blinth backed up as the sludge hit, a buying-time move that would've played better on level ground. The sloping marsh did him no favors, causing Blinth to slip, slide, waver. Wax's Foti blade cut close, slicing into the man's Kance armor, drawing sparks and gashing through, splitting Blinth's breastplate. The guard swore as Wax, double-gripping the Foti blade, flipped his wrist and sent it back, continuing to walk forward.

Until he flew to his left, smashed by something Wax didn't see. He tumbled, the Foti blade flying from his hands as reeds caught his fall. Wax's right shoulder ached, dirt crushed against his left cheek, and before Wax could reel his feet under him, a thin sword point pressed into his neck.

"Just kill him and be done with it," Blinth snarled. Wax wanted to turn and look, see who held him, but every time he twitched his neck, that sword point pressed in harder. "He's ruined my mail."

"You ruined it, letting him hit you," Silvrin replied. "A Kance royal guard, struck by a Vis? You should be stripped of your rank this very second."

If Blinth had a ready reply, he didn't say it.

"What, you won't kill a Renewal?" Wax said, his voice mushed against the earth. "Too mean for you?"

"Noctia won't allow it," Silvrin answered, simple enough. "Die by a fiend, die by disaster, the world mourns. Die by our hand, and it's our necks that pay the price." Wax felt the sword lift, started to move only to get a hand on his side, pushing him over and flat into the mud. "Move again without my permission and you'll spend the night unconscious. It's not your death we want. Nor hers."

"Then what?"

The answer came with a search. Blinth replaced Silvrin as Wax's prime captor, keeping the Vis pushed into the ground. The man's hands, freed from his gauntlets, performed a fast pick-pocketing, delving into Wax's ruined clothes and coming away with the necklace, the Foti skar attached to it.

"Where's the other one?" Blinth asked, his breath hot on Wax's ear.

"Don't have it, you moron."

The cuff came quick, splattered Wax's other side into the mud. Cold, yet somehow soothing on the aftermath of his burning assault on the bubble fiend.

"Where?" Blinth asked again.

"My other Guardian has it," Wax replied. "Don't you know what the skars do?"

Blinth cursed, put his hand on the back of Wax's head and pressed him deeper into the mud. "He says he doesn't have it. Says it's with the other guardian."

"The one Akido has?"

"Answer her," Blinth hissed at Wax.

"He's got nothing you want," Wax replied. He kept his ears open for a chance to lie, to misdirect, but nothing offered itself. If the guards wanted the Vis skar bad enough to trek back to Bliss and Torny, well, that would be a great decision for Wax's survival. "Bliss needed it to heal."

Blinth repeated the words.

"Then get off him. There's no going back to that outpost. We have the three from Eujo, his fourth gets us our reward. It's nearly dark enough to get them cast off. Akido will be back soon. Then we leave."

"Where are you going?" Wax asked as Blinth jerked him to his feet. "Off to a party?"

"Of sorts," Blinth replied, flashing teeth somehow still a perfect white. "Too bad you won't be joining."

Blinth pulled Wax along the marsh while the woman

picked up the unconscious Eujo. Together, the trio marched through the reeds to the west, away from the main river and parallel to the raft city. Dusk deepened into dark, starlight and Sichi serving as a fortuitous guide to the march. Wax peppered the pair with questions, but both Blinth and Silvrin went quiet as the walk began, as if falling into some long-designed plan.

"All I want to know," Wax said finally, having run through his insult retinue, "is how you made it off the roller? With that fiend and its vines?"

"Our armor is light enough to let us float," Blinth answered. "The ship broke and we went to the surface. A pity you won't have the same luxury."

"I'm a good swimmer."

Blinth just laughed. The reason why came about soon enough, when they reached a sturdy boat bobbing in the water. The purple and black trim spoke of Najahn allegiance, though no Noctia soldiers waited. A small canvas cabin covered the middle, with spots for oars along the front and back. Silvrin dumped Eujo in the center. Blinth put Wax in with her. Stuck Wax's Foti blade nearby.

A bold move, a reckless one to leave the weapon so close to its wielder.

The Kance guards pulled out thick rope, the kind used to tie a boat to its moorings, and lashed Wax's hands together with Eujo's, their backs to one another. Blinth guided the pair to the boat's bow, being gentle enough with Eujo's head.

"This is how you treat your Queen, is it?" Wax asked. "Hardly honorable."

"Two Queens," Blinth answered, taking his spot at the oars behind Wax. "We choose which one we serve."

The man fell silent again as he focused on the oars,

putting them into the waters and lurching the boat forward. Both Kance guards worked in unison, propelling the boat through shallow pools until it connected with another river, this one's current slow enough for them to push against northward. Wax couldn't guess how much time had passed, except to know his stomach rumbled, his throat itched for thirst, and they'd all taken turns to void themselves over the boat's side. Eujo, returned to consciousness, had nothing save glowers for the guards.

At some point, the boat brushed up against a muddy bank and the third Kance, Akido, boarded. Claimed he hadn't secured the skar, but the other Guardian would serve well enough as a warning, as a diversion. The oars picked up again and the marsh fell away, the lake growing wider and wider as they pushed north. Behind every oar strike, now, grew a rushing noise, steady and endless.

"I know where they're taking us," Eujo said, soft.

"Think I've figured it out too," Wax replied, glanced at Blinth. "No murders, right? Only disasters?"

"The Renewal is a dangerous undertaking." Blinth grinned. "So many die along the way."

CHAPTER 26

THE BEACH BAIT

Nothing came the first night. Quiet waves and little else, save the city behind them prepping defenses and falling asleep. The prisoners, left to fend for themselves, curled up and slept in the sand or sat with eyes on the horizon, watching and not caring whether anything showed up.

These prisoners are useless. Kill a few and maybe Jochi will reward you.

Maena ignored the voice. She'd been working on it in the lonely hours, Svarde snoring nearby. The others around the smoldering fire. The cold wind, occasionally spiced with snowflakes, kept Maena shivering. Yet, those bodily discomforts became a weapon wielded against the voice, blunting it, driving it and its growing madness away.

She could take a loan out on her sleep. A practice she'd honed for a long time on Rana ships, slicing across the water with little help waiting, no second chances if a wayward wave or reef took your vessel and tore it apart. Sleep could come with calm seas, with a dock and a dry bed.

For Maena, that comfort came during the day, with a cloth pulled over her eyes to shield the gray sky. Svarde stood watch. Other prisoners played games, found ways to hone their weapons. Jochi tossed along provisions, shovels to dig latrines.

Said the fiends must be taking their time.

They did, at least till the second night. Hunched over their fire again, this time with fish and more, always more, potatoes, the group made it halfway through before a horn blew from the tower nearest them. Blasts followed from the others, rebounding around the foothills in a sonic cascade.

"You can see it," Svarde nodded past the fire, towards the ocean.

White crests. Shadows. Shapes moving against the horizon, winter clouds obscuring what little light there would be.

A loud twang sounded from the near tower and a burning dart soared into the dark. A gold radiance getting brighter as it went, nearly reaching the white crests before it exploded in a spark shower wide enough to cover the whole beach.

And show that the enemy, the things crashing towards them, weren't fiends at all.

The prisoners shouted, stood, Maena among them. The shadows racing in weren't monsters, but sloops, cutters, frigates belonging to a Rana fleet. In that flash, too, it became clear those ships weren't perfect. Ripped sails, gouged hulls, some chugging along deep in the water with ropes linking them to larger vessels.

"If there's been an attack here, it's on them," Maena said. "This is a trap."

"And not for us." Svarde picked up broad metal blade. "Get ready."

"We're not fighting our own kind," Rasslebeck said. "No way—"

Rasslebeck's words cut off as another prisoner, arms high and mouth hollering, ran back towards Jochi's line, calling the warlord a coward, demanding he help the sailors. Those words ended with a single crossbow bolt, the quarrel sticking out from the man's chest and driving him to the ground.

"The offer," Jochi's voice bellow, beating down the waves, the clamor with its sheer force, "stands. Destroy the enemy, win your freedom. Do not, and die."

The ballistas opened up as he finished, the first long bolts lancing out towards the coming ships. Two missed, two hit home, blowing into a cutter pair and sending wood, bodies into the sea. Both craft lurched, listed. Another fifteen remained, still barreling in.

"They can't mean to fight," Rasslebeck said, his hands hanging limp. "There's no victory for them."

"Don't think they mean to," Pennifer replied. "I think they're running from something worse."

Maena nodded, the sick twisting in her stomach growing as the ships neared, the wounded on those decks coming clear even in the dim light. The ballistae fired again, three hits now, the fourth sailing over its target into the water. The main frigate took the damage, the giant bolts hanging off it like some spiny growth.

The artillery wouldn't get another shot: the Rana closed too quick, skilled sailing despite the damage, their wounded crew.

Metal scraped around them, prisoners seeing their choice and making it.

"Do we fight, Maena?" Svarde asked.

"You're asking me?"

Svarde didn't answer, but gave her a level stare that served as well. These were her people, she was their commander.

An easy sacrifice for your life. Svarde should kill them just like he did me.

Svarde asked her for honor's reasons, but that would only go so far. The man had a goal, and he would do what he could to achieve it. Dying on this beach served nothing.

"Follow me," Maena said. "We'll make it out, souls intact."

"Big promise," Pennifer muttered, but the three, and Kivi, trailed Maena as she made her way forward off the line, then left near a ballista tower's base. The stout door in had been bolted, sealed, but that wasn't her goal.

Instead, Maena moved them around to the tower's front, putting them closer to the waves, the ships now seconds from landing, but blocked from Jochi's view.

"Keep your arms up," Maena said, "but make no attack. Only defend, and maybe we'll make it through."

"And watch our friends die," Rasslebeck cursed.

"You knew that would happen the second you signed up for my crew. This is the price you pay for a chance at something better."

"Wasn't on any contract I saw."

Maena snaked up her rusted saber, stuck its point into Rasslebeck's gut. The older man just snarled at her, didn't move, the stone tower at his back.

"Then do what you want, Rasslebeck. Throw your life away." Maena withdrew the saber. The first Rana ships ran themselves aground, sliding up the sand. "Don't make me do it for you."

The words didn't mollify the raider—Maena figured nothing save a stiff drink and a few dead rockbiters would do that—but Rasslebeck didn't try to cut her head off either.

Nor did he join the charge as the desperate prisoners ran down the beach towards the landing Rana ships.

For their part, the Rana kept what composure they could. Maena recognized the vessels, the people onboard. Raiders, yes, but sanctioned ones, professionals prowling the seas for cargo they could find from anyone Rana had a disagreement with.

Which meant, mainly, Whent and Kance.

The Najahn had a crap navy, one occupied ferrying soldiers and supplies from their outposts. Without much presence on the seas, Rana's tiny isle could take what it needed within reason.

But theft had a way of haunting the thief, and those Rana paid that debt now at the rusted, scared hands of a trapped people.

As sailors jumped off the landing ships, they found themselves pressed by the motley. Snow spinkled as red spattered, weapons finding their mark. Rana crossbowmen fired into the charging crowd, drawing their own blood. Well-armed raiders carved up prisoners that didn't strike with surprise, batting aside inferior arms and using their sabers to vicious effect.

Maena's group held firm. Whether because they weren't a part of the chaos or through random luck, the fighting broke up around them as the Rana professionals found their footing, pushed back the prisoners. The forced rabble broke here and there, poor souls choosing to dash up the beach in hopes of . . . what, Maena wasn't sure. The only thing they found were Whent crossbows ready to fire, black bolts burying deep in rags and ruin.

Maena didn't even need to see the shots. The clicks, the screams, were enough.

"Such a waste," Svarde said, standing next to her. "All these lives lost when we should be fighting the fiends, pushing into the Dark Below."

"Or just living," Maena replied. "We don't know what put these people into the Pits, but there's a better way."

"What would they do on Rana?"

Svarde's tone said he knew damn well what they'd do on Rana. Criminals would get exiled if the offense wasn't too terrible, dropped on Foti or Noctia. Much worse and the executions came quick, tossed off a boat with a weight wrapped around the ankles.

Steal some food and you'd find yourself doing forced labor on the rice paddies, cleaning fish for nothing more than a meal. Finish your sentence, though, and Rana would see you cleared.

"Foti's no better," Maena countered.

We're all monsters.

"Foti's a miserable, blasted isle," Svarde replied. "Thing is, so's every one, save Vis. There, at least, the people seem happy."

"Because they barely know we exist."

The odds continued to turn worse for the prisoners. Rana flowed onto the beach, and Maena blinked more than once to confirm what she saw: wounded sailors getting offloaded, dragged down boarding ramps in a hurry and up onto the beach while other Rana cleared the way with sweeping sabers, twanging crossbows.

More, Rana voices started to overpower the prisoner cries. The seafarers weren't making their own battle songs, no, but were instead shouting, begging the prisoners to back away, calling for the Whent archers in the tower—ones who, Maena noted, had yet to fire any close range shots—to hold their quarrels.

Red water ran along the sand, lit now more by lanterns on the boats, torches on the sand, than the pink sneaking through the night clouds.

"This isn't an assault, then," Svarde muttered.

"It's a slaughter, is what it is," Rasslebeck added.

"Why'd they choose to land here?" Pennifer asked. "It's the dumbest thing. There had to be another choice."

You know why, don't you?

"They won't be far behind," Maena spoke soft, steadying her grip.

Svarde nodded, sighed. Maena would've done the same, but she had no emotion left. Just a cold stare as the last prisoners broke, ran, died. The Rana disembarked, some watching Maena and her group, not bothering to attack.

"Hold!" Jochi's voice again, bellowing. Closer this time. "No Rana is allowed on this isle without permission, and I have granted you none."

Maena slipped back, looked behind the tower to see the warlord, flanked by four rock-armored soldiers, standing before the fortifications. Jochi held a wrought, gilded horn to his mouth, one magnifying his voice.

"You'll return to your boats, or I'll see you cut down where you stand, wounded and all."

The Rana, though, didn't stop. Kept unloading, faster now with the fighting done. Bodies slung off the ships, hit the dirt where other sailors scooted them up, at least till one of the Whent in their tower fired a bolt into the dirt.

"Cross that mark, and you'll meet the same end too many of our criminals did. The worthless bunch." Jochi laughed. "Did you see your own friends as you cut them down? The Pits were full of Rana. We gathered them all and brought them to you. I hope you enjoyed the reunion."

"The bastard," Rasslebeck muttered.

"He's baiting them," Maena said. "They're tired, desperate. Jochi wants that to become anger, so they can die on this beach."

"Why?" Pennifer asked. "What's the damn point?"

"Because he doesn't want to feed them when this becomes a siege," Svarde replied.

"Fiend's don't siege."

"They might now."

Maena gulped down Svarde's words, turned her eyes back to the sea. The Foti had it right. No ordinary fiend, even a group, would be able to defeat a Rana fleet like this. Wild animals could cause damage, cause chaos, but they could be outsmarted, destroyed by that unique human trait.

No Rana stepped forward to counter Jochi's demand. They didn't have to. The sea did it for them.

Back out into the black, a quiet line grew against the horizon. Slow and building, heading steady towards the shore. Shouts started on the Rana ships, the Whent towers, passed back through the crowd into the city.

A single ballista shot, the long lance streaking beyond the light to strike the wave with a crackling, clashing ring. An unnatural noise, one Maena and Svarde knew too well.

Metal.

The wave, nearly as tall as the towers now, parted. Broke and splashed away to reveal a crusted-over sloping bow, not a sail in sight. Upon its soaked shell were carved lines, designs even at this distance coming clear to Maena in their twisting undulations, all guiding the water to twin fins off either side, ones moving up and down at frantic speed, driving the vessel, twice as large as the Rana frigate, towards the shore.

Kivi snorted. Svarde nodded.

"Now, the real battle begins."

CHAPTER 27

CAUSE LOST, CAUSE FOUND

By the time Bliss and Torny made it to the outpost's edge, ready to step off into the mud, nightfall and looming exhaustion both waylaid their hopes. Torny acted on it first, grabbed Bliss's arm and held her back as she tried to go on into the marsh.

'Then we take a torch and follow,' Bliss said, when Torny put a voice to her objections.

"You want to take a tiny flame out there and go looking around?" Torny asked. "You, who's shaking where you stand? Who would've been dead asleep by now? What happens when that charge runs off and we're deep in that muck?"

'It won't. I won't.'

Bliss believed it, too. Quik's awful appearance and Wax's vanishing blended into a strong cocktail, and she'd run to the ends of this isle and the next before dropping down for a nap.

"Then how about we try something different?" Torny asked, backing up further, as if to invite Bliss to sanity. "We know it's those Kance guards who took'em—spare a prayer for the roller's captain and crew, by the way."

Bliss almost winced. She'd not thought of those four, the ones who'd carried them up the river. No sign since the fiend attacked. Had she grown so callous as to simply move on?

Or had it become a necessity in a more dangerous world?

"That's what I thought," Torny continued, nodding at Bliss's expression. "We're running so fast we're losing our thread."

'Our thread? What's that got to do with the roller crew?'

"What's the whole reason we were sailing up this way?"

'The skar?'

Torny nodded. "Right. If those guards hated the Queen, which, deserved, but that's neither here nor there." Bliss scowled, Torny shrugged. "Anyway, point being, they could've knifed her any moment between Foti and now. They had nights with her in that roller where they could've done her in and nobody would've known."

Bliss glanced back to the marsh. Torny had a habit of getting long winded, and every minute spent listening to her spout theories was one they could've burned sponging along the mire with an eye for Wax.

"Stay with me, Bliss, because I'm untangling this as we're talking and I think I'm on to something."

Bliss rolled her eyes, but sent them back to Torny. 'What, then?'

"I'm saying they want the skars, same as us. Which means, if they've got Eujo, there's only one place they'll be heading. Maybe they're taking Wax along for the ride."

'You're saying they're going to the Whirlpool?'

"Think it's a better guess than stumbling blind through

all that."

A better guess, a better plan. Bliss flicked her fingers as she pushed past Torny, heading the opposite way. 'Could've said all that at the start.'

"Didja miss when I mentioned I was working it out?" Torny replied.

She ran after Bliss all the same.

At night, the damaged outpost hustled as those with limbs and life left struggled to get their homes rebuilt, or at least in a state of survival. The couple working hearths burned, cooking soups, the smell a nice reminder to Bliss as she ran that, once again, she'd be giving up a cozy night for one in the wilds.

The thought almost brought her to a stop. If the Kance traitors were taking the Queen and her brother to the Whirlpool, and if Bliss and Torny meant to follow and catch them, they needed one thing: a guide.

"Not a chance," Castilan said, half-asleep in a chair back in the central warehouse, now serving, as every standing building seemed to, as an infirmary and inn. "With Reathe getting ready to go south with the worst of the wounded, I'm the sole Najahn left. Can't be taking off in the night, even for your Renewal."

"Isn't that your job?" Torny asked, the two of them standing before Castilan with their best glares on. "Isn't the whole point of the Najahn to help the Renewals, or are you a coward?"

"We work for the Circle, not your Renewals," Castilan snapped, then softened. "Not that I'm ungrateful for what you've done. Destroying that fiend saved our outpost. I'm not going to risk it now by leaving."

"Oh, what's going to happen, all your friends going to loot the place?"

Castilan sniffed, "Maybe."

He held up a lone finger before Torny could whip up another sarcastic reply. "I think what you're doing is stupid, to try and go onto the lake at night. But there's boats aplenty missing owners now, and the sky's are clear, so I'd say you have half a chance." Castilan sat up. Leaned forward, like some ancient storyteller about to divulge a tale. "You want to find the Whirlpool, grab your ores and go north. You'll hit it."

"That's it?" Torny asked.

"That's it."

"No secret password? Hidden cave? A switch to find and flip before fiends tear us limb from limb?"

Castilan flicked his eyes towards Bliss, who shrugged.

Getting a clear direction only boosted Bliss's energy. Torny refilled their waterskins, snuck some soup bowls out to the dock for the pair to wolf down before jumping in a halfway decent gray boat. Their chosen vessel had a couple seats spanning its width, a length about triple Bliss's own height, and enough room to store a couple more when the rescue, inevitably, came back successful.

'Thanks for coming with me,' Bliss signed as they ditched the bowls, stepped into the boat under Sichi's pink light. 'I know it's been a long day.'

"Yeah, I do know. I lived it." Torny sat back with the oars. "Learned how to use these things only a few hours ago, so don't expect much, captain."

'Captain?'

"You see anyone else on this boat?" Torny made a show of looking left and right. "I sure don't, and I am equally sure I'm not captain material."

Bliss smiled. Torny had a way of making the awful bearable, sometimes.

"Just remember, as captain, anything goes wrong it's your fault. I'm blameless on this enterprise."

'Agreed. Now shove off and let's go rescue my brother.'

HER ENERGY FLAGGED before the outpost and its cozy orange glow disappeared. Bliss's muscles began aching almost from the get-go, every stretch and strain tugging at skin that just wanted to heal. Her head pulsed, telling Bliss to find herself a bed before she passed out.

Even Torny fell quiet quick, the bandit focusing on moving the oars so as not to knock the boat into a spin. Bliss figured out the groove quick enough, not so different from anything else with her arms and legs. Keep them in sync to get where you needed to go.

The Whirlpool, too, didn't hide its presence. If the outpost's light dimmed, a great noise to the north grew. Some monstrous beast roaring, like a hanoko in its prime. The sound gave them a direction. The lake didn't fight them either, a night for once without whipping winds, as if the fiend's death prompted nature to hold a solemn vigil.

"You know," Torny said, her tone not matching the words, a near-shout to get over the Whirlpool's roar, "this whole thing might be pretty neat, if it weren't for the death and all."

Bliss nodded. With her hands occupied by the oars, she had no other way to respond, and with their goal so close, no reason to slow down.

"Makes you think, maybe, after all this Renewal junk is over, might be nice to take a tour of the Isles. See the sights without the skars. You could show me why Vis doesn't deserve the slander."

Bliss would've snapped something at that comment,

would've questioned what slander her home deserved, but Sichi's glow had picked something out ahead and to port, a silhouette where the water started to speed up and head in a great circle.

Letting one oar go, Bliss pointed, and Torny caught it quick enough.

"Of course they're going in," Torny said. "If that's them, and who else would be as stupid as us to be out here, then we've gotta haul, Bliss."

They tried. The oars slapped the water hard, churning against the Whirlpool's edge and its pull. The smacks loud enough that the boat had to notice them, had to see what they were doing. But the pair couldn't get closer. Couldn't outfight the Whirlpool, and Bliss's arms were about dead.

"Hey," Torny said between smacks, "I don't think we've got this one." Bliss started her oars around again, only to feel Torny's hit the other way, slow the boat's spin. "We've gotta save some strength to get out, Bliss, or that thing will take us down. They must have some anchor to stay that solid."

Their target hadn't moved, though there'd been motion aplenty. Too far away, too dim to make out exactly what, and the Whirpool's din, now forcing Torny to holler just to reach Bliss a couple arm lengths away, made any listening impossible.

But Bliss could see well enough when two shapes, two struggling shapes, moved to the boat's bow.

"Oh, what's this now? Is that your brother?" Torny asked.

Bliss couldn't tell, but her heart, its sudden tightness, told her it was. Two shapes, armor glinting in the pink light, rose and went towards the pair, but the bound couple jerked away, falling over the side into the water.

Torny cursed. Bliss wanted to scream. Not in horror, but in anger, frustration. They'd been right, they'd known where to go, and still, still, hadn't made it in time.

That'd been Wax. And now he was lost somewhere up there, buried in dark water.

"Maybe he'll get carried this way?" Torny shouted, but nothing more than pity lay in her words.

Bliss didn't bother giving the bandit a listen, a look. She locked her eyes on the boat, one with oars springing from its longer body. The anchor pulled up hard, those oars hitting the water as the weight cleared, rocketing the boat towards them.

Up till now, Bliss and Torny had kept their own oars moving, backing their boat up enough to the Whirlpool's very edge, where the whisking current didn't yet threaten to tug them inside. From there they watched the approach, the glint as moonlight found Kance armor, Kance blades.

If Bliss and Torny bent their boat at the right moment, turned their oars, they might get a burst long enough—

"No," Torny said, quieter, but the words cut through anyway. "We're not doing it, Bliss. Even if we could, we'd just die tonight, and I'm not ending today on a rapier's point. We're going back."

Bliss glared Torny's way, tried to muster some counter, some clever plan to beat the guards, steal their boat, their strength and go dashing after her brother.

Instead, she saw truth in the bandit's solemn eyes, in her own aching limbs.

"We turn now," Torny said, "we can leave before they know who we are, what we saw. We get back, we get rested, and tomorrow, we do what I'm best at."

'Which is?'

"Revenge."

CHAPTER 28

A TRAITOR'S TOWN

Sawi stuck to the buildings as she descended into Mottilan proper. The cliffs sported stairs now, rough-carved steps that made her feet ache with every stride, her legs burning from the impact with the mountain wall up above. At least her pursuit slowed as it entered the city too, those chasing calls dying down to murmurs, as if to respect the night.

Not that they needed to: Mottilan seemed to defy sleep. The port below hustled with nighttime fishermen launching out into the waves or skimming the shore. Late deliveries scooted in, their catch and cargo rushed to baskets, crates, or cook fires. Those orange dots sent their sweet smoke up Sawi's way, bringing with it happier conversation, flutes and drums making music.

Not all that unlike Kitaye, then, whose own evenings often descended into a soft party. A day alive on the Seven Isles was worth celebrating.

An attitude Sawi would've adopted if she thought she might make it to see the next sunrise.

Around her, cozy cabins made a calm labyrinth, one

disorienting without the canopies Sawi was used to. How could these people like sleeping on the ground, away from the trees, and still call themselves Vis?

Then again, going by what she'd heard, Mottilan didn't seem all that interested in sharing culture with the isle's other towns.

Sawi's stumble pushed her in a general direction, her limping scampers across narrow streets angling in one particular way: to the inn she and Gladdring had reserved.

Yes, Sawi figured it likely the people who'd taken Gladdring would know where they were staying, but if Sawi was going to find help, the inn seemed a good place to start.

Travelers would be there, sailors from other isles. Maybe even a Najahn or two. Someone who wasn't on the side of those toughs, who wouldn't be as keen to throw Sawi to the gang.

If not, well . . . Sawi refused to think about that. Panic's edge only allowed a little planning.

The inn's light wood door pushed in easy, Sawi almost falling inside as it swung open. A fire's warm crackle, glib conversation greeted her. A glance picked up somewhere around eight people drifting among the few tables, wood cups bearing the fruit wine. As Sawi let the door swing shut behind her, more than a few of those eyes looked her way, noticed what must've been a rough appearance.

"What happened to you?" the chef, innkeeper, and all around matronly lady asked, coming out from the back with several more wine cups. Two she set on a table, the third she kept in her hands, leaving its intended staring after her with an unasked question on his lips. Instead, the innkeeper shoved the glass at Sawi, who took it, along with the woman's arm in hers. "Come on over here, there's a chair and we'll get you seen to."

The wine went down sticky and sweet, orange and perfectly cool to match the night. Sawi collapsed into the chair, one near enough to the stone fireplace to catch its warmth. A shiver broke out, a tear or two made threats, but Sawi blinked them back.

Remember, Gladdring's endless suspicion came to her, trust is your enemy.

"Tell me what happened," the innkeeper said, returning to Sawi's side with a wet cloth, one smelling of years soaking up wine spills. Nonetheless, Sawi let the coarse fabric wipe away the blood around her cuts. "I've a bath being drawn for you as we speak."

"Thank you," Sawi replied. "We can pay for it."

"I'm sure you can. Now, out with it. What's gone wrong, and where's your friend?"

Before she spoke, Sawi caught the quiet. The inn's crowd had fallen nearly silent, saved for a few mumbled words. She'd be telling the story not to the innkeeper, but the entire inn.

Best make it a good one then, as Wax would say.

So Sawi weaved what she could, kept as close to the truth as she dared. A ragtag group after her and the Najahn. She'd run after their lives were threatened, slipped and fell a few times getting away in the dark, the Mottilan paths unfamiliar.

And where was the Najahn? Somewhere out there still. She'd gone to get help.

"Up the path, you say?" the innkeeper asked when Sawi had finished.

"Near the top," Sawi replied. Close enough to the house where Gladdring was held.

"Odd place for bandits to be," the innkeeper muttered. "Odd time, too. Scoundrels hang up their knives when the fiends come. Gets too dangerous to be out in the jungle." The innkeeper handed Sawi another cup of wine. "You sure that's what they were? Thieves?"

"Near as I could tell."

The innkeeper threw a look, a wave at a triple-set table, the one she'd stiffed on the wine earlier. The three men there, all looking about as tired as Sawi, nonetheless snapped up to their feet and made for the inn's exit.

"They'll take a look, see if they can find your friend," the innkeeper said. "All of'em can throw a mean punch, and I know Tok's carrying a skinning knife." At Sawi's blank stare, the innkeeper smiled. "Now, about that bath?"

THE WATER KEPT the innkeeper's promise, its warmth softening Sawi's wounds, the dirt floating away. The tub sat in a large room at the inn's back along with several others, thatched partitions giving the bathers some small privacy. Another wine cup made its way to the small table near Sawi's bath, though she'd left it untouched so far.

The sugary drinks were already muddling her head.

Was the innkeeper telling the truth? Was her sympathy, this bath all an act to keep Sawi here? Or were things, as the woman down on the beach suggested, more split in Mottilan?

Or was Sawi going to find a dagger slipped between her ribs tonight?

That thought robbed the bath of its remaining enjoyment, prompting a fast stand up, weave slip-on, and exit. Sawi went to her room—Gladdring was kind enough to pay for rooms for the both of them, trading more Najahn trinkets—and collected her rope, her water skin, her satchel. That last still had some heft from the fruits, mushrooms, and herbs she'd scavenged on the way across the mountains. As Pan used to point out, treasure often lay underfoot so long as you paid attention.

Things gathered, Sawi looked towards the small, square room's sole door. The innkeeper hadn't made any checks and nobody had come calling after her. Waiting, perhaps, for the party to return, or maybe Gladdring's captors had made their own appearance, changed some minds as to Mottilan's future.

The window, then.

Sawi tugged away the tight netting across the diamond exit. Big enough to squeeze through for her, not so if Gladdring needed to make a hurried escape. Good. Maybe his enemies wouldn't consider the route.

Sawi poked her head out, looked down. The inn's roof extended away from her, the structure's back rooms and storage billowing out into a star- and torch-lit square. Mottilan still hummed, but nobody pointed her out.

First went the satchel, then the water skin. Sawi dropped them both with her arm hanging out the window, letting them plop onto the grassy thatching.

Whether someone heard those thwacks and reported it, or Sawi's time had run out, a knock on Sawi's door prompted the Vis gatherer to move faster. At least, as fast as her still-sore body could allow.

"My friend," the innkeeper asked, "are you in there? I couldn't find you in the baths."

Sawi, one leg about through the window, hesitated. Buying time. that's what she needed now.

"Just getting myself cleaned up," Sawi said, throwing her voice towards the door. "I'll be down soon."

"Don't take too long. We've got some good news!"

"Like what? Did you find him?"

"Come see for yourself! I wouldn't want to spoil the surprise."

The tone broke something in Sawi. The innkeeper had seemed so kind, so friendly and ready to help. Now, that same earnest voice held a toxic lining, every word bearing false. Was the innkeeper as bad as the ones holding Gladdring, or merely under their thumb?

Sawi didn't care, didn't ask. Repeated that she'd be a couple minutes and dropped from the window.

The satchel and skin landed hard on the thatch, Sawi struck on her heels, rocking back into a sit, the sharp twigs and leaves adding new marks to her battered skin. Better, though, than the rocky cliffs.

Sawi looked up at those now, the pathway up lined with torches despite the hour, ensuring Mottilan's most powerful could come and go without risk.

Up there lay Sawi's only option. The rooftop confirmed no scuffle in the city, no protesting kidnappers being brought to justice.

Her hope lay back at the Najahn outpost. Sawi would need to make it there, convince the guards to come this way, and pray Gladdring lived long enough for a rescue.

Or, or Sawi could just leave. Get herself on the path and keep on walking. Sawi took a breath. A decision, anyway, that could wait until she made it to the Najahn outpost. Then she could see if Gladdring had bought her loyalty.

Sawi slipped to her left, crouching and stepping along the roof to its edge in the same way she'd walk along a narrow frond. No strong pressure on any one point, her right arm holding the inn's structure for balance.

One more drop into a quiet alley, one Sawi managed without difficulty. Once more on the run. To the left led the wraparound to the city's square, more people. To the right, quieter residences, fewer eyes, and a tougher stair to reconnect with the upward path.

Better to take the harder climb than chance another run.

She made it three steps before the inn's back door opened. Thrust wide before her, the innkeeper following its swing with a Kance metal pot in her arms. She dumped the slop right there in Sawi's path, letting a false surprise play up on her face as she sighted the gatherer, "Well now, how'd you make it out here?"

"Got lost." Sawi spun on a heel, kicked off in the other direction, heading towards the square.

At least her lungs worked well, and the bath must've had some good effect, because Sawi started the run at a great speed, her feet barely hitting the ground before striking off into the next stride. Her arms pumped, she dodged around one surprised person after another, bounded over a fish cart, and used a sturdy torch as a pivot point, her hand gripping strong as she swung around the pole to start on the path up.

Shouts followed her, calls both curious and predatory. Sawi ignored them. Kept running. The way straight, the path clear. Torches lit either side.

She ran and the houses flew by, Mottilan fell behind her. Sawi would get away, would make it.

Until a shape crossed into the path before her. Ragged, ugly, barely able to stand, but shadowed in the torch light. Gladdring forced Sawi to slow, his hands outstretched.

"Stop," Gladdring said, a simpering sound with none of his usual guile. "Stop, or you'll kill us both."

"Run, and we might survive," Sawi countered, but Gladdring already had his head shaking.

Sawi started to run again. If Gladdring wasn't interested in saving himself, that made her choice that much easier.

"Sawi, please."

Gladdring reached for her as Sawi went by, the Vis dodging the Najahn's grasp with little effort. Harder, though, was what followed: a dart, small and swift, striking Sawi's neck. Its shooter stood up the path, an easy aim delivered on.

Sawi stopped, the burn already spreading. She slipped the satchel off her shoulder, let it hit the dust.

"I told you," Gladdring said to her back.

He was right, too. There was no fighting a Mottilan dart. No escaping her fraying muscles, her dying spirit.

Sawi sat, saving herself another fall when the blackness came, and come it did.

CHAPTER 29
WHIRLPOOL

ax never hit water without a whoop, and this time was no exception. That the water in question shocked with its chill, that Wax's hands and feet were bound not only to each other but to Eujo, the Kance Queen, only gave his yelp added vigor.

Then he sucked in what air he could, because the lake's roiling waters crashed over his head. Eujo struck first, a motion owing to her steadfast refusal to engage with her guards during the rowing towards the Whirlpool. Wax wasn't so quiet, delivering verbal barbs one after another until the soldiers stopped responding.

When that fun ran out, when it became clear what was about to happen, Wax tried to give his limbs a stretch, flex them as much as the bonds would allow, because now, with the water dark and thick rushing around him, the current pushing Wax and Eujo deeper, any chance at all relied on his ability to move.

They'd discussed it in the final seconds, when Blinthe and Akido overruled Silvrin's idea of honor to go for their rapiers. Make the Whirlpool's job easier with a stab first.

Maybe they didn't think Wax would hear, but he'd spent a life listening to the softest jungle noises.

A quick whisper with Eujo. Work together. Move as one. An easy idea damn hard to execute when your world tumbled, turned, tossed.

But he felt Eujo. Her legs kicking, her hands trying to move with what little room they had. Wax responded, keeping his eyes closed, his lungs already starting to burn. He moved his legs anyway, matching Eujo's flutters, the ropes keeping their legs together so they moved less like a person, more like a fish, pushing through that dark in the current's direction.

There would be no escaping the Whirlpool. Only embracing it. The skar, so Eujo said, would be inside. There had to be a way to survive its pull.

A crazy hope. Wax couldn't have reached for it, didn't even have the necklace anymore, but as his head began to fuzz, as his body asked for him to open his mouth, take a breath of that fatal water, he wanted the skar, the chance to embrace its warmth one more time.

Who knew, maybe Vis could turn water into air if it meant life.

Eujo's guards had them now. Wax's Foti skar, Eujo's triple set. What they were going to do with the gems, Wax didn't know. The guards didn't elaborate, their sole concern getting Wax and their Queen killed in a clean fashion.

Those thoughts tumbled in twisted panic in between bouts of kick, kick, kick.

Don't move any other muscle. Keep those eyes closed.

The Whirlpool pulled harder as they neared its center, the raging water sucking them inside. Wax felt his head, his neck stretch as his top moved closer than his toes, a surreal yanking threatening to snap him in half.

And maybe it would've, except Wax fell. Surged free from the water and plummeted, Eujo alongside him, down a funnel. He opened his mouth, gulped air as he and the Queen rolled end over end. Water surged up and down around him, dark and wild.

One breath, two, the fall picking up speed. Wax tried to push against Eujo, doing what he'd learned so long ago as a child on Vis: fall with your feet, not your head.

Eujo proved herself a quick learner, tumbling with Wax and pointing their toes down. They hit the pool, a warm splash rising around them, a numbing shock traveling Wax's legs. But they knew what to do, they knew how to survive, they knew how to kick.

Together, Wax and Eujo broke the surface. The barest gray light split the clouds, filtered down into the Whirlpool's great center. One emptying, it seemed, into a broad cavern beneath a narrow hole. Water gushed through it now, raining about Wax and Eujo like a temperamental storm, the pair treading as best they could amid the drops.

"There," coughed Eujo, though she couldn't point and Wax couldn't see her way.

"Go, I'll follow," Wax replied, his words waterlogged.

Eujo started, a hard kick that sent her plunging into the water while Wax wound up doing a back stroke. Looking up at the Whirlpool, the horrifying nexus, brought a strange calm over him, a sense that he'd either defied death and lived, now, on borrowed time, or that he'd already died and Noctia's afterlife was a cruel joke.

Those thoughts ended when Eujo flipped him, submerging Wax while they kept on treading. He held out till Eujo stopped kicking, giving Wax just enough warning to slow his own legs. In the dark water, his head brushed the rocky landing hard enough to leave a mark, soft enough to leave him alive, breathing as Eujo sat up, giving Wax a chance to get his head through the surface.

"Thanks for that," Wax said, wincing.

"Hard to see. I don't know if you noticed."

Eujo called it right. The Whirlpool's bottom proved the sole light in the place, its barest remnants making their way over to this landing. There, the light caught a silver line, a strip either made by human hands or a very convenient ore vein. The line rose onto a flat landing, where littered the markers of human progress, or at least human travel.

"Any ideas on how we get up there?" Wax said, the pair continuing to kick. "Or are we going to swim till we can't anymore?"

"Haven't you ever been tied up before?"

Wax snorted, water leaking from his nose. "Uh, no? Is that a thing on Kance?"

"Follow my lead."

Eujo kicked to the left, then leaned towards the landing. Wax felt her guide their bound wrists towards the stone, whereupon she began rubbing the rope on the rough rock.

"I get it now," Wax said, wincing a bit at how dull the words sounded. "Fray the rope, free us. Good stuff."

"Good stuff, indeed."

The rope wasn't cheaply made, though, and didn't part ways quick, giving time for Wax, as his mind adapted to his continued presence among the living, to ask Eujo what was going on.

"You've been cagey this whole time," Wax said. "Ever since the roller. We knew the guards weren't your buddies."

"Focus on freeing us. Your feelings can wait."

Well then. Wax could do just that. If Eujo didn't want to talk, then he'd just give his all at moving his wrist up and down, feeling the slow fray matching the growing fatigue in his legs, muscles that'd already had a long day. But, unlike his legs, the rope gave out with a sudden split, one matching a gasp from Eujo. Wax fell forward in the water, his arms, wrists sore, surging ahead to catch himself on the rock. With their legs still bound, Wax found himself bent at an awkward angle.

"Climb, idiot," Eujo said.

"Working on it."

The rock ledge had grip aplenty, wet though it was. Wax leaned on his fingers, found crevasses. Eujo worked her legs back against Wax, swinging her arms around to hold onto Wax's waist as the Vis pulled them up onto the stones. There, lying on the cool rock, with Wax's face again mashed on rock, Eujo worked their bonds till the rope came free. The Queen curled up off Wax one last time, standing with a sigh and a curse.

Wax figured he'd take a minute or two to just lie there. Not a comfortable spot, but it beat standing, moving.

Eujo seemed to have the same idea. She sat at the water's edge, dangling her legs into the cool cave lake and massaging her calves.

"Well that was something, wasn't it?" Wax rolled up too, sitting flat on the rock. Their clothes were utterly soaked, half shredded from the Whirlpool and the brushes with sharp rocks. Wax felt like he had a thousand small cuts and bruises. "Not every day we get thrown into a lake and left for dead."

"For you, maybe."

Wax winced. Maybe he'd misread the Queen. Eujo's tone didn't have a smidge of pity, self or otherwise, in it. Sounded, in her way, like his own parents when Wax had been much smaller, less wise to the ways of the world.

Whether he was wise at all now was anyone's guess.

"Not going to elaborate on that, then?" Wax asked after the requisite, water-rushing silence had gone on long enough.

"I don't know where you get the idea that I need to tell you anything," Eujo replied. "I tried once before, to warn you, but you didn't listen, and now we're down here. Thank you for the roller, but I think we're done."

"Oh, now, when we're all alone at the bottom of the Whirlpool, now's when you want to split up?"

Eujo stood. Wax felt the glare even though shadow hid her face, where they'd come ashore.

"After, then," Eujo replied, not giving in the slightest. "We survive this, then we go our separate ways. Two Renewals again."

Wax matched Eujo on his feet. Followed her look towards the cool distance, the dripping dark where the cave continued on.

"Two hopeless Renewals, you mean. Your guards took our skars."

"I'll get them back."

"How?" Wax laughed. "Eujo, they beat you, they beat Quik and I. Wouldn't say you've got good odds here."

"I'll have surprise. that's all I'll need." Venom dripped from her tongue. "They'll split up, whether on the street or at an inn's bathroom. When they sleep, or when they think they're safe, I'll be there. I'm a Kance Queen, Wax, and they didn't kill me when they should've."

"Apparently not."

Now it was Eujo's turn for a grim laugh. She punctuated the sound by walking forward, her voice echoing on the walls around them. Wax, with nothing better to do, followed, away from the Whirlpool's glow and into the dark.

Only to stop, not three strides later, as they hit a flat wall. The cavern's end, and one smoothed out by human hands.

Lines wrapped around the stone, grooves cut in an obvious spiral.

"The center, then," Eujo said, her hands shoving Wax's out of the way. She pushed, nothing happened. "Damn."

"Guess they're smarter than a Kance Queen."

"I don't see any ideas coming from you, Vis."

"That's because I prefer to think before I speak."

Eujo chuckled. "Wax, I've known you only a few short days, and already I know that's not true."

While she spoke, though, Wax had his own fingers running along the stone, finding its outer edges. There the smoothness vanished, replaced by uneven lines. Jutting triangles, circles, and squiggles. Wax followed the pattern all the way to the floor, where the smooth surface narrowed to a clean line before picking up again on the right side. At the top—Wax could reach, touch the low cavern ceiling— the line smoothed out again.

"What are you doing?" Eujo asked, moving back a step to give Wax space. "Wasting time?"

"Yep, that's it, Eujo. Here I am, stuck in a cave with no food, nothing but a bunch of rags on, and I'm wasting time. Sounds like me."

"It kind of does."

"You're lucky I'm thinking right now, or I'd take these insults personally."

While Eujo had been speaking, Wax had kept his fingers moving, digging into a growing idea. The circular lines ran in towards the center, true, but the outermost line wasn't a solid circle. It had an end, a point towards the bottom.

The same spot someone coming to the Whirlpool might

enter. Wax moved a finger inside the line, dropping it into the gap between the outermost groove and the next one. When he did, Wax felt the stone descend beneath his tip. Not far, and not more than a thumb print's worth.

But that press guided his thumb forward, and Wax ran it along the stone whirlpool in the dark. As he did, the lifeless grooves picked up a phosphorescent blue, much like some jellyfish Wax had seen. The blue glow traced Wax's hand as he ran it between the grooves, the little press continuing until he reached the whirlpool's center, washed in iridescent light, like a liquid blue sky.

"Guess I was wrong," Eujo said as Wax pressed into the whirlpool's center.

"I won't hold it against you."

At his press, the stone door shivered. Some lock on the door's far side clicked, and the portal slid open.

At the sight, Wax wanted to give a whoop, but the cavern felt so close, he settled for a whistle instead.

CHAPTER 30

OBSIDIAN FIENDS

The vessel broke through a Rana sloop on its way to the sand, scattering the wood with wrenching cracks. New dunes rose as the craft's momentum collided with the earth. The ballistae had proven ineffective, at least so far as Maena could tell, though the vessel, now catching torchlight, bore deep cuts throughout its frame. As if someone hacked at it with a giant sword.

"The Aegis," Svarde answered the unasked question. The man had his weapons out as fleeing Rana, the few other prisoners streamed by them towards Jochi's lines. "They might be different, but these are still fiends. Treat them as nothing else."

"Never seen a fiend in a boat before," Rasslebeck said.

Maena kept them in the tower's shadow, not least because she couldn't discount Jochi deciding to murder them all. The crossbow fire in at the Rana, at the prisoners, had stopped once the fiend vessel appeared, but a glance around their tower defense showed the flight halting at Jochi's sandbagged walls.

Rana begged for mercy, for aid, for relief from what

must've been a terror. Maena had been in her share of ship pursuits, chasing down slower prey, boarding, and looting their holds. She'd been on the other side just once, her second time out, and the Najahn frigate making chase filled every moment with a tooth-gnashing tension. Death only a few waves away.

A storm had saved her then. The cloudy skies now, their snow flickering down in casual flakes, would do no such thing.

"Svarde's right," Maena said. "We wait and see what comes out of that thing, and then we try to use it."

Use a fiend? Bold.

Bold, maybe, but better than being Jochi's pincushion.

"What if it comes for us?" Pennifer asked.

"Then we do what we came here to do," Svarde answered. Kivi snorted her agreement. "This is a preamble, nothing more."

Beyond the continual crashing waves, a gradual silence fell over the beach. Jochi's barricade stopped the flight, and the Rana found their dignity as calls for help went unanswered, instead sorting themselves out as best they could on the rocks between sand and civilization. Every eye not watching a wound focused on the charred, rounded thing waiting, wondering.

Is there a signal? Something they're expecting?

Surrender, maybe. Or an all out assault leaving the attackers vulnerable.

Then why don't you go see?

I thought you didn't want to die again?

Maybe there'll be another one that'll suck you away and give me back my body.

Or maybe there would be a fiend that'd take away this voice, this person that didn't deserve to live.

Don't lie to yourself. You need me now.

The fiends interrupted. A clacking series, a thousand locks coming undone one after another, rattled through the night. The vessel shook. New cries to let the wounded through echoed after, their fear leaving its taste on the air.

When the crackles ceased, the vessel's top half shuddered, a motion Maena could see only because the gathering snow slid off in glittering dust. As it shook, the vessel's very top split, much like Maena might crack an egg. A sudden parting, a slim line becoming an arcing gap.

Blue poured forth, an eerie, flickering color the shade of flowers, of Vis waters on a warm tropical day. Maena's hands gripped her cutlass tight.

No limbs signaled the emergence, no ladder or hook rose to the surface. Instead, there was the blue glow alone, and then the glow moved. Flew. Shot up into the air, though only a short distance, before swinging back towards the ground.

"Another," Svarde said.

Maena had been watching the first, but she saw a second flash, then a third. Each one half as tall as a ballista tower, thudding into the beach with enough weight to throw up sand in wild geysers.

The trio stood tall, their blue glow not some light but instead fire's intense flicker. Still some paces away, well beyond weapon range, Maena felt the heat pouring off the creatures, saw the sizzling as snowflakes winked from existence before touching their skin.

Skin? You think these things have skin?

Not, Maena realized, that she could see. The flame framing their bodies ended in legs and arms, four of the latter, with a shorter pair erupting from the monster's shoulders. Their legs ended in broad stumps, ones appearing like a candle's burning wick. Their heads cleaved obsidian, dark and sparking with the fire's heat.

"They're armed too," Rasslebeck muttered. "Not any normal fiends."

"Bad news for the isles if this is what we're facing now," Pennifer added.

Each one looked to carry some sort of molten whip, a long chained menace wrapping around their bodies, ending with a hooked prong dangling off an arm's end. An unusual weapon, but then, who knew what these fiends considered normal.

The three fiends took in their opponents, burning in the sand. Smoke rose around their feet, what few things flammable in the dirt bursting into orange. The burning blue flashed onto their black rock heads, outlining circles and slashes whenever the heads moved before fading away.

No arrows fired, no shouts to attack came from Jochi. Two sides studying one another.

"Do we get on with it then?" Svarde asked.

"I'm inclined to let the rockbiters fight first," Rasslebeck said. "Let 'em take a lick, then we take the glory."

"No glory in finishing the scraps."

"Glory isn't important," Maena cut them off. "It's the opportunity."

What are you cooking up?

All her life, Maena had seen fiends as that rare nuisance, something that came about near a Renewal and meant carrying a saber at all times. Violent beasts needing to be cut down and nothing more. These three, though . . .

"They're not fighting, which means they're waiting for something else," Maena said.

"Yeah, an opening," Pennifer added.

"Then let's give them one. Either they kill us, or say they come in peace. I think it'll be the latter."

"Then you're not paying attention. Our raiders were running. They're wounded."

Maena nodded, "That was in the open sea. Now we have the advantage. I think these fiends see that."

Maena started forward, taking a long step onto the sand. How she'd communicate with these monsters seemed an impossible question, but the idea was there. She had to try.

Why?

Simple. These things had come from The Dark Below. They knew what waited in its heart. Might know, then, how to stop the onslaught and bring an end to the terrible chain tying the isles together.

Or maybe they're just here to destroy us all.

A risk she'd take.

The closest fiend, the center one, turned its immense, eyeless gaze on Maena as she approached. The Rana captain threw her saber to the sand. Made a clear show that she held no weapons, secret or otherwise. Behind her, far up the beach, and on the tower tops, clanks and rustles sounded as Jochi's forces maneuvered to some other end.

"Can you understand me?" Maena asked.

The fiend, those glazed outlines flashing up and around its head over and over again seemed to stare right through her. The heat this close had Maena wincing, sweat breaking out. Still several strides away, too. How could these fiends survive?

Morever, how could they even interact? Maena figured the monsters would set a house on fire if they stepped inside, burn up a ship should they come aboard.

Yet, maybe the answer lay in the craft the fiends had

piloted up here. A changeover in society from one of woods and thatched roofs to one of metal.

You're getting carried away.

A daydream on the edge of oblivion.

"Please, tell me." Maena repeated. "Do you understand?"

The fiend's face flared brighter, its full constellation glowing. Two three-circle columns on either side, split by six small diamonds twinkling up the middle. The flash vanished as quick as it came, the fiend rising up to its full height.

A roar built, the growling chorus of a fire filling out to its peak. Almost as one, the fiends swung up their clawed hooks. And broke.

The center fiend, the one closest to Maena, lunged forward. The thing would've buried her if not for Kivi, the ferrite darting faster than the fiend to knock Maena aside, cover her with its stone shell as the fiend lumbered past.

Though lumbering wasn't their goal. As alarmed shouts broke out, the fiends whipped their grapples towards the ballista towers, each one soaring high and landing on their targets with stone-crunching force. Rocks blasted, the fiends following their grapples with leaps to land on the tower sides, using the stone to shield the creatures as they scaled the walls.

Beneath the middle tower, Svarde, Rasslebeck, and Pennifer lay in the sand, trying to escape the awful heat. Maena rose, found her saber, though who knew what good the small weapon would do against these monsters, and watched the fiends ascend the three towers.

As they reached the top, wood battlements, the ballistas themselves burst into flame, great orange gouts rising up like pyres in the snowy night.

The first counters came from Jochi's force, crossbows launching their bolts into the blaze. Whether they hit, whether they hurt, Maena couldn't tell. The burning Whent bodies diving off the tops told a different story clear enough.

The fourth ballista tower found its will, though. The guards rotated their massive weapon, a loud thwack sounding as an iron missile launched right at the nearest tower. When it didn't appear on the tower's other side, when, instead, the fire moved, a blue-burning fiend appeared, tumbling off the tower's side to land, missile sticking up like a grave marker, lifeless in the sand. Cheers rang out.

Cheers that died a moment later when the third tower sent a burning missile of its own, thrown by the fiend on its top, to slam into the remaining ballista and break it apart. Screaming, scrambles, and flame rained.

The last fiend added to it, lancing burning ballista bolts down at Jochi's fortifications. Each one glowed orange as it whistled through the air, striking those sandbags and bursting them alight. Impossible to counter, impossible to fight.

Maena looked up at their tower, the fiend at its top beginning its own burning assault. She glanced back towards the waves, the Rana sloops resting on the sand. A possible escape there, into the chill night.

"We fight," Svarde snarled, rising up to his feet. "No running, Maena. We won't leave this town to die."

Maena sniffed, picked her way over the sand to the tower's base. Kivi followed.

"Caring for other people, Svarde?" Maena asked. "Unlike you."

"It's the fiends I don't care for. It's the fiends that scare me," Svarde replied. "I won't let them do it."

"How do you suppose we stop them, then?" Rasslebeck asked. "Unless you want to go toe to toe with one of those things?"

"We'll find a way." Svarde pointed an axe up towards the tower's top. "First, we need to get up there."

"Kivi," Maena said, "open the door. Lead the way."

You're sounding confident.

As the fiends continued their barrage, as Jochi's forces began a haphazard retreat and the first buildings caught fire, Maena found a smile. She had an idea, and for the first time in a long while, she had real hope.

CHAPTER 31
TRACKING TIME

When Bliss couldn't sleep, she prepped. The outpost around her did much the same, the Najahn and Rana using their sudden safety to rebuild a ravaged ruin. Bliss focused on her satchel, her water skin, her staff. Torny did too, though the bandit's constant looks Bliss's way said she didn't quite have the same urgency.

Quik, oblivious and exhausted, kept sleeping.

"It's not that I think we shouldn't go after them," Torny said as the pair stuffed fruit and salted fish inside the rough woven sacks, "it's that we're outnumbered and, let's be real here, Bliss, out-skilled."

'Your alternative is what, then?' Bliss signed back.

"See if we can't get into the Whirlpool and find your brother?"

'You saw him vanish. He's gone.'

"Well, yeah, but maybe not the body. The skar."

The Foti skar would've still been with Wax, sure. But what did that matter? Who cared, if his chance at a—

Bliss stopped, glared Torny's way. 'What, you want the skar to sell?'

Torny didn't bother looking embarrassed. Instead, her slight form picked up a stiff spine, facing Bliss straight on.

"I'm saying we're still alive, Bliss. If your brother's not, then we're not Guardians anymore either. Which makes us alone on a random isle overrun with fiends. We don't have a roller, we sure don't have the goods to pay for a ship off Rana." Torny spat to the side, through a narrow slit between slats. "I'm not going back to work for another grabby innkeeper."

'So your choice is to loot my brother's body?'

"What do you think he'd want, Bliss?"

'He'd want his killers down there with him. Pack your bag, Torny. We're leaving at dawn.'

The bandit, at least, knew when to let an argument die. The two went back to their satchels, and, when those were full, fell onto straw mats. Despite the noise around them, the day's battle, the rowing, the anger and loss threw Bliss into a fitful sleep, one flush with nightmares and hot rage.

Those dreams led to a cold sweat, a hard waking to fresh-cooked fish and roasted mushrooms, something Bliss had plenty of back home on Vis, something that'd always bring her stomach to life.

Gratitude for saving the outpost bought Bliss, Torny, and Quik breakfast. Their older brother, despite the Vis skar, limped and looked unable to make a trek. Even the fire that came into his eyes when Bliss relayed the story dimmed at the idea of breaking south after a group already rowing ahead.

'Then wait,' Bliss signed between bites. 'Look for Wax. Vis ought to get to say goodbye.'

"Won't last that long," Torny muttered, and at the glares from her fellow Guardians, the bandit shrugged. "What. It's close to winter now. You won't get an easy ride down to Vis, and his body won't keep, even if you do find it down there. Better bury it here, and take a token—"

'If you say the skar, I'm going to leave you here right now.'

"Was going to say whatever you could find." Torny looked away. Off to the east, where the marsh rolled into the large river they'd traveled on an eternity ago. "You're being too sensitive. This is it. This is life now. It's grim, it's hard. Sentimentality just makes it harder."

The day seemed to share Torny's perspective. A gnashing wind blew, and clouds kept up their cover. Snowflakes idled in the air, as if unsure whether to land. The water lapped gray and cold against the outpost.

"For once, I'm with Torny," Quik said. "The skar might be useful, and it could buy us a ticket home." He put a hand on Bliss. "And don't count your brother out. He's a tricky one."

'He was bound, and he fell overboard.'

"But if they wanted Wax and Eujo dead, they could have killed them, Bliss. Could have put a block around their feet, or done any of a dozen things to ensure they drowned." Quik looked north, towards the Whirlpool. "There's something we're missing here, and I'm not going to count Wax out yet."

'Wish I could have your hope.'

"Then earn it. Find those bastards and get them to tell you everything." Quik flashed a dire scowl. "And when they're done, do what they couldn't. Make sure they pay for it, Bliss."

Torny snorted. "Big talk. Two young girls going up

against three Kance Queensguard?"

Bliss, though, rose to her feet without any fear. The calm, perhaps buttressed by the grim morning and her cold purpose, kept her steady.

'We're not on Kance, Torny. They're in the wilds, and that's my home.'

Well, not quite. The marsh didn't match Vis's jungle. The thin trees didn't offer swinging opportunities. Vines and large fronds weren't ready to speed her along. Nevertheless, Bliss eschewed an offered boat by the grateful Najahn, leaving Torny confused but understanding as they started off south.

The Kance guards had taken the western river, an offshoot, so the Najahn said, both sloppy and slow-going, especially at winter's onset, with less rain and low water forcing a more meandering path.

Cut straight south at speed and the two could make gains. The marsh seemed to understand their purpose, too, with the chilly weather hardening the mud, making their walk easy. Their clothes were, in a way, the biggest hindrance: the thick linens, upgraded from the light Foti versions back in Riroca, proved able to get caught on any grasping thorn or bush. If the earth held their footsteps, the wind attacked their walk with vigor, blowing Bliss and Torny around and stumbling them into unfrozen ponds. Before long, their feet were soaked, and blisters followed.

Torny voiced her complaints with the usual invective, hurling curses at the weather, at the Rana for not building a road through the marsh, and ultimately at the Kance traitors for forcing this awfulness upon them.

A comforting cadence, in its way.

The first night came and went on a mossy rock listing atop a small knoll. While the western river trickled by, Bliss and Torny settled down in their furs, pressing near enough to one another for body heat, as Bliss didn't want a fire.

Who knew if the Kance were paying close attention, or what else a fire's light might bring. Fruit and dried fish sufficed, with Torny chewing on some particular weeds after the meal.

"These?" Torny said when Bliss pointed at the serrated leaves. "Try one."

The burst came from the first bite. Bright and fresh, enough to make Bliss's eyes pop. She gnawed on the leaf, trying to place its flavor and finding no comparison.

"Never had mint before?" Torny asked. "You can find it everywhere on Rana. A few other places too."

'It's not on Vis.'

"Yeah, I'm getting that." Torny laughed, leaned against the rock and waved the mint leaves in the air. "See, Bliss? There's so many neat things out there you haven't seen."

'I could show you something just as cool back home.'

Torny nodded, "I'd like that. If, you know, we make it through this murder quest of yours."

'We will.'

A slight smile, "Wish I had your confidence."

The next day boosted that confidence further. The western river continued to refuse a straight track south, winding instead between islands and around clumping trees. Bliss and Torny cut straight through, the marsh dwindling as it mingled with more firm and fertile terrain. The first rice paddies, long harvested for winter, appeared, with lonely thatched farmhouses sprinkled in between.

Actual paths upped their speed further, though Bliss wondered at the utter absence of people. A question Torny tried to answer by pointing out the harvest was done and fiends were about.

"Would you stay here alone all winter, not knowing when some monster might come crashing through your door?" Torny asked as they passed by a ragged barn. "I know I wouldn't."

Back on Vis, the outer towns had indeed emptied—or been slaughtered, like the one Bliss found with Deshiva. Going towards the fortified cities made a certain sense, though Torny found her own advantage in it.

"Look," the bandit said as she went to work on the simple lock on a squat home's door near the day's end. "I'm sure whomever's house this is won't mind a couple Guardians using it for the night."

'So we're Guardians again?'

"When we need to be." Torny held up a finger when Bliss started to sign. "Don't you dare go giving up an advantage when you don't need to. There's no such thing as honor, Bliss. It's survival, that's it. That's all that matters."

Bliss couldn't say she agreed with that, but she had to admit Torny's plan had merits: the house had real beds, food stores well beyond what the two could eat, consisting of rice, root vegetables, and the ever-present fish pickled in thick barrels. A stove made for hot food and a warm night, one Bliss filled by signing through Vis legends for Torny until the day's walk knocked them out.

The third day's afternoon brought the sight Bliss was looking for. After the marsh, Rana grew hilly, with rice paddies climbing up and down the slopes. The western river ran around the rises, an inefficient slough south. From the top of one, Bliss spied the boat, the Kance making their slow way down.

"No oars out," Torny noted, standing next to Bliss. A clearing day, for once, though the sun barely seemed to touch their skin. "They're really coasting."

'Why?'

"Asking the wrong bandit." Torny snapped her fingers. "Wait, I've got it. They want to make it easy for us."

'That makes no sense.'

"Sure, but if we don't have any other ideas, why not go with that one?"

Torny's logic seemed flawed, but for once the bandit didn't act like they were about to be skewered, so Bliss let her have it.

They sped on, vigor replenished at the sight. A small Rana town lay ahead too, the buildings poking up, over, and around trees. A place, perhaps, for the Kance to stop for the night. They'd need food, water. Vulnerabilities Bliss hoped she could exploit.

The thought brought a smile. Look at her, thinking like the hunter, seeking weaknesses, making plans to catch her prey. Deshiva would be proud.

They kept their pursuit near the river, popping up every now and then to catch sight of the boat, making sure the Kance did indeed make their way to a docking at the small town. Their targets were predictable, the trio tying up their raft and heading in, all while Bliss and Torny watched from a nearby grove.

"Slit their throats in the night, then?" Torny asked as they lingered beneath the leaves.

'We need one alive to tell us what they did with Wax. And why.'

Torny nodded, appraised her. "You're a cold one, Bliss. Know that?"

'Like you said, Torny. It's about survival. I don't think the Isles will let you live any other way.'

"Just don't, you know, lose yourself so completely. Don't be like Sledge. Or Eggrad."

Bliss stared at Torny. 'When all this is done, then maybe I'll think about who I am. Until then, let's find out what happened to my brother, and hurt the ones who did it to him.'

CHAPTER 32
TAMAS TURNABOUT

The chill woke Sawi more than the light, and what a grudging, slow awakening it was. As if her every bone and muscle needed attention to come back to life. Not that the rising did much good: rope bound her hands and legs, leaving her feeling the grass beneath her thighs and the rough stone at her back.

The view had more to recommend it. A sweeping vista, the height almost dizzying to Sawi, who preferred her lofts with canopies all around rather than the clear, sheer drop to surf and savagery. But Mottilan's tallest cliff didn't partake in jungle fantasies, instead offering little more than skinny shrubs and a glaring group busy building something nearby.

"She rises," Gladdring said, the man sitting next to her, equally bound. "It warms my heart to see you alive, Sawi."

"Strange, because mine's still cold."

Gladdring bore his bruises, scratches, and general rough handling like someone who was, somehow, used to it. No tears leaked from puffy eyes, he neither slouched nor winced, and a bloody lip stayed firm. His robes, likewise, kept a certain dignity despite their rips and tears.

Less dignified, grumbling to one another, with grimaces abounding, were the five Mottilan men and women erecting what seemed to be a crane. A large bamboo cage sat nearby, its purpose not all that hard to guess.

Certain stories, certain legends Sawi hadn't heard since her earliest days, suggested wars between Kitaye and Mottilan demanded punishments, and Mottilan's were of a distinctly terrifying variety.

"What'd you do to them?" Sawi asked, keeping her voice low. Gladdring might not know what she'd heard, and Sawi wanted to get his side, wanted to know how much he'd put her in danger. "Why do they hate you so much?"

"Misunderstandings and mistakes, on my side and theirs." Gladdring sighed, a heavy one that rolled through his whole body. "Patience is always the first to fly when the fiends return."

Yet patience kept Sawi quiet while the Mottilan work continued. Gladdring fell silent too, refusing to elaborate on his sole phrase. They watched, Sawi trying to ignore her hunger, her thirst, her physical needs. Easy to do that when the Mottilan job concluded, well before the sun hit midday.

They stood their construct up, about twice Sawi's height and made of a thick wood base, follow by a board reaching out over the cliff's edge. At its end, looped through a metal ring stolen from some fishing boat, was the thick rope connected to the cage.

The Mottilan leader, Korrus, turned his baleful look towards his prisoners.

"I don't see any surprise, so you must know what this is," Korrus said, giving them a moment to interrupt.

"It's war, is what," Sawi said. "I'm just a guide. When Kitaye hears—"

"Hears that you've been aiding a Najahn traitor? No Vis city will risk Noctia's help now, not for you." Korrus softened. "Not that we wanted this to happen. If you'd kept to yourself, you wouldn't be here. I've had enough of Kitaye meddlers showing up where they don't belong."

"I'm so sorry for you."

Sawi's bite earned her nothing. Instead, Korrus walked forward, grabbed Sawi by the shoulders and lifted her up. With her legs bound, the Vis woman couldn't do anything as Korrus carried her over to the bamboo cage and deposited her inside its open door.

"I can walk myself," Gladdring said when Korrus turned back for him.

The Najahn stood, revealing his own legs and arms weren't tied like Sawi's, and marched his own way to the cage. Sized about the same as a large bed, the two could sit, couldn't quite stand without hitting the bamboo top, but it was room enough.

Sawi wanted to ask why Gladdring wasn't bound, but the question didn't have a chance to launch, as Korrus waved for the Mottilan crew to set the cage swinging.

"You'll hang here until our demands are answered," Korrus said as the Mottilans tightened the rope, raised the cage off the ground. It swayed from the first tug. "Twice a day, we'll pass food and water to you. The chill will rob you of your comfort, the sun will burn your shoulders, and should a storm come through, your deaths are all but assured. I hope your Najahn take it seriously."

"And I hope you realize the mistake you're making," Gladdring replied, surrendering nothing to his captors.

Sawi pushed away her own fear, her own bewilderment. Somehow, she'd gone from picking fruit under safe guard to, as the cage swung out over the cliff, dangling in the air over a rival city with no help, no defense.

"I'm sure I will," Korrus replied as the cage went off the cliff, into open air. "But you, betrayer, will not be alive by then."

The cage jostled in the breeze as Korrus and his crew finished pounding in heavy stakes, setting the rope into its position, a taut spot an arm's reach from the rocky cliffside.

Then, without any further word, the Mottilans left, leaving Sawi and Gladdring alone with the birds, the wind, and winter's bite.

The plan, as Gladdring described it in those first hours, was a simple one. Persuade the Mottilan coming to give them food and water to end the torture and set them free. From there, a run down the mountainside and a vanish into the jungle.

"That easy, huh?" Sawi asked, huddled in the corner, her arms and legs pulled close. Her weave was not built for the weather, and she'd been shivering all morning. "Just say a few words and we're free?"

"It will be as I say."

"Then why go through the whole thing in the first place, if your honey tongue can get us what we need?"

"Because they had numbers. One, maybe two, I can turn. More is beyond me."

"Turn?"

Gladdring, his hands inside his robes and his eyes watching the sea, shook his head. "You'll learn more when the time comes. What matters, though, is what will happen next."

"What's that?"

"When they open the cage, you will subdue them."

"With what?"

Gladding nodded at her hands. "Use what your god has given you, Sawi. You know how."

"I'm a gatherer, not a hunter."

"False. You are what I need you to be."

Sawi's denial died before she could even find the words for it. Instead, confidence welled in its place. Gladdring wasn't wrong: she had done far more than simple gathering on this journey alone, not to mention all the expeditions with Wax and Pan. She could handle knocking a Mottilan head or two.

"You didn't really answer my question earlier," Sawi asked. "Why are they so angry? In real words, please."

"Because we made a deal. One that didn't work out as they hoped, despite my making no promises that it would."

"Sounds like a bad deal."

"I gave them an opportunity. They didn't capitalize. Now they blame me." Gladdring closed his eyes. "How easy it is to put your own fault on others."

"But won't the Najahn take revenge for you?"

"As I said on our way here, Sawi, the Najahn isn't one whole. We are individuals, thirsting for power or fighting to keep it. If avenging my death would help someone, then troops might sweep Mottilan clean. More likely, another bargain will be struck, much the same as mine, in return for casting my death as an unfortunate accident."

"Noctia sounds like an awful place to live."

Gladdring snorted. "Everywhere has its rules, Sawi. You either play by them, learn how to break them, or fail because of them. Noctia is no different, no better or worse, than anywhere else."

Sawi laughed. Gladdring could say whatever he liked, but Kitaye had yet to do anything so brutal.

Maybe that's what adventuring was: finding out the home you started with really was the best place after all.

Gladdring's plan had its first test in the afternoon, when a Mottilan pair, Korrus among them, scaled the cliff with some moldering mangos and a small water skin. Korrus's partner wheeled the crane back over land, settling its bulk on the grass. Through the slats, Sawi, unbound by Gladdring, could feel those little stalks, could imagine breaking across them.

Korrus reached over the crate's top, opened a small section cut for that purpose, and dropped the food inside. The water skin followed. Gladdring took a sip, handed it to Sawi. He didn't touch the mango.

"Don't starve yourself, Gladdring," Korrus said. "It's going to be cold tonight. You'll need all the food you can get."

"Some of us can handle ourselves, Korrus."

"As you so obviously are."

Korrus waved, the crane moved back over the abyss, and the Mottilans left.

Sawi didn't follow Gladdring's example, digging into the mango without relish, with need. After, her hands sticky, she threw a glare Gladdring's way.

"Wanted to keep us in here a little bit longer, did you?" Sawi asked.

"Korrus isn't our target. He's too invested in the success. We need a weaker pair."

"What if he comes every time?"

Gladdring frowned, "Then I have truly been outplayed, but it's a long walk up here. Korrus has to make his threats to the Najahn, to Kitaye now if he's to get his reward. That will take time. We'll have our chance."

"Wish I had your faith."

"You will."

Gladdring's patience paid off as the sun made its way down the horizon, settling their world into a harsh purple-orange twilight. Again a Mottilan pair emerged up the cliff, carrying fish and more water.

Korrus not among them.

"Be ready," Gladdring said. "The opening will be small."

Sawi, whose whole body seemed on the verge of going numb, nonetheless scooted closer to the cage's gate. The crane shifted, swinging the pair back over land. As it did, the second Mottilan, carrying food and water, moved towards the crate and reached for the upper opening.

"You don't want to die, do you?" Gladdring said to the man, who stopped his reach, flicked a suspicious look Gladdring's way. "Korrus plays with a force beyond his imagining. The Najahn will scour Mottilan, they will destroy your family. Your home. Your city. All this, because Korrus feels slighted."

"You all right?" asked the other Mottilan, back by the crane's base.

"Fine," replied Gladdring's target, never once moving his eyes off the Tenet.

"The way out is simple. Open the door. I will ensure your survival. Your reward. Mottilan lives. Your family thrives."

The man's hand wavered. His partner asked again what was going on.

"Do it," Gladdring ordered. "Save yourself and the ones you love."

Like a reflex, the man's hand snapped to the cage's gate. He flicked lock on its outer pole open, releasing the wide door. Sawi, her legs and arms barely working, stumbled at the chance, but caught herself on her palms, her toes, and kicked forward.

Fear, hope, anger did the rest. The Mottilan man seemed stunned by what he'd just done, didn't even get a hand up before Sawi tackled him, drove him back into a hard hit on the stone.

Yelling, the second Mottilan came running up behind, a club held in his hand. The man didn't reach Sawi: Gladdring, stepping from the cage, stuck out a long leg and tripped the charging enemy, sending him sprawling. Sawi tore the club from the Mottilan's hands and, at Gladdring's nod, delivered what she hoped wouldn't be a fatal strike.

Both their captors groaned. Sawi and Gladdring scooped up the water skins, the food. Sawi was about to break off running, but Gladdring stopped her.

"Put them in," Gladdring said. "We'll dangle them over the cliff. From distance, they'll look enough like us to buy some time."

Moving bodies should've been harder, but freedom gave Sawi energy, a rush not near spent by the time the crane once again swung its cage over the open air, not spent by the time she and Gladdring ran down the cliff, beyond the grass and back into the jungle's warmer, welcome darkness.

CHAPTER 33

THE RIVER SKAR

As if anticipating most travelers wouldn't have torches beyond the Whirlpool's sucking powers, the room beyond the spiral door offered the same glowing moss Wax had seen in caves on Vis. The purple-blue flora ran along a narrow path expanding, after several strides made in awed silence, to a carved stair. Down those steps, in gouged lines, ran water, a glittering liquid that at first had Wax stumped.

"Silver veins," Eujo said, kneeling at the soft pool near the stair's base to inspect the deposits, a shimmering circle whose overruns trickled to the sides and vanished into invisible holes. "Wax, look."

Following Eujo's own stare led Wax around the chamber, taller than his treehouse back home, and caught out the twinkling walls. Between the moss, the rock, wandering silver lines writhed. A fortune for Foti miners or Rana traders, but none had taken advantage.

"Because the Najahn won't let them," Wax muttered.

"It's the same on Kance. Our skars are near a whole nest of sky diamonds, but we're not allowed to approach." Eujo didn't look all that happy about it. "If we could, so many of our stragglers could be helped."

"I didn't think royalty cared about commoners." Wax winced as he spoke. "Sorry, that came off harsher than I meant. We don't have people like you on Vis."

Eujo, if she took any offense, didn't show it. "You know how Kance chooses its queens, Wax?"

"You know how Vis chooses its elders?"

Eujo laughed, the sound echoing off the burbling water, the Whirlpool's distant roar.

"I don't," the Queen said. "But, before we get caught up in the tragedy of our separate lives, let me say this. On Kance, one queen comes from inheritance. The daughter, if one exists, of either the current queens, is chosen when one dies or gives up her throne. The other, always, is picked from the streets."

"And you were that one?"

A nod. "That's also why Kance has a history of killing its queens. We don't see eye-to-eye, the other Queen and I, and she apparently thinks her luck might be better with someone new."

Eujo spoke the words with a defiant apathy, as if this was the way things were, so no sense in pushing against them. Wax though, read a stiffness, an anger and disappointment in the pose. Something he'd picked up having to measure Bliss's mood based solely on gestures for so long.

"You would do the same to her," Wax said, "if you had the chance."

A flinted glare, a turn back to the watered stair. Eujo pointed towards the top. "Let's keep moving."

The steps held no secrets. A simple scaling to the top, their feet catching the running silver from time to time. As dust leaked in around his toes, Wax felt the mild grit, cold and pure. Who knew, maybe if enough caught in there he could sell the Rana shoes for a good meal. The leather itself would be worthless, so drenched, destroyed, and muddied by river, marsh, and whirlpool, but the silver?

Maybe more than a meal. Maybe a ship's passage to Whent.

Delusions of grandeur kept Wax occupied till they crested the stair's top, a flat landing crowded with just the two of them. The room's gradual narrowing came to a finish not far over their heads, a point suffused with silver and near blinding to look at. The direction, instead, seemed to be a tunnel ahead, one sloping hard down. Water poured into it, with enough splashing off to run along the stair at their feet.

"Who designed these things?" Wax asked, staring at the hole. "Every skar, it's like, why?"

"Noctia claims these are the hearts of the gods," Eujo replied. "That we're journeying to the most sacred place on every isle, where the god's last essence remains."

"Sounds like mystical crap to me."

Another laugh. "Either way, we only have one option."

"What, you don't think we can swim back out the Whirlpool?"

Eujo smiled, "It's good you're joking again. I prefer you that way."

"Glad to meet your mark, Queen."

A sigh, then a sudden dash. Eujo threw up her hands, gripped the tunnel's ceiling, and launched herself down into the dark. Wax gaped, cursed himself for being slow, and followed.

The cold water stole his breath. The tunnel's smoothed floor couldn't match its rough sides, ensuring Wax earned new scrapes with every bounce, every hard turn. Drops came and went with a speed he couldn't fathom, his stomach leaping up and slamming back down more times in mere seconds than Wax had ever felt before.

All in total darkness.

Whether he rushed along those twists and turns for a few seconds or a few minutes, Wax didn't know, couldn't guess. He found his breath at last, let out a whoop into the cave, his arms and legs tucked up close. His last cry?

No. The Vis Renewal launched out into open space, a wide fall into a dark chamber followed by a splash into the deep pool. His feet hit something soft and Wax splashed away, only to hear a cursing, sputtering Eujo in his wake.

"You could've waited a minute," Eujo said into the black.

"How was I supposed to know what this was? What if there was a fiend at the end and you needed help?"

The two again treaded water, again could only follow their voices to one another. Wax, still tired, still running on little more than excitement, felt the burn returning quick. They'd need to find land, or an escape before long.

"I suppose expecting you to be patient is unreasonable," Eujo said. "Any ideas?"

"One. Look down."

Below his feet, deep in the murk, another silver glisten. The only light in the place, and Wax couldn't judge how deep. Eujo suggested they search the chamber first, which, other than the water from the tunnel, proved itself quiet. It also seemed to have no exit, just rock walls all the way around, coated in a thick slime. No glowing plants here.

"So we dive, then," Eujo said once their search ran through, after Wax complained, not for the first time, that he could only swim for so long. "We go for the silver. As deep as you can."

"Grab it, then come back up."

"Unless you see a way out."

"No." Wax shook his head. "That's not the way we do it, Eujo. Together. Grab the silver, come back up. You see a way out, you share it. Then, we go together."

"You're stubborn."

"It's a rule. You don't leave your friends behind in the jungle, and you don't leave them behind in a place like this either."

"Quaint, Wax."

"Not quaint. Necessary."

"You're serious about this." Eujo's mocking edge disappeared. "Why?"

"Because it's meant my Guardians don't want to tie me up and throw me in the drink."

"A fair point, Vis."

They counted off, taking a big breath on four and diving on five. Wax kept his eyes open, kicked his legs into the deep. Below, the silver glittered. Eujo was invisible save for the motion created by her strokes, the two of them pushing down, deeper towards the gemstones.

Wax's ears grew taut, the water pressing against him. His kicks seemed to be lost in an infinite, without direction as the world fuzzed out. Only the silver, everything else was dark. But he kept moving, kept pushing.

Vis demanded no less, and Wax wouldn't see his isle lose to Kance. Not now, not here.

The silver split as they neared, resolving from a single white and gray mass to separate stones, all nestled in a scalloped pit.

The skars. They had to be.

The sight gave Wax energy, the thrust he needed to get the rest of the way down, to reach and grab a silver stone.

The warmth, the whispers flooded in, demanding Wax return to the surface. He flung his body around, tried to figure out which way was up.

His breath ran out. He had nothing left. Those legs that'd brought him this far found themselves floundering, their kicks lacking vigor. Wax had heard of people drowning, usually swimmers who'd gone too far out, been caught in the wrong current. Pulled off shore till no strength could get them back.

This might not be the ocean, but death would come the same way.

The skar, though, declared otherwise. Its whispers surged to a yell, one Wax didn't understand, but one that propelled him forward nonetheless. His legs stopped kicking in and of themselves, instead aligning with his arms, his back, his head to move in a singular motion towards the surface. Water gathered below him, pushing Wax up like some giant hand.

Wax broke the surface and flew out, landing back in the pool with a hard splash. The skar's whispers dwindled to a quiet murmur, Wax's hand gripping the stone hard. He took breaths, floated, stared into the dark. Tried to piece together what'd just happened.

The skars were so much more than he'd been told, than anyone on Vis seemed to talk about. They all seemed to have some power, some strength given by the gods. How to draw out that strength, to use it in a way less random than Wax had seen, that seemed to be the question.

One nobody had asked, or one answered and kept secret?

If anyone knew, it would be the Najahn. The Circle. Those masters sitting in Noctia with the world on their string.

Wax started at the thought. Masters. Rulers. Queens. Where was Eujo?

He swirled around, unable to see anything in the dark. The Queen hadn't breached the surface. Panic flashed. The skar surged in his hand at the thought, the need to go back below and find her. Wax curled, dove back into the black depths.

The darkness died when he held out the Rana skar, its silver light shining out and beating back the gloom. The answering glows came from deep below, yes, but also to his left, a sole light drifting amid the deep.

Wax kicked that way, the skar again urging him to faster and faster speeds. This time, Wax resisted, kept his arms and legs under his own control. Something he might've found harder if not for the Foti, the Vis skars own whispered urges in the past. He had to keep that in mind: the skars weren't smart, they were instinct, ready to burst forth at their own will.

Eujo floated, looking at the skar in her hands. Her eyes open, her mouth closed. No panic in her, no struggle. Wax swam up to her, saw her eyes flick to the skar. She pointed a finger at her mouth, and smiled.

Then, she opened her lips. A translucent sheen came over Eujo's mouth as she opened it, and Wax saw her lungs expand while not a drop seeped inside her mouth.

Breathing, breathing underwater.

As if jealous of Eujo's ability, Wax's own skar snipped and sniped. Its aim seemed obvious, so Wax opened his own mouth. At first, water ran in, but before he could take a panicked swallow, the surge stopped. Only air followed. Wax coughed once, twice, the water coming up and out his throat but without being replaced.

The first breath tasted ugly, metallic. Unclean. But still,

air. Eujo watched him, grinned as Wax found his comfort. After several minutes kicking underwater, breathing through the skars, Wax glanced upward and Eujo nodded.

Together they broke the surface. Together, they saw each other and burst into exclamations about what they'd just done, how close they came to certain death. The magic of the skars, the possibilities waiting for them. As they spoke, both Wax and Eujo held out their glittering stones, and with their light, the cavern no longer hid its secrets.

"The way out," Wax said, seeing it first.

Carved, above a casual arm's reach, lay the first of many grooves. A ladder leading up, towards a gap in the chamber's ceiling.

The Queen nodded. "Lead on, Renewal."

CHAPTER 34

TOWER FALL

Whent knew stone. The rockbiters earned their name through more than their thick skulls, and as much as Maena hated admitting it, the tower was a clever construct. Svarde used his ample shoulders, with Kivi's rocky bulk providing knee-height impact. The sturdy wood handled the first thwack, splintered at the second, and with Rasslebeck trotting out a jeer, Svarde growled into a third ram to break it apart.

All that happened with Maena and Pennifer keeping close, ash and cinders mingling with the falling snow as the flame fiend duo continued their barrage. Jochi's retreat escalated, with Rana and the few prisoners joining the scramble. They climbed and jumped over stacked sandbags, many alight as the fiends launched flaming arrows and rocks from atop their perches.

If the fiends were going to get tired anytime soon, Maena saw no sign.

Inside, the tower's craftsmanship revealed itself in winding notches carved into the sides, an ascending spiral going all the way to the top. Chains mingled with the mechanism, pulleys that'd work to slide the ballista platform all the way down from the tower's top to its base. An easy way to restock ammo, to fix a damaged ballista, or change shifts.

"Wait," Pennifer said as Svarde moved to a large lever built into the tower's stone floor, near the door and inside its alcove, beyond the tower's middle. "You're going to bring that thing down?"

"The heat's going to fry us alive," Rasslebeck added. "You can't."

Do it. Destroy the fiend.

"He will," Maena countered. "Do it, Svarde."

The Foti, grinning, pulled the lever. A creaking heave sent gears spinning throughout the tower, their all-too-many chains jerking into motion. The building rumbled. Maena's feet shook. Overhead, the dark disc noting the tower's top began its descent.

"Now we change the game," Maena said. "Kivi, get back outside. Climb the walls, get as high as you can. Bring these two after you."

"Bring?" Pennifer asked. "Kivi's not that—"

"You'll climb," Svarde said. "Go."

Still looking confused in the scant light filtering in through the tower's open door, Rasslebeck and Pennifer nonetheless followed the lizard.

Above, a blue-orange glow shaded around the descending disc.

"You think this will work?" Svarde asked.

"Are you reading my mind, Foti?"

"I hope so. Otherwise Rasslebeck had it right."

Maena and Svarde stayed in the entry alcove, their weapons ready. The beach and its cool breeze behind them.

The platform came closer. Thumps, an angry snapping joined the chains and their grinding gears.

"Stay close to the door," Maena muttered. "We keep it in here."

"It won't like that much."

"I'm counting on it."

For all the anticipation, the platform fell faster than Maena expected. The air became a cross-section, a battle between chill and fire, every breath mixing the two into a scalding, freezing mix. Maena's eyes winced as the fiend's full form sank into view, the platform it stood on immolating slowly at the heat from the demon's body. That form stood tall and silent on the platform, the clawed chain dangling from its lower left hand while its others held molten ballista ammo.

The triangle obsidian head met the pair square, those golden flashes flaring up as it took them in, realized their alcove would be too small for an easy exit.

Svarde crossed his axes before himself. Maena raised her rusted cutlass, a pitiful shield before the fiend, but one worked with what they had.

Hopefully, the fiend wouldn't realize what was happening until it was too late. Hopefully, Kivi and the others would get their time.

The fiend, though, didn't seem interested in games. In its right hand, it hefted another ballista bolt, the massive arrow a sure kill if it hit either Svarde or Maena this close. A massive arrow the fiend tried to throw, cranking back its hand only to have the missile's tail strike the tower, snap apart amid the intense heat.

The fiend threw the scraps anyway, the tower's tight confines giving it a poor angle, little power. Maena and Svarde back-stepped as the arrow scored off the alcove's side, breaking off rock and showering the pair in embers, burning bits. Maena brushed at them, felt the fiend's heat rise.

The obsidian face flashed faster, brighter.

Yes, make it angry. Good move.

Her only move, more like. Better, too: it proved these fiends weren't icy tacticians. They had emotions, had pride, could be manipulated. The fiend, soundless, began hurling more junk their way, burning wood, stone chunks, pieces of the tower's chain breaking apart under the pressure. Maena and Svarde retreated further, pressing themselves into the alcove behind the ruined door remnants. Poor cover, but Maena kept the scratches, the sears only to her limbs, her hair.

"Any moment now," Svarde bellowed. "Get out of here, you damn thing."

The fiend obliged. With a skeletal jangling, the chain claw flew up, a long toss sending the weapon at the tower's top. The fiend's arm extended.

"Now!" Maena called.

Could they hear her? Would they know what to do?

The fiend, apparently, didn't see a problem. The chain bit in, stone falling around them, and the fiend began climbing its own grapple. Maena and Svarde crept out as the heat receded, watching the fiend spread its width across the tower to straddle the thing, pressing upward with its legs while its arms tugged on the chain.

"Now it's our turn," Svarde said, and the pair moved quick.

There wasn't much science, much method to their actions. Mere seconds were on offer, and they used those seconds in the simplest way they could: if it was sharp, they stuck it in the charred platform, the battered base, with its pointy end facing up.

Maena's cutlass, the metal end of the ballista's arrow, busted spikes from the ruined platform's gears. All found opportunities to stand straight up in the bubbling morass the fiend had left behind. Maena jammed her sword into an ashen pile, left it there. Would it withstand much pressure before toppling over?

No, but would it need to?

"Time's up!" Svarde called and Maena didn't question him, beat back to the alcove, out the door.

Up above, from the outside, Kivi, Rasslebeck, and Pennifer showed clear against the burning city's glow. The other fiend, for its part, didn't seem to notice its partner's predicament, happy to still be launching bombs into the city.

"Cut it now!" Maena cried.

The call rose over the din, sharp and vibrant with a commander's edge. The trio jumped, spread, with Pennifer and Rasslebeck throwing their weapons at the fiend, anything to slow it down. Kivi went for the grapple, something Maena couldn't see from the ground. The ferrite's jaws needed a bite, maybe two.

If they needed three, the fiend would have them.

A single blue burning hand appeared on the tower's lip. A clang sounded, Kivi jerking back—Maena and Svarde rotated around the tower's base, keeping the ferrite in view. The tower rumbled as the fiend struck its walls from the inside. Still, the hand clung. Rasslebeck and Pennifer, empty, backed away, their looks trailing down the tower to the sand.

A fall too far to survive.

Kivi had no such fear. The ferrite scuttled over to the

clinging hand, opened its jaws again, and bit down on the blue fingers. A single snap, with Svarde yelling encouragement, cursing the fiend and lauding the ferrite in Foti bellows, did the deed. The hand vanished, the tower shook, and the beach trembled when the fiend struck the earth.

"Drop the claw!" Maena called up, Rasslebeck and Pennifer already moving towards the obvious end.

The large grapple, still biting into the tower's lip where Kivi left it after snapping the chain, proved hard enough to pry off. Not that Maena and Svarde watched: they ran back to the alcove, the ruined door, sweltering.

Facing them, a hand and head trying to force their way through the door, was the fiend.

Where blue fire had been perfect before, now dead patches loomed, spreading white flakes across the fiend's body, or what little of it they could see.

"A human bruises, these fiends turn to ash," Maena muttered as Svarde tossed her a scrap axe.

Not that the weapon would do much good. Even wounded, even attempting to burrow its way free from the tower, the fiend remained too hot to near.

Instead, the pair did what Rasslebeck and Pennifer had done before: they threw their weapons at the monster. Let the rusted iron fly through the air to bounce off the hand, to knick the head. The fiend stopped at each impact, that obsidian stare regarding them with what Maena could only feel was utter loathing.

"It's a damn hard thing to kill," Svarde said, the pair again retreating, bringing strides between themselves and the fiend.

The monster's chosen path to freedom seemed to be through the sand, through the burning. Shoving stone. The alcove buckled, the tower shuddered again. No mere rumble this time, but the foundations questioning their hold. Sand shifted as the fiend's arms, legs, dug at the dirt beneath it.

"Hurry!" Maena yelled towards the tower's top.

Pennifer and Rasslebeck, with Kivi biting away the grapple's holds, pulled the claw aloft, the weapon almost as large across as their two bodies. For a striking moment, the two lifted the thing as if it was a trophy, before casting it down, those jagged prongs aiming at the fiend, into the tower's burning abyss.

If the fiend hadn't made much of a noise before, the claw's strike gave Maena a withering hiss-pop, like a campfire hitting sizzling steam within a wet log. The fiend's face, the outstretched arm digging towards them, shivered. The fingers twitched once. The head leaned forward, burying its face in the alcove debris. The ash-white followed.

Pennifer cheered. Rasslebeck and Svarde let curses fly. Maena allowed herself a smile. A nod that the plan had, for once, worked out as she'd hoped.

Kivi, between Pennifer and Rasslebeck on the tower's top, opened her vents. The orange glow steamed out into the night, a victory light.

"Got'em," Svarde said. "One down, one left."

They turned towards the last fiend, atop its tower, expecting to see the monster absorbed in its bombardment. Instead, the blue-flamed fiend seemed to be done. Seemed, instead, to be staring at them.

With its left hand, the fiend reached, snapped off a sturdy stone from its own tower's top. Bracing itself, the monster leaned back.

And Maena knew what was about to happen, her feet beginning to give her distance even as she screamed for the others to get down, to get away.

The fiend launched the stone, its tumbling mass a shadow in the night. The rock struck their damaged tower with a muffled bang, rippling the structure, sending all those beautifully molded lines crumpling.

Rasslebeck, Pennifer, and Kivi sank with their tower, crumbling towards the beach as sand and snow flew.

Behind it all, a light covered by a rising dust curtain, the fiend leapt, hit the sand, and began stomping towards them.

Well, captain. Your first plan worked. You have another?

CHAPTER 35

COMMON CRIMINALS

They stalked. They watched. They waited. The Rana town obliged. Some sparse guards, obviously drafted from the townspeople by their loose saber holds, their ramshackle thick leathers, paced the sole main street as night bled on. Bliss and Torny neither earned their attention nor sought it, instead lingering in a sloppy alley near the inn.

Torny had picked out the spot as part of restraining Bliss, keeping the Vis from a more obvious course. The slop came from old soup, from bath water and rain remnants given nowhere to flee. Overgrown patchwork stones marked the alley's middle, while aged crates and barrels waited for action.

Bliss rested her chin on one, a sturdy metal-rimmed construct about her height. From it, she could see the inn's entry, the few people milling about the place. Someone plucked at a lute, an instrument Bliss had never heard before coming to this isle, but had quickly learned to appreciate after the nights and days working the taverns further south.

The Kance had gone in and not left. That they were staying the night seemed obvious now, as did the impossibility of going inside after them. Bliss might've felt revenge's stifling itch, the inability to consider anything other than the decimation of her brother's killers, but the hunter remained sane enough to hold her rage at bay.

There would be time, as Torny said, to catch one, then two, then three.

But the wait for one was proving longer than expected.

A rustle and Bliss turned, hand reaching for her staff. Only Torny, slinking back into the alley with a head shake.

"They weren't stupid, then," Bliss said.

"Nothing on the boat save the things you'd need to move it," Torny replied. "The watch here is a bunch of chumps, but I think even they'd catch us if we tried to row the thing away."

"I wasn't going to run."

"Not run, Bliss. Lead'em into a trap. You're supposed to be a hunter. Think like one."

"I'm waiting for an ambush, aren't I?"

"Grudgingly." Torny tapped Bliss's shoulder as the Vis turned back to the inn. "Here, picked this up on the way back."

A crusted rice cake sat in Torny's hand, one Bliss took with a grateful nod. Her stomach about matched the lute in volume. Stalking prey could satisfy some needs, sure, but it left others woefully ignored.

"Let me guess," Torny continued while Bliss ate, alternating bites with her water skin, as the rice cake had dryness aplenty. "you're thinking we stay the whole night out here, watching the door and waiting?"

'You have a better idea?'

"Look. I know one thing: as a thief, it's much easier to take what you want when your target's distracted."

'By?'

"The whole town's on edge. They've gotta think a fiend's going to attack at any moment. Why don't we make that happen?"

'How's that going to get the Kance moving?'

Torny's eyes glittered in the town's torchlight as she grinned. "They can't lose their boat. Let's make'em save it."

Torny's plan proved to be more than idle chitchat. Bliss listened as the thief laid out the steps, one after another in a strict sequence, a masterwork that had Bliss re-evaluating her friend. Torny had sarcasm, had a strange charm Bliss couldn't seem to shake, but now cleverness too?

Where'd Torny been hiding this?

The thought buzzed Bliss's mind as she settled near the docks, low in the reeds. A silent count ran in her head, ticking off the numbers along with her heart beat. The sweet rush she'd felt just before taking on the fiends back on Vis ran with Bliss now, anticipation tightening her grip on the staff.

Wax. This is for you.

Torny's shout rang the air. The thief hollering off to Bliss's left that there was a fiend, a monster in the waters.

Bliss burst forward at the words, sloshing and swinging the staff wide. She splashed, struck several small crates on the wood boards on her left while keeping her head low, making her way towards the Kance boat. At her waist, its length hidden beneath the water, ran one of Torny's knives.

The thief howled and ran, paying no attention to the shouts following her from the frantic watch. Someone started to ring an alarm bell. Soon, feet, eyes would be at the docks, soon they'd find nothing there.

Nothing, save a single craft drifting away into the current.

Staying low, kicking her feet beneath the surface, Bliss pedaled to the Kance boat. With the staff floating in her left hand, Bliss drew the knife, worked it against the rope tying the Kance boat to the dock. Its threads frayed, though the water made the cuts slip, the knife not biting.

And Torny, ever lackadaisical, hadn't kept the blade as sharp as it should've been.

Bliss thought up curses as Torny's shouts ran out. The thief would be vanishing, disappearing into the trees to avoid any close questioning. Running steps neared, the first hitting the boards.

Her time was—

The rope snapped. Bliss pushed the boat, gave it a kick off the docks before sinking beneath the surface herself. Holding her breath, she angled to her right, back up the coast to those sheltering reeds. The darkness would help hide her, though the biggest aid would come from her pursuit's own cowardice.

Torny judged the town unwilling fighters, people pressed through desperation to take up some small arms against horrors. They wouldn't try hard to find any.

That guess played true as Bliss surfaced seconds later, many strokes away from where she'd dove. Only her head peeked above the river's surface, lilies and other grasses clinging to her hair—while the two had left most of their gear back in the alley, the river's chill water was draining Bliss's stamina. She clambered onto the bank, the cold grasses and reeds doing little to warm her. Shivers rose up, cramping her muscles.

Still, Bliss looked, caught the rabble at the dock's end waving their torches over the river. Some noted the crates she'd toppled, and more still pointed to the Kance boat, drifting further out.

Nobody dared jump in after it.

If she wasn't shivering, wasn't occupied more with her own survival after the icy swim, Bliss might've sighed at the sight. On Vis, courage would rise up. Someone would've saved the boat.

Instead, Torny had to play her second part.

The thief, her face already slathered in mud before her shouting run, would be bursting into the inn about now, calling that someone's boat had been cut free by the fiend and was drifting away.

The real question wasn't whether the Kance would go after their boat, but how many, and could Torny and Bliss capitalize on it?

Bliss, rubbing her arms and legs, the water in her hair starting to freeze, felt her teeth chatter as Silvrin, for once not in her armor but just a linen tunic, some thick pants, ran through the crowd to the docks end. She took a long look at the boat, then asked the crowd to borrow on of their own.

Someone at least proved willing to risk their own rowboat, pointing the Kance to another tied up craft. Silvrin, joined soon enough by a second Kance—Bliss couldn't tell from distance, in the blurry torchlight, which one—kicked off the boat and rowed into the river after their drifting vessel.

Which left one alone back at the inn.

Bliss forced herself up, feet slipping some on the hard ground. The staff helped get her going, pushing into the thicker grasses and trees beside the river, a winding way back to town.

"Hey," Torny whispered, emerging from the dark

several minutes later as Bliss neared the inn's back. "Come over here."

The bandit had their gear, scavenged from the alleyway and ready. Bliss threw on the weave, wiped away the wet on her ragged clothes. Ragged, yes, but still better than skin in the cold. They left the satchels behind, advancing armed and ready on the inn's dim rear.

The sturdy two-story building, standing on bricks and mud, gave way to Rana's ever-present wood and thatch roof. Narrow windows, filled with splotched glass, picked out the seven or eight rooms the place offered its guests.

Torny and Bliss didn't have the time to investigate them all—already, the two Kance would be rowing back to the dock—so they started with the back, and of the four windows there, only two had lanterns lit inside, like spread eyes in the night.

The inn's back door had its own lantern too, hanging from the door's top on a metal line.

Torny, whirling her grapple and launching it at the inn's roof, used that line as a quick step, leading Bliss up the inn's back, feet on stone while her hands gripped the grapple's long rope.

For Bliss, working her fingers back into gripping strength took some real kneading, drew enough of a frown from Torny that the hunter willed her muscles to work, her nerves to feel again.

At least her staff, slotted into its sling along Bliss's back, came along easily enough.

Torny pulled the grapple up after they'd both ascended, keeping low as townspeople filtered back to their homes. Some insisted they'd seen a fiend, others claimed it was a lie, and still more declared their fast action scared off the monster.

Bliss snorted at the last.

"Hold the rope," Torny whispered. "I'll take a look."

The thief was as light as she appeared, though Bliss dug her heels into the roof's slight lip to keep Torny level as the bandit dropped down, using the grapple to hang just outside the windows. The first took a second for Torny to shake her head, whisper that the room belonged to an older couple. From there, Bliss slid along the thatching, moving her feet one after another, while Torny kicked along on the inn's outside.

Easy enough on the inn's back, in the near dark. Damned impossible on the front.

But Vis was with them. At the second window, Torny waved.

"This is the one," Torny said. "Kance stuff everywhere. And it's empty!"

Before Bliss could ask what they'd do now, Torny brought her sleeve to her mouth, letting her one hand and her feet keep her balanced against the inn. With her teeth, the thief tore her sleeve off at the elbow. Keeping the fabric in her mouth, Torny wrapped the cloth around her hand, bit it tight, then delivered a sharp jab with her covered hand to the window.

It rattled. Stayed firm.

"Damn." Torny cursed, let the fabric fall. Drew her knife. "So much for the quiet approach."

This time, the thief smacked the dagger's hilt into the window, shattering the glass. Kicking off the building's side, Torny rocked back, lifted her legs, and twisted inside the small window.

Bliss felt the rope go slack. Stared at it. This hadn't been part of the plan. Torny was supposed to identify the guard's room, then Bliss was going to lead the way inside. Now, well, now Torny was alone.

No, not quite.

Bliss turned, found the grapple's edge and set it into the roof. Drew up the rope. She could let it down, climb along and get into the—

"Hey! What're you doing up there?"

Bliss looked at the shout, saw several people, the innkeeper and a member of the town's watch standing below. The innkeeper had her eyes on the broken glass, the watchman had his hand on his saber as he repeated the question.

And Bliss had no answer. Had no idea what to do when Torny cursed below, the thief's fiery words streaming out the window, followed by blades striking one another.

A plan, a masterwork, a mistake.

CHAPTER 36

GRIM PROMISE

Midnight in the jungle mountains would've been magical under better circumstances, like if Sawi had been ducking beneath ferns and brushing past vines with Wax by her side instead of a grumbling, stumbling Gladdring. However smart the man might be in Noctia's political playground, he struggled in the natural one, and Sawi spent as much time turning 'round to help him over some root or leaf pile as she did keeping them heading in the right direction.

"Always have a point to walk towards," Sawi said when Gladdring asked her how she could navigate the dense forest. "Pick a tree, a mountain, anything that isn't moving and walk at it. It's the first thing we learn."

"Why?"

"If you don't, you'll find yourself walking for hours in a circle." Sawi clambered over a fallen log, turned to guide Gladdring between its gnarled branches. They were both sweating despite the cool air, though at least the insects weren't so bothersome. A small blessing. "Every young Vis learns that."

"A difficult lesson for those on a smaller isle."

"Maybe you need to get out more."

Gladdring chuckled, sat on the trunk with his hands on his knees. "My friend, I've been to every one of our seven isles. Just, perhaps, not this far off the path."

That choice, though, had been strategic. Korrus and his Mottilan gangsters would doubtless be searching for the escapees, and the easiest way to look would be along the sole road journeying from the cliffside city over the mountains and down towards the Najahn outpost and Kitaye. Instead, Gladdring wanted to stay hidden, at least as long as they could.

Such a limit seemed to be rapidly approaching. Sawi gauged her own body, ravaged after the previous night falling across the cliffs, a day spent dangling in a cage with little food, and now an evening fueled by flight's rush. The hours were creeping up on them, and Sawi felt it every time her foot slipped, her eyes mistook a shadow for a tree, her ears the wind's rustle for a hanoko's stalking paws. Gladdring bore the weight worse than her, his stopping more frequent, complaints about blisters and bruises coming not as clear words but through sighs, muttered curses, and ever more questions about where they were, what lay ahead.

"We won't outpace them," Sawi said while Gladdring took his break. She brought herself some relief leaning against a smaller tree, its trunk cold, coated with fluffy moss. "If Korrus wants to catch us, they will. Our only chance was to outrun them on the road."

"Outrunning was never the plan, Sawi."

So he'd said, time and again when Sawi pushed for a turn back to the road. Instead, delay. Grind the hours in slow progress to let Korrus and his team move ahead, fear they'd made a mistake and abandon the chase.

"They hate you. They won't stop." Sawi rubbed her shoulders. Her thin weave wasn't meant for this. "They'll come into the jungle eventually."

"Then tell me, how close are we to the first inn?"

Sawi flicked her eyes up to the sky. Clouded. No help there, not that she knew this route well enough to gauge their place. She could only use the time they'd been traveling, the distance they'd gone down from the Mottilan cliff.

"An hour. Maybe two if the jungle stays this thick."

Gladding nodded, "Then I think it's time. Point me towards the path."

"Point?"

"I want you to head to the inn as fast as you can," Gladdring said, picking up a sparkle, a life. The kind Sawi noticed whenever Gladdring found something tasty to sink his mind into. "If my friends are at all what I think, you'll find them there. It's been long enough. They will be looking for me."

"Friends?" Sawi tilted her head. "I thought you said the other Najahn were your enemies?"

"Depending on the situation, they can be either one. That, though, is not your concern. Go to the inn. Find them. Bring them along the road to me." Gladdring stood, brushed off dirt from his hopelessly torn robe. "If I evade Korrus, then we are saved. If not, then my friends will effect the rescue."

"Why?"

Gladdring waved her off. "When I have more breath, a mug of ale, and a crackling fire, I'll explain it all to you. I have too much dirt on my hands, too many bugs in my clothes. Get going." As Sawi stepped off from the tree, Gladdring said her name. "Remember, helping me through this helps you too. Both of us are in the adventure together now."

Whether Gladdring had that last part right or not was a question Sawi pondered as she whipped through the jungle. However tired her body was, jumping into full-speed swinging brought her back some life. Vines and ferns opened their ways to her, letting Sawi leap through pink-gray shadows, grappling thick plants and slipping along giant leaves. She wanted to whoop—Wax would've—but kept her voice quiet, embraced the jungle's night and gave nothing away to listening ears.

She reached the inn fast enough to, Sawi figured, set a record time if anyone had been tracking. As if all the stress from the last few days served to tense her up, so the flight cut her loose and brought Sawi jogging up to the inn's front door. The building, really a network of rope bridges and ladders to a massive tree just off the path, offered a warming house not much larger than a Kitaye home. Behind it, those ropes and walkways sprawled to individual treehouses. All were dark, though that didn't mean unoccupied.

Blankets, furs, were enough in Vis winters, and putting a flame in a treehouse was a risk accepted in a Kitaye home, among family, but not one taken with strangers. Instead, the innkeepers would lead guests to their houses, settle them in, and leave them until dawn lit the way back down.

Until then, though, pipe flutes and drums would make music. Fresh fruits and soups would serve as a meal, and, at the base, a growling fire fueled by the jungle's cast-offs would give warmth. Sawi took that in now, letting herself inside and shutting her eyes for one small moment, basking in the hot wave waiting for her.

"Sawi?"

Gladdring's warning prepped Sawi well enough. She didn't jump at her name, didn't shy away from the person saying it: the Najahn guard captain. The man, with two other Najahn by his side, sat at a small rounded table. Their chakrams and voulges rested nearby, though the trio looked too exhausted to lift them. Wood cups that would've held fruit wine sat stacked on one another at the table's end, waiting for another round.

A promising state for Gladdring's would-be rescuers.

Sawi dished the story out fast, clipping it to a simple betrayal and subsequent flight. Skars and planned deals stayed well hidden, and when Sawi arrived at Gladdring's imminent danger, the trio wobbled to their feet.

"You hardly look like you're ready for a rescue," Sawi said, watching them struggle to get their chakrams on their backs.

"Najahn are always ready," the guard captain replied, mustering up a half-assed grin. "Nothing on Vis can handle us, even a few rounds in."

Sawi blinked. Thought about pushing that remark. Instead, she held her tongue. Already learning Gladdring's lessons.

The Najahn left behind some cured jerky to pay for their drinks, a delicacy the innkeeper accepted without complaint, and the foursome ventured back onto the path. Sawi's lids felt heavy, her legs more so, but the fire gave her enough to keep on going. Just a little longer, and after the Mottilan bunch were scared off by the Najahn, she could collapse in one of those tree houses and find some sleep.

And Sawi had little doubt Korrus and his jokers would be scared off. Even a little shaky, the Najahn still held a majestic threat in their armor, their gleaming weapons.

They jangled as they walked, heavy boots padding into the path's stiff dirt. The captain pestered Sawi for more details, and Sawi gave them, suggesting the Mottilans weren't warriors, just fishermen and woodworkers frustrated they didn't get the Renewal. Wanting to take it out on Gladdring.

"Like so many others," the captain laughed. "Gladdring has a way of making enemies."

"I'm seeing that."

"Don't let his golden tongue get to you, Sawi. The man's always scheming. He'll use you as long as he can, then leave you behind."

As if those words could surprise her now.

"He said as much."

"The spider telling you about his web as he weaves you into it," the captain replied. "Keep your guard up, is all. Make sure you have a way out."

"Then why are you trying to save him, if he's so terrible?"

"Duty. Nothing more, nothing less." The other two guards muttered their agreements. "We're Najahn, he's a Tenet. Our jobs, our families rely on keeping him alive and safe. Besides, Gladdring's games are above us. We're not the flies he's trying to catch."

Should she mention Gladdring's suspicions? The question hung in her mind as the steps continued, as the path wound into a rocky pass. The clouds broke, Sichi's pink rays dancing between the shadows, marking rose lines on the ground. Highlighting, halfway down the pass, Gladdring's form and Korrus standing above it. Flanked by another Mottilan. The pair turned as Sawi and the Najahn came forward.

The guard captain whistled, chakrams flying off the

trio's backs and into their hands. He pushed Sawi off to the right, clearing their view.

"Mottilan," the guard captain announced, any fuzziness from the wine long gone. "Step away from the Tenet. Leave, and we'll forget we saw you here."

Korrus folded his arms. Sawi gaped at the gesture. The man wasn't running? Him, standing there in little more than a fisherman's garb, with a short club at his waist meant for bashing in a lively catch? Had the Mottilan lost his mind? And Korrus's partner too, also standing up straight and baring teeth.

Were they asking for a slaughter?

The defiance threw the Najahn guard too. The man's mouth worked for a second before he found his duty. Brought the chakram to his side, ready for a slinging throw. The other two Najahn stepped to the path's edges, forcing Sawi up onto the sides. Clearing their lanes.

"This won't end well for you," the guard captain said. "Last chance. Leave the Tenet alone."

Gladdring, for his part, looked up. His face, splashed in pink, bore fresh batters. Bloody pools splashed the stone around him.

"Help me," Gladdring said, his voice a hoarse struggle.

"Come and take him, if you can," Korrus barked.

Called out, the Najahn did as they were trained to do. The three stepped forward, arms pulling back their chakrams. Something whistled past Sawi, then another, and a third. Rocks flying from behind, striking the Najahn hard enough to rattle their armor, turn them around. Softer missiles followed. Small darts Sawi knew well, fired from a Mottilan quartet that'd left the trees behind them for an ambush.

The darts hit home, striking necks and cheeks. The

Najahn reeled, stumbled, fell. Their muscles shook, froth and spit ran from their lips as the Mottilans dashed up and relieved their enemies of their weapons. Sawi watched, frozen both with exhaustion and shock.

Even if she could scoop up a voulge, what could she do with it besides die?

"The prize is yours," Gladdring said, his voice climbing into the quiet air. "Ensure nobody finds the bodies, and I'll keep your secret."

"And your end of the deal?" Korrus asked, bringing the Tenet over as the Mottilans stripped the Najahn. Every armor scrap, every knife and satchel came off. "You'll get the trade?"

"Your city will be richer than ever before," Gladdring replied. Sawi, sitting on the stones, could only stare as the pair spoke, as if what'd just happened had been a mere game. "Noctia and Tamas both will offer their boats to you."

"No lies?"

Gladdring pointed at the Najahn trio, left in little more than their underclothes. The Mottilan loaded their spoils into several large satchels, the armor an awkward fit but tied on nonetheless. A long journey back, but none looked tired at the prospect.

"There are some debts I will always repay, this among them." Gladdring held out a hand and Korrus pulled a small satchel off his belt, put it in Gladdring's palm. "Mottilan's time is coming, Korrus. Be patient a little while longer." Gladdring kicked once at the guard captain's head, knocked it to the side. "And ensure these three are never found."

Korrus's eyes glittered. "Hanoko will handle it." He looked over at Sawi. "And her?"

"She's with me. Part of our deal."

Korrus nodded. "Done, then. Don't disappoint me, Gladdring."

The Tenet offered Korrus nothing more, instead came and sat next to Sawi. The Mottilan continued their work arranging their spoils, with three breaking off to drag the drugged Najahn off into the jungle.

"Does it disturb you?" Gladdring asked.

Sawi, gulping, tried to find her voice. It came out less as words, more as a rasp, a fevered rush.

"You killed them."

"Those three would have killed me as soon as they'd finished with Korrus," Gladdring replied. "Fassle ordered it before we left Noctia. Korrus offered an opportunity. Not quite what I planned, but the man was reasonable enough."

"Korrus? He wanted us killed?"

"No, he wants his city to prosper," Gladdring took a deep breath. "A few Najahn guards can't offer him what I could. He just needed to see it."

"So you used me? You told me to bring those guards here?"

"A chance. If they'd not been at the inn, my position would've been weakened. I would've needed to offer Korrus much more than I did." Gladdring leaked a half-smile. "Perhaps the man would've let his rage get the best of him and killed me. But you found my would-be murderers. I would've been fine with mutual slaughter, but this is truly the best outcome."

"Three Najahn dead is the best outcome?"

"For me, yes." Gladdring put a hand on Sawi's shoulder. "For you too. Now, Sawi, let's get to our feet. One more walk until some much needed rest. Tell me it isn't far."

It wasn't. Though as she walked, Sawi focused less on

her aching muscles, her tired bones, and instead on where she sat within the spider's web. Was she a fly, waiting for Gladdring to eat her alive?

One sidelong look at the Tenet, eyes focused on nothing as they walked, gave her the answer.

CHAPTER 37

WET RESCUE

Sleeping on wet, mossy rock turned out to be both necessary and devastating. Wax and Eujo climbed the rough ladder from the skar cavern up and then up some more, their hands gathering scrapes and blisters aplenty by the time they rose from the small hole onto a small, flat island. Eujo gauged them north of the Whirlpool, gauged too that several hours had passed since the Kance threw them off the boat.

No rescue waited. To the south—a direction easy enough to estimate with the flowing current rolling around them—the Whirlpool's great bulk churned. Their island spread a few strides in every direction, sloping down to the lapping waters. Moss and a few scant weeds dying in the winter's chill were their only partners.

Well, that and exhaustion.

Wax sat down first, when no other route presented itself. Eujo followed. The cavern had blocked the outside wind, had given some shelter, and now they had neither. Soaked clothes offered nothing, and the river water carried even more cold.

"We'll freeze to death," Eujo said, her teeth starting to chatter. "There's no way out."

Going back down wasn't an option. Only the pool waited, not somewhere they could rest. Swimming offered no easy choices either: south, towards the outpost, meant outpacing the Whirlpool, a prospect so impossible Wax wanted to laugh. Any riverbanks were beyond sight in the night's dark, and tired muscles made a chance attempt at a crossing in icy currents a truly desperate move.

Which left one choice.

"We stay close," Wax said. "Hunters do it on Vis, if you're caught out in the mountains on a cold night. Body heat."

"As if it'll be enough."

"It will be."

Eujo looked his way, "So confident."

"Never lack it. Besides, if it doesn't work, we won't know or care."

They found the driest patch on the island. Used their hands to scrape away enough moss to leave flat stone, then, lying down, piled that same moss back over them. Dirt, dead insects, and random roots all formed a natural blanket, albeit a chilly one. Almost without words, the cold keeping mouths shut, minds numb, the two curled into their makeshift bed.

"A long way from your Kance palace, isn't it?" Wax muttered, his cheek on stone, face looking out into the river's constant rumble.

"From your jungles too, I'd wager."

"There's nothing like'em, Eujo. I didn't think I'd miss it, but here, now, it's hard not to."

"They are beautiful. The Great Sana almost matches our peaks."

Wax coughed a dry chuckle. "Almost?"

"Our soaring spears are beyond anything you've ever seen, Wax. They rise up near the clouds, sky diamonds catching the sun's light and tilting it to rainbows all across our isle. At night, Sichi covers the peaks in glittering ruby. Stand anywhere on Kance and you can witness a marvel."

"You sound like you never wanted to leave."

"I left *for* Kance, to protect it. Didn't you do the same for Vis?"

"Vis can protect itself. I'm doing this to keep a promise."

"To who?"

"A friend," Wax started, and when Eujo asked for more, he plunged in, talking about Pan, their adventures among the ferns and the vines until his voice ran hoarse, until the soft, steady breathing against his neck told him Eujo had fallen asleep.

It didn't take him long to follow.

MORNING CAME WITH AN ACHING BACK, sore muscles, and a stomach in dire need of food, but morning did, at least, come. Wax blinked open his eyes, found the sun high up in a brisk sky. Eujo stood nearby, looking over the water. Their clothes remained damp, but no longer quite so cold. The sunlight helped too, scant as it was. As did the Rana skar, clutched in Wax's hands and warm to the touch.

Shaking off the moss, Wax joined Eujo at the island's edge. Her stare went south to the Whirlpool and, beyond it, to shapes moving on the water.

"Boats?" Wax asked, then bent to drink some of the river's water.

A bit perilous to sip directly from the river, but better than dying of thirst. Wax also figured he'd inhaled enough of the stuff during yesterday's forced swim to ensure he'd catch any sickness lingering in its waters. As it was, the cold liquid went down easy, massaged his throat back to life.

"That or a fiend," Eujo said, her eyes squinting, hand shadowing the stare. "Though even if it was a monster, I'd take that to a day spent here."

"I'm such awful company?"

"No, but I might eat you in a few minutes if we don't find something else."

"So quick to cannibalism?" Wax asked, his own look going to the rushing water.

Clear enough at the surface, but the coming chill, the Whirlpool's proximity meant any fish had gone missing. Nothing lingered near enough to grab, the depths too muddy to see deep. No improvised hunting.

"I'm ahead of you in the Renewal race," Eujo said, shrugging. "I think that means you have to give me a leg. An arm, if necessary."

"Official Noctia rules, is it?"

"Very much so."

"Well, before you take a bite out of me, why don't we try waving, shouting? Maybe they don't see us?"

"Aren't you Vis all about your cries?"

Wax stood, stretched. "Just listen."

The whoop came easy, loud and happy. What made Wax even happier was the reply, echoing back from beyond the Whirlpool.

"I know that voice," Wax said when Eujo asked. "Sometimes, a brother can be a good thing to have."

Quik, Castilan, and several Najahn skirted the Whirlpool's edge, taking turns at the oars until they reached the island. Eujo and Wax indulged in the water skin, the food-stuffed satchel on board, telling their story beneath blankets while the rescuers rowed them back to the bustling outpost. In its first full day fiend-free, the town hummed with repairs, with livelihoods returning. Smoke rose to the sky, the air moving from the river's clean wet to the outpost's hot, industrial taste. Fresh fish, harvested marsh plants roasted over barrel fires, making the return a succulent one.

At least for Wax, who found his appetite insatiable. So much swimming had stripped his body raw, and he tried to make up for it in a few hours, a drive that petered out only when he asked about Bliss, about Torny, and caught his brother's damaged scowl. Quik said the pair hadn't left long ago, at the morning's earliest light.

"They thought you dead, and wanted vengeance."

"I'm touched," Wax replied, started to stand from their place around the fire in the same centerpiece where the group had first gone when arriving at the raft city. Already, the ramshackle clutter had been cleared, returned to its rightful homes. A cleaner center now, one with Najahn purple banners unfurled. "We need to go after them."

"Not yet." Quik nodded Eujo's way. The Kance queen, wrapped up in those blankets, had fallen asleep again after her own lunch. "We all need to rest, Wax. I'm injured. You're exhausted. So is she."

"You're telling me to let Bliss, our Bliss, she of the hottest heads, go on her own against three Kance Queens-guards? Those awful asses who beat us up yesterday?"

Quik found a deeper scowl, turned his glare at the fire. "What's to think it'll be different next time, Wax?"

"So don't try?"

"Try what? Bliss and Torny are going to fail. They'll give up, or get beat like us, and we'll find them down south. Then we can all go home."

Wax sat down again, blinked. "Quik, you're not sounding like the brother I know."

"I'm being practical, Wax. Like I always have been. They took the skars, you said. We can't win the Renewal without them, so why put ourselves through this? Why risk our lives again and again when we can go home?" Quik touched a scabbing gash along his shoulder where a Kance rapier had left its mark. "Don't you miss the trees? The songs? Sawi?"

"Sure. I miss mom and dad too. Mangos, the birdsong every morning." Wax spread his hands, raised an eyebrow. "We knew we weren't going to see them for a long time when we left, brother. It's not been so long, has it?"

"Weeks."

"And if I become the Aegis, what then, Quik? I'd never see home again. Never leave Noctia. That didn't stop me. When I took that skar from Pan's hand, I made a promise, and I'm keeping it. At least till I can't anymore." Wax pointed at Quik. "You made that same promise when you asked to be my Guardian. Are you giving up?"

A cruel move, maybe, to push Quik like that. To call him out. Wax might've spared his brother except, dammit, he'd just been shoved in the Whirlpool, just survived a frozen night on a river rock. Going through all that only to throw up his hands and give up wasn't, well, wasn't something Wax could do.

Not yet.

"Then what, Wax? What do we do?" Quik asked. "They have the skars."

A blanket flopped to the floor. Eujo stood, eyes hot. "We take them back."

"Easy to say, hard to do."

"They're heading south. They'll need a boat, and my captain won't give them mine," Eujo said. "Not if we beat them to it." She swept a look from Quik to Wax and back. "When they're trapped, we take what's ours."

"How?" Quik looked down at himself, the wounds. "They'll kill us."

"They fight like soldiers," Eujo said. "The way I see it, there's no soldiers here. We don't play by their rules."

Wax nodded, and even Quik didn't look quite so glum. "We have to find Bliss and Torny too."

"We do that in the city. If we move fast, we'll beat my guards there. They only have a small boat and they don't know the waters. Your sister and the bandit will show up later. Our reinforcements."

"If they're not caught first," Quik said.

"If they're caught, then we'll do what you did for me and save them." The Queen took a long, deep breath. "Come on. There's still a few hours of daylight left. Let's find ourselves a raft and get going."

CHAPTER 38
MAKING GLASS

Svarde hurled a rusted axe at the fiend, the flimsy metal going up in a green burst without making the monster so much as twitch. Beneath its feet, the sand melted to glass, the shimmering kicking up the flame's reflection, broadening its glow, until Maena seemed to see nothing save an immense candle trudging towards her.

"Run?" Svarde asked, both stepping backward on the dunes, the sand getting more loose as the flattening waves grew distant.

"To where?" Maena replied.

A fire wall raged at their backs, Jochi's fortifications turning into tinder. A blaze likely to burn half the town behind. Ahead, other than the sea, sat the crumbling tower and, within it, Rasslebeck, Pennifer, and Kivi.

No rescue offered itself.

The fiend made plain their fate, wrestling its clawed chain free and looping it in lazy arcs over its head. Another moment, maybe two, and the weapon would be in range.

Maena didn't like her chances of surviving a strike.

"Then we stand our ground," Svarde answered, the stoic Guardian flattening his stance, doubling his grip on the remaining axe, as if the thing would help.

It gives him courage. Something you could use.

Maybe, but Maena didn't have something to grab. Something to hold. Her hands caught snowflakes and nothing more.

The fiend smashed its foot into the nearest dune, plunging its fireball into the mound and scattering the molten glass. With the step, the fiend threw its left shoulder forward, whipping the chain towards Maena. Fast for some, maybe, but the strike had distance, had bulk.

Had nothing on a swift saber's swing.

Maena jumped to her right, the clawed hook slamming into the sand and missing her with space to spare. As Maena rolled with the fall, hands and feet trying to get enough leverage to stand, the fiend yanked its weapon back, dredging a deep farrow.

"You alive?" Svarde called.

"And well," Maena answered.

She found purchase, stood and put herself into a run, dashing forward as the fiend, content with its position, swung its weapon again. Maena dove, the flail launching overhead. A poor show.

Well, they've never tried to hit you before.

This time, Maena had the sand's number. She tucked into a small dune's side off the dive, using its upward slope to stop her momentum, rebound back to her feet.

And felt an idea.

The shard stuck her wrist, a small gash, but a useful one. Fresh and hot, right from the fiend's own presence.

"Right!" Svarde's yell, off to her left, and Maena obeyed with a soldier's speed.

The flail's clawed head swept back through where she'd been, recoiling its destruction along the sand.

Maena scooped her hand with the sidestep, gripping a loose pile. She ran to the dune's top, Svarde yelling at her to stay down, and felt the fiend's heat blast her. Several long strides away, the eyeless obsidian regarded her with its implacable golden fires.

"Eat dirt," Maena muttered, at once upset with herself at the line's lack and exuberant at the idea.

She threw, the sand losing cohesion as it went to strike the fiend more as a cloud than a ball. The dirt sparked, fizzled, and melted, the black glass sticking to the fiend amid its fires. The monster stopped, its flail's spin dropping to the dirt as it regarded itself, or at least seemed to point that dark rock face down.

"What did you do?" Svarde asked, scrambling near, though not so close a single lucky shot could nail them both.

Always pragmatic, the Foti warrior.

"The sand." Maena scooped up another, threw it.

The second cloud followed the first, sprinkling into the fiend's skin and sticking. Enough, now, to break through the fiend's burning shell, black mars on its beautiful, horrifying body.

"Into glass," Svarde murmured. "It could work . . . "

"Break!" Maena shouted, moving right. Heading towards the ocean.

And away from any reinforcements, I might add.

If Jochi wanted to help, he would've already done so. The warlord would be hoping whatever remnants still lived outside his burning wall would weaken the fiends, distract them, buy him time.

Maena would destroy it instead, and buy her salvation.

The fiend crackled, dredging up its flail again and following Maena. She glanced back as she ran, trying to time her dodge, and fell on a crab's hole. She pitched forward, stuck in sand. Wet, thick sand.

The fiend advanced, the flail swung. Maena rolled, saw another cloud strike the fiend from its right side. Saw a green gout emerge as the fiend brushed at the dirt, the glass. The flail again dropping as Svarde threw his other axe into the monster's weapon arm.

Distractions. Vital ones.

This time, when Maena scooped her hand through the sand, it clung together. A thick ball, and one that sailed when she threw it. The missile collided with the fiend's chest, breaking and blackening, a dark chink in its fiery armor. Svarde struck with another cloud, then a second, both hands pitching dirt, and not at the monster's chest, but its feet.

The blue leg grew dark at the ankle, around the top, the glass finding like stuff where the foot touched the beach. A trap, but the fiend wasn't simple. With its right hand, it reached down and punched, shattering the sand seal.

And found another dirt ball slamming into the striking hand, sticking the fingers together. Svarde followed with more clouds, Maena seeing her friend less as a body and more as a flitting shadow.

The glass tied more knots, bound the fist to the foot. The fiend tried to break them free, a hard move with more dirt pounding into its legs, its chest, its arms. Maena kept her arms pumping, scooping and throwing as fast as she could.

Accuracy mattered, but not so much as just hitting the thing. Every glass bit weighed the monster down, threw off its balance, and seemed to pain the creature. Enough so when it strained its trapped fist, the glass shattered and the fiend overbalanced, falling backward to land deep in the sand.

Grains flew up, mingling with the snowflakes, and landed on the fiend, coating it in sudden glass. Svarde stopped throwing at all, simply scooping all the sand he could find and shoving it onto the fiend.

Maena joined him, running up to the right side, kicking and throwing sand along the way. It felt ridiculous, insane, wild, and absurd.

Welcome to my life.

The fiend crackled, its own body working against it, melting the sand and fusing its limbs to the ground. In seconds, only the beast's head could move, the obsidian's baleful glare following Svarde and Maena as they buried the monster in a shimmering, glossy tomb.

Even with the glass in the way, getting near enough to the fiend to shower sand on it struck Maena with more heat than she'd ever felt, the very air seeming to lash against her skin, steal away any breath, and force her eyes shut to keep them from boiling. The only spot with any relief was the thing's head, the obsidian blocking the flame, a lone barricade whenever the fiend looked her way.

"Stop," Maena said after one last toss, fusing the monster's neck in the shimmering deep brown glass. "Not all of it."

"No?" Svarde asked, on the monster's other side, body a sweaty sheen. Both had ashen ends where their hair had come too close, caught a spark. Their clothes, what little they had, sizzled on the edges. Maena's own skin crawled with a red ache, but they lived.

"This thing came from the Dark Below, Svarde. We have

it trapped." Maena stumbled back, legs drawing down as the battle's thrill faded. "We might be able to learn from it."

Or, as the Rana might otherwise say, use it. A key commandment of the isle was just that: a raider must seize anything of value, miss no opportunity to claim a resource.

Svarde accepted her logic, gave the fiend a wide berth as he came around to her side. The fiend watched them, sparks writhing the obsidian in a dazzling, angry dance. The glass prison crackled, melting and hardening over and over again. At least, for now, the monster seemed stuck.

A look north towards the city saw its people fighting back. Water brigades, or Jochi's soldiers pressed into civil service attacked the sandbags and burning buildings, beating back the scattered flames. The winter snow kept up its mild assault too, the flakes filtering around the pair and the dunes.

"We should search for our friends," Svarde grumbled, lurching to his feet.

"Go," Maena replied. "I'll watch this one."

"Yell if it's breaking free."

"You'll hear it, Svarde."

"You say that like my ears haven't been burned away."

Nevertheless, with a lone hand landing on Maena's shoulder, the Foti warrior stomped off towards the ruined tower and the bodies that likely lay inside.

Maena kept her look on the fiend, watching those sparks. Fascinating in the night.

What do you think it's saying? Free me?

Weapons, a vessel. These fiends were far from mindless. Svarde had fought smoke creatures when they'd first come to Whent, fiends organized, and, so the man had said, able to speak in a vague form. The memory thief below also worked with more than a predator's instinct.

And don't get me started on those awful eyes.

What was so different this time? Why were there so many fiends reaching beyond the snarling savagery that'd been their status for so long?

"What are you?" Maena asked the monster.

The sparks stopped. Pure black rock looked at her.

She repeated the question.

A single burning line, white-gold, carved up the obsidian's center. The spark went to the stone's absolute middle, glowed for a long second, then burst into seven motes. Those seven spun around the smoldering center in a lazy arc. As they moved, the motes began to dim, while the center, again, grew brighter.

Until, with an orange flash, only the center remained, hot and alive, until it too disappeared into the stone.

Well what do you know, Maena. You might've been the first to talk with a fiend.

"You understand me?" Maena asked, trying at the same time to press what she'd just seen into her memory. "You know our words?"

This time, though, the fiend offered nothing. Only its dark stare. Maena, again, repeated the question. The fiend did not respond. The glass crackled, melted, cooled in its endless cycle.

Maena tried one question after another, a barrage with everything she could think of while the snow began piling up around her. The fires in the city dwindled, the people gaining the upper hand. Behind her, Svarde called out every successful extraction. Kivi, Pennifer, Rasslebeck, wounded but alive.

The fiend did not answer.

Till dawn threatened, her throat long parched, the questions only rasps, Maena asked, and still the monster didn't reply. Only when Svarde, returning to her side, pointed out that the glass no longer broke and crackled, did Maena stand to see the reason, or at least one, why the obsidian stayed dark: the fiend's fire had gone out, and all that remained were its massive, charred bones.

CHAPTER 39

PRISONERS

In Kitaye, justice ran two ways. If the elders found you guilty of a crime, you were offered a chance to labor to make up what you owed. Harvest, fish, hunt, or do what your skills allowed to benefit the community until the city agreed you had repaid the debt. Anything too severe for such remedies ended in exile. Banishment into the jungle or across the seas.

The Najahn were always willing to take in stragglers, reform them or, so Bliss heard, send them swiftly beyond this life to the next.

The Rana town took a harder tack. Both Bliss and Torny, once the bandit had been disarmed by Blinthe, were hauled to the town's center and given an immediate, late night trial. Bliss, who'd only seen a few sentences, who had no way to respond to the questions asked by the town's watch, let Torny deliver their defense.

"The only thieves here are these three," Torny began, a stiff declaration to the half dozen or so civilians bothering to watch, alongside all three Kance.

Torny sprinted through the story, adding in choice invectives as she reached moments, like the casting of the Renewals into the sea, that earned the expletives. The bandit impugned character, wound up the tale with the dire consequences of killing a would-be Aegis, and ended on a plaintive note, asking the town to understand they were merely trying to restore honor, as Guardians, to their slain charge.

That last shook Bliss, a hollow ringing marching in as her own exhaustion mingled with the shock at hearing her brother called dead. Surreal enough with Pan, with all the bodies in the fiend-ravaged town, but to hear the same state given to Wax . . . her head dipped, she pushed back tears. An emotion shifting quick to red anger, and if her hands hadn't been bound, Bliss might've charged the Kance guards right then.

"If your story is what you say, then why not come to us?" asked the leader of the watch, a stout man with more gray in his hair and beard than not. "If these three are heinous criminals, then why skulk after them in the darkness? We might have helped you, or at least offered a fair hearing for both sides."

"That's what I'm—" Torny's wind-up died as the man drew his saber, leveled the curling point her way.

"We're not some regal court, equipped with police and judges, jails and juries," the man said. "Out here we make our calls quick, as there is other, more pressing work to be done. You shattered a window, you assaulted a paying guest, and some suspect the fiend we saw tonight might have had its origins with you." The man waited a breath, his eyes boring into the pair. Torny glared back with equal measure. Bliss kept her face blank, her attention still on

Wax. "Regardless, this isn't a time for deliberation. The innkeeper has taken what she is owed from your satchels. I would cast you out of this town, but these three have agreed to take you into their charge." The man motioned at the Kance guards.

"You mean the ones I just accused of killing our Renewal? Our friends?" Torny asked, and even Bliss's mouth dropped at the idea.

"Accusations only," the man sighed. "And they have offered to pay for you, a trade we can hardly refuse." To his dismal credit, the man didn't seem too proud at where the trial was heading. "They've promised to take you south to the Riroca, where you can press your claims in a place where they'll matter."

"They'll slit our throats as soon as you're out of sight," Torny countered.

The Kance trio, throughout all this, kept their faces stern, their voices quiet. Even when the town's leader looked their way, hoping, perhaps, for some refutation of Torny's remarks, they shifted not one bit. Iron and strong.

"They will not," the leader said, straightening. "We have one last trader, who would have waited until spring to make the journey, but who can go with you in the morning. Her boat will follow yours, and should your bodies find the water, justice will at least find these three."

At that, at last, the Kance resolve cracked. All three sent sharp glares the leader's way. Blinthe even dropped his hand to his rapier, though Silvrin twitched her own hand and stalled the draw.

"Agreed," Silvrin said, "though we won't forget these last additions."

Weariness suffused the leader, "I assure you, I don't

care. Between fiends, the winter, and people like you, the Isles are fast becoming a place I no longer wish to be."

Akido and Blinthe stuffed Bliss and Torny, hands tied, into their boat's bow. Neither, pressed against one another back-to-back, could find much comfort in the hard wood. The cold air snuck around and between them too, their shivering at least giving a measure of warmth. Their captors, with one staying aboard to keep watch, returned to the inn to snatch what sleep they could.

Torny didn't bother. Like Bliss, she worked at her bindings. Unlike Bliss, she gave up soon.

"They're done too well," Torny said, the bandit's head lying, like Bliss's, against the ship's forward rail. The boat bobbed in the tiny bay given over to the town's docks. "These aren't ones we'll be escaping."

Bliss wanted to tell the bandit to keep trying. That to do anything else was to damn themselves to a quick death. No matter what the leader said, the Kance guards could kill the two of them, and any following idiots, without much effort. So she tried, rubbed the ropes against each other, against the wood. The knots had to fray, had to give, had to . . .

The knock woke Bliss up, her head banging against the wood rail as the other two Kance guards loaded up the boat with fresh provisions, their own satchels. Torny's curses rose with the birdsong too, the bandit lighting into the guards.

"Shut it," said Silvrin, finally. "You called it right, rat, when you said we were going to slit your throats beyond the town. Keep up the talking and we'll do it anyway."

"As if you won't, you wind-spitting murderers."

Silvrin took a long stride over to them, while the other

two cast the boat off the dock. She bent down, clad in her glittering Kance armor. A gauntlet hand reached out, snared Torny's ragged shirt. Lifted her up from their narrow stick.

"Say that slur one more time, and I'll gut you right here." Silvrin's other hand made its way to Torny's throat. "We didn't outright kill your Renewal because we're not the devils you think we are. You and your friend don't fall under that protection. If I snapped your neck and threw you overboard right here, nothing would happen. That trader, she won't say a word. Your bodies would be picked over by whatever sad fish swim in these waters. By sunset, only your bones would remain. So choose, rat, whether you want to live another day."

Torny started to move her mouth, gathering up for a spit. Bliss shoved her elbow into the bandit's side, an awkward move, but anything to get Torny to reconsider, just once, making their captors mad.

A quick death here wouldn't get Wax revenged.

"Why?" Torny croaked. "Why bother leaving us alive?"

The woman flicked an irritated look back towards the town, "Because I think that man meant what he said. Because we're Kance, through and through, and word will travel. Reputation matters, rat, though it might not to you. Stay quiet, and maybe we'll even let you live. Keep talking, and I'll not give you another warning."

Maybe it was the prospect of life, maybe it was Bliss's ribbing, but Torny held her tongue. Kept her mouth shut as the day wore on, as the Kance guards rotated turns at the oars, speeding down the river. The following trader fell behind, all but disappeared.

Yet the Kance didn't kill their hostage pair. Fed them,

slipped water skins to their lips, and all the while Torny kept her insults quiet.

At least till night fell, when most boats would've sought refuge and a camp on the river. Instead, the Kance kept up their rotation, the ship cruising down the thin, winding water, always heading south.

Bliss had spent the time nursing her own anger, toying with revenge, mingling it with breakaway daydreams of home, of a life spent without swords and solemn oaths.

"It's easy to be brave when you have nothing to lose," Torny whispered, stars glittering above, water lapping at the boat's sides. "I've spent so long there that it's habit, you know?"

Bliss offered a shrug. Something that'd pass through their touching shoulder blades.

"When Wax died, and you started this little crusade, I fell back into that habit. Kill'em or be killed. But that's not the way it is, right?"

Another shrug.

"I mean, there's still a life out there. Maybe not as Guardians, but what you told me. Going back to Vis, showing me Kitaye. That can still happen. When she had me by the throat, that's what I thought about, Bliss. That's what I say going away when you shoved your damn pointy elbow into my ribs."

A nod this time, hair brushing hair. Torny had it right. Vengeance was a must, but if Bliss could keep herself alive in the process, well, that would be nice. Would be ideal.

"So that's what I'm saying. You and me, we see this out. Maybe we get off this boat alive, get onto another. Go home."

Bliss hesitated. Waited for Torny to come round to what

really mattered. When the bandit didn't, Bliss shook her head. Heard Torny's soft laugh.

"Okay, okay. We kill these bastards first, then home. Right?"

A nod. A promise.

She started working the binds again.

CHAPTER 40

TO THE SEA

Riroca, Rana's southern metropolis, gilded and flush with returning raiders hunkering down for a winter's reprieve, welcomed the Najahn boat with little more than a murmur. The river piers, largely emptied as ships slipped into dry dock, seemed stunned to see another craft coming in from the north, much less one from an outpost little seen, little heard.

Reathe guided the slim craft in, several others onboard gathering up satchels flush with tradeable goods, a couple others with their packs ready to relocate for the cold season. The stay would be short, the path back up north growing more perilous every day.

Not that Wax, Eujo, and Quik would ever go that way again.

"Once in the Whirlpool was enough, thanks," Wax said as Reathe bade goodbye.

The trio did pick up one clue from their docking, though: two more recent arrivals, a trader already making ready to leave, and another group that'd sold their ship as soon as it landed, a sale Reathe invalidated when she claimed the boat as their own. Stolen from the Najahn, a taint no Rana trader would accept, and one Reathe mollified with repayment.

The thieves didn't look as such, vanishing into the city with their glittering armor and two serving girls, or so the dockmaster said. When pressed, he didn't have more to add, claiming he wasn't some spy.

"With their gear," the man offered, "and attitude, I'd say they were heading to the sea port, though good luck getting a real vessel this late in the season."

"Obvious," Eujo said as they left, descended into the town with a straight on objective. "My captain won't let them take my ship without me, so they must have another plan."

"Where would they even go?" Quik asked, Wax's brother recovered well enough from the Vis skar and the long ride down. The man's gauntlets hung at his waist, ready to draw real blood. "All the way back to Kance?"

"With the stolen skars?" Wax added.

"I don't know," Eujo replied. "Silvrin must have a buyer, or some other plan."

"Doesn't tell you everything, does she?"

Eujo grinned, wicked and cold. "If we talk, it's a war of words, Wax."

They reached the port near midday, the hustle as constant as ever, though, like the river docks, less effort went towards unloading and more towards wrapping sails, oiling wood, and tamping down ships for turbulent winter storms. Sailors, some already many mugs deep into their offseason, sang and laughed. A loud scene, a happy one.

"Celebrating what they stole," Eujo muttered as the trio passed by one crowded tavern after another. "Rana's not only raiders, but Noctia ought to clamp down on them. Blockade this city until they put away their arms."

"Why allow it at all?" Wax asked.

"Near as I can tell, it's tradition. Whispers, though, suggest Fassle and the Circle collect tribute in bribes to let it continue." Eujo nodded at a war-going galley, svelte and still bearing its grapples, a deck-born ballista. "Foti makes the weapons, Rana and Whent use them."

"Kance makes the sails, and Tamas brews the ales," Quik added. "It's an industry."

"And Vis gets what?" Wax asked.

"Left alone," Eujo replied, steering them to the pier leading to their own vessel, the nicest one left in the port. "Nobody cares what you do, because you're not a threat, nor a player."

"Thanks, I think?"

Eujo's captain, a stalwart, silver-and-blue uniformed, man introducing himself as Deux, claimed her guards had tried to buy him off the day before. They'd come by with satchels, with two women they called servants but that looked, with their angry stares and filthy clothes, more like hostages. Or worse.

"So you did what?" Eujo asked, the four sitting in *Storm's Edge*'s mess, around a refined beachwood table. "Let them go?"

Storm's Edge had beauty from afar, but up close its craftsmanship forced a reevaluation of everything Wax had seen before. Kitaye's treehouses used to seem incredible for him, nestling as they did between every curling branch and wrapping trunk. Next to the ship's clean lines, her glistening silver-painted body, though, the finest Vis construct seemed a haphazard folly.

The main deck graced their boarding with smooth

floors, every board a perfect fit with the next, the bolts clamping them together painted over to seem like black stars on the near-white wood. Furled sails slotted up against the three masts like both were a single joined thing, a butterfly waiting to open its wings. The cabins, too, offered clean windows, full beds. Storage space for gear.

The Najahn and Foti ships they'd ridden on, in contrast, pressed sailors into tiny bunks, everything inessential stuffed into large lockers in the hold. Even the Kance cutter Wax had taken from Vis to Foti seemed lackluster compared with *Storm's Edge*.

Deux, with a deckhand's help, even served them their first meal on ceramic plates, with real glass cups.

"I suspected," Deux said, "but I couldn't do anything. I'm no fighter, and neither are the few staff onboard. They, though, are no sailors either. We were at an impasse, and rather than push the problem, they left."

"Left where?" Quik asked.

"Another ship," Deux replied. "A Noctia vessel. Some trader scalping the last of the raiding valuables, I'd expect. Squeezed them onboard." Deux forestalled the next question with a raised finger. "They set sail quick in the afternoon. Faster, I'd expect, than the Noctia wanted to. They'll be moving."

"They'll be reckless." Wax read the look in Deux's expression.

"As reckless as you can be in the northern seas this time of year," Deux replied. "The first ice flows are already in the ocean. Any journey now takes risk, and a fast one doubly so."

"But we will ask it of you anyway," Eujo stated.

Deux nodded, "Whent is close enough, their western

ports will still be open for another few weeks yet. We can leave tomorrow, well-provisioned, and—"

"We're leaving today. We're going after my men, Deux."

"The traitors? Let them go. We can deal with them when you return to Kance."

At Eujo's angry look, Deux asked for more and the Queen gave it. With the skars stolen, there would be no victory, no need to go to Whent.

"And if you won't sail," Wax added, "we'll find someone that will."

"No Noctia can out sail you, right?" Eujo said, words everyone understood to be a challenge.

Deux met the Queen's stare with one of his own, a look that continued past Eujo and out the mess's rear window, one looking past Rana's port to the grey sea.

"A chase now risks not only my life, but everyone on this ship," Deux said. "There's a fair chance the Noctia vessel has already met an unpleasant end, one we would never see." Deux flicked his eyes to Wax and Quik. "I'm sorry about your Guardians, and the skars, but adding more tragedy won't bring them back."

"Are you refusing me?" Eujo asked.

"I—"

"Because if you are, then I order you to leave this ship. I will go into one of those taverns and find a sailor good enough, drunk enough, or dumb enough to do what you will not, and we will try."

Deux snorted, "Then you would die."

"A problem you seem pretty able to prevent," Wax said. "Either way, the day's going. Your call, captain."

A curse ended the meal, and set *Storm's Edge* to sail.

Daylight's last hours gave them a good start on the chase, the winter winds catching the Kance sails and sending *Storm's Edge* flying over the waves, often literally, with the ship's barest bottom kissing those white crests as it zipped along.

Quik, claiming exhaustion, retreated to his cabin and collapsed. Eujo stayed with Deux, discussing strategy or relaying the story about the north, which left Wax to walk the ship himself, admiring the construction and watching the waves, trying to keep from focusing so much on Bliss.

Both she and Quik had already sacrificed so much for Wax, from the very beginning of this journey up to this point. They'd been hurt, been held hostage, and so close to worse. All so Wax could chase a dream likely out of reach. With this delay, and Eujo proving Wax's first skars had been slow in coming, what were the odds they'd even succeed? And who really wanted to be the Aegis anyway, stuck on that stone throne getting assaulted by fiends?

Wax found himself at the bow, leaning forward, an overcoat offering some protection from the cold, if not the occasional sea spray. The water flicked his face, nestled in his hair, the sun hidden by clouds as it set behind him. A revitalizing mix, one burying his doubts one by one.

Questions, yes, Wax could have those. Needed to, or else he'd be swinging blind, so confident in his next vine that he'd fall to the floor. But doubts? Hesitation? That'd kill you just as quick.

So no. Wax could thank his siblings, could love them for what they'd done, but he couldn't doubt their decision. Couldn't doubt his own.

He'd keep on trying to be the Aegis, keep on pushing against anything standing in his way, because that's what the journey demanded, that's what he owed Pan, and, dammit, that's what Wax wanted.

He didn't go inside till the ship slowed, settled in a

calmer part of the sea. Deux declared the night too cloudy to keep sailing, not when ice might be around. They'd make up more ground in the morning.

The trek from Rana to Noctia would take at least five days in good conditions, or so Deux said. That, too, with a Kance ship. The Noctia vessel would take at least a week.

"When will we catch them?" Wax asked as the whole group, including Deux's several deckhands, first mate, and cook, gathered around the mess table for a fresh fish—always fresh fish around here—dinner.

Deux bared his teeth, "With good weather and simple sailing on their part, we'll have them by the afternoon. This time tomorrow, we'll all be dead, or dining with your sister."

CHAPTER 41

TWO SOULS, STITCHED

Maena stood again upon the wet sand, the icy waves lapping up to her boots every so often. Exhaustion pressed in on her temples, despite the full breakfast and loamy coffee offered up by the city in their thanks. Her eyes scanned the snowy horizon, watching flakes by their thousand land upon the water or the Rana ships, now being dragged up from the surf to an inevitable dry dock.

Too damaged to take to the sea again this winter, they and their crew were now Whent prisoners. Or, rather, their fodder.

Jochi made the offer around his ruined defenses. While food emerged along with the dawn, the first repairs beginning in a burnt city that found itself still standing, the Whent warlord delivered a sermon of sorts to the survivors, chief among them Svarde, Maena, and their wounded trio.

Pennifer and Rasslebeck didn't hear the words, as they'd been pulled onto waiting wagons, carted off to the city's hospital, a venerable offshoot of the university. There, so Jochi promised, they would receive the best care, coupled with the most promising experiments Whent scientists could divine.

Any further questions on the matter had been brushed aside by the growing crowd, the confusion, and the need for Jochi to stake his claim again as leader.

And he had, by doing what Maena had done, what glory-seekers always did: he made a promise.

"We will follow the trail left by these burning aberrations," Jochi had declared in the cold gray light, standing on half-burned sandbags, his beard snarled with ash. "We will find their homes and obliterate them, we will close the gate through whence they came and seal off their evil forever."

Particulars came next, though Maena found herself hard-pressed to pay attention. Something about an assault on the Dark Below, led by both Whent and Rana forces. Svarde, leaning back on sandbags of his own, openly slept, snored.

That uncommon alliance should've garnered Maena's interest, but its forging came through force, not compassion. The Rana captain—Maena would remember her name later—must've agreed to terms with Jochi, terms that left her remnants alive. Terms made to send them to a deeper, grimmer death.

And you're going with them?

The realization pushed Maena back to the beach after the meal. Jochi had declared a time and place to meet, back near the University, that evening to plan. There the serious work would begin again, another dive into the depths, this one with an Isle's full backing.

Not just old-timers with nothing to lose, you mean?

And with provisions to match. Maena would press Jochi to set up supply lines, establish outposts all the way down.

Not an expedition, then, but an invasion? How merciless.

All the isles had been content to live atop a bomb all these years, accepting and ignoring the detonation lurking below the surface. The momentum was there, at last, to take a serious stab at what mattered most.

Murdering the fiends?

A younger, more naive Maena might have tried to find a better word for it. Something with more diplomatic verve, something more fit for legend.

But yes, murdering the damn fiends. That's what they needed to do, and do it well enough so the monsters didn't come back.

There's my captain. I've missed you.

Maena nodded at the waves. She'd missed herself too. Something down there had shattered her, split Maena apart and left her reeling. She'd lived with that rift too long now.

No more.

Trying to get rid of me already?

Maena knelt in the cold sand, felt the chill leak through her new cloth pants. Looked down into a tide pool at her feet, the lingering water giving a murky reflection. Her captain's visage was long gone, only dirt and ragged energy remained. New scars molded with old, all in a red sheen now thanks to the fiend's fire.

You're ruined, just like me. That'll never go away.

Maena took the glove off her left hand. Reached it into the pool. The ice shot through her skin, and along with it a comfort, a pressure rose on her face, against the same cheek her hand held below.

I could say that I am you, but you already know that.

There were magical things that happened across the Seven Isles. The Najahn explained them away as the leftovers of the gods, while the scientists worked to prove their foundations in natural laws. All Maena knew was right now, right here, she needed to right herself.

Then stop fighting me, fighting yourself.

The reflection scowled. Maybe Maena did too. Not that it mattered. She worked the glove off her right hand, dropped it to the dirt and sent her fingers into the pool to join her left, cupping her reflection. Again that cold, that pressured warmth.

Let me in.

One life, one body, one soul. Only one. Split, maybe, but like any wound, such a split could be healed. Had to be, if Maena was journeying back into that dark place.

A wave crashed in, ran over the pool, buried the reflection in froth. Maena closed her eyes against it, held onto that warm pressure, right where her fingers touched, until, with the wave, the pressure went away. The tide pool leaked with it, the sand holding it together draining aside. Empty, wet dirt remained.

But Maena heard nothing, felt no whispers in her mind.

THE DOORS OPENED as she neared, Jochi's guards pushing them in and revealing the dinner's spread. Svarde, refreshed from a long day's nap, beckoned her to an empty seat near him, the only one left at the table. An arrangement awaited Maena, ranging from academic cloaks and colors, to Rana blues, to Jochi's furs and bright grin.

"At last, our final member," Jochi thundered.

The room matched his voice, a high ceiling at the university's top, broad windows split by crackling fires. Below, the city hard at work fixing the damages. A meaty meal let its thick scent suffuse the air. Ale mugs waited, filled.

Yet, despite all this, Maena saw few smiles. Shoulders were stiff, hands tense, as if searching for weapons to grab.

A war council.

"Now," Jochi said, "we eat, we drink, and we discuss how to do to these monsters what they tried to do to us." He planted his elbows, leaned forward on the table. "Noctia will not help us. The other isles have their own problems. We must be enough."

Svarde again nodded at the open seat, but Maena ignored it. Went instead to the table's foot, across from Jochi, and put her hands palm down on the thick stone slab. Swept a fiery scowl around the group.

"Svarde and I tried once, failed once. We will not fail again." She reached forward. Svarde saw the gesture, passed her an ale mug. Maena took it, held it aloft. "Let's murder those monsters."

Cheers, jeers, and gestures, though no grins were as wild, as hungry, as Maena's own.

CHAPTER 42

CAGE MATCH

The binds didn't come undone. Every time the ropes frayed, the Kance on watch would replace them. Not a one acknowledged Bliss's efforts either, just put a rapier point to her side while another shifted the rope, put fresh strands in the right spots.

After the third time, Bliss stopped trying. Took the opportunity to sleep, however uncomfortable it was. At least the river made for pleasant noise, at least their captors were quiet. No beatings, no random threats. Compared with Sledge and the Foti bandits, these three were postively saints.

Torny and Bliss repaid that kindness in the city. The Kance trio stacked their satchels in the two women's hands, hiding their bindings—shifted to the front—and keeping the pair burdened enough to stall any getaway. The weight, the ropes, those gleaming rapiers spoke of what would happen should the two try to run, so they stayed put.

And the Rana, so wrapped up in their own preparations for winter, didn't seem interested anyway. Torny, at one point, after their fivesome had sold off the boat and ditched the trailing trader, seemed like she was about to holler for help, when Silvrin stopped, faced Torny direct.

"Make any noise, make any trouble, and you'll be dead before you hit the ground," Silvrin said. "Anyone asks why, we'll tell them the truth. You're criminals. Attempted thieves and killers. Not a soul will care."

Good enough to keep Torny's mouth shut, good enough for Bliss to focus her efforts on what really mattered: timing.

If Foti had taught her anything, it was that chances came and went. A moment would come when the Kance relaxed their reflexes, some opportunity would offer itself, and if she was ready, if she took what sleep she found and stole what food she could, then Bliss could take advantage.

That moment arrived on their second day at sea, aboard a slick Noctia caravel headed towards her home port.

The vessel lacked the Foti galleon's raw heft, the Najahn frigate's power, but the caravel nonetheless cut an impressive line through the winter waves. Seasickness normally clinched around Bliss like a vice, but the boat kept its rocking controlled, leaving Bliss with only a vague rock in her stomach. Hardly the reckless vomiting she'd become used to.

That relative health coupled with Torny's sharp eyes and sticky attitude as the pair watched the water roil from a squat cage several levels in the trader's depths. The Kance had put them there, stuck them in a pen meant for livestock. Moldy straw lay strewn about the corners, and the odor of not-quite-cleaned manure pervaded. All the same, Bliss was dry, warm, and her sore muscles had found their strength after the hard journey and the burning battle with the fiend.

"So you're ready now, is what you're saying," Torny

sighed, her back matching Bliss's against the ship's hull. "Everything up to this was just a fun romp?"

'Biding my time.'

"Could've told me."

'You seemed busy.'

Unlike Bliss, Torny had spent the journey testing the limits, and she'd earned some bruises from her breakaway attempts. Once, during the last change of their bindings, Torny had thrown herself overboard, kicking to try and stay aloft. She'd called to that following river trader, hoping for help and getting none.

The Kance had pulled her out first by Torny's hair, the missing chunk obvious near the bandit's right ear. After that, her spunk had dimmed, finding fight in muttered curses and little else.

"Not that it's going to do much good." Torny bonked her head, slow and firm against the dark-grained wood behind them. "We get outta this, all we're earning is a swift punch to the gut and a return to where we came from."

'Don't want to swim in the sea?'

"You try taking a bath in this ocean and you'll freeze up in a minute. This isn't your Vis paradise."

'So we throw them in.'

Troyn flashed a grin, "As much as I like the sound of that, not sure I buy the confidence."

'All we need is an opening.'

"And how're we getting that, Bliss? Ask'em nicely?"

Bliss shrugged. The idea was there. Now, she just had to wait.

Slop for lunch. A thin bowl filled with a rice gruel. A small Rana apple. Blinthe came into their cage, planted the bowls and the flimsy spoons at their feet. Drew the rapier and, with his other hand, reached past and undid the knot keeping the pair bound to the post. A step back, keeping that rapier pointed, and Blinthe nodded at the slop.

"Eat up."

Bliss shrugged from her bonds, leaned forward. Took the bowl, the spoon, raised the food to her lips. The caravel made a slow climb up another wave. Blinthe compensated, leaning towards the pair, that rapier so level, eyes serious.

The caravel moved, the slightest turn as it crested the wave. Bliss used it. Fell forward, throwing the bowl out before her. The slop splattered out, some rolling off onto Blinthe's boot. The spoon bounced off the cage's right iron bars. Bliss felt the rapier's point at her back in an instant.

"Try nothing," the guard hissed.

And cursed, a half second later, as Torny's bowl struck his face. Bliss felt the slop rain around her, the rapier loosing its point a hair, enough for Bliss to reach, grab, and scoop Blinthe's left boot off its hold, aided by the caravel's gentle descent down the wave's other side.

Blinthe fell back, tunic and cloth pants—the armor, apparently, could be left off in the ship's secure confines— making a soft thud as they found obstacles.

Torny cackled as she ran past Bliss, throwing herself on the guard and pinning the rapier to his stomach. Bliss came up to a crouch as Blinthe swung his left fist, socking Torny in the side and throwing her off, just in time to catch Bliss's kick to his face. The strike rebounded the man's skull off the iron bars, sent his eyes crossing.

The rapier wavered. Torny came back at it again, and as Bliss delivered a second snapping kick, Blinthe's grip went limp.

'See?' Bliss signed as Torny lifted the cage keys off the guard. 'Easy.'

"You didn't take a punch," Torny grimaced as they left the cage, shut the door and clicked it locked behind them.

"You could've dodged.'

"I do that, and you'd be skewered about now."

Torny's words faded as they looked around, the surroundings getting a new complexion with freedom. Several other cages matched their own, though these had been stuffed with crates. No other animals on the short journey. Rana rice and spun fabrics, swamp spoils and things Bliss couldn't name pressed in about them, a narrow path marking the only way forward.

"How long till someone comes looking for us?" Torny muttered as the pair started ahead, Torny leading with the rapier. "A minute? Five?"

Bliss would've signed a reply, but Torny's eyes were forward. Instead, she looked past the bandit, measured her steps, the caravel's creaks. Beyond their own, the boat shivered with other boots hitting hard, rushing around. The ordered calm in place yesterday seemed to have dissipated.

She tapped Torny's shoulder, flicked her eyes above.

"Yeah, I'm hearing it too," Torny replied. "Betting that's why we had Blinthe solo today. Something's up."

'Close to Noctia?'

"Not unless this is the fastest ship ever built." Torny bit her lower lip. "Rana wouldn't raid a Noctia ship either. I'd bet fiends."

'Might be the only time I'd be happy to see them.'

"Right up until they eat you, I'll wager."

The two stopped at the slanted ladder leading up to the next floor, with grooved steps to make walking easy. The open door up offered little protection. Conversation, urgent and snapped, filtered through. Preparations being made for a fight.

'Not fiends then,' Torny signed, her fingerwork getting better with every practiced day. 'They don't give you time to plan.'

'Then what?'

'Doesn't matter. What does, is how we're going to wait this out.' Torny nodded back down the ship's length. 'Come on, let's go back to our pal.'

Torny's reasoning came well enough on the walk back. Even if the duo somehow fought and surprised their way through all the guards, the ship's crew, and the captain, they'd then be stuck alone on the seas with a ship neither could sail. Any lifeboat, if the Noctia vessel even had one, would put them in a freezing ocean. Better, then, to use the card they had.

"We keep Blinthe hostage," Torny said, pointing the rapier at the senseless body in the cage. "Hold the line down here till we dock. Trade his life to be let free."

'You think they'll do that? Let us go?'

Torny nodded. "We're bargaining chips, Bliss. Don't mean anything to them. Bet we're more annoying. They'll ditch us the first excuse they get."

'So all my brilliant move earned us was a wait outside the cage instead of in it?'

Torny held up a single finger. "What you gave us, Bliss, was choice." She frowned at the spilled slop. "Though you could've waited till after lunch. I'm starving."

CHAPTER 43
CALL AND RESPONSE

Wax waved the rapier through the chill wind. The blade had a nimble feel, as if it could dart and dash with a wrist flick. Deux, the captain, had spent a few hours over the last day giving Wax a few pointers, correcting the stance, the swings, both different from the heavier Foti blade.

That weapon Wax presumed lost, vanished in the northern Rana swamps after the Kance guards jumped him. If he was lucky and the Queensguard kept it, maybe Wax would find it stuffed aboard the Najahn trader.

If he was lucky, Wax would end the day alive, unharmed, and victorious.

Deux expected to come upon the Noctia ship that afternoon, and the captain held true to his word: at first a dark blue shadow on the horizon, the trading ship resolved itself against the waves and the gray sky as minutes spun. Wax and Quik threw on their linens, the latter still with his gauntlets, and stood on the bow. Eujo remained with Deux on the ship's bridge, talking strategy.

"Or deciding to turn us in," Quik said.

"Because that makes sense," Wax replied, staving off a shiver. Linens aside, winter came on hard up in the north. "She'd do all this just to, what, have her guards gut us?"

"I don't know, Wax. After Foti, and now this, I don't know how you can trust anyone that's not part of our family."

"I choose to, Quik. That's how."

His older brother shot Wax a classic look, the one with a single raised eyebrow saying Wax needed to get a grip on his naivety. A younger Wax might've been infuriated, prone to snapping back.

This one, the Renewal about to get his skars back, only smiled.

"Good thing you don't have to worry about it," Wax said, slipping bravado into his words, just as he might if they were back on Kitaye and Wax was proposing an expedition. "Just follow my lead, brother, and you'll be fine."

Quik, at least, could laugh at that.

Deux's other crew assembled as best they could as the Noctia trader drew near. Three deckhands, rapiers and grapples at the ready, joined Wax and Quik. Informed them, too, that Eujo and Deux would be remaining on the Kance vessel.

"Too scared?" Quik asked.

"Too important," came the deckhands reply.

Eujo did, though, come through with a plan. Wax and Quik had precisely zero experience with ship-to-ship combat, much less a boarding operation. Eujo seemed to understand that, seemed to understand, too, that numbers wouldn't be on their side. A Kance deckhand couldn't handle a Queensguard in a fight, much less a Noctia crew.

So Eujo settled on a bribe, one called out to the Noctia trader as the two ships drew alongside. The Noctia ship's upper deck clustered with workers, easily double the deckhand's number, most looking at the armed Kance crew with something akin to stupefaction.

Raiding, after all, wasn't the Kance habit, particularly during a Renewal's peacetime shroud.

"A trade," Eujo called from the vessel's top deck, Deux standing beside her with an imperious scowl on his face. "The three traitors and their captives on your ship, and in exchange, you get their armor and weapons."

When Wax, standing with the deckhands and looking across the narrow abyss between the ships, heard that offer, he scrunched up his nose, glanced at the queen. A few suits of Kance armor hardly seemed worth it.

That impression, though, died quick when he heard the deckhands whistling and whispering around him.

"Guess that's a big deal," Quik muttered.

Big enough, anyway, for the Noctia trader to agree in seconds, only to declare that he couldn't force the Kance guards to leave his ship. The Noctia captain, a squirrely man with hands always moving in and out of his thick robes and their pockets, declared only that he and his crew wouldn't stand in the way.

"So generous," Wax said.

"A merchant's way," Quik added. "There's no profit in joining the fight, only in picking up the spoils."

Those spoils, Wax figured, might earn themselves a few more dings and dents before the battle was over.

The Noctia captain allowed a boarding ramp to slam down between the ships, the walkway shifting with the waves, but easy enough for Wax and Quik to walk. The deckhands followed, rapiers drawn.

"Where are they?" Wax asked the Noctia captain as he

set foot on the black wood. Sails snapped overhead, but otherwise as much silence as the sea allowed reigned.

"We've three decks," the Noctia captain said, his face tanned and dry. "Your prize will be in the second, their captives in the third."

Wax started off that way, then stopped. "Why'd you allow them passage? You had to know they carried unwilling prisoners."

"They paid a good price," the Noctia captain said. "You're offering a better one."

"The more I see of the world, the less I like it," Quik said, behind him. "How many ways down?"

The Noctia captain pointed to a single open, downward ladder. Large enough to hoist a massive cage, with ropes and pulleys alongside it. "That's the only one. I'd expect they know you're coming."

"Then we need to find a better idea," Wax said.

Bravado was one thing, rushing headlong into sword fighters more than able to tear him apart was another. Wax, looking at the portal down, nodded. "Quik, we've got prey backed up in their hole. How do we get'em out?"

Quik grinned. Looked across the deck to the waves beyond, eyes getting a distant glaze. A hunter getting pulled back into the game. "A couple options, but here, I'd say a little break, a little quake."

"You're not sinking—" The Noctia captain started, only for Quik to reach, put those sharp wood claws at the man's throat.

Rapiers fled sheathes, and the Noctia crew, those loyal enough to the trader to do more than retreat back a few steps, pulled out their own daggers, clubs, and sabers. A motley battle about to break on the rolling seas.

"Hold on, hold on," Wax said, spinning slow—harder

than expected on a ship's deck—to throw placating palms up to the whole crew. "It's a play. They think they're going to get sunk, they come up, nobody gets hurt. See?"

Now Wax just had to hope the Kance weren't listening in, but at least the weapons dipped, the scowls flattened into suspicious stares. No stabs, no spears, no smashed skulls.

"Then do what you want," the Noctia trader snapped, pushing himself away from Quik. "If you hurt my ship, however, I'll see to it the Najahn come calling. I have friends with them, you know."

"I'm sure you do," Quik replied. "Wax, you want to do the honors?"

"Happy to."

The idea came from home, swimming in the inlet. Dive underwater when someone dove off the dock and you'd hear a rumble roll through the water. Get a big enough jump and Kitaye sailors on the lily leaves would feel their feet tremor. The Noctia ship's wood ought to carry the same shakes, might even give some good cracks. The question now, with deckhands and Noctia crew alike staring daggers at each other, was how to get that rolling thunder going.

Deux had the answer, and it lay in the great weighted anchor at the *Storm's Edge*'s prow. The ocean's depths meant it wouldn't hit the sea floor, but a few rapid hauls and drops would get the noise Wax wanted. With any luck, it wouldn't smack the Noctia ship . . . Much.

The plan readied up in record time, both ships staying tied tight to one another, drifting over waves on the gray, snow-drift day. The Noctia trader kept up his muttered complaints, ignored by everyone. Quik and Wax had their eyes on the ladder below deck, listening now to a frustrated fight between Akido and Silvrin below.

"They're suspicious," Quik said as Wax joined him, the *Storm's Edge* making its first drop.

The anchor plunged into the ocean, splashing up water with a thunderous smack. Both Silvrin and Akido stopped the chatter for a long second while Deux's deckhands began hauling the anchor back up.

"They should be," Wax said. "They need to be scared."

The anchor dropped again. Another smack. The current pulled the anchor's great chain this time, brushing against the Noctia ship in a creaking scrap Wax heard and felt through his feet. The Noctia trader squawked, his deckhands cursed. Nobody, though, made a move. Wax waved at Deux, standing near his crew and looking immaculate, as ever, to drop the anchor again.

The captain complied, the anchor dropped, the loud splash, another tremor. Silvrin and Akido started up another violent chatter, their words just too quiet to make out. Quik leaned closer to the ladder, trying to listen in, when the words cut off. A stomping commenced, but the wrong way, heading deeper into the ship. Wax met Quik's frown with his own, started to voice a new plan: take Silvrin, alone, and get the others after.

That plan died with a deckhand's shout, with the anchor's chain pulling the wrong way. With a clanging yank, the chain broke free from its handlers. The *Storm's Edge* lurched in towards the Noctia ship, the boards linking them cracking. The reason why revealed itself in the next instant, a deep purple, writhing limb rising from the surface and slapping the *Storm's Edge*.

The Noctia ship jumped, rose up from the water and tilted. Quik fell, vanishing down the opening to the lower deck while Wax rolled past for a moment before the craft settled, something new, something awful rising in the sudden gap between the two ships.

A fiend?

Wax tried to square the awful luck, the low chances, until a continuing grinding noise drew his eyes back to the *Storm's Edge*, to the anchor still drawing out, and had his answer. Now, as the air filled with curses, orders, and screams, they had to survive.

CHAPTER 44

BELOW DECK

Blinthe did not like being locked in the cage. As the guard woke, he started shouting, and the ship did little to keep those sounds suppressed.

'Let me take the lead,' Bliss signed, swiped rapier in hand as she occupied the narrow hallway between stacked crates.

There'd been a huge lurch moments before, but the ship's rocking seemed to have settled for reasons neither Torny nor Bliss cared to speculate. Blinthe's constant cursing, threats, and cries for Akido and Silvrin drowned out the muffled noises from elsewhere, leaving them in an odd pocket.

Hope for rescue wasn't something Bliss dared dance with, not at this point. Better to trust only in her grip on the blade, and her chance for surprise.

That chance came when the first armored leg hit a visible rung, Akido calling out a question to his shouting friend. Where was Blinthe, where were the two prisoners, how safe was it?

Not safe at all.

Bliss, whose skill with a sword sat somewhere between nil and marginal, pressed her only advantage and ran straight at Akido with the rapier held out like a spear.

The move might've worked on someone less skilled, on someone dulled by ale or time, but Akido, his back facing Bliss, either heard or predicted the charge and turned, sweeping his own rapier with his right hand to deflect Bliss's move and send her stumbling past towards the ship's aft.

Akido dropped the rest of the way as Bliss pushed off a soft crate, turning to see the enemy's rapier coming in for a heart-stopping stab. She fell back, her own short height coupling with the distance to give the guard a grazing blow and no more.

Not that Akido would give her any opportunities. The rapier jerked back a hand's length, then jutted in again, this time aimed at Bliss as she kicked away on the floor. The blade pierced her side, hot pain coming with it. She tried to scream, her butchered voice a mangled yelp instead.

Bliss flailed with her own rapier, sending the blade towards Akido with enough wild rage that he took a step back, batted the strike away. With his left, the man drew the dagger at his waist, again leveling the rapier.

"Drop the blade, and you might live," Akido said.

Bliss only spat in response. She pressed her left hand to her side, felt the hot, sticky wet, the pain constant now, but not enough, not enough to make her surrender.

She kicked back, bought herself a stride's space and threw her shoulder against the crate to her left, leaning on it to keep herself upright.

Akido only sighed. Came in again with that leading stab.

Silvrin shouted up above, a warning about something

gone wrong. To hurry. Akido's eyes glinted, a sane glare. Finality.

Bliss raised the rapier, shot it forward. A hard stab, one the guard deflected with his dagger, sliding the blow away and past his left side. The killing riposte should've followed, but Akido stiffened instead, his mouth dropping open in both shock and surprise.

Not death.

"If you killed her, it's gonna be so bad for you," Torny hissed, her head appearing around the guard's shoulders. Those bandit eyes found Bliss, tracked to the placed hand, and went dark. "Oh, you—"

Torny's curse died in a yelp as the ship shuddered once, then broke hard to port, cracking sounding through wood planks suddenly rising, breaking around them. The large crate near Bliss, its rope restraints snapping, surged forward as the hallway tilted. Dropping her rapier, Bliss tried for an instant to push back on the crate.

It cared not.

Neither did the ship, continuing its roll and throwing Bliss across the hallway into falling crates on the opposite side. Her nemesis continued, breaking through its ropes and sliding towards her, about to smash Bliss into so much slime.

But Vis live and die by reaction, by instinct, and Bliss rolled to her right, farther away from Torny, Akido, and the falling crate. The wood-and-metal box slammed down behind her, breaking through its target. Rana ceramics shattered, their sound mingling with a furious crackle, a noise Bliss wouldn't have known save for one terrible night:

The Rana roller, sinking at the fiend's vines.

Wincing, drawing her left hand away from her wound, Bliss pulled herself to a leaning stand, the ship finding some equilibrium now at an angle. The water roiled somewhere beneath her feet, icy cold.

The crate's devastation left, at least, a damaged path back towards the ladder, towards where Torny tussled with the guard. The pair didn't fight so much as scrabbled, striking each other and falling junk with every close range punch and kick. Bliss would've expected Torny to lose a fight like that, save for the knife sticking out from Akido's shoulder blades, right in the crease between his armor. The same red staining Bliss's side leaked there, and as Bliss limped towards the tangled pair, the knife's work slowed punches, left them weak. Akido knew it too, taking any chance he could get to scrounge for another weapon, to reach for a rapier.

Convenient, then, that the falling crate, the listing ship, had left Bliss's blade sticking up from the cargo now at her feet. She tugged at it once, found the point embedded deep. Another pull, still nothing save a groan.

Torny cursed, drawing Bliss's glance in time to see the bandit take a kick, falling back along the hallway to the ladder's edge. There, halfway down, glinted more armor, moving gingerly.

The sight and its sure end made Bliss's decision an easy one: charging in wounded without a weapon, even as Akido retrieved his own, would be the worst form of suicide.

Torny would have to hold on.

Gripping the hilt with both hands, Bliss didn't pull, but pushed. Leaned on the rapier's hilt, shoving with her legs. The ship shuddered, something distant snapped. Blinthe screamed, a pure echoing terror.

And the rapier's tip broke.

Bliss stumbled forward, dragging the broken blade free. On her right, the slanted hallway offered splintered handholds, the crates and cargo a battered, treacherous line. At its end, though, lay Torny, trapped and looking between the guards on either side.

The path to her target might've been tricky, but Bliss dealt with the ill footing like she'd tackled every thorny frond, every vine as likely to drop under her weight: with speed and sure steps.

One stride forward, her left foot landing on the edge of the hole created by the plummeting, crashing crate. A push-off, angling left and up, giving her right foot a chance to catch a grip on the tilted hallway floor. The rapier flipping to her left hand so Bliss could snag the ruined rope restraints, still tied to the boat's ceiling and offering just enough to keep her moving.

Just enough to jab the rapier forward, faster than Akido dodged.

The strike bounced off Akido's back, the rapier's jagged point sliding up the smooth Kance armor and wedging beneath his helmet. A useless blow, save that it brought Bliss charging, pushing, flying into the guard, and together the pair mashed into Torny.

Or, at least, that's what Bliss thought would happen. She figured in the moment the rapier glided off the Kance metal, that she'd blown it. Cost the pair their lives at long last. Yet in that tangle, buttressed by the wall holding the ladder between decks, Bliss looked up and saw the ever-nimble bandit squeeze against the hallway and stay on her feet.

"Perfect timing," Torny said, snatching Bliss's broken rapier from a groaning Akido. She swung the blade up and right, parrying Silvrin's stab. "Any more tricks, maybe?"

One. As Silvrin moved in to press Torny, Bliss reached across her own face to snag the dagger jutting from Akido's shoulder. She yanked it free, Akido screaming in the process, and jabbed it against Silvrin's ankle as it stomped down near their struggle. The dagger glanced off the hard armor, but in the way surprise attacks do, the stab drew Silvrin's attention.

Just long enough for Torny to counter, stab into Silvrin's heart. The rapier's jagged end blitzed again off the hard armor, but the blow forced Silvrin to retreat, a maneuver turned into a mistake when Akido, in apparent pain and without his mind, tried to rise up. His shoulders struck Silvrin's retreating knee, knocking her to the ground with a heavy wallop.

In a flash, Torny stepped up over the two, had the busted rapier ready for a mortal strike.

"Give up," Torny announced, her voice more than a little deeper than before, "or, you know, suffer the consequences."

Bliss shoved herself free from Akido, stood to see one pallid face, eyes almost closed, and another angry glare.

"You haven't won yet," Silvrin replied.

"Looks pretty good from my view," Torny shot back.

"Only because you aren't listening."

As if she'd pulled back some veil, Silvrin's words brought in the outside noise. The continued cracking and snapping around the ship as whatever had collided into it continued its breaking advance. Sailors called out to one another, words speckled in with raw fear. Splashes sounded too, distant thuds as things heavy and alive hit the frigid waters.

"Guess we'd better kill you quick and get outta here," Torny said.

Bliss tapped the bandit's shoulder, 'We need those skars.'

"Oh yeah," Torny said, pushing the rapier's edge closer to Silvrin's unarmored mouth. "Where are you keeping those?"

"In our cabin, where else?" Silvrin shook her head before Torny could ask the follow-up. "I'm not helping you—"

"Torny! Bliss!" Quik's voice followed his head as the Guardian leapt down the ladder, those big gauntlets on and wanting blood. "You're alive!"

"No thanks to you," Torny said as Silvrin flicked her eyes between both of them. "Try to take longer next time. It really helps."

"We're under attack by a huge fiend, in case you didn't notice." Quik looked down at the guards. "Looks like you've got these two?"

When Quik returned his eyes to the pair, looking them over to see if they were hurt, Bliss signed the story, with Torny interjecting. A succinct summary, ending when the boat rattled again, water making its presence known in a rush not far below their feet.

"To the cabin then," Quik said, starting to turn. "This ship's not going to last long."

"Hold on," Torny said as Bliss made to follow. "We left these three to drown in a roller and they made it. Not making that mistake again."

Torny didn't wait for a discussion, but neither did Silvrin, who swept her arm, her whole body across. The swing knocked Torny's rapier aside, Silvrin not stopping there. She threw her left arm back, its gauntleted hand gripping Torny's rapier blade. A jerk pulled the weapon free from Torny's hand and—

Bliss kicked. Hard, straight, and right into the Kance leader's chin. Her head snapped back, those eyes went hazy. The rapier clattered to the crates on the floor. Bliss raised the dagger, stopped. She'd never done it before, killed someone in cold blood. An animal, prey, a fiend, one thing. But a person?

"Do it," Torny said. "Or give it to me and I will."

The ship cracked. Began listing back to starboard. Bliss and Torny braced themselves on each other, arms spreading across what'd been the hallway. Quik spread his own, the gauntlets carving into the ladder's side and crates still held fast on the other. Both guards tumbled over one another, a heap at Bliss's feet.

Both still alive, both deadly enemies.

"Bliss, we need to leave!" Quik shouted.

And still she held the dagger, trying to decide.

CHAPTER 45
GODS AND THEIR GIFTS

L ike a nightmare come to life, the fiend rose up from the churning waves. The ocean's foaming vortex spoke of the thing's arrival before its body cracked the surface near the two vessels, the boarding ramp and grapples straining to keep both ships together. With Quik dashing down the ladder after the Kance guards, looking for Torny and Bliss, Wax stumbled up top, hearing sailors curse and fall around with him. The rapier bounced from his hand, lost as Wax steadied himself on the railing, looking over at the monster and recognizing it.

The gargantuan thing that'd terrorized Kitaye was here, again. No, not the same fiend: while this one bore scars and damage like the other, its colors differed. More purples and blacks as the tentacles rose up from the waves and slapped the ship's sides. A deckhand—Wax couldn't tell if they belonged to the Noctia trader or Eujo's crew—tumbled off the side, plunging into the water and vanishing. Someone fired a crossbow at the monster, the pitiful bolt lancing into the creature's side and prompting nothing, no recognition from those hideous yellow eyes.

"Wax!"

He looked up, hands gripping the railing like iron. Saw Eujo on her own upper deck, her face a Queen's stoic mask.

"There's no winning this! Get your Guardians and let's go!"

Wax wanted to laugh. How, how was he supposed to get his brother and sister out of this? He could barely keep himself standing straight. Nevertheless, he wheeled back towards the ladder, took a single step, and found the ship rising beneath him. The tilt swung the boat to port, putting Wax's back against the railing. More sailors flew by, some quick enough to hold on, others missing their grabs and falling away. The wood beneath his feet shook, a violent quake accompanied by creaks and cracks. Boards breaking.

Water would follow. Wax didn't have to be a sailing expert to know this ship wasn't long for the surface.

The choice to flee or stay didn't wait for him: the fiend's approach came with slapping rage, one bent first on the ramp between both vessels, already cracked after the splitting lift of the Noctia trading ship. The fiend simply rammed through the remainder, Wax catching full view from his railing grasp. Bigger than either ship, the fiend seemed to be making its way through, and damn anything unfortunate enough to be caught. Its forging shoved both craft apart, Wax lurching forward now as the tentacles pitching the boat port-side slithered away, leaving the fiend's bulk to move the ship opposite.

Again wayward sailors and miserable deckhands tumbled. This time, Wax followed them. His grip, the wrong way for a forward fall, slipped on the wet railing. He moved his feet on instinct, kicking them ahead so he slid down with his eyes up, just like Wax would on a massive fern frond deep in Vis's jungle.

Unlike those ferns, Wax's path had an opening right in his way. Beyond it, the cracking ship left a clear run right to the roiling sea.

After experiencing the chill in Rana's wintry lakes, an ocean with literal ice floating on it promised an uncomfortable swim.

Wax crouched as he slid, aiming to duck right inside the ladder to the lower decks. Where he'd go after that was a problem for another second, a problem Wax didn't get to solve as the ship rocked again, pushing further away from the fiend and sending Wax into a sudden leap. He flailed his arms, kicked his legs, and found no vine, no sturdy tree to grab hold of. His stomach dropped, his eyes locked on the roiling water, until his world shifted and Wax swung straight into the buckling boards.

The hit blew out his air, left Wax's eyes swimming. Blood ran from a bit lip, and Wax felt a dozen splinters find new homes in his legs, but for a moment he hung there, just below the opening.

"Got you." Quik strained, pulled Wax up. Dumped him over the lip. "But I guess we're not going this way?"

Wax shifted, pushed himself almost all the way inside before Quik stopped him. A look into the lower deck revealed Bliss and Torny waiting behind, both grappling with ropes, broken boards, and ruptured cargo to keep moving towards the ladder. Wax's sister held a knife in one hand, looking back at a dark drop. As if making some decision, Bliss flipped the knife away, getting both hands helping her balance. If any Kance guards remained behind, Wax didn't see them. Down below, what should've been the boat's dark hull was instead the blue-white sea, lit by silver beams coming through cracks in the sinking ship.

"The ships are split apart," Wax gasped as the quartet

looked at one another, around them for answers. "Eujo's ship is gone."

"Well that's a problem," Torny replied. "Specially 'cause I don't like getting wet." She nodded down towards the sea, its churning waters approaching with dire speed. "Already been soaked once on this trip, would rather not repeat it."

Wax could agree with that sentiment, but he didn't like their chances. Any lifeboat, if the Noctia trader even bothered with one, would already be gone or destroyed. Surviving a float on wreckage might be possible, but Wax hadn't ever seen a shipwreck before, much less been a part of one. How easy would it be to get out of here and drift on a board?

A whisper, though, offered a different idea.

"Did you get the skars back?" Wax asked, flinging the question at all three.

Quik turned a curious look at the other two. Bliss eyed Torny, who shook her head.

"Silvrin hinted the stones were in their cabin, but that's back there," Torny pointed aft, away from their opening and through a whole disastrous tangle.

"Then don't wait, get going after it. All of us."

The three others didn't move, looking at Wax with a sort of pity, as if the man's commitment to the Renewal now meant he'd doom himself. Not something he had time for.

"Follow me, you morons," Wax cracked, ignoring his battered self to kick away from Quik.

The ship's inside held little in common with his favorite jungle, but that little bit was the most important: hand- and footholds offered themselves up with every motion, be it a hanging bit of rope, a cracked board, or a dangling hammock that'd lost half its pegs. Bliss and Torny let Wax go by, and Wax didn't bother looking to see if they'd follow.

He only said the words:

"We get those skars, we get out of here alive."

A foolish promise, maybe, and one made as Wax ducked beneath a tentacle breaking apart the ship above him, but the only words Wax could think of that'd get his friends moving. With mutual curses from Torny and Quik, Wax soon heard the cracks and clutter as the trio followed, meeting him at the ship's aft, where two cabins waited. One, below Wax, had already lost its door to the sea. In between it and the other cabin sat the opening to the lowest deck, where Wax heard more cursing and metal clanks.

Apparently Torny, Bliss, and Quik had left someone alive.

The door before Wax had lost a hinge and hung askew, revealing cots and belongings. Enough to reckon it a good chance, because they'd only get one. Balancing on a broken board, Wax tried to tear the door away, but the remaining hinge held itself firm. Trying to open the door wouldn't work either, the handle a tough reach at an angle without leverage.

"Move," Quik ordered, and Wax pressed himself back against what used to be the deck's floor.

His older brother stepped past and swung his right arm, the heavy gauntlet slamming against the doorframe. Splinters flew, the door broke, and the hingeless half dropped into the drink. Wax whooped, and Quik kept right on going, hitting the door again to clear the lower end away, save for a small square clinging to that stubborn hinge.

Following Quik inside, Wax stood on a cot as water began leaking in below. Both of them, joined fast by Bliss and Torny, ripped open satchels and pried up the lone lockbox. Frowns abounded as hands came up empty.

"This isn't Kance stuff," Torny said a few seconds in. "Noctia, all of it."

The wrong cabin.

Everyone had the same thought, eyes going back to the exit. Wax hit it first, scooping himself out and back to the balancing board. Below, their target disappeared beneath the sea. Water flowed into the lowest deck through the opening, and the sinking seemed to be going faster now.

"There's no time," Quik said, voice dead and defeated.

"Always time for something," Wax replied, and dove off the board.

As he jumped, Wax reached into his pocket, caught the Rana skar as it started to fall free. Its whispers had been growing as the sea came closer and closer, pulling Wax towards the water, and now those same whispers grew to a burbling cacophony, rougher than Vis, continuous, unlike the Foti skar's aggressive bursts. Whether those noises meant anything, Wax would find out.

He struck the water, Wax's head, shoulders, chest, and his whole length went numb almost in an instant. The cold stole his breath while the bubbling churn forced his eyes closed. Wax tried a kick, pushed himself to the right towards the cabin and its ruptured door, or at least where he hoped it was. He felt the first stroke, the thrum in the roiling water, but not the second, as ice stole the sensation away.

Hitting the cabin came less as a sharp knock and more as a stubborn stop to Wax's progress. He forced his eyes open, accepting the blurry gray and the salt's sting that came with it: the pain would be better than death.

Yet, as fast as that sting came, it vanished. The pressure

on his breathing faded, and Wax pulled himself inside the cabin, following the blown-in door's lead to a sunken space flush with floating cots, with baubles and bags drifting around. One in particular caught his glance, a tied-off gray pouch poking its way from a satchel.

Wax had seen the Kance put the skars in that pouch way back on the Rana river, and he reached towards it now. He couldn't feel his fingers close on the bag, but he saw his grip as bubbles, froth swirled. Wax pulled it in, made to move back towards the door, the Rana skar pounding in his skull.

The little stones were miracles.

Miracles with limits.

As Wax tried to kick towards the door, he didn't move. The water barely shifted. Instead, he sank towards the room's bottom. The Rana skar kept Wax from needing to breathe, kept his heart thundering in his chest, but Wax didn't know how, couldn't call on the stone to push him up and out. He tried to focus on his legs as he settled on the room's bottom and came up empty, his commands going to nowhere, as if Wax floated detached from his own body.

The only part with any feeling now came from his left hand, the one holding the skar pouch. Wax tried looking that way, found even that simple movement sluggish. Still, his fingers on that hand responded when he found them, when he told those tips to dig for the warmth, opening the pouch just enough to reach inside, to find what Wax hoped waited there.

Two Vis skars, two Foti skars, and they all leapt at Wax's touch, their voices mingling in with the Rana roar. They flooded Wax's growing panic, the Vis skars flushing away the numbing chill, as if Wax had stepped into a warm bath. The Foti skars made that warm bath a reality, suffusing Wax with a desperate heat. Bubbles ran away from him on all sides, the temperature throwing the room into roil.

One more whisper came through, a sly and slithering voice speaking the same word over and over again. It seemed to play with the other skars, and as it did, Wax felt his body lighten. The sinking reversed, Wax using his left hand to grab as many skars in that pouch as he could, but holding most to this last, strange one. He rose in the room, kicking legs that, again, had feeling. With the Rana skar in his closed right hand, Wax swam in awkward glory through the broken door.

And rose.

As if he, too, were one of the many bubbles around him, Wax bobbed through the boat's wreckage. He burst through to a dark surface, the trading ship's hull slivers overhead. Around him, almost oblivious to Wax's return, were his brother, sister, and Torny, all with their mouth's above the water gasping for breath. Their skin looked blue, their motions slow.

Torny didn't even have curses left.

She wouldn't need them. The Foti skars told Wax what they wanted, not in words he could understand, but in tones he knew well. Shoving his left fist, the pouch and the skars, up against the hull, Wax felt the stones rush, a sudden flare burned his body and the dark wood exploded.

CHAPTER 46

THE GRAND BARGAIN

Sawi and Gladdring picked up the scholars at the Najahn outpost, beneath the Great Sana's sky-spiking glory. Gladdring spun the narrative, aided by some dirt, some scratches, and plenty of real exhaustion pasted onto their skin and clothes. The Najahn guard captain and his two friends had come upon Sawi and Gladdring under attack by a fiend in the mountains, the pair making their return from Mottilan after successful negotiations. Fearless, the guards threw themselves at the fiend, buying time with a fatal sacrifice.

A true tragedy.

If the Najahn leaders at the outpost bought the story, or questioned it, they didn't say. Instead, they held an impromptu memorial service for the fallen, raised their mugs, and sent Sawi and Gladdring to get cleaned up.

The march to Kitaye passed with words throughout the day and late into the evening. Gladdring kept Sawi close, peppering her with stories of his travels, of Noctia and the Najahn. His motives weren't hard to guess, and the Tenet spelled them out clear as Sawi's home treehouses came into view.

"I want you to come back with me," Gladdring said. "To Noctia."

Just two months ago, Sawi had told Wax no to such a thing. Eight weeks picking fruit and wondering whether she'd made the right decision. At the time, it'd been an idle musing, as she had no other choice.

Now, again, the branch was being offered. An escape from a life she'd wanted, then realized was missing the thundering roar she wanted more.

"Because you want someone loyal?" Sawi asked.

"Because I want someone who can see with different eyes," Gladdring replied.

The ambush and murder of the guards had settled into a subtle shock, starting quick that same night on the mountain pass. Gladdring's excuses made incursions on her opinions, chipping them away until anger, confusion, and doubt turned into acceptance, understanding. If the Tenet saw his world as one of knives and turncoats, then were his actions really that surprising?

Were they excused?

Vis worked on trust, honor, and efficient kindness. All things Gladdring kept saying were commodities on Noctia. Sawi should feel like taking his invite would be poison, a walk into a dangerous, alien prison.

But she'd seen the alternative. She'd climbed the sana, waited till her watchers said Sawi and her satchel could descend. Nights alone, or with new, haphazard friends wondering whether another fiend might emerge to terrorize the town. Wondering what her real friends were doing, out there among the isles.

"This chance comes around once," Gladdring continued, the first Kitaye traders calling out their offers as the Najahn party hit the city. "If you say no, I'll understand, but you will never get to reconsider."

"If I say yes, what will we do?"

Gladdring, jostled the satchel tied to his hip, hidden beneath his robe. In it, Vis skars rattled.

"We'll save our Seven Isles, Sawi."

CHAPTER 47

AFTER SHOCK

Coming back from death took shock, took desperation, took the dark wood all around her breaking apart in a fiery curtain, scattering boards, bolts, and all that went with them into the icy sea swallowing her whole. Her body numb, breath catching, eyes locked above, Bliss wasn't in any position to do, well, anything save panic.

The day's light, at once clean and clear, cut through her frozen mind. Not just because the gray stood in harsh contrast to the dark wood, but because there before her sat the sloping, slimy fiend. Its back half, rising from the sea like some soaked stone, flinched at the wood barrage, the huge creature sliding away, its tentacles sweeping with it. The water chased, pulling Bliss, Torny, Wax, and Quik into its path.

A great yellow-green eye, far larger than Bliss, angled their way and Bliss felt she could see herself an infinite number of times in its glimmering iris. Could see, too, its tightening glare.

The fiend's tentacles swept in from all sides. Bliss

couldn't do anything save kick and paddle, even that faltering in the cold water, so when a tentacle took her, drew her up from the sea in a broad arc, Bliss found herself immobile. The wind replaced the water, equally effective in stealing her breath, freezing her muscles. The tentacle itself was a pressure, Bliss's ribs aching as it wrapped around her.

If death seemed ready to claim her, Bliss at least had a good view before she would go. Down below her feet, tentacles snatched at the others, bearing not just Torny, Quik, and Wax but other squirming and dead forms too. Bashing them against each other or flinging them into the air. Nothing remained save a burbling whirlpool where the Noctia ship once floated, spare wreckage drifting without aim.

Hopeless, save for a blowing horn off to Bliss's right.

She turned, matted hair a frozen cloak along her cheeks, and saw Eujo's ship, sails unfurled heading not away, not in a sane escape, but instead changing its direction. A charge, the Kance bow pointed right at the fiend, a creature whose eyes, whose focus, bore in square on Wax. Why?

The explosion. At first, Bliss wrote it off as a fortunate tentacle smash, but that wouldn't explain the heat that'd caressed her in that instance, at once too hot and yet so very welcome against the numbing cold. Wouldn't explain, either, the fiend's sudden rage.

Wax, always pulling tricks.

Not that this one would matter.

Bliss's tentacle seemed to recover its purpose, realize that dangling Bliss above the waves wasn't worth it anymore. With an unfurling snap, one Bliss watched ripple out from the fiend's moldering base, the tentacle brought Bliss down towards, again, the icy water. She couldn't do anything, couldn't move her arms, couldn't—

No. A hunter, like its prey, had to use everything she could. Every possible weapon.

Bliss bit. Leaned forward and chomped with her chittering mouth, sinking her teeth into the dark ribbon holding her fast. The skin parted, rubbery, with little defense. Something hot gushed into her mouth. Bliss coughed, retched, but the tentacle jerked, stopping the downward thrust and curling, like a reflex, in towards the fiend's body. Bliss's feet brushed the waves, her boots long since fallen off.

What worked once might work again.

Bliss attacked a second time, as big a bite as she could manage. Again the tentacle spasmed, but this time it whipped free, recoiling and throwing Bliss across the waves. She bounced once, a hard hit off the water, rolling, only to smash into the fiend's body. Slime coated Bliss in an instant, gumming up her hands, her legs, her hair. And yet, the slime brought a certain dead warmth with it, an instant cloak.

How, perhaps, the fiend could survive such chill waters. How, now, Bliss could catch her breath for all of a second, plastered there against the great monster's body as the fiend thrashed. Her eyes tracked Wax, her brother, the Renewal, flying away as the tentacle holding him launched Wax into the air. A speed and distance that ought to mean certain death.

He plunged into the sea with a broad splash, vanishing beneath the waves.

Despair, though, would have to wait. Before Bliss could react, could process the chaos, the fiend lurched, rising up from the water and twisting, bringing Bliss's side up and tilting towards her back, so that the Vis huntress rolled in a goopy mess across the fiend's body, along one of those great eyes, and into the soupy mass on its head.

There Bliss saw the reason for the fiend's distress.

Eujo's ship, that great Kance vessel with its wind-slicing profile, stuck from the fiend like a gigantic spike. Eujo herself, along with the deckhands still aboard, stood at its bow with rapiers in hand, stabbing at the fiend. They paid for their bravery in ichor, in the writhing beatings from confused tentacles. More bodies splashed into the water as the fiend gave up its attentions, the tentacles pushing Eujo's ship away, sliding the fiend apart from the spear. An awkward escape, managed more by shoving Eujo's ship off course than by speedy swimming.

A prisoner on the monstrous island, Bliss tried to move. Her body tingled all over, the slime bringing feeling back to her arms and legs. Enough to try to rise, the slime sticking with her like a living blanket. The fiend fled, leaving a wake and, behind it, floating people calling for help. As Bliss stood, she saw Eujo's vessel drop its two life boats into the water, those deckhands reaching out with oars for the desperate and dying.

Not that they'd reach her. Not, at least, if Bliss stayed atop the fiend.

She took a step, slipped, fell and planted on the fiend's gross skin. Tried to plant both hands to rise again, slipped a second time. The fiend drew further away from rescue. The cold water, Bliss noticed as she put her elbows beneath her, came nearer too. The fiend wasn't just swimming away, but descending beneath the surface. Whatever distant dreams Bliss might've had of living on a fiend island in the sea were dashed.

As if.

Bliss imagined Torny cursing her out, for slipping and

faltering, and forced herself back to her feet. Turned towards Eujo's ship, hoped they saw her, and took one, two sloppy strides before the slime had her slipping again, this time rolling, falling off the fiend's side into the choppy sea.

The water closed about her, yet didn't touch her, save around Bliss's face, the one part that'd missed a direct smack against the mucus. Bliss kicked her arms, her legs, and found the surface fast. The slime seemed to buoy her, bob Bliss above the waves. Light enough even, she dared entertain, that Bliss might be able to swim near enough Eujo for a rescue.

The thought, like a Foti forging lighting in her stomach, spurred Bliss into frenzied action. She slashed the water, attacking every wave like it was her most hated enemy. One spared glance behind her confirmed the fiend's retreat, the creature disappearing with nary a hint of its rampage. Only the wreckage lay around Bliss, her body amid boards, cargo, and random ruin.

Whether Quik, Torny, or—

Her hand brushed something soft yet solid. The mucus clung to the object, and Bliss slowed her swim enough to look. A pouch, its drawstring half undone. As her fingers gripped the fabric, some small warmth came through the bag's base. A familiar kind. Bliss turned the pouch, reached inside as her legs paddled against the sea. Inside sat two stones, both warm, both surging different whispers into her mind.

One she recognized, the calming sounds of Vis. The skar leaped to life as she grasped it, finding Bliss's wounds and attacking them with tickling ferocity. The other, though, lay in wait, so quiet as to seem nearly asleep. When Bliss brought her other hand over, swapped the quiet stone, she understood: Foti. A skar that, to believe Wax, required aggression to be awakened.

Wax.

Bliss swung herself around, searching and seeing nothing. The fiend had thrown her brother in this direction, and the pouch confirmed it. He wouldn't be far, but where? How could she . . .

There. Turned over by a wave and now, as if guided by some gentle hand, angled right side up. His nose and mouth barely breaking the water. Bliss threw herself towards him, every battered bone in her body doing its best to carry her through one wave after another. She burned with the effort, Vis skar be damned, and reached Wax only to fall limp at his side, the slime keeping her afloat.

Her brother's eyes were closed, his head a bruised patchwork. Wax's left shoulder hung at a sharp angle, too sharp to be healthy. Blood pooled around his legs where the water, as sharp as any stone at Wax's impact speed, left its scarring mark. With all that, too, Bliss found his skin near to ice.

But his fists were clenched, both, and Bliss figured she knew what lay inside. A bulwark against the worst, but not an invincible barrier. He needed help, needed a chance for the Vis skars to do their work.

Bliss couldn't give him that chance. Not that she didn't try, treading the sloshing water, at first putting her hands beneath Wax to try and prop him up, then slipping her arms around him when it became clear Wax wasn't going to sink. Was, in fact, a life raft for her. She held him tight, felt the water's chill begin to encroach as the fiend's slime slowly, slowly washed away.

Eujo and her vessel grew more distant with every second too. Bliss tried raising an arm, waving it, but not a soul there seemed to be looking out towards the horizon, hunting for specks on the sea.

Soon her legs would give out. The slime would wash away and she would freeze, or the skars would keep her on the brink of life till some sea creature devoured her and Wax. Or they starved, adrift in the ocean.

Adrift.

The thought, coupled with her own fatalistic musing about the Vis skars, had Bliss looking closer at her brother's closed hands. How was he keeping himself afloat? Wax never mentioned that power within the life-giving stones. Revelations, and with them hope, flashed from one to the next: Wax being here meant he had to have survived the Whirlpool, which meant he likely had a Rana skar.

And those Kance guards had looted Eujo too, and she'd had a stone from the isle. Both of those might explain why Wax drifted atop the waves as if untouched. Either one might be something Bliss could use.

She shifted down Wax's torso. Found his left hand, lifted it from the water with her own and placed it on her brother's stomach. Still kicking with her feet, bobbing in the waves, Bliss pried Wax's hand open. Three stones fell, landing on his soaked linen. Bliss recognized the Vis and Foti skars, but not the glittering silver third. Kance? Rana?

Wax gasped, a pained sigh as his body sank into the sea. Acting quick, Bliss scooped the stones up, shoved them back into Wax's hand as the first wave washed across his face. By the time it drained away, he was back to being a placid raft.

More riddles solved. The silver skar kept Wax afloat. The Vis skar kept him alive. Foti would be useless, or nearly so in the open sea. But what about his other hand?

With her legs starting to go numb, Bliss lunged over her

brother, grabbed his right arm and pulled the hand across his chest. Pried it open like the other one, this time doing a better job to cup the stone inside between her right hand and Wax's own. Easier to scoop it back if he fell. Except the teal skar didn't seem to have an effect as it tumbled from Wax's palm into her own.

But the whispers, the whispers that came pouring into Bliss's head at the skar's touch. They urged her to go, to just kick her legs and she'd find the sea her willing servant. Not literally, of course—Bliss couldn't understand the words themselves—but the rush now was one of triumph, power, and home.

She cupped the skar in her right hand, used her left to grab Wax's own arm, and looked back at Eujo's vessel. Still searching for survivors.

Two more were on their way.

CHAPTER 48

THE WILD LIFE

He woke and fell back asleep too many times to count in the days that followed, as Eujo's ship continued on to Noctia. Someone tied him into a bed, necessary, so Eujo said, to keep Wax from falling out. He'd twitch, spasm, roll and thrash about in his sleep, or so the Queen said every time her visits coincided with his lucid moments. Occasionally Bliss, Quik, and Torny would be there too, though they all looked about as bad as Wax felt.

The skars, those miracle stones, appeared at their limit, though Wax heard their whispers raging in his mind, a furious hissing onslaught as the Vis skars attacked his wounds, knit his skin and bones back together. With only two skars and so many wounded, though, those attacks only happened here and there, when one could be spared.

Wax, apparently, wasn't so close to death that he qualified ahead of the deckhands, ahead of his own brother and sister.

He'd lost consciousness when the fiend flung him down into the water, regained it on the bed, and took his first free steps in the hour after the Kance ship docked in the Ringed City's port. Eujo was there to help him up, offering her arm and keeping any winces and worries off her face. Wax's gratitude for that little gesture ran deeper than she'd ever know.

A flat sun marked his exit, a slow walk in cleaned Kance linens, onto the ship's deck. Eujo, after confirming Wax had never seen Noctia before, took him to the boat's prow, let his eyes wander over the gray, sloping city in silence.

"Pretty ugly," Wax whispered.

His voice felt charred. His left leg weak, where some exploding metal from the sinking ship had found a home. Nobody knew how to cut it free, so it festered there, sealed in by the skars. Eujo said he'd have to learn how to deal with the imbalance, that he would, with time.

If those two things were his only problems, maybe Wax might've found a sly word to say, something clever at the sight of the Isles' stone seat. Instead, he wanted nothing more than to turn around and crawl back to the bed. There, at least, no fiends would find him. No killers would tie him up and throw him away.

Death wouldn't be so close.

"There's a lot to see," Eujo said. "It would do you good to go for a walk."

"Would do me better not to die," Wax replied. "Myself, I mean."

"Not the words for a Renewal."

Wax shrugged. "You have a ship and more skars. If you want the Renewal and whatever sits in that city, it's all yours. I'm done."

"Quitting isn't something a Renewal can do, Wax."

"Oh no? Watch me."

Before Eujo could say another word, Wax turned on his

heel and limped back inside the ship. Walking was hard. Locking the door to his cabin and falling on the bed was easy.

Q̲ᴜɪᴋ ᴡᴏᴋᴇ ɢᴀsᴘɪɴɢ ꜰᴏʀ ᴀɪʀ, something he'd done every day since the fiend nearly drowned him. He still felt the ocean's hungry waves burying him, freezing him, closing in like a vice. His right wrist, wrapped and set after the break, responsible for saving his life. As the fiend's snapping tentacle let him go, the hunter had reached out with the gauntlet, those pointed ends snaring the fiend's flesh and calming Quik's descent at the cost of bone. The pain, then, should've blacked him out, but Quik could master pain, could control his body, and he shoved away the dark in time to fall from the fiend and splash into the water not far from Eujo's vessel.

Kicking, struggling, grabbing onto a floating board to stay alive as his skin froze, his lips turned blue, Quik held out till a small life boat found him, pulled him onboard and wrapped him in thick blankets. Eujo herself did the wrist wrap, a technique every Kance urchin learned at one point or another, broken bones being a common ailment in the sky cities.

"Falling," Eujo said, as warm as Quik had ever seen her, "has its consequences, and you fall a lot growing up on Kance."

He took his turn with the Vis skars along with everyone else, though like Wax, Quik found himself keeping inside the ship. Every time he'd wander to the railing, see those waves, his chest grew taut, his muscles wavered. A coward's feel, but he couldn't find a way past it, no matter how much he tried.

His cabin, at least, offered some relief. So, too, did Noctia.

With a silver Kance cloak on, fresh gray linens wrapping his chest and legs, Quik ducked off Eujo's vessel. They were docking for days, at least, for repairs from ramming the fiend—Eujo's call, that—and possibly longer if the ice kept the path between Noctia and Whent closed. Not that Quik minded: The Ringed City felt sturdy beneath his feet, a sensation he'd prefer to keep as long as possible.

Bliss and Torny, to hear Eujo tell it, were already off the ship and in the city. Quik hadn't made friends with any deckhands, so he wandered into the metropolis alone. His height, bulk, and curious hand, coupled with the gauntlets hanging from his waist, ensured a wide berth as Quik navigated the port, always angling deeper into the isle, and higher.

He had a destination in mind, questions that he might get answered, and possibilities to explore.

Quik had seen Wax precisely one time since the fiend, and his brother seemed a faded man. No grins, no tricks, only haunted eyes and a broken body. If Quik had lost any love for the sea, Wax had lost any love for life, for adventure. The Vis Renewal was shattered, and with that end came a choice: home to the isles, or somewhere, something else.

Parvi, back on Foti's coast, had left Quik with an opening. The Najahn were always looking for new recruits, and the possibilities were limitless.

If Wax was done saving the world, well, Quik could still fight for it under the purple and black.

. . .

THE RAMMING SAVED TORNY. Literally knocked into the fiend right beneath her tentacle, severing the wet limb and sending both her and it crashing onto Eujo's deck. Sure, the weight snapped the railing and made an ugly dent in the Kance ship's wood, but hey, Eujo earned a bandit for her troubles. Torny, bearing a few bruises but little else, rolled off the tentacle and took a spot on the prow, pointing out people for the lifeboat to rescue.

Including Bliss, who'd emerged amid a growing desperation with Wax in tow. Torny's rapid fire invectives drew everyone's attention to the struggling Vis, and Torny had spent the next few days at sea making sure Bliss, Quik, and Wax never missed a meal.

"And you owe me for all that," Torny said as she and Bliss shared an ale in the Rat's Fang. The first proper drink she'd had in far too long, and the malty caramel warmed her up just like it should've. "I'm not your mom, and I'm not your maid."

'But you are my friend,' Bliss signed back.

The Vis seemed a little nervous at first, here amid all the bustle of the Isles' largest city. Torny, though, calmed the jitters with facts and frivolities, pointing out all the places in the massive port where Bliss could see or score things that she'd never find on Vis.

Theater troops from Tamas, live zephyrs from Kance ready for racing, golden raiments woven on Rana and for sale by desperate traders trying to clean out stock before Winter froze the northern routes, all for the viewing and the taking. The rush brought a vital color back to Torny's cheeks, a pulse to her heart.

She'd run from this damn place, and she wouldn't be doing it again.

'You lived here?' Bliss signed.

"Did, once. Loved it too. But things change, right?"

Bliss glanced down at herself. Torny followed the look and fought off a frown. Unlike Wax, Bliss had kept herself mostly unscathed, minus the scratches, the gashes, the bruises worn by everyone on the ships that day. No, the Vis seemed to turn inside more often than not, counting down the lives lost between both ships, and how close Wax was to numbering among them.

When Torny had asked, on the second day, why Bliss seemed to obsess over the dead, Bliss replied that she'd seen so many in such little time. Life on Vis hadn't been so hard, so murderous, and being so close to so much loss was getting to her. A pressure she couldn't seem to shake.

Back then, on the ship, Torny hadn't known what to say. Nobody leaned on her shoulder asking for advice, for comfort.

Now, with a bit of boozy confidence, she had some words.

"This is it, Bliss," Torny started in, building up like water running down those sloped Noctia roofs. "You had your charmed life, but the Isles don't work that way. They're hard, brutal, stained with shit." She hesitated. Timing, in a speech like this, was everything. Torny had learned that much from Sledge. "But it's beautiful too. You've gotta move past the dark, find the good. Look at what we've done, the people and places we've saved. That Rana outpost? Torched if not for us. All those skars? Lost if we don't chase those Kance jerks and slow them down. I bet your brothers would be dead a dozen times over if you hadn't come with'em too."

Bliss laughed. 'You're right there.'

"And guess where I'd be without you?" Torny continued. "Back on Foti, either dead in that Najahn raid, or sweating in a forge, working the iron. You saved me from that. It's not your fault what happened back there, so don't you let it hold you back. Your brothers need you, and so do I."

The Vis wasn't much of a blusher, but Torny saw some definite red in those cheeks. Before Bliss could find some way to demure, to dodge and deflect, Torny raised her glass, pushing Bliss into a clink, a bond.

"To this wild life, and winning the Renewal," Torny said.

The smile, when Bliss touched her glass, meant everything.

CHAPTER 49

RENEWAL'S PROMISE

Dark came early in the winter, and with it, the ship burst into a golden life. Deck hands, most still recovering or mourning lost friends, nonetheless found some solace in duty and lit the lamps. Beyond, the Ringed City sparkled up along the mountainside. Almost beautiful enough to make Wax ignore the guarded parapets, the frigates out at sea watching for encroaching fiends. Not that he could see all that much out the small window from his bedside.

After making the journey to the deck, he'd come back, settled beneath a blanket that somehow felt lighter than air, and drifted through a dead sleep. A knock had jolted him out, given Wax just enough time to observe the evening spectacle, before the door's lock turned.

"Hey," Wax started as Eujo walked in, decked out in leathers, complete with a Kance rapier at her hip, that suggested an evening lacking in quiet. "I was—"

"You were doing nothing important." Eujo cut him off. Hard steel, as ever. "You're leaving. Now."

"What?"

"You said it yourself. You're done. My ship, my people, my resources are supporting my Renewal, not your moping. So leave."

Wax blinked, sat up straighter. Felt a thousand hot arguments begin to bubble up. All the danger he'd faced, the injuries he'd suffered, the guilt-tinged fear as his siblings dodged death for Wax's quest, each one rose as a knife ready to stab Eujo's cold words.

"Unless," Eujo said, drawing the word out, those eyes getting a mischievous crinkle Wax had never noticed before. "Unless . . . but no. You're not ready."

A tempter's trick. A lifetime with jokers like, well, himself made it easy to recognize the trap Eujo laid, but what waited on the other side? A lost man could find comfort in a road revealed, and Wax had nowhere else to go, so he took the step on the path Eujo offered.

"What?" Wax asked. "What am I not ready for?"

"I've lost my Guardians, if you can even call them that," Eujo replied, her hand tracking to the bracelet on her forearm, where four skars gleamed. "Deux and the ship's crew can sail me around, but they're not going to follow me to the skars. Your brother and sister, and the thief, all seem capable enough." She slowed again, curled up the slightest smile. "A deal. You can stay here, lay here in your self-pity, if you ask your Guardians to join me instead."

An offer Wax could refuse. An insult, trying to steal his Guardians. Wax slipped from the bed, stood, tried to put on some rage and remembered he wore only a slight Kance shift. Clenched fists and a scowl could only do so much with nightclothes as the backdrop.

Eujo laughed, though her mocking edge didn't grace the sound. "At last, some emotion out of you."

"I'm not dead," Wax sputtered.

"Could've fooled me, and everyone else on this ship." Eujo dropped the mirth, put a pointed finger on Wax's chest. "Do you agree? Your Guardians and your pitying bed?" A miserable silent second to let Wax stew. "Or do you have a different idea?"

Wounded, distraught, afraid. Wax could be all those things, true, but he was also Vis's Renewal. He was still the man who'd promised his friend to see the journey through, no matter how many scars and skars he'd have to collect on the way.

As those thoughts took root, the endless whispers from the Vis, Rana, and Foti stones hummed. Mostly, they were quiet, but at Eujo's barbs, as Wax gathered up his will, the Foti skar jumped to life. It flared, a rush pushing Wax to reach for the necklace around his neck, the metal running hot. Eujo followed the move, saw the ruby glimmering with a forge's fire, and her eyes went wide.

"Wax, don't burn my ship."

"I won't," Wax said, sweat beading on his skin in the chill room, his whole body running hot. Another skar mystery? Would he immolate himself? Did it even matter against Eujo's dare? "I won't give up my Guardians either. I'm a Renewal, same as you. You want my Guardians, then we get your ship. All the way through Kance."

Eujo tilted her head, "I already have my home skar."

"Through Kance, or we leave now and you go alone."

The Queen returned his hard look, then nodded. "You have yourself a deal, Wax. Or, should I say, Renewal. Welcome back." She ran her eyes up and down Wax's length. "And get yourself dressed. It's time for dinner, and Noctia has food you've never seen."

Eujo turned and left, and as she did, the Foti skar quieted. The heat dissipated, the raw fire fading from his fingertips, his feet, his forehead. Yet, when Wax took a step towards the trunk with the linens, the floor behind him bore two blackened footprints.

The skars saved his life. How many more might they help? How far could their power go?

As Wax looked out the window, at Noctia's endless lights and the black cliffs behind them, he wondered whether the stone chair was really the answer. Or if salvation, instead, lay in the whispers and the raw power around his neck.

"You and me," Wax muttered to himself, to the skars. "We'll save everyone together."

What he didn't know, what those blackened boards asked, was whether they'd would destroy everything first.

THIS CONCLUDES 'THE WRATH OF RIVERS' - read on for an excerpt from The Seven Isles Book Four - The Bonds of Stone. For more adventures, visit us at Black Key Books:

AN EXCERPT FROM THE BONDS OF STONE

THE SEVEN ISLES BOOK THREE

Torny took a lower road. She'd tailed Bliss for a few minutes, keeping careful enough to drag behind towns-people and stay out of sight. The Vis did exactly what she ought to be doing, wandering along and scoping the build-ings, the earthworks, the animals on offer. Once Torny established Bliss didn't have some ulterior motive, Torny slipped downward at the next break. The thin switchbacks descended alongside cavern crannies, not their official name but what everyone called the narrow homes build into the rock. Supported with heavy beams and not much larger than a small boat, the crannies nonetheless served as housing for, well, everyone that couldn't afford something better.

And that everyone included more than a few of Torny's former friends.

Thankfully, another not-so-written law of owning a cavern crannies was keeping your door shut. Most opened outward, right into the walkway, so Torny avoided any uncomfortable chance encounters as she wound back and forth several times, always getting closer and closer to the in-and-out waves.

Noctia's southern side bore the goddess's angry whims, the shallows crusted over with jutting rocks and swirling pools. Black sand beaches offered options to those with little else to entertain them, and they were empty now with winter's cold. A summer day would've brought laughing children, tired parents, and couples looking for a little romance. No ships would dock here, no business save some brave food stands, broke in on the fun.

Torny fought away any memory, instead focusing behind the beaches, to caverns and cutaways too old and unstable for any sustained business, for any home. Any, that is, save the one she was going to find. Her boots crunched on the stiff grains as she walked past a few sightseers braving the surf, drawing little and less attention. Like on Foti, everyone here knew to keep to their own affairs.

Catching the wrong eye could ruin so many good things.

The third tidal cave, a saw tooth number whose rock overhangs looked crusted over with salt, still smelled true to Torny, a faint whiff of pipe smoke and snacks drifting out. The bandit gave one last look around, found nobody on her tail, and slipped inside. A few steps warmed the air with a fire's comfort, those flickering flames soon drawing up on the dark, pitted walls. Noctia's caves carried with them a bleak history, one written not in purity of Foti's black lava rock or in the packed sediment of Vis's living caves—something Torny had only heard about. Instead, Noctia offered a lifeless swill mashed together, as if someone had taken a stale gruel, thrown in some old black ash, and swirled it together before baking it into bricks. Smooth, dull, and altogether worthless, was Noctia rock.

Less so were the people clustered around the fire and the whole cave, a deceptively large room that looked like a spoon expanding out from Torny's tight entry. The deeper the cavern went, the more the ceiling rose, and Torny could see all the way to the top thanks to the globes strung about the place. The lights gave sight to hammocks and beds carved into the walls, along with lockboxes aplenty. Racks on the floor held both weapons and tools of a certain trade, one practiced by all the faces now realizing who'd found their way in.

"You just letting people find their way here?" Torny asked by way of introduction, directing her words at the older man crouching near the bonfire, pestering it, as he always seemed to be, with a metal poker. "A new recruitment method?"

"Hardly need to look for new thieves these days," the man replied, matching Torny's look with a single-toothed one of his own. "Especially when missing ones return."

Yarvick delivered a lot with his look, not least the sledgehammer blow of his own visage, so gnarled by vices unknown that he resembled a fleshy tangle of tree roots all coming in together. One good eye shown out from the mix, with a second replaced by an opal, one actually a Noctia skar for those savvy enough to see, or deep enough in the Nimble Fingers to know. His old hair had long since shriveled away save for a sole thick, black strand he kept tied and coiled about his neck, a dry and shifty snake. The rest of him lay buried beneath a cloak so patchwork any shot at identifying its original color or fabric had long since past.

"What brings you back here, Torny?" Yarvick continued. "Come to offer some payment for your debts, or should I have let my boys skewer you outside?"

"I'm here for a job, Yarvick." Torny didn't hear, didn't

see the shifting around the cavern's edges, but she knew it was happening. She'd have a few more sentences to buy her life, and Torny planned to use them. "That debt wasn't getting paid on Foti, so I'm back to do what's right."

Yarvick laughed, full-throated and strong. "What's right? Torny, I don't care about what's right. I care about what's mine." He pulled the poker from the fire, held its orange end up. His opal eye caught the glow, made it seem his very face burned. "And what's mine, what has always been mine, is you."

This concludes the excerpt from 'The Bonds of Stone', The Seven Isles Book Four, available at your favorite retailer. For more adventures, visit us at Black Key Books:

Thanks for reading!

Acknowledgments

There's this idea that writing is a solitary act, but that couldn't be further from the truth. Every writer depends on friends, family, and, yes, the readers to keep spinning their stories.

Specifically, I'd like to thank my wife, Nicole, who's endless love and encouragement make every day brighter. My brothers, Jonathan, Justin, and Matthew, and parents, Bob and Mary, who help keep a smile on my face.

And, of course, all of you readers that make this life possible.

Thank you.

ABOUT THE AUTHOR

A.R. Knight writes sci-fi and fantasy in the frozen north of Wisconsin. With a pair of cats keeping him company, he enjoys delving into adventures that are as much about the villain as the hero.

After getting a degree in journalism and touring the country installing healthcare software, A.R. Knight thought it would be good to get back to what he loved. So now he's got a small office and early mornings to spin whatever tales come into his imagination.

When he's not writing, A.R. Knight tends to travel anywhere he can, whether that's islands off the coast of Ecuador, the rainforest, snowboarding in the Rocky Mountains, or sipping scotch in Edinburgh. That's the nice thing about the writing life, you can take it anywhere.

To contact or see what he's up to, visit www.blackkeybooks.com

arknight@blackkeybooks.com

For Art and Val

Copyright © 2023 by A.R. Knight
All rights reserved.
ISBN:
Ebook — 979-8-88858-042-4
Paperback — 979-8-88858-043-1
Large print — 979-8-88858-045-5
Hardcover — 979-8-88858-044-8

Published by Black Key Books

This book or any portion thereof may not be reproduced or used in any manner whatsoever without the express written permission of the publisher except for the use of brief quotations in a book review.

This is a work of fiction. Any similarity between the characters and situations within its pages and places or persons, living or dead, is unintentional and co-incidental.

www.blackkeybooks.com